CROSS
FIRE

A Holly Novel

By C.C. Warrens

RECOMMENDED READING ORDER

Dedication

To Jesus, the One I would most love to hug, for shaping my world.

To my family, for their love and support.

CROSS FIRE

A Holly Novel

By C.C. Warrens

1

The aroma of sweat and coconut shampoo filled the room, bringing to mind a tropical sweat lodge. I paced the outside of the rubber mat, casting wary looks at my opponent.

He was roughly ten inches taller than me—putting him at an even six feet—and he had a lean muscular build that made my runner's physique pale by comparison. His eyes, which reminded me of a clear blue sky, sparkled with amusement as he watched me.

"You actually have to get close to me to hit me, Holly," he pointed out.

My hands were sheathed in fingerless purple boxing gloves, and I interlaced my fingers, twisting them anxiously in front of my stomach. I reached the end of the mat and spun on my heel to pace back in the other direction.

Up until this point, our training had been entirely nonphysical. I had mirrored his movements, albeit less gracefully, from a safe distance. We had touched on the possibility of sparring during our last lesson, but I wasn't ready to plunge into it.

"I'm not sure—"

"Jordan's not gonna hurt you, Holly," a smooth voice with a touch of Southern said from the back of the room.

I glanced at Marx, who leaned against the wall by the door, arms folded and ankles crossed in a relaxed position. He was wearing jeans and a black T-shirt—his casual wear for when he wasn't on duty—but as an NYPD detective, he was never truly *off* duty. He always carried his gun and badge in case he was called away unexpectedly to a crime scene.

I doubted I would ever truly feel safe with a man, but I trusted Marx more than any other man. He knew my secrets and my fears, and he was always mindful of them. He understood that I wasn't comfortable being alone with Jordan yet, and he made it a point always to be here with me.

"I'm not gonna grab you," Jordan assured me. "We're not there yet. We'll work on breaking out of holds when you're more comfortable with it."

When I was more comfortable with it . . . right. So, never? Yep, I was comfortable with never.

"I'm gonna stand perfectly still." He held out his hands shoulder-width apart in front of him.

I sighed and walked across the mat in my workout toe socks. I stopped four feet from him. We had an agreement: he remained at least four feet from me at all times except in an emergency, and we didn't touch one another. He was asking me to break that agreement . . . and then punch him.

"Can we just go back to mirroring the movements? I like that better," I said.

"I can teach you the punches, kicks, and blocks until you can do them in your sleep, but it doesn't teach you how to connect them or how to recover if you miss. It also doesn't teach you how to dodge if someone is trying to hit you."

The last time someone had taken a swing at me, I had curled into a ball on the floor and covered my head with my arms. That sort of counted as dodging, right?

"This is important, Holly," Marx said. I met his eyes and saw worry swirling in their green depths.

He knew as well as I did that Collin hadn't decided to pack up and leave; he would view the cops surrounding me as a challenge, and he savored a challenge.

Collin was my foster brother, the only biological child of the foster family who took me in when I was fourteen, and he had developed an unhealthy fascination with me.

I had spent the past ten years in hiding—moving from city to city, working odd jobs under the table, never drawing attention to myself—in the hopes that he wouldn't find me.

I had managed to hide from him for two years in New York City, but then I made a mistake: I gave a statement to the police after two men attacked me in the park, all but lighting up a blinking neon sign that read, "Holly is here."

The statement I gave to the cops, which was logged into a "secure" police database, was accessed by an outside source. I didn't doubt for a moment my foster brother was behind the breach of their system.

He hadn't made an appearance yet, but he had called me on my birthday a month ago just to let me know he was watching.

I knew what he would do to me if he got his hands on me again, and I couldn't let that happen. I had decided not to run this time, which meant my only hope was learning how to fight.

I tapped my fingers on my hips nervously as I looked at Jordan. "What if I hurt you?"

His lips twitched in amusement. "You're not gonna hurt me. You're not gonna hurt anyone from that far away." He motioned me closer with his fingers. "Come on. Across the border."

When we first met—or rather, re-met—in Kansas this past November, he had jokingly dubbed the invisible personal bubble around me "the border."

I chewed on my lower lip and then crossed over the invisible boundary. I pushed my red braid back over my shoulder and sank into the stance we'd practiced for the past three weeks.

"Make sure you don't bend your wrist too much. And focus on the form of your punch rather than the strength of it for the first few swings. Here's your target." He waved his right hand.

I folded my fingers into a fist and planted it gently into his gloved palm. I repeated the movement a few more times, practicing until I felt confident I wouldn't accidentally miss and punch him in the face.

"Okay, let's see what you've got," he said.

I exhaled heavily and then swatted his open palm with my fist. When he didn't say anything, I hit his hand again.

"I think I just got high-fived by a gnat," he commented, completely deadpan. "Put a little force behind it, Holly. Hit me like you mean it."

I glared at him, and he gave me one of his trademark charming yet playful smiles. I smacked my fist into his hand again,

3

and he arched a blond eyebrow at me, which apparently meant "punch harder."

"I think he's doubtin' your abilities, Holly," Marx said, and I glanced over at him. He inclined his head in a silent signal.

I darted forward, kicked Jordan in the back of his knee, and swept his legs out from under him while he was off balance. I scampered out of reach as his back slapped the mat.

He wheezed in surprise and then unexpectedly started to laugh. "Seriously?" He propped himself up on his elbows and looked at me. I grinned, and his gaze slid to Marx. "I did not teach her that."

Marx smiled proudly. "I taught her that."

He and Sam, his friend and fellow officer, had demonstrated that technique for me repeatedly until I was able to simulate it solo. Jordan was the first person I had tried it on. I hadn't expected it to go so well.

Honestly, I thought I would trip myself.

Jordan sighed as he sat up on the mat. "I just got taken out by a 110-pound woman. That stings a bit."

"As it should," Marx informed him.

"Yeah, well, I'm ready this time." Jordan climbed to his feet and made a show of brushing off his clothes before looking at me. "No more cheap shots."

I hesitated at the edge of the mat, anxiety sparking in my stomach. "You're not gonna retaliate, are you?" The last thing I wanted was to be body-slammed on the mat for taking his legs out from under him.

"Not if he wants to keep breathin'," Marx muttered under his breath.

Mischief danced in Jordan's eyes. "I'm not gonna retaliate. But I do think you owe me an ice cream cone for bruising my ego."

My eyebrows crept up. "It's twenty-three degrees out."

"Then I guess we won't have to worry about it melting." He held up his hands again. "Left hook this time."

4

Satisfied that he wasn't going to tackle me or twist me into some sort of pretzel in retaliation, I walked across the mat to join him.

"Try putting your body behind it this time," he suggested. "You're not getting enough force by just using your arms."

I shifted my stance a little, trying to figure out what he meant by putting my body behind it. I was pretty sure that if I was punching someone, my body was naturally behind my arm.

"Do what I do, okay?" He raised his fists and demonstrated a right hook. He moved as fluidly as water, and I pitied anyone who came in contact with the other end of that punch.

I tried to mirror him, but after watching his easy movements, I felt as inflexible as a stick. I wondered if I could even touch my toes without bending my knees. I glanced down at them, curious, and decided I would have to try that later.

"Twist with the punch," he said.

"I *am* twisting!"

"No, you're turning your whole body."

"What's the difference?" I demanded irritably.

I watched him a few more times, trying each time to make my body do what his did. Judging by the frown line between his blond eyebrows, I was failing.

"Don't step forward. Keep your back foot behind you, and just move from the core up," he explained.

I could throw a decent punch if I stood perfectly still. How was I supposed to concentrate on swinging without bending my wrist too much, not moving my feet, and twisting but not turning all at the same time?

"Why can't I just use my fists?" I huffed in frustration.

He bit back a sigh and ran a hand through his hair. "Because you'll be lucky to knock out a mosquito, let alone an actual person."

I glared at him.

"Here, just let me . . ." He reached forward and his fingers grazed my waist before I danced back beyond his reach with a flutter of fear.

"You said no grabbing!"

5

He froze where he stood, and realization flickered across his features. "I'm sorry." He stepped back with his hands raised. "I didn't mean to invade your space. I just forgot."

I wrapped my arms protectively around my midsection and tried to ignore the anxiety crawling the walls of my stomach.

Jordan tried to respect my boundaries, but he had a difficult time remembering I wasn't as free with touch as most people. What might be a casual or unconscious gesture for others could twist my nerves into knots.

Marx peeled away from the wall and said, "Okay, we're done for the day."

Jordan opened his mouth like he wanted to object, but then exhaled and dropped his arms in defeat. "Yeah, okay."

His expression was a meld of confusion and regret. He didn't understand my fear, and I didn't think I could explain it to him.

"We'll work on it more next time," he said. He offered me a smile that was too thin to be reassuring and then left the room.

I dropped back against the wall and slid to the floor, frustration and disappointment clinging to me.

Marx sat down beside me and leaned back against the wall with his legs stretched out in front of him. He always gave me space without me having to ask.

"You did good today," he said.

"I don't think we're remembering the same lesson, because that"—I gestured to the room—"was a disaster."

He gave me a gentle smile. "No, it just feels that way because you're frustrated with yourself." He was quiet for a moment before saying, "It's okay to be scared, Holly. It's okay to need space. After everythin' you've been through, nobody expects you to just *get over it*."

I averted my eyes and rubbed at the palms of my gloves.

"You've made a lot of progress. It's been what, four and a half months since you've considered slammin' a door in my face?"

I smiled at the memory.

We had met in October when a serial killer was stalking me. I had vehemently disliked him due to the fact that he was a man, a cop, and imposing at five feet ten with a gun. When he'd shown up at my apartment the next day with more questions, I had very much wanted to slam my door in his face.

Now I considered him a friend.

"You never thought you could trust a cop, let alone a man. Now here I am sittin' about two feet from you and you're not even scared," he observed.

I looked at the doorway Jordan had disappeared through. "It's . . . harder with him than it is with you."

I was trying to rekindle the friendship Jordan and I had as children, but there was an insurmountable barrier between us. And it wasn't the eighteen years we had spent apart.

"It's because you know he's attracted to you," Marx said after a thoughtful pause. At my surprised look, he gave me a sad, knowing smile. "You curl in on yourself whenever you think about intimacy, like you're subconsciously tryin' to protect yourself."

I hadn't realized I had wrapped my arms around my stomach and drawn my knees into my chest until he pointed it out. I tried to force my body to relax.

Marx was in no way attracted to me—maybe because he was forty-seven and I was twenty-eight—and it made me feel safer with him. But Jordan had made it clear that he was, and I was on guard every moment we were in the same room together.

"It'll work itself out. You just have to be patient with yourself," Marx said. "Now come on. Let's go get a terribly unhealthy lunch before I drop you off at home. It'll make you feel better."

"Tacos?"

"If that's what you want."

"And sombrero-sized tortilla chips with cheese dip?" I asked hopefully.

He laughed. "Of course." He stood and offered me his hand, but I ignored it as usual. One of these days I would let him help me up, just to see the look of surprise on his face.

7

2

I sighed contentedly in the passenger seat of Marx's car and resisted the impulse to rub my overstuffed stomach like a pregnant woman.

He glanced at me, his lips curved in amusement. "I don't think I've ever seen you eat that much."

"I love cheese dip."

He chuckled. "Apparently."

Something vibrated in the car, and I looked around curiously. Marx pulled his cell phone from his pocket. He frowned at the screen and then flipped it open.

"Marx," he greeted crisply.

He was driving with one hand.

"Can I do that the next time we practice driving?" I asked, pointing to his lone hand on the wheel.

He gave me a look that clearly communicated, "No, absolutely not."

I was going to try it. What was the worst that could happen?

I had intended to wait to learn to drive for fear Collin would use the license to find me, but considering he had already found me, I accepted Marx's offer to teach me.

"I'm busy right now," he said into the phone. He paused to listen to the voice on the other end of the line. I couldn't understand the words, but I picked up on the notes of panic. Someone was terrified. "How urgent?"

He clenched his teeth and veered onto an empty side street, doing a u-turn that I was pretty sure was illegal, and pulled back out onto the main road.

"I can be there in five minutes, but if I get there and you're wastin' my time . . ." He listened for another moment and then released a tight breath before snapping the phone shut.

"I'm gonna guess that wasn't your mom."

"No. If I ever accused my mother of wastin' my time, she would smack me back to third grade."

I laughed and slid down in my seat, propping my feet on the dashboard. I was pretty sure I would like his mom.

Marx frowned. "We had the conversation about your shoes on my dashboard, did we not?"

Wow, that had been months ago on the road trip to Kansas. "But it's comfortable," I protested.

He arched a single eyebrow that somehow managed to be both admonishing and mildly amused. He had a thing about his car.

Fine. I lifted one foot off the dash and pulled off my sneaker, dropping it on the floor. I repeated the process with my second foot and returned my toe-sock-clad feet to the dashboard. I wiggled my toes. "No more shoes on the dash."

He sighed, but there was a hint of a smile on his lips. "You are a very dangerous young woman, you know that?"

I tilted my head quizzically. I didn't really consider myself dangerous. Apparently I couldn't even throw a punch properly, and the last time I used a gun, I had accidentally murdered my front steps. "How so?"

"Because you're cute and you know it." He gave me a stern look. "I expect you can get away with just about anythin'."

"So I can put my shoes back on the dash?"

"No."

I grinned and looked out the window. I watched the buildings pass by in the opposite direction of my home. We turned onto a street that made me sit up a little straighter in my seat. There were some places in the city that sane people just didn't go. "Um . . . where are we going exactly?"

"I just need to make a quick stop."

"Here? In this neighborhood?"

This was where people were murdered in broad daylight and all five of the witnesses had permanent amnesia or they wound up permanently six feet under. This was also very active gang territory.

9

"I don't have time to drop you off at home," Marx said, changing lanes and pulling into an alleyway. "And I'm not riskin' droppin' you off somewhere else when we have no idea where Collin is."

I looked at the rusted, run-down buildings around us as we drove deeper into the inner-city alley. The smell of trash, alcohol, and other odors I couldn't place filtered into the car, and I crinkled my nose.

The alleyway spilled out into a cramped space that had probably once been occupied by a building, but had since become a scrapyard for broken vehicles and apparently, refrigerators. Oh, and shopping carts.

"Are we making a drug deal?" I asked. "Because this looks like a great place to score some drugs before we die and our bodies are never found."

He sighed. "We're not gonna die. And drug deals are for Wednesdays. It's only Monday."

Ah, of course. What was I thinking? "So . . . we're just vetting our drug dealer ahead of time, then?"

He gave me a look. "This has nothin' to do with drugs, Holly. And where on earth did you come up with the word *vettin'* anyway?"

"Isn't that what you people say?"

He arched an eyebrow at me. "You people?"

"Detective people."

He chuckled quietly and shook his head. "No, I don't often use that word. Now, I need to meet with somebody and you people—by which I mean tiny women who are not cops—need to stay in the car."

I lifted my chin. "You're only eight inches taller than me. You're not that tall."

"Only," he muttered, unhooking his seat belt and reaching across the car to the glove compartment.

I didn't flinch away from him like I would've at one time, but I drew my feet onto the seat to put some much-needed space between us.

He pulled a radio from the compartment, turned a dial that made it buzz loudly, and then clipped it to his belt beside his badge and gun. He closed the glove compartment and said, "I'm done."

I lowered my feet back to the floor and cast him a worried look. "You hardly ever take that with you. Is this dangerous?"

"I don't expect trouble. But it's better to be safe than sorry."

"Can I come with you?"

"No."

I turned in my seat to look at him. "This is not a safe neighborhood." I didn't like the idea of him meeting some random individual in this neighborhood without backup or witnesses.

"I'm aware of that, which is why you're stayin' in the car with the doors locked."

"That's not fair. You're no safer in this neighborhood than I am, maybe even less so because you're a cop." There had been a rash of violence against inner-city cops lately, and it worried me.

"I'm much safer than you, trust me. Not only do I have a gun and trainin', but I somehow doubt any of the gangs in this part of town are gonna want me to be their date for the afternoon."

"Not really interested in dating?" I teased.

He gave me an unamused look. "Not at the moment, no." He pulled a canister of pepper spray from the center console and handed it to me. "Please, Holly. Stay in the car."

His tone was pleading, as if he expected me to do the exact opposite. Like I ever did that . . . okay, occasionally I did that. I silently accepted the canister.

"I'm gonna be right over there." He pointed toward an abandoned factory about two hundred feet away. "And in the event that somethin' does go wrong, call Sam. He'll be here within five minutes."

"Can you at least tell me who you're meeting?" I wanted to know at least that in case something went wrong.

"He's a confidential informant."

"What's his name?"

"I can't tell you his name, Holly. That's why it's called a *confidential* informant." He opened his door and then paused to look

11

back at me. "Keep the doors locked. Do not open them for any reason. Understood?"

I chewed on my bottom lip as I considered it.

"Holly," he prompted with a note of impatient warning.

"Yeah, I hear you." I held up my phone and slumped down in my seat. I wasn't promising anything because I had no intention of staying in the car if he needed help.

"I won't be long." He closed the door and locked it with his little black button, which Jordan had informed me was a *key fob*. What sort of ridiculous name was that? Key fob.

He weaved between the cars toward the factory. A slender man with almond skin paced in the opening, his mannerisms reflecting barely controlled anxiety.

I knew the way he moved; it was the way I had moved for years, and occasionally still did. He was afraid and on guard. When Marx approached him, he did so like a man approaching a wild deer that might disappear back into the brush at the snap of a twig.

He said something to him, but I couldn't hear their voices through the closed doors of the car. The man hesitated and then removed his hands from the pouch on his hoodie, holding them out palms up.

Marx stepped up to him and patted him down. If a cop ever tried to do that to me, I would get arrested for assault, because I would resist—violently.

Apparently satisfied the man was carrying no weapons, Marx stepped back. The thread of trust between them must have been very thin if he was concerned the man might come to their meeting armed.

I was pretty sure I saw Marx's lips form the word "talk."

His informant flipped back his hood, revealing coal-black hair and a tattoo on the side of his neck that, as I squinted, resembled a Star of David. I quickly realized he was a hand talker, because he gestured with agitated emphasis as he spoke.

Curious about what they were discussing, I slid into the driver's seat and cracked open the door. I heard a Hispanic voice say something about heroin.

Ha! And Marx said this had nothing to do with drugs.

I was too far away to hear more than the occasional word or two, but his informant mentioned something about three kids overdosing.

I wasn't sure what the statistics surrounding drug-related deaths were, but three deaths sounded high to me, and the fact that there were children involved made it even worse.

Something metallic squeaked from somewhere to my left. I yanked the door shut and smacked the lock down. I was not about to be murdered by a gang just because I was disobediently snooping.

I wasn't the only one startled.

The informant bolted back into the factory at the sound, and Marx swore; I couldn't hear the swearing, but his lips were moving and he wore his I-wanna-slam-someone's-head-off-the-hood-of-my-car expression.

A clattering sound echoed through the lot, and Marx drew his gun, eyes sweeping over the graveyard of cars. His gaze fixed on a single point, and I looked through the rear window to see what had captured his attention.

An older woman in a threadbare jacket was pushing a shopping cart between the cars and appliances, perusing the items like she was searching for the best pasta option on a grocery store shelf.

Marx lowered his gun, clearly relieved. His gaze shifted to me, and he mouthed the word "stay" before following his informant into the building.

Irritation trickled through me. I didn't appreciate being told to stay like a dog. I slumped down in my seat and looked around the car for something interesting to do. I opened the glove compartment and rummaged through the contents, finding nothing more interesting than a road map, a registration card, and spare keys.

Men were boring.

I searched the compartment between the seats next. I pulled out an oblong-shaped object and turned it over with curiosity. My eyes widened when I realized it was full of bullets, and I dropped it.

Probably shouldn't mess with that.

"Ooh, gum."

I fished out the pack of mint gum and pulled a piece out. I unwrapped it, popped it into my mouth, and chewed happily. I put the rest back and was just about to close the compartment lid when a sharp knock on the driver's side window made me jump and nearly choke on my gum.

I looked up, expecting to see Marx, but it was the old woman. Her cloudy gray eyes looked at me from a lined, weathered face. She motioned for me to follow her before turning away.

Ummm . . .

I looked around for signs of danger, but everything was still. How dangerous could one old woman be? She motioned me forward with her fingers again.

Okay then. It couldn't hurt to make sure everything was okay. I tugged my shoes back on, gripped the pepper spray tightly in my palm, and opened the door. "Do you need help with something?"

She nodded emphatically. "He's dying." Her voice was frail and cracked with age, but it wasn't the sound of her voice that grabbed my attention.

"Who's dying?"

I glanced at her cart behind her. It was filled with things most people discarded: old blankets, bottles, boxes, another pair of boots that looked no better than the holey pair she wore now.

She was homeless.

I had lived on the street from time to time while on the run from Collin, and it was a hard life. No place was truly safe, the winter was unbearably cold, there was never enough food, and most people regarded you as a nuisance or a leech on society.

She didn't answer my question; she just wrapped her hands around her cart and started pushing it back down the cluttered aisle of the lot. I looked back at the factory, but there was no sign of Marx.

He's gonna be so mad at me.

Maybe I could help her and be back before he realized I ever left. And if he didn't ask, I wouldn't need to tell him. I got out and closed the door soundlessly behind me.

"Wait," I whispered, walking in the direction the old woman had gone.

I stifled a noise of surprise when my foot landed on something soft and it let out a warped, dying giggle. I looked down at the naked, armless baby doll lying on the ground. The giggle faded, and her single blue eye blinked lazily. Oh my word, that was creepy. I gave the doll a wary look as I tiptoed around it.

"Hello?" I whispered.

She was a seventyish-year-old woman with a squeaky shopping cart. She wasn't a ninja. Where could she possibly have gone? I wandered deeper, looking for her.

Male voices drifted across the scrapyard from somewhere to my left, and I froze. My eyes darted over the cars and heaping piles of trash in search of them.

Why had I left the relative safety of the car?

"You see his face?" one of them asked.

"You mean what was left of it?" another replied. "He ain't gonna be runnin' his mouth no mo'."

Laughter reminiscent of a pack of cackling hyenas broke out, and I realized with a sinking feeling in my gut that the men were coming this way. I looked back in the direction of Marx's car.

It was too far.

"Man, I could go for a line right now."

"Not me, bro. I got a six pack and a smokin' little blonde waitin' for . . ."

I took a few steps back when I saw a dark head bobbing closer, and sucked in a sharp breath when I bumped into a pile of junk and something clattered to the ground.

"Sh!" one of the men said loudly, and the conversation died. "You hear dat?"

I looked around for a place to hide. I retreated between two cars and peered through the broken rear window of a purple-and-pink one. It was as good a place as any. With one final glance in the direction of the approaching voices, I climbed through the window into the backseat.

I hunkered down behind the passenger seat and tried not to think about the filth littering the floorboards. The sound of glass breaking just behind the car had me shrinking down.

God, please don't let them see me.

Something shook and rattled, and one of the men taunted, "Out shoppin'?"

A female whimper drew me up from my hiding place, and I peered through the rear window at the old woman. Five men crowded around her, laughing and taunting her as they shoved her cart and tossed her belongings to the ground.

I could see her fear in the slump of her shoulders and the jerkiness of her movements, and I wanted to help her. She caught my eye and gave a subtle shake of her head.

She didn't want me to help her?

"Whatcha got in here, Grandma?" one of the men asked. He overturned her cart completely, and all her belongings spilled onto the pavement. "Oops."

They deliberately stomped all over everything, crushing the cans and bottles she had collected. Two of the men stretched out her blanket while a third shredded it with a knife.

Their cruelty sent anger scorching through me, and my fingers curled into fists. She had so little, and they were destroying it.

God, what do I do?

I knew what I *wanted* to do.

The man who had tipped over her cart shoved her, knocking her to the ground, and that solidified my decision. I wasn't sure what I could do against five men and a knife, but I couldn't sit by and watch them hurt her.

"Filthy old hag," he spat.

The men laughed and kicked her things as they walked away. Were they leaving? I hesitated, watching them from my hiding place. Maybe I wouldn't have to fight them to try to protect her.

They passed by the car, and I held my breath, praying silently that they would keep walking. The breath left me in a shaky rush when they disappeared from view.

I waited until their voices faded before I scrambled back out the window to help the old woman.

"Are you okay?" I asked, crouching beside her.

Tears left shining tracks down her grimy cheeks, and my heart ached for her. There was no reason for her to be treated with such disrespect.

I helped her to sit up and then began collecting what was left of her belongings. The bottles and the blanket were ruined, but everything else was just scattered.

"I'm Holly," I said, handing her a boot. "What's your name?"

"Agnes."

"Agnes, why didn't you want me to help you?"

I suppressed a flinch when she reached out a hand and touched my cheek. Her gray eyes that had seemed so distant and confused when she first approached me were suddenly full of awareness.

"Pretty girl," she said, patting my cheek. "They would do worse to you."

I swallowed uneasily. Those men had been looking for someone to torment purely for the fun of it, and if I had stepped in to help her . . .

Marx probably would've had to shoot people.

"Do they bother you a lot?" I asked.

"Sometimes." She searched inside the shoe I had handed her and pulled out a picture. Joy filled her eyes as she showed it to me. It was a picture of a couple holding hands. She pointed to the woman. "Me." And then at the man. "My husband."

"Where is he?"

17

Sadness and grief overshadowed her momentary joy. "Gone." She tucked the faded and cracked photo back into her boot for safekeeping. Her face darkened with renewed worry, and she looked back at me. "He's dying."

Confused, I asked, "Your husband?" But I thought she just said he was gone.

She shook her head and took my hand, trying to pull me to my feet with her. She didn't have the strength, so I stood and helped her up instead.

"What about your things?" I asked.

"Just things. Come."

"Agnes, I d—" I began to protest, but she pulled me along behind her.

"This way."

I glanced over my shoulder in the direction of Marx's car. I was worried those men might come back and catch both of us out in the open.

"Dying," she reminded me, and I let her pull me along toward whomever or whatever she thought was dying.

We bypassed a few more stripped, graffiti-covered cars and . . . a bathtub . . . before she stopped and pointed. I stepped around her and inhaled sharply.

A German shepherd lay on the ground, his stomach rising and falling slowly, and his eyes glassy. A red stain spread through the fur on his side and spilled over onto the pavement.

I crouched cautiously beside him and looked him over. There was a shiny tag around his neck. I reached forward, pausing only when he let out a pained wheeze, and then caught it with my fingertips. The name engraved into it made my breath catch.

Riley.

Could it be the same Riley?

Then I saw the snapped leash dangling from his collar, and I knew it had to be him. How many German shepherds named Riley had a habit of breaking their leashes?

This was the same dog who had saved me last autumn. I knew it hadn't been chance that put Riley and his owner on that walking path in the park. I had prayed for help, and it had come in the shape of a former police dog.

Riley suffered from PTSD, and the sound of my screams that night had made him break his leash and rush to my aid.

"Riley," I whispered, brushing my fingers through his coarse fur. The old woman was right: he was dying.

What had happened? Why was he here? Where was his owner? I looked around, half-afraid I would find a body, but I didn't see any sign of the old man Riley belonged to.

I lifted my eyes to Agnes. "What happened? Who did this to him?"

Her mouth drew down at the corners. "Found him."

"Holly!" Marx shouted, and I flinched in surprise. He must have returned to the car and realized I wasn't there. So much for my plan to be back before he noticed I wasn't where he'd told me to stay.

Agnes stilled, and I saw fear flicker through her eyes. She hugged the boot with the picture to her chest and stepped closer to me.

"It's just my friend," I assured her.

"Holly!"

"Here!" I hollered back. "By the blue car with . . ." I leaned sideways to read the letters spray-painted across the doors. Oh, I didn't use that word. "Past the bathtub!" I said instead.

I heard the creepy death giggle from the doll I'd stepped on earlier and knew he was on the right track. His expression was frosty with worry and anger when he finally arrived.

He looked me over to make sure I was in one piece and then holstered his gun as he snapped, "Are you tryin' to give me a heart attack? I told you to stay in the car." He spared a glance for Agnes and gave her a polite nod.

He would be even more furious if I told him about the troublemakers who had come through. Maybe it would be better to keep that detail to myself. "We have to help him."

He crouched down alongside me and looked at the dog. He examined the wound and Riley let out a pained whimper. "Holly, this is a gunshot wound. A bad one. There's nothin' . . ."

"It's Riley."

It took a moment for the name to register. "The dog from the park? The one who saved you?"

I showed him the name tag. "We have to do something."

He pursed his lips and looked at Riley. I knew that expression; he didn't think there was anything we could do, but he didn't want to tell me.

"Please," I pleaded, and tears burned my eyes. "He's suffering. Even if all we can do is take him to a vet so they can put an end to the pain. Please."

"Holly . . ." He trailed off when he met my eyes, and whatever objection he was about to offer died in his throat. He sighed. "Okay. Get the rear car door, and I'll carry him."

We packed Riley into the backseat with his head in my lap, and I rubbed the fur between his ears as he whined. Marx climbed behind the wheel and glanced back at me.

His serious expression melted when I brushed at my damp cheeks and forced a smile. "You ready?"

I nodded, and we pulled out of the scrapyard. Marx called his captain to fill him in on the conversation with his informant as we drove to the nearest animal hospital.

"I realize it's not much to go on, sir," he said after a pause.

I heard his captain's faint voice through the speaker say something about not wanting to waste one of his best detectives on a tip that provided so little information, and that he needed more to justify opening a case.

Marx exhaled. "I'll see what I can do." He hung up and tossed his phone into the passenger seat in irritation.

We pulled into the animal hospital, and Marx stayed in the waiting room with me for the next two hours while they operated on Riley. When a tall, dark-haired woman finally came out to talk to us, I nearly plowed into her.

"Is he okay? Can I see him?"

She offered me a patient smile. "Riley survived the surgery. He lost a lot of blood and he's severely dehydrated, but I expect him to make a full recovery."

Relieved, I asked again, "Can I see him?"

"He's still unconscious, but you can see him for a minute. I would like to keep him for observation for a couple of days just to make sure there aren't any complications."

She took Marx and me back to visit with him. I petted him and kissed his head, and then we left him in the vet's very capable hands.

I insisted we stop at a store to pick up a new blanket and a few boxes of granola bars for Agnes. I told Marx he could wait in the car while I tracked her down, and he gave me a flat stare before getting out. Apparently he didn't like that suggestion.

It didn't take us long to find her; she was rummaging through the scrapyard for anything interesting. I thanked her for finding Riley and told her he was going to be okay. She hugged me when I handed her the blanket and food and then, much to Marx's discomfort, hugged him too before we left.

3

Dear Jesus,

Today I'm thankful for a blue sky and sunshine, and I'm grateful beyond words that You love me just because.

I kept a daily journal of gratitude. I had learned early on that this world we were passing through was riddled with darkness, but there were flickers of light if we were just willing to see them. I made a conscious effort to see them. It kept the pain and suffering in this world from swallowing me whole.

PS: Thanks for whoever came up with chicken nuggets, I added after another bite of my lunch. I set down my pen and flipped my journal shut. I chewed slowly, enjoying my last chicken-flavored nugget.

I heard a car pull up, and dusted off my hands before climbing onto the metal chair in front of my kitchen sink to peer out the window.

The downside of living in a basement apartment was that the windows were more horizontal than vertical, and they hugged the ceiling, which meant I had to do chair aerobics to see outside.

I was expecting Marx, but it wasn't his car that rolled to a stop along the curb. I was about to dismiss it and climb down when the occupant of the car—a tall, lean man in his thirties—slid out of the driver's side and started down the path that would lead him to my front door.

There was a youthful spring to his stride as he came down the steps onto my patio. I stiffened when he knocked on the door. I didn't open the door to strangers even in broad daylight, and I definitely didn't know him.

I considered pretending I wasn't home, but he had probably seen me watching him from the window like some sort of paranoid weirdo. I hopped down and approached the door warily.

"Who is it?" I asked.

A muffled tenor came through the door. "Nathan Whittaker, your new landlord."

Mr. Stanley, my former landlord, had been murdered last autumn. I heard a rumor that someone had bought the building, but I hadn't met them yet.

"Ms. Smith?" he asked when I didn't respond.

I frowned at the name. Mr. Stanley had died before I discovered my real name—Holly Marie Cross—so whatever records the new landlord had about me were outdated.

"Um . . . what can I do for you?" I asked.

A pause. "Do you mind opening the door so we can talk face to face?"

I curled and uncurled my fingers at my sides anxiously. I had assured Marx that while Collin was in the area, I wouldn't leave my apartment alone or unlock the door for anyone I didn't know and trust. But I couldn't very well ignore my landlord.

"Just a minute," I called back. I grabbed my cell phone and sent my best friend Jace a quick text for clarification:

> What's our new landlord's name? And what
> does he look like?

I knew I was probably just being paranoid, but after everything that had happened the past few months, I couldn't help but be overly cautious.

Jace's reply was instant, cementing the fact that her phone was glued to her fingertips:

> Nathan Whittaker. Thirtyish? Black slimy
> hair, and he gives me the heebie-jeebies. Why?

That sounded like the man at my door. I didn't reply to her question. If she was that curious, she could just look out her window and see him standing on my patio.

I summoned my nerves and unbolted the door, cracking it open. The man standing on my patio was maybe closer to forty given the fine lines around his eyes and the thin streaks of silver in his slicked-back hair.

"What did you wanna talk about? I dropped my rent money off," I said. I was meticulous about dropping it off on time simply to avoid this kind of situation.

His eyebrows climbed up a fraction as his gaze swept over me, and my grip tightened instinctively on the door. "You're Ms. Smith?"

He sounded surprised.

"Were you expecting a man?" My sharp tone drew his eyes back to my face where I preferred them.

He smiled, and I knew instantly what Jace meant when she said the man gave her the heebie-jeebies. It made him look like a predator on the prowl, and I resisted the urge to slam the door in his face and lock it.

"I've introduced myself to all of the other tenants, but you've been pretty hard to pin down," he said.

I shrugged. "Been busy. In fact, I'm leaving in a few minutes, so . . ." *Please go away*, I wanted to say.

"I'm updating the tenant records, and I would like you to fill out this information card for me."

He offered me a note card. I skimmed over the questions that covered the front and back, and frowned. It required a lot of details I either wasn't comfortable sharing or didn't know. "Mr. Stanley never made me fill one of these out."

"You seem to be the exception."

He pulled a sheet of paper from his coat pocket and unfolded it for me to see. The top of the form read Tenant Lease Agreement, and it was blank except for a note scribbled across the top in a man's handwriting: Holly Smith. Basement. BA placement.

BA must have meant Beth Anne. She had been the one to arrange the apartment for me.

Mr. Whittaker refolded the paper and looked at me in a way that made me want to fidget. "I'm curious *why* he made an exception for you."

Mr. Stanley might have been a grouch, but he was never heartless. Beth Anne, the woman who spoke with him about the vacant basement, had worked with him on housing arrangements before, and she had vouched for me.

"I haven't caused any trouble," I said, "so I'm not sure why—"

"I require this information of all my tenants." Mr. Whittaker tucked his hands into his coat pockets. "No one else has had a problem answering the questions."

I studied the long list of questions. Some of them were simple enough—do I have pets, do I have a criminal history, do I have a reliable source of income, etc.—while others struck me as unusual. "I don't understand why some of these questions are relevant to me being a tenant."

"It's just for record keeping."

Right. "I'll um . . . fill out what I can and get it back to you. Thanks for dropping it off."

When I tried to close the door, he pressed a hand against it to keep it open, sending my heart rate skipping. "I'm sorry, but we also need to talk about your keys."

His eyes flicked to my ring of keys on the kitchen counter beside me, and I grabbed them, gripping them protectively in my fist. "What about them?"

"This seems to be the only apartment I don't have keys to. I'm not sure if the former landlord misplaced them or if he just neglected to make copies, but in either case, I'll need to borrow yours so I can make copies for myself."

I had been afraid this might happen.

"Mr. Stanley and I had an agreement," I said.

"Oh?"

"He didn't have to pay for the locks and I got to keep the only set of keys."

His eyes narrowed. "Are you hiding something in there you don't want anyone else to see?"

He leaned forward to see inside, and I clenched the door tighter, holding my ground. I didn't want to back away and give him the impression he was welcome to enter. "I'm not hiding anything. I just like my privacy."

"I'm not Mr. Stanley, Ms. Smith, and I'm afraid that's not gonna work for me. I require keys to every lock on my property, and your apartment is no exception. Of course, if the keys mean that much to you . . ." The scheming glint in his eyes made me uneasy. "I'm sure *we* can come to an agreement too."

"What kind of agreement?"

"An extra two hundred a month ought to cover it."

I gaped at him in disbelief. Income from my photography was slow during the winter months, and the small amount Georgetta sent me from my father's book store in Kansas wasn't enough to cover much more than what I paid now for rent and utilities.

"I can't afford that."

"I'm sure you'll find a way. Otherwise I suggest you start packing, because I'll be putting your apartment on the market by the end of the week."

Anger momentarily overshadowed my anxiety, and I snapped, "But I haven't done anything to warrant eviction, and I can't pay you that kind of money. Business is slow during the winter."

His lips curved into a self-satisfied smile. "If money's an issue, I'm sure we can make other arrangements."

I didn't immediately understand his meaning until his gaze flickered over me appreciatively. I stiffened. Was he suggesting what I thought he was suggesting?

I was about to slam the door in his face when a familiar Southern voice pulled my attention past him.

"Get your hand off her door."

The anxiety my landlord had stirred up drained away at the sight of Marx. Mr. Whittaker snatched his hand off my door, as if the metal had suddenly scalded him, and turned around.

Marx must have detected the tension between us, because he scrutinized my landlord as he descended the steps to join him on my patio. "And who might you be?"

My landlord lifted his chin proudly. "Nathan Whittaker. I run this place."

Marx's tone was distinctly unimpressed. "Good for you."

"He's my new landlord, and he wants me to fill out an information card for his tenant records." I offered the card to Marx.

Mr. Whittaker started to object. "That's not for . . ."

Marx scanned the questions, and I watched his expression cloud with suspicion. He flipped the card over and then pinned my landlord with a look that probably made every one of his suspects squirm in the interrogation room.

"Tell me, Mr. Whittaker, what exactly does her relationship status have to do with her bein' a tenant?"

"That's a normal question."

"Marital status, maybe, but whether or not she's in a relationship is none of your business. And why are you concerned with the names of her kin and what they do for a livin'?"

"In case of an emergency."

Marx pointed to the bottom of the card. "No, that's the emergency contact down here. Information about her next of kin is none of your business. Neither is it your concern how long she's lived in this city."

Mr. Whittaker tried to snatch the card back, but Marx pulled it out of his reach.

"We'll fill this out for you and you can be on your way." Marx fished his pen out of his pocket and filled out my updated name as well as three additional lines on the card. Next of kin: Richard Marx. Employment: Detective at the NYPD. And a phone number where he could be reached.

He handed the card to my landlord, and Mr. Whittaker swallowed hard as he read the information. "You're a detective?"

"Mmm hmm."

Mr. Whittaker's eyes shifted between us before he asked with uncertainty, "Are you . . . her dad?"

"Is that a problem for you?" Marx replied.

Mr. Whittaker blinked. "No. It's just . . . there isn't much resemblance. I mean . . ." He studied my naturally red hair and honey-brown eyes and then looked back at Marx.

"She takes after her mother."

I most certainly did take after my mother, except for my ears and nose. Those had come from my dad.

"Stanley didn't have a record of a next of kin," Mr. Whittaker said.

"Because next of kin was none of his business either," Marx pointed out, and Mr. Whittaker flushed.

"There was nothing about a dad who was . . . is a cop. Not even in the emergency contacts."

"Stanley didn't keep very good records. I'm sure you'll remedy that."

"Of course, but . . ." Mr. Whittaker hesitated. He glanced at the locks on my door and seemed to wrestle with whether or not he wanted to make an issue of them now that Marx was here. His gaze shifted to me. "We can talk about the keys another time."

"If you have a problem with Holly havin' the only set of keys, we can discuss it now. I'd rather you not bother her later," Marx said coolly. Yep, he had definitely sensed the tension. "I had these locks installed for her protection after your predecessor invited himself into her apartment and then let a serial killer in."

Mr. Whittaker blanched. "A serial killer?"

"Mmm hmm. Killed Mr. Stanley for the keys. How unfortunate for him that he had them. And I should point out that the last two men who entered her apartment without her express permission are dead."

Mr. Whittaker must have interpreted that as a threat, because he paled and took a step back. "I see. Well, thank you . . . for thee, um, information on the card and, uh . . ."—he looked at me—"Never mind thee, um . . ."

"Arrangement?" I offered when he struggled for the word. I couldn't keep the disgust from my voice.

He paled even more and cast a worried look at Marx before returning his attention to me. "Right. That. That was just a misunderstanding."

I folded my arms and narrowed my eyes at him. "Good, because my answer will always be never. Just in case you think about *misunderstanding* again."

He shot another worried glance at Marx. Apparently he was scarier than me. "If you need anything, Ms. Sm—" He glanced at the information card and corrected himself. "Cross, please don't . . . hesitate to ask."

He nodded to Marx and then scampered up the steps and retreated into the main apartment building.

I puffed out a breath and rested my head against the door. "I could've handled that." I slanted a look up at Marx. "I had a plan."

He arched an interested eyebrow.

"Okay, fine. I was planning on making a plan after I slammed the door in his face. I just hadn't quite worked out all the details yet."

The corners of his lips twitched with amusement. "In my defense, it's in my nature to be protective, like it's in your nature to stumble into trouble. You're lucky I haven't wrapped you in bubble wrap."

I grinned. "I would just pop it."

The humor faded as he asked, "What did he mean when he said never mind the arrangement?"

I considered whether or not to tell him everything. I was worried he might lose his temper.

Mmm . . . maybe less was better.

"He said he would let me keep the only set of keys if I pay him two hundred dollars a month on top of my rent," I explained, straightening. "If I refuse, he's gonna evict me and put my apartment up for rent."

Marx grimaced. "That's not gonna happen."

"You think he's done this to other people in the building?" My thoughts turned to Jace, and I felt a spark of anger.

"Undoubtedly. People like him exploit others for their own benefit. He probably uses those information cards to figure out who the most vulnerable targets are. Most likely single women with no next of kin, who haven't lived in the city long enough to form connections or relationships they can rely on."

I lifted my chin and narrowed my eyes in mock indignation. "What are you trying to say?"

He clicked his pen and tucked it back into his jacket. "You know exactly what I'm sayin'."

"Is that why you let him think you're my dad? So he wouldn't view me as an easy target?"

He gave me a warm smile but didn't answer my question. "I'll have Sam speak with the other tenants. If Mr. Whittaker made any *arrangements* with them, Sam will find out and pay him a visit."

Sam would probably terrify my landlord. It was a combination of the monotone way he spoke and the sheer size of him that made him intimidating. He wasn't tall, but he looked like he could punch through a brick wall.

He was one of the officers who volunteered to be a part of my protective detail in October. That was when he'd met my best friend, Jace. I liked him well enough, despite the fact that we had a tendency to clash like orange juice and toothpaste. He genuinely cared about Jace, and he spent a lot of time with her, which meant he would have no problem setting Mr. Whittaker straight. In fact, he would probably do it with a concise, bullet-point list that left no room for error. He was just that maddeningly logical.

I grabbed my coat and pulled it on over my sweater. "Ready to go?" At Marx's nod, I locked up my apartment, and we left for the student-driver parking lot so I could learn how *not* to run things over.

Thirty minutes later, I was glaring at the orange cones in the side mirror. I had pulled forward through them without so much as a hiccup, but for some reason I always managed to flatten them like roadkill when backing up.

I looked at the gear shift and chewed on my bottom lip.

"It's the R," Marx reminded me.

The first time I had driven a car had been in Kansas. I had more or less highjacked Jordan's car and then backed it into another vehicle. After nearly running him over in the parking lot. It had taken me a while to reason out the letters on the gear shift.

"R for rewind, right?" I asked, keeping my voice completely serious.

Marx gave me a pained look. "Reverse."

I laughed softly to myself. I knew the R was for reverse, but I couldn't resist the temptation to tease him. I put the car in reverse and lifted my foot off the brake. The car drifted slowly backwards.

I winced when I ran over the first cone. I swerved to miss the second and flattened the one on the opposite side. I breathed a sigh of relief when I eventually cleared the strip of obstacles and put the car into park.

All but one cone, the one I had swerved to avoid, were dented and toppled on the pavement. Marx observed the disaster and said evenly, "Congratulations. You just murdered seven pedestrians."

"Yes, but it's one less than last time," I said with false brightness.

He gave me a small smile and stepped out of the car to set the cones back upright. I groaned and rested my head on the steering wheel. I was never going to get this right.

Marx's phone rang, and he answered it in his normally brusque way. "Marx." He was setting up the second-to-last cone when he suddenly straightened and asked, "What? Are you certain?" That wasn't his good-news tone of voice. He looked at me briefly and then said, "I'll be right there." He walked to the driver's side and opened the door. "Scoot over."

"But I have to run the cones over five or six more times," I explained.

"You can run them over tomorrow. I have a crime scene."

He climbed in, shifted the car into drive, and we pulled out of the parking lot quick enough to make my head spin.

4

Marx rolled the car to a stop about twenty feet from the yellow crime-scene tape that roped off the area. Bystanders gathered on the street and sidewalks, their grim and curious expressions caught in the flickering glow of red and blue lights.

"Vultures," Marx grumbled under his breath as he flung off his seat belt.

"You should've let me drive," I said. "It wasn't that far."

"I wanted to actually make it to the scene, not become one on the way," he replied dryly. "And you shouldn't even be here."

I lifted my chin. "You could've taken me home."

Truthfully, he had intended to, but my apartment was in the opposite direction of the crime scene, and after sitting in stalled traffic for ten minutes, his temper and impatience had gotten the better of him.

"Stay in the car."

He didn't give me a chance to object before he climbed out and closed his door. I swallowed my pointless protests and huffed out a frustrated breath as I watched him weave through the people toward the scene. He showed his badge to the officer standing outside the tape, and the officer jotted something down on a clipboard before lifting the tape and letting Marx pass beneath it.

It annoyed me that he was always telling me to stay in the car. I might not be able to help at a crime scene, but I could at least get out and snoop around. I glanced at all the other people. There were plenty of other civilians on the sidewalk.

And I hadn't *promised* to stay in the car.

I unhooked my seat belt and slipped out the passenger side. I hopped onto the sidewalk beside the other onlookers and snuck behind the cars parked along the curb to see what was happening.

A body lay in the middle of the street. A sheet had been draped over him, but I could still see the distinctly male arm

32

sprawled across the pavement, and the multiple red stains on the sheet where his wounds had bled.

Marx crouched down alongside the remains and lifted the corner of the sheet with a gloved hand. I braced myself for the gruesome sight, but his position blocked most of the body.

"Did you see what happened here?" an officer asked someone behind me.

"I ain't seen nuttin," a woman replied.

I exhaled sadly. A man was lying dead in the street, and even if someone had witnessed his death, no one would say a word.

Marx lowered his head and rubbed a hand over his face. He dropped the sheet back over the body, but not before I saw the Star of David tattoo on the side of the man's neck.

Oh no. His informant.

It had only been three days since I saw the man pacing anxiously in the factory doorway. He had been frightened but alive, and now . . .

"You lost?" a tight voice asked from behind me, catching me off guard.

I turned to see a middle-aged Latino woman standing two feet to my left. Her chocolate eyes regarded me with unwarranted suspicion.

"A little pale to be up in this part of town, no?"

I glanced around, noticing for the first time that the other bystanders were predominantly Latino, and I didn't exactly blend in.

I swallowed my nerves and said, "I'm working on my tan."

Her lips pinched together in an unfriendly smile as she looked me over. "Not police, I see. Reporter?"

I shook my head. "I'm here with a friend."

She gave a disapproving grunt. "Just a nosy girl, then."

I started to disagree with her, then decided against it. I could've stayed in the car, but curiosity had gotten the better of me. Maybe that did make me nosy.

"Why won't anyone tell the police what happened here?" I asked.

"Police are no friends of ours."

Well, I guess it was a good thing I didn't tell her the friend I came with was a cop. "But this is wrong." I gestured to the body lying in the street. "Someone has to care enough about him to—"

"You don't know this life, pequeña," she cut in icily. My Spanish was rusty, but I was pretty sure she had just called me "little one." Like she had room to talk. "We care, but people die in drive-by shootings all the time here." She added something under her breath in her native tongue, and I fumbled through my brain for a translation.

I didn't know the first word, but the last three sounded like "is the life." Judging by the resignation in her tone, it was the Spanish equivalent to "such is life."

"I wanna help," I said, and I stumbled over a phrase that had stuck with me from freshman Spanish class. "Por favor?"

She smiled tightly. "You should not speak Spanish. Your accent is . . . painful, and there is nothing you can do. Nothing any of us can do."

I saw the crucifix resting against her chest, and offered, "I can pray." It was the only thing I *could* do. "I just need a name so I can pray for his family."

She considered me for a long moment before saying, "Ruiz. Analucia's boy." She jerked her head toward a woman folded over on the ground, weeping.

She was completely alone; the other bystanders had cleared a space around her and left her to grieve without so much as a drop of comfort.

"Why isn't anybody with her?"

She muttered something in Spanish that sounded vaguely insulting, but when I just waited patiently, she sighed. "Don't talk. That's the rule. Her son talked. Who knows what else he brings on his family. If she is next to die . . ." She pressed a hand to her chest and shook her head. No one wanted to be near the woman who might also be a target.

I could see the sadness in her dark eyes as she stared at the mourning mother. It wasn't a lack of compassion that kept these people from getting involved; it was fear that they or the people they loved would wind up dead in the street next.

"Go home, pequeña," she said, and her eyes moved over the people nervously. They landed on someone in the crowd, and I saw fear flash across her face. She looked away before I could follow her gaze to the person who'd scared her. "Go," she insisted. "Before something bad happens to you."

She gathered up some of the younger women and children from the sidewalk, cast another wary look over her shoulder, then ushered them quickly up the sidewalk to a well-lit house.

I turned back to the street with a quiet sigh.

Marx stood and murmured something to the officer who approached him. Judging by the way the officer flipped through his notes and shook his head, he was explaining that he didn't have any witnesses. Marx surveyed the throng of uncooperative observers.

I froze when his eyes landed on me. Frustration rippled across his features before melting back beneath a neutral expression. Oh boy. He was mad. I smiled and gave him a little anxious wave of my fingers.

He grabbed the attention of a uniformed woman with a camera and made a sweeping gesture to encompass everyone on the sidewalk. She nodded and broke away from him to take snapshots of the surrounding faces. Knowing Marx, he intended to bother everyone on this street whether they wanted to be bothered or not.

I watched the woman taking pictures and wondered if maybe I could freelance as a crime scene photographer during the colder months. Probably not, since I only had a high school freshman education.

I spent hours at the library reading books when I had the opportunity, but I doubted they would accept reading hours in place of a high school diploma. Maybe I could get my GED someday.

The hairs on the back of my neck prickled, and my instincts whispered that I was being watched, a feeling I knew all too well.

I turned and searched the faces around me, expecting to catch a glimpse of Collin, but I didn't recognize anyone. What if he was hiding in the back of the crowd, waiting for an opportunity to drag me away?

Fear burned all the way through my insides at the thought, making me queasy, and I suddenly regretted getting out of the car.

Marx won't let him drag me away. And there's too many cops. He wouldn't be able to.

Maybe Collin wasn't even here and the older woman's fears were just contagious. Still, I found myself searching the faces for his one more time.

My eyes connected with a stranger's, and the frightening intensity in his gaze almost made me take a step back. Was he the reason for my unease?

He leaned against the metal guardrail of a staircase leading up to one of the houses. A green serpent tattoo snaked up from beneath his hoodie and coiled around his throat, the head opening its mouth into a fanged hiss on his cheek.

His attention clung to me for a long moment before shifting to catch something over my shoulder. I turned my head to see Marx ducking under the police tape, his eyes fixed on the Latino man with the tattoo.

The man shrugged his hood up over his head, hunched his shoulders, and walked away. Marx stepped onto the sidewalk beside me, and I could almost feel the suspicion wafting from him as he watched the man disappear into the crowd of people outside the police tape.

"Do you know him?" he asked, pulling off his rubber gloves.

I shook my head. "Never seen him before. Why?"

"Because he seemed awful interested in you. He's been starin' at you." He looked me over and pinched his lips together in what struck me as disapproval.

I looked down at my skinny jeans paired with red flats and my black wool coat. I frowned up at him in confusion. "What? Should I have worn sneakers to party crash a crime scene?"

"This isn't a safe neighborhood. There's a lot of gang violence and racial tension, and you stand out like a target."

I lifted my chin. "I can't help that I'm pale. What do you expect me to do, spray-paint myself and wear a wig?"

"No, I expect you to stay in the car."

"But I was curious."

He frowned at me. "Do you have any idea how frustratin' you are?"

I tried not to smile.

"Don't you smirk at me. I'm angry," he grumbled. He shoved his used gloves at a passing officer and demanded, "Back to the car."

I arched my eyebrows at his curt tone and dug in my heels. He drew in a frustrated breath and let it out slowly before adding with obvious difficulty, "Please."

I started walking in the direction of the car, and he fell in step beside me. "I can walk myself," I pointed out, slipping between two onlookers that Marx nearly had to push out of his way. "I did make it this far without being murdered."

His expression darkened, and I realized it was probably too soon to be making murder jokes. It had been less than three months since a serial killer tried to murder both of us. Apparently it was still a sensitive subject for him.

"If I leave you to walk back to the car alone, who knows when or where I'll find you," he said. "You'll sneak away before you ever get there."

If he could grab my arm and haul me back to the car, he probably would, but he tried never to force me to do anything against my will. He was the first man I had ever managed to trust, and he wouldn't risk fracturing that trust just because he was irritated and impatient.

"Are you purposefully walkin' at a snail's pace, or are your legs just that short?" he asked.

I grinned and continued my leisurely stroll toward the car. He had to walk at my pace, and I walked nice and slow.

My eyes landed on the grieving woman as we passed by. It bothered me to see her so alone during a time when she needed someone.

I ignored Marx's protests as my heart tugged me in her direction. I knelt in front of her. "Analucia?"

She drew herself up to look at me, her grief-crumpled face glistening with tears. The desperate, lost look in her eyes pierced my heart.

"I'm sorry about your son," I said.

"He was all I had. Mi niño, my baby boy," she managed to say. She folded over and pressed her face into her hands as she wept. I knew what it was like to lose everyone, and to her, he was everyone.

I stretched out a hand, hesitated, and then placed it gently on her shoulder. She reached up and wrapped her fingers over mine, craving the bit of comfort I was offering. I didn't really know what to say—I wasn't good with words—so I just sat with her while she grieved.

I looked up at Marx, expecting him to be annoyed with me for pulling him away from the crime scene when he needed to be working, but he was watching me with a thoughtful expression.

I stayed with her for a while longer before leaving her to grieve alone. There was nothing more I could do for her. I said a silent prayer that God would be with her in this time of mourning.

"Sometimes you amaze me, Holly," Marx admitted as I fell in step beside him.

"When I'm not being *frustratin'*?" I teased.

A smile ghosted across his lips. "Or stubborn, yes. You have an amazin' capacity to care about people you don't even know."

I pointed up toward heaven and said, "That's His fault."

He shook his head, smiling. "It's not a fault."

He opened the passenger door when we finally arrived at the car, and waited for me to slide in. He leaned in the opening.

"Promise me that you won't get out of this car and that you'll keep the doors locked." When I fidgeted unhappily at the idea of promising that, he said, "I can't do my job if I'm worryin' about where you are and if you're okay. If you don't promise me, I'll call Sam and have him pick you up."

"He's on a date."

"I don't care if he's in confession."

"He's not Catholic."

He frowned. "Regardless. If I have to call him and ruin his evenin' because you're too stubborn to stay in the car, that's on you."

I sighed. "Fine. I promise to stay in the car."

"Good. Call me if you need me." He closed the door and locked the car before walking back to the crime scene. I slid down in my seat and put my feet on his dashboard.

5

We pulled up to the curb in front of my apartment building, and I started to unbuckle my seat belt. Marx placed a hand over mine, stilling my fingers before I could press the button.

"Holly, I need you to trust me."

He rarely touched me without permission, and I would've pulled away from him, but the gravity in his voice drew my eyes to his. He was staring beyond me through the passenger window. I followed his attention to my apartment.

A man lounged against my front door, completely relaxed with his hands in his jeans pockets and his legs crossed at the ankles. His dark hair was closely cropped, and the two years since I'd seen him last had shaved what was left of the baby fat from his cheekbones. His icy blue eyes sparkled with mischief beneath long black lashes.

Seeing him in person made every muscle in my body tighten, and I struggled to breathe.

"Holly."

I heard Marx's voice from a distance, but I couldn't pull my attention from the man on my doorstep. I was certain that if I looked away for even an instant, he would appear outside of my car window, and then it would be too late to run.

He winked at me, and his lips curved into a wry smile as if he knew exactly what I was thinking.

"Sweetheart." Warm, gentle hands cupped my face and forced my focus away from the window. I stared into Marx's deep green eyes as he said, "Breathe."

My throat made a choking sound as I sucked in a deep, trembling breath.

Marx brushed away the tears that spilled down my cheeks. "It's gonna be okay. I'll take care of it."

It wouldn't be okay; there was nothing that could make this okay.

He slipped from the car, and I pounced on the locks. I would choose a claustrophobic space over the man outside my apartment any day.

Marx walked around the car with one hand resting on his gun. The man in front of my door shifted his attention from me to the approaching detective, and an interested light sparked in his eyes.

"Ah, she sends the detective in her stead," the man said with a taunting smirk. "The perpetually troublesome Richard Marx, I presume."

Marx stopped a few feet from him. "Collin Wells."

"In the flesh." Collin spread his arms and inclined his head in a mockingly gallant bow. "You've made visiting my sister a very challenging ordeal with all of your bodyguarding and chaperoning."

"My sympathies," Marx replied flatly. "And Holly is not your sister."

"Well, not by blood thankfully, because that would make our relationship"—he hissed through his teeth—"awkward."

My stomach twisted at his words, and I made a valiant effort not to vomit all over Marx's floorboard.

"Whatever relationship you forced on her is over," Marx replied. "You're not gettin' anywhere near her."

"So you're the knight in shining armor. Or is that the sheriff? It really is hard to keep you all straight. There's a Mexican in the mix somewhere."

Sam had been born and raised in New York City, but he had very strong Latino heritage. It was obvious in his dark eyes and warm almond skin tone, but he wasn't Mexican.

"So you're a rapist *and* a racist," Marx said with obvious distaste, and I cringed. "What other endearin' qualities do you possess?"

Collin clucked his tongue in disappointment. "Let's not name-call, Detective. You're from the South, and the lack of intelligence inherent in that inbreeding area of the country doesn't equip you well enough to exchange insults with me." He paused for a moment and then added, "That means I'm smarter."

Marx grunted at the insult. "I don't care how smart you think you are. You prey on defenseless girls, which puts you one step below a cockroach in my book."

Collin pressed a hand to his chest and adopted a wounded expression. "That's hurtful. It makes me wonder what kind of stories my little sister's been spreading, because I'm just here for a long overdue visit with her."

"Like you visited her in Pennsylvania?"

Collin's lips curled up at the corners. "Something like that. But our last visit ended sooner that I would've liked. I'm hoping for more of a prolonged reunion this time."

I saw the muscle in Marx's jaw flex. I had never given him the details about Pennsylvania, except to say that Collin had found me, but he had drawn his own disconcertingly accurate conclusions.

"What's the matter, Detective? You look a little . . . tense. Is it because you can't arrest me?" He lifted his eyebrows in question. "Because even if I had done something to Holly in Pennsylvania, and I'm not saying I did, that state's a little out of your jurisdiction. You can't touch me."

Marx stepped closer to him, his voice lowering with tightly controlled anger. "You're in my jurisdiction now. And if you try to *visit* her—if you so much as touch her—I will redecorate this pavement with the insides of your head. And then I will kick back with a beer, in my Southern, inbred way, and celebrate your blessed passin'. I might even indulge in some fried chicken."

Collin's smile curved into an intrigued grin. "That sounds a little dark for you. What would Holly say?"

"Holly thinks life is precious. I think yours is a waste of good air. Now leave before I haul you in for trespassin'."

Collin tilted his head and pretended to think for a moment. "It only qualifies as trespassing if I'm inside the apartment or touching something that belongs to her." He rapped a knuckle on the outside of the metal door. "This belongs to the apartment complex. Now these"—he pointed to the three dead bolts—"these have Holly written all over them."

When I moved in, I had two more dead bolts installed as added protection against him; I didn't want him to be able to get to me the way he had in Pennsylvania.

"It's almost as if she's afraid someone might break in and hurt her," Collin said, humor in his voice.

The front doors to the main apartment building opened, and Sam stepped onto the porch. He must have been upstairs visiting Jace. He folded his arms across his broad chest and leveled a glare at Collin, looking far more menacing than I had ever seen him.

"Ah," Collin breathed. "Enter the Mexican."

"You're not welcome here. Ever," Marx said. "So I suggest you be on your way before I decide to arrest you."

"What exactly is it you think you're going to arrest me for, *Detective?*"

"Gettin' on my nerves."

"That sounds like an abuse of power. And let's be honest," Collin began, tucking his hands back into the front pockets of his jeans. "You don't have much power to begin with. You detectives—you're really just bloodhounds on a leash, constrained by the law while you sniff out the criminals too ignorant to cover their tracks. Even if I had committed a crime, you wouldn't be smart enough to catch me."

My fingers tightened on the door.

Collin left a trail of pain in his wake, and he was still walking free. I had told the police what he was doing to me and the other children, but nothing changed.

He was untouchable, and he was going to come after me again. I needed to leave. Now. I needed to protect myself.

"I like New York," he said. "I think I might stay a while, take in the sights, visit a few places, and become reacquainted with . . . what would you call Holly? An old flame?"

Panic gripped me.

I couldn't let him hurt me again. I scrambled across the seat, flung open the driver's door, and bolted.

"Holly!"

Marx's worried shout chased after me as I fled into a twisting maze of alleyways and side streets.

I should never have stayed. I knew better than to linger in one place for too long. Collin was always one step behind me, and I should've run the moment I realized he was in New York.

Now I had to flee with nothing: no money, no food, no plan.

I sprinted across a busy street, narrowly avoiding a yellow cab that took a corner too sharply. The driver's angry curses and beeping nipped at my heels as I sprang onto the sidewalk on the other side and darted down another side street.

I ran until my body gave out, and I stumbled to a stop against a metal building, wheezing for breath. I needed to rest, but it wasn't safe to stand out in the open.

I fumbled my way into the run-down building through a sliding door that hung at an angle and sank down in a cobwebbed corner.

Tears slipped from my eyes without my consent, and I buried my face in my knees as they quickly turned into sobs of grief. I didn't have the strength to hold them back.

Everything I had worked so hard for—my home, my small, simple life, my sense of independence and security—was all crashing down around me. I didn't know where to go from here.

But I knew sobbing in this corner wasn't going to save me. Lifting my head, I swiped at my wet cheeks and drew in the pain, stuffing it down deep so I could think clearly. It took far more effort to wall off my feelings than it used to, and I wondered if that had something to do with the people I had let through my emotional barriers.

I didn't have time to contemplate that at the moment. I needed a plan. I could probably rest here for an hour or two, give my body a chance to recover, and then—

The door beside me screeched open without warning, and a figure appeared in the opening.

I gasped and scrambled back, bumping into a shelf and sending what sounded like cans tumbling to the floor. I groped for the pepper spray in my coat pocket.

"Easy, Holly," a man's voice said, and the figure took a step back.

I brandished the can of pepper spray in a shaking hand as I huddled in the corner. I blinked at the veil of tears in my eyes until the man's features sharpened. "Sam?"

"Yeah," he breathed heavily. He leaned against the door frame and bent forward to rest his hands on his knees. "You're ridiculously fast, you know that?"

A strangled noise of relief escaped me, and the tension melted from my body, leaving me limp. "I thought . . ."

"You thought I was Wells," he said when I trailed off. When I nodded, he grunted. "Understandable."

I brushed away the remaining tears from my face. "Why did you follow me?"

"Because I'm faster than Marx."

That hadn't exactly been what I meant. "I didn't even know you were behind me."

"I was pretty far behind. You left some angry drivers in your wake who were more than willing to point me in your direction. I would've run right by this building, though, if I hadn't heard you crying."

I winced. Of course I had to stop and cry, and of course he had to hear me.

He pulled his cell phone from his pocket, punched a number on the screen, and put the phone to his ear. "Yeah, I got her. She's upset, but she's okay." He relayed our location to the person on the other end of the line, whom I could only assume was Marx. "We're definitely gonna need a ride. I'll stay with her until you get here." He ended the call and slid the phone back into his pocket.

My exhausted legs didn't want to support me when I pushed to my feet. "I won't go back."

He straightened when I stepped toward the door. "Holly—
"

"No." I snapped up the pepper spray. "I'm not going back. I can't . . . go back there, and you can't make me."

He held up his hands, palms out. "I'm not gonna *make* you do anything, so don't spray me with that. Let's just talk."

"Talking won't fix it." I eyed the door, wondering if I could slip past him. I didn't think he would grab me and hold me here until Marx arrived, but I was leery of getting close enough to him to find out.

"And running away will?"

"Maybe. Just . . . move and let me go."

He shifted into my path but kept his hands raised. "I know you're scared because Collin hurt you, but running—"

"How do you know that?" I demanded. "Did Marx tell you he hurt me? He said he wouldn't say anything, and I didn't tell you."

He sighed and dropped his arms back to his sides. "You just did." He glanced at the pepper spray, which was still aimed in his direction, and explained, "It wasn't hard to figure out. The way you reacted when he called on your birthday"—I'd had a panic attack that left me gasping and sobbing on my bathroom floor—"and the way you're reacting now . . . I'm not blind, Holly. I recognize terror when I see it."

I shifted my weight, feeling vulnerable and exposed. How much did he know? Did everyone know?

"What happened between the two of you?"

So he didn't know.

"What did he do to you?"

My stomach clenched painfully at the memories. "It doesn't matter."

"It does matter."

"No, it doesn't! All that matters is not letting it happen again. I have to go. So please just . . . get out of the way and let me go."

He didn't move.

Fine. There had to be another exit in this building, and it couldn't be that hard to find. I turned and started walking in the opposite direction.

"Where are you gonna go, Holly? Your life is here. Everything you own or care about is here. You need to think this through."

There was nothing to think through. Collin had made the decision for me when he showed up at my apartment.

"You told me you've been moving from place to place for ten years. But he still found you. How is running now gonna change anything?"

I tried to ignore his question as I visually scanned for an exit, my eyes sweeping over blankets and food wrappers—evidence that other people were using this building as a shelter.

"What will it change, Holly?"

"I don't know!" I shouted, whirling to face him.

Nothing I did ever seemed to make a difference. No matter how far I ran or how careful I was, Collin always found me. Running only delayed the inevitable, but what other choice did I have?

"I don't know," I said again, weariness seeping into my voice.

Sam approached cautiously. "When you run, does it discourage him from following you? Does it make him change his mind about hurting you? Or does he just find you and do it all over again?"

I let out a trembling breath and looked away.

"You're perpetuating the cycle by running, Holly."

I flinched and glared at him. "This . . . isn't my fault." But even as I said the words, old, familiar doubts whispered through me.

I wasn't the only person Collin had tormented, but he had hurt me differently. Maybe I had done something to attract his attention. Maybe I deserved this.

I wrapped my arms around myself, not wanting to believe those cruel whispers. "I didn't ask for this. And it's not my fault."

"I wasn't suggesting it was. I know you, and whatever he did to make you this afraid of him, I know there's nothing you could've possibly done to deserve it. None of this is your fault."

Hearing those words from someone other than myself loosened the knot of guilt and shame that had been growing like a tumor in my chest since I was fourteen.

"Collin is a grown man capable of making his own decisions, and it was his choice to hurt you. But the fact of the matter is, if he's been following you for over ten years, hurting you or attempting to hurt you, he's not gonna stop."

I knew he would never stop, which was why I had to live with one foot out the door for the rest of my life.

"If this is what he does, then it's what he'll continue to do until someone stops him. Unless you wanna be stuck in this cycle of you running and him tracking you down for the rest of your life, *you* need to change. *You* need to do something different."

I shrugged hopelessly. "What do you expect me to do, Sam?"

"Stay. Fight back."

He was out of his mind. "I . . . can't fight him. I've tried."

"I don't mean physically. That wouldn't even make sense." At my frown, he added quickly, "Not that I'm saying you're incapable. I just mean . . ." He struggled to find the right words and then let out an exasperated breath. "Don't run. He wants you to run so he can get you alone. Don't give him that opportunity. Stay here and stand up to him."

"There is no standing up to him. It just makes things worse."

"You're not alone anymore. If you stay, you have me, Marx, and Jordan to stand with you. There's no better time to fight back and break the cycle."

I shook my head. "You don't get it, Sam. Staying, fighting— it'll just make things worse."

"How?"

I squeezed my eyes shut and let out a breath heavy with memories. "Because people's lives are like a game of Jenga to him.

He will pull apart my life one piece at a time just to see how long it takes me to crumble. And he'll start with the people I care about. When he finally comes for *me*, none of you will be left to stand with me."

Sam's jaw hardened. "He's just one man, Holly. Let him try to come after three men in law enforcement."

"Sam—"

"At least give us the benefit of the doubt."

He had no idea how badly I wished I could. If I could trust them to protect me from Collin, then I could stay. "I'm sorry."

I turned and walked toward the nearest exit. I pushed open the door and stepped outside, only to freeze when I saw Marx's car pull into the alley.

6

You never realize how loud silence can be, until no one is willing to say what needs to be said. It just hangs over you like an ominous rain cloud, and you wait with apprehension for the storm to break loose.

I could feel the unspoken words between us, pressing on me as I sat in the chair beside Marx's desk.

I had finally caved to his pleas for me to get in his car, and he had driven us to the precinct, but all of his questions had been met with silence.

There were some things I just wasn't willing to talk about.

I tugged at the wool blanket he had wrapped around my shoulders shortly after we arrived, and took a sip of my hot chocolate.

I flinched in surprise when he spoke, breaking the long stretch of silence. "If you're still cold, I can get you another blanket."

A fine tremor in my body sent tiny ripples across the surface of my hot chocolate, but it wasn't from being cold. I gripped the cup with both hands and tried to will calmness into my body. All my anger and panic had drained away, leaving my nerves trembling with the echoes of fear.

"I'm fine."

He sighed when I said nothing more and returned his attention to the file he was reviewing. His expression was carefully blank, but his agitation was apparent in the quick, quiet tap of his pen on the desk.

I drew my knees into my chest and surveyed the abandoned squad room, scrutinizing every shadow. I half expected Collin to materialize outside one of the windows or come striding through the stairwell door.

My eyes snapped to a room behind us when I heard a man clear his throat. A pale glow illuminated the blinds of an office, and the plaque on the door read Captain McNera.

I exhaled slowly, trying to relax.

My attention trailed back to Marx, who was jotting down notes on a pad of paper. The tense quiet between us had stretched on for too long, and it was making me uncomfortable.

"Are you working on a case?" I forced myself to ask.

"Mmm hmm."

Okay, he wasn't going to make this easy. I tried again. "The drive-by shooting that killed your informant?"

His pen paused midword. Without lifting his eyes from the page, he asked, "How do you know the victim is my informant?"

I pressed my lips together. Maybe reminding him I had disobeyed him twice when he told me to stay in the car wasn't the best idea given his mood. "Mmm . . . the Star of David tattoo on his neck. I kind of also know his name is Ruiz."

"Why am I not surprised," he muttered. "And yes, *that* case." He resumed working without further elaboration.

I tapped my fingers on my cup. My body was exhausted and anxious at the same time, and I was having difficulty sitting still. "Do you want some coffee?" It was late, and I knew he must be worn out. "Or a doughnut?"

"No, I want you to talk to me," he said.

I sighed and stared down at my hot chocolate. It needed marshmallows. Big, fat, fluffy marshmallows that would make me feel better. "I don't wanna talk about . . . what you wanna talk about."

"Well, then it's gonna be a long night, because I'm not lettin' you out of my sight until we discuss what happened this evenin'." Despite the frustration in his tone, he kept his voice soft. "And then we're gonna come to an agreement."

I glanced at him warily. "What sort of agreement?"

"The kind where you agree never to run away again." He set down his pen and looked at me.

"I—"

51

A door slammed somewhere, and I almost jumped out of the chair. My gaze flickered wildly around the room, but I didn't see anyone.

"It's just the janitor, Holly."

I relaxed a little when I saw a man in overalls emerge from the bathroom with a bag of trash. He hummed to himself as he went about his work.

It took a moment for my heart rate to return to normal. If I wasn't so terrified that Collin was lurking around every corner, I might have had enough energy left over to feel embarrassed by my jittery reaction.

"Collin can't hurt you here."

That might be comforting if I could move into a police station. My phone made quiet water drop noises, and I pulled it from my coat pocket. Jace had sent me a text message:

> *Sam bailed on our movie. Said sumthing about an unwanted visitor at ur place. Am I missing sumthing? Everything ok?*

I exhaled a shaky breath and texted back:

> *Fine. Talk later.*

I snapped the phone shut and slid it back into my pocket. I could feel Marx watching me, and I chanced a quick look at his face. "Are you mad at me?"

The tightness in his expression eased. "No, I'm not *mad* at you, but I am upset. I'm upset that you didn't trust me enough to protect you."

If I wasn't mistaken, there was a twinge of hurt in his voice. "I do trust you, but . . ."

"You got scared," he said, when I fell quiet. "I know. I realize that comin' home to find him standin' on your doorstep was a shock, and after everythin' that man has done to you, I don't blame you for tryin' to protect yourself the only way you know how. But—"

"Can we talk about something else now?" I asked, scratching anxious patterns into my Styrofoam cup with my thumbnails.

"No, we can't. Because I need you to understand that no matter how scared you get, you're safe."

"Safe." A small choked sound somewhere between a laugh and a sob escaped my throat. I wasn't even in the same hemisphere as safe. "You don't understand."

He leaned forward in his chair and rested his forearms on his knees as he looked at me. "Then talk to me."

"Why do you always wanna talk about everything? I don't like . . . talking about him." Even thinking about Collin made me feel sick to my stomach.

"I know you don't like talkin' about him, but he's here now and we can't just pretend he isn't. I need you to tell me everythin' you can about him."

"You promised you wouldn't ask me anymore questions about him, or about what he did to me," I reminded him. That was the bargain we had struck last autumn.

"I made that promise under the condition that he wasn't an immediate threat, which he now is."

"You can't make me talk about him."

He clenched his jaw in frustration. "Why does everythin' have to be a battle of wills with you?" When I just stared at him, he sat back in his chair and scrubbed his hands over his face. "Okay," he exhaled, wrestling with his Southern temper that seemed to flare up every time it collided head-on with my stubborn resolve. He crossed his arms over his chest and said with deliberate calm, "I'm not mad."

"You look mad."

He grimaced and grumbled, "Well, I'm not."

He uncrossed his arms and returned his elbows to his knees, his insightful green eyes studying me, no doubt trying to unravel the threads of emotion I was fighting to keep wrapped up tight.

"Look, Holly," he began, his voice low and gentle. "I realize that talkin' about the man who hurt you is painful. I've also learned that when you're scared or hurt, your defenses come up. But you don't need to hide behind those defenses with me."

I stared into my hot chocolate.

"I promise you, sweetheart, I will put that man behind bars or in the ground if it's the last thing I do, but I need to know who I'm dealin' with."

Experience taught me that no one could protect me from Collin, and I would have a better chance of survival on my own. But the determination in Marx's voice made me want to believe him.

If nothing else, I believed he would do everything in his power to protect me.

I drew in a deep breath and let it out slowly. "He has this . . . fascination with pain. He gets some sick satisfaction out of hurting other people."

"He's a sadist," Marx said matter-of-factly, as if he dealt with people like that every day. Maybe he did.

"He would always find new and creative ways to scare and hurt us. If one way didn't get the reaction he wanted, he would . . . try something else."

My mind offered up graphic images and sound bites of crying children, and I tried to blink them away.

"When you say 'us,' you mean the other foster children?"

I nodded.

"But he fixated on you."

"I . . ." The words caught in my throat, and I nearly choked on them. "I was his . . . favorite."

I could only guess why: because I fought to deprive him of a reaction when he inflicted physical pain, because he was determined to find a way to break my spirit, because . . .

"Because you were a teenage girl?" Marx asked, his words echoing the next thought in my head.

Tears clung to my eyelashes when I looked at him. "Maybe." Maybe if I had just given him what he wanted, if I had cried the way the other children had, he never would've—

"Okay," Marx exhaled, derailing that painful thought. "He enjoys hurtin' people, specifically people who are younger or smaller than him. What else?"

I watched the agitated rhythm of the pen as he bounced it off the desk. "When he was hurting us, he would ask us how it felt. He wanted us to describe it to him."

I tried not to shiver at the memory of Collin's voice whispering in my ear, "How does it feel, Holly?"

A muscle ticked in Marx's jaw. "He likes mind games. Can't say I'm surprised."

"In the beginning, I think he asked because he was curious about something he's never experienced, but after a while I think he just did it to taunt us."

"What do you mean 'somethin' he's never experienced'?"

I tried to prepare myself for the blatant disbelief that would inevitably follow my explanation. "He bleeds and bruises just like everyone else, but he can't . . . feel pain."

The pen abruptly stilled, and I glanced at Marx's face, trying to gauge his reaction. His eyebrows were pinched together in confusion or doubt. Maybe both.

"You don't believe me."

Why had I bothered trying to explain? The only other cop I had told about Collin hadn't believed me either. But that man's disbelief hadn't stung so deeply.

I started to climb out of the chair, but Marx caught my arm. "It's not that I don't believe you. I'm just havin' a hard time wrappin' my mind around it."

I slipped my arm from his gentle grip and asked suspiciously, "You don't think I'm making it up or *misunderstanding*?"

"No."

The lack of hesitation in his answer surprised me so much that I plopped back down in my chair. "Really? Why?"

"Because I know you would never lie to me; withhold information, yes, but never lie. And you lived with the man for eleven months. That doesn't leave a lot of room for *misunderstandin'*."

I let out a breath and felt my shoulders sag in relief. It meant a lot to me that he believed me.

"What more can you tell me about this mysterious condition of his?"

"I looked it up once, but I don't remember what it's called. I know it's rare. People who have it aren't expected to make it to adulthood."

Collin would be the one to make it, I thought bitterly.

The pen started tapping again as Marx tried to work out the facts in his mind. "I assume he didn't just volunteer this information about his condition."

I shook my head as I looked down at my feet on the edge of the chair. "I figured it out when I tried to fight back." Fresh tears gathered in my eyes. "I tried—I did—but he's . . ."

"Holly." The softness in his voice drew my eyes back to his. "You were a fourteen-year-old girl, and he was a grown man. It wasn't a fair fight."

"I wasn't fourteen when he came after me again in Pennsylvania." Anger and frustration sharpened my voice.

Marx sighed. "I know what you're thinkin'. That maybe if you'd tried harder, *fought* harder, you would've gotten away. But the world doesn't always work that way. No matter how hard you fought, he had the advantage. He's bigger and stronger and he can't feel pain."

"I stabbed him."

Marx's eyebrows climbed up in surprise.

"When I got free, I stabbed him with a pair of scissors that I kept under my bed. And I pushed him down a flight of stairs after . . ." My throat constricted against the words. "After he—"

The bitter taste of bile on the back of my tongue was my only warning. Marx plucked the hot chocolate from my shaking fingers and thrust an empty trash can in front of me a split second before everything in my stomach came back up.

He held my hair back with a sigh. "I had a feelin' that was comin' at some point. I'm surprised it waited this long."

I dry-heaved into the trash can until I was so weak I thought I might fall headfirst into it.

When my stomach spasms finally subsided, I curled back into the chair and hugged myself. "I'm sorry I threw up in your trash can."

That was twice in the time we had known each other that he'd had the unfortunate pleasure of watching me vomit, only this time there had actually been something in my stomach.

He offered me a tissue to clean up with, and I took it, my fingers still shaking.

"It's just a trash can, Holly. And I've seen people's insides on their outsides before. An upset stomach doesn't even compare."

"It's technically my insides," I said halfheartedly.

"It's technically food."

I tried to take slow, normal breaths through my nose.

"I know that talkin' about what he did to you is hard," he said. "But if it helps you to share the details with somebody, I'll gladly listen."

I shook my head and wiped at the few silent tears trickling down my cheeks. I had never told anyone those details, and I had no intention of doing so now. Some secrets—some nightmares— weren't meant to be shared.

"If you change your mind—"

"I won't." I drew myself up in the chair, trying not to appear as brittle as I felt, and said, "I'm gonna get you some coffee now." He didn't object as I unfolded myself from the chair and walked away toward the break room, but I could feel him watching me.

I flipped on the light and looked around the small room. I twisted the sleeves of my shirt anxiously between my fingers as I shuffled over to the coffeepot. It was empty. That was fine; I would just make some.

I snooped through the cabinets for the filters and coffee grounds. It had been years since I made coffee, but I was pretty sure I remembered the basics. I found the coffee grounds and popped open the lid. No scoop.

Hmm. I guess I could just estimate.

I shook a heaping mountain of dark granules into the coffee filter, filled the pot with water, and hit the brew button. I stared at it expectantly, but nothing happened.

I nudged the coffeepot with an impatient finger. "Work."

When a low, male voice rumbled through the squad room, I stiffened and looked through the vertical blinds.

A uniformed officer strode toward Marx's desk, and some of the tension melted from my shoulders. It was only Sam. I hadn't realized it was already time for him to come on duty.

He looked around the room, searching for something, and it took me a moment to realize it was probably me. He spotted me in the side room and gave me a brief nod before sitting down in the chair I had just vacated.

His voice was barely above a whisper as he asked, "How's she doing?"

"As well as can be expected."

He leaned forward, elbows on his knees. "I remember you mentioning a few months ago that this guy was a threat, but you never gave me any details."

"The details aren't mine to give."

Sam stared at him, as if searching his unreadable face for more information. "What I saw out there today in that abandoned building—she was terrified beyond rationality. She was ready to go nowhere with nothing just to get away from this guy. Who is he?"

Marx tapped his pen on the desk again. "Her foster brother."

"I take it he's not here for a family reunion."

"Oh, he's here for a *reunion*, but I don't intend on lettin' him get close enough to her for that to happen."

Sam drew in a breath to speak, hesitated for a beat, and then asked, "I know he hurt her—she as much as said so when I confronted her about it—but did he . . ."

Marx gave him a look I couldn't interpret, and Sam let his question trail off with a heavy sigh.

"All I can tell you," Marx began, "is that she was abducted three months ago by a man who tried to kill her, and she barely blinks an eye at the mention of him. But you mention Collin, who hurt her two *years* ago, and it makes her physically ill."

Sam glanced at the trash can I had vomited in and grimaced. "I've known the guy for five minutes and I already wanna pound him into the floor."

Marx grunted, then asked, "You find anythin' when you went back to her place?"

"No, he's gone and no one saw which way he went or what he was driving."

"I wanna know where he's stayin', and I wanna know everythin' he's done since he's been here. He's been in town at least since her birthday. Why show up on her doorstep now?"

"You want me to stalk the stalker?"

"See what you can find out on the street. If there's a way to make him legally disappear, I wanna know about it."

The coffeepot made a horrible noise—like rocks in a blender—and my eyes widened as I took a cautious step back. Was it going to explode? Black liquid began to filter down into the pot, and I relaxed. The dreadful odor of coffee filled the room.

I grabbed two mugs from the cupboard and watched the coffee drip painfully slowly into the pot. Some people, like Jace, weren't morning people, and they had two personalities: pre-coffee and post-coffee. I had seen Jace pre-coffee, and that person was short-tempered, hopelessly clumsy, and prone to irrational fits of tears over the smallest things—like a missing sock.

If this was the pace that all coffeepots brewed, it was a wonder pre-coffee people didn't smash them to bits in a hulking rage. The grinding finally came to a stop and the pot leveled off.

"How's your case going?" I heard Sam ask.

"It isn't," Marx replied. I glanced at him as he flipped through the file. "It looks like your average drive-by shootin', but the timin' is too coincidental. And not a single person on that street would give a statement. Apparently they're all blind, which leaves me exactly nowhere."

My hands still shook a little as I poured the coffee, but doing something normal helped to ease my nerves. I puffed out a breath as I picked up both cups and walked carefully back into the squad room.

Don't trip, don't trip.

Marx gave me a small smile that didn't reach his eyes as he took the mug I offered. "Thank you, Holly."

I offered one to Sam, and he hesitated before Marx gave him a look. "Um, thanks," he said, accepting it begrudgingly. He stared into the murky liquid as if it were poison. Well, in all fairness, I had served him roofied punch once, but that hadn't exactly been my fault.

Marx took a sip, grimaced, and swallowed with some difficulty. "That's"—he cleared his throat—"flavorful."

Sam choked on his sip and pounded a fist against his chest. He set the mug down on the desk. "Flavorful is one way to put it."

I slid my hands into the back pockets of my jeans and sighed. "It's awful, isn't it?"

"It tastes like battery acid," Sam confirmed.

"Sam," Marx scolded.

"What?"

Marx forced down another swallow of his, but I suspected it was just to spare my feelings and not because he enjoyed it. "It's a little bitter," he admitted. "But it was very thoughtful of you to make it."

I bounced on my toes as I stared at the folder next to his coffee cup. "About your case. I heard . . . a rumor, I guess you could call it, that your informant was killed because he talked. I assume because he talked to you."

There was a silent moment of surprise before Marx asked, "Where did you hear that?"

"At the crime scene." *When you told me to stay in the car.*

"From whom?"

I lifted one shoulder in a shrug. "I don't know her name. It was a Latino woman who lived on the street. If it helps, she went into the house two sidewalks to the left of where the snake guy was standing."

Sam frowned. "Snake guy?"

"One of Holly's afternoon admirers," Marx muttered as he flipped the folder closed and dropped the pen into a cup on the desk. "If we drive through the neighborhood before headin' home, can you point out the house to me?"

The trace of anxiety in my stomach expanded at the word "home," and I shook my head.

"No, you can't point it out?" he asked with a puzzled frown.

"No, I can't go home." If sending me home was his plan of protection, I couldn't stay. I wouldn't be safe there.

The two men exchanged a look, and then Marx clarified, "Not your home, sweetheart. Mine."

Stunned, I asked, "You're . . . inviting me into your home?"

"That's the idea," he replied with a shadow of a smile. "I know you practically live in a bunker and you're the only one with keys to it, but I'm not comfortable entrustin' your safety to a few dead bolts and panes of glass. Not with Collin knowin' where you live."

The thought of him rekindled my instinct to flee while I had a chance, and I found myself staring at the stairwell door as possible escape routes raced through my mind.

"And I don't want you disappearin' again when he tries another surprise visit," Marx said, drawing my attention back to him. His gaze flickered to the door and then back to me, letting me know that my thoughts hadn't been as private as I would've liked. "I'll feel better if you stay with me. I have a guest room and it does have a lock on the door. You think you'll feel safe enough?"

I knew what he was asking: would I feel safe enough not to run? Truthfully, I didn't know, but I was too tired to run anywhere tonight. "Maybe."

"I'll take it. Let's call it a night." He shrugged on his coat and grabbed his gun from his desk drawer before the two of them escorted me out of the building.

7

We gathered a few essentials from my apartment and then drove through the neighborhood where Marx's informant was found. I pointed out the house of the woman I had spoken to, and then we headed to his place.

His home was a second-floor apartment in an old brick building. I followed him quietly up the steps and waited in the long hallway as he unlocked his door.

This scenario reminded me too much of my childhood. The State of Maine had shuffled me through twelve foster homes, and each time I stood on the doorstep of someone else's home, bag clutched in my hands, I wondered how long they would let me stay.

I might not be a little girl anymore, but my well-being was still contingent upon how long Marx would let me stay. He hadn't specified how long this invitation would last, but I had packed my emergency bag—a few changes of warmer clothes, hygiene necessities, some money, and some food—in case the situation changed and I needed to leave the city quickly.

I wasn't as confident as Marx and Sam that they could find a quick and easy resolution to my foster brother's arrival. Marx pushed open the door, flipped on the light, and moved aside to let me enter.

I took a few tentative steps inside, then stopped. I studied his impeccably clean apartment. A leather couch, a coffee table, and an entertainment system occupied the first room. There wasn't a trace of clutter, unless the open car magazine on the coffee table constituted clutter.

"You're very, um . . . neat," I said.

He smiled at the surprise in my voice. "I don't like chaos."

The next time I was in his immaculate car, I was going to leave a straw wrapper on the floorboard just to see what he would do. I bet he would freak out.

"Am I allowed to touch your floor with my shoes, or is it like the dashboard of your car?"

He narrowed his eyes. "Are you gettin' smart with me?"

"It's my natural disposition."

"Cute," he said with a faint smile. "Yes, you can wear your shoes, but don't put them on my couch. If you do, they might just disappear the next time you take them off."

He crossed the room and pulled the curtains shut to block out the night, or anyone who might be inclined to watch us through the window.

Fresh unease crawled through me. "You think he's watching?"

He glanced at me as he pulled the last drape shut in the living room. "He's not gonna get to you here. Even if he could scale the side of the buildin', the windows are always locked, and the front door is sturdy."

I glanced over my shoulder at the flimsy-looking door; I wasn't sure we were thinking about the same door. Maybe I was just unfairly comparing it to my metal barricade with three dead bolts. His door only had one lock. But then, Marx was a trained cop, so he probably wasn't worried about intruders.

"If by chance he does manage to get inside, I'm gonna be standin' between you and him with a gun. He might be immune to pain, but he's not immune to bullets."

"I don't know about that," I muttered. Logically, I knew Collin was only human, but he had haunted me for so long that it was easy to think of him as something more.

Marx's eyes clouded with sympathy as he approached. "I know you're scared, but you're safe here." He took the travel bag from my stiff fingers and carried it to the kitchen peninsula. "Try to relax and make yourself at home. You don't have to hover by the door."

I rubbed my sweaty palms on my jeans and took a few steps inside. I didn't know how to make myself at home in someone else's home. I always felt awkward and out of place.

"So . . . did you do the cleaning when you were married?" I asked, examining the unnatural tidiness.

"My wife was not what one might call"—he considered his words carefully as he closed the curtains over the kitchen sink—"domestic. If she tried to vacuum, she destroyed the vacuum by runnin' over rubber bands and bobby pins. If she tried to run the dishwasher, I had to unload it and reload it when I got home because it looked like an explosion had gone off inside and nothin' was clean."

I arched my eyebrows as I walked to the counter. "What happened when she did laundry?"

"We had to go shoppin' for new clothes."

A small, surprising laugh bubbled out of me.

Marx smiled. "It's good to hear you laugh, even if it is at my wardrobe's expense. Come on, I'll show you to your room."

He grabbed my bag and led me down the narrow hallway to one of the two rooms. He opened the door across from the bathroom. "I'm sorry about the size."

The space was the size of an average walk-in closet, with barely enough room for a bed and nightstand. I felt a claustrophobic flutter in the pit of my stomach as I stood on the threshold of the room, but I tamped it down.

This was infinitely better than where I would've slept if I had succeeded in running away. Condemned houses and closed factories weren't exactly warm and cozy, and then there were the rats.

"It's wonderful. Thank you."

Marx set my bag on the end of the bed and looked around the sparsely decorated room. "If I'd known you were comin', I would've gotten an eggplant pillow for the bed."

A faint smile touched my lips.

Eggplant purple was my favorite color, something I had only mentioned once in passing, but it was a fact he had apparently committed to memory.

I slid my hands into the back pockets of my jeans and surveyed the small room. New places made me nervous, which seemed odd considering I spent so much of my life on the move. But new meant unfamiliar and unpredictable.

I could maneuver through my apartment with my eyes closed, but I would stumble into everything in this space.

I walked slowly through the room, familiarizing myself with the dimensions and looking for anything I might be able to use as a weapon.

I unplugged the ceramic lamp on the nightstand and slid it closer to the bed so I could throw it if I needed to. The drawer would be a good place to stash a kitchen knife. Just so happens I brought mine.

I heard a sigh from the doorway and flicked a brief glance at Marx, who was watching me with a shoulder propped against the door frame.

"You're doin' that thing you do."

"What thing?" I asked, mentally counting the steps from the end of the bed to the door where he stood. Four steps, not unlike my front door to the invisible boundary of my living room.

I could remember that.

"Takin' the measure of your environment. I didn't notice it until we were in Kansas and everythin' was new to you. I watched you do it in the diner, and I'm pretty sure you did it at the Inn."

I looked up at him in surprise. I hadn't realized my behavior was so transparent.

"He's not gonna make it into your room, Holly. You don't need to plan an exit strategy."

I knew, inevitably, Collin would come for me, and I couldn't risk being unprepared when he did. My only advantages against him were my speed and my knowledge of my environment.

A hint of sadness touched Marx's voice. "I suppose after livin' in fear for so long, it becomes ingrained in who you are and everythin' you do."

Fear had kept me one step ahead of Collin for most of the past ten years. It provided me with an edge of constant awareness, and I had spotted him coming more than once.

I shifted my feet, uncomfortable with the direction this conversation was taking. "Not unlike being a cop."

He perceived and reacted to the world like a cop, even when he was "off duty." It was just a part of who he was.

"The difference bein' I chose to live my life as a cop. You didn't choose to live the past fourteen years of your life in a constant state of fear."

I forced a shrug. "Life doesn't usually ask us what we want."

Sometimes life fired one bad experience at you after another, and all you could do was dodge the bullets and hope you come out in one piece on the other side. I had a lot of scars—inside and out—but I was still mostly intact.

Marx rested his head against the door frame. "You deserve to feel safe, Holly. What can I do to make that happen?"

The simple knowledge that Collin was out there in the city somewhere destroyed any hope of ever feeling truly safe.

I rubbed at my arms as I turned toward the window and peered through the slitted blinds into the quiet street. I half expected my living nightmare to coalesce from the darkness and come for me, but the street was oddly still.

"Rewind time," I said beneath my breath, wishing it were possible to melt back through the years and save my family.

I would be able to see the beautiful person my sister would've grown into, I could hug my dad every day, and I never would've met Collin.

I felt the tightening of tears in my chest and closed my eyes. It was foolish to dream of impossible things.

"I wish I could," Marx said quietly.

It took me a moment to realize he was responding to my comment about rewinding time. I hadn't actually meant for him to hear me, but somehow it didn't surprise me that he had.

I cleared my throat and decided it was best to change the subject. "I assume Sam told you about our conversation in the warehouse."

"Mmm hmm."

His nonchalant response had me turning back toward him. "So you realize that by letting me stay here, you're putting yourself in danger."

"Mmm hmm," he repeated in that same calm, unruffled voice.

"You're not"—I grappled for the right word—"worried?"

Tiredness made his smile slightly lopsided. "I've put a number of people behind bars, Holly. Some of those people walk out of prison with a chip on their shoulder that has my name on it. I'm not unaccustomed to somebody holdin' a grudge against me, or tryin' to upset my life because they blame me for their much-deserved stay behind bars. Collin isn't exactly a new experience for me."

"Has that ever turned out badly for you? The grudges, I mean."

"Once or twice, but nothin' that caused irreparable damage. It comes with the territory. My job isn't to make friends; more often than not, it tends to be the opposite."

"What, the criminals you take off the streets don't wanna be pen pals?" I teased with a weak smile.

"We both know they wouldn't be able to read my writin' anyway."

His writing was nearly illegible. His ex-wife had likened it to chicken scratch. I thought it looked like something a chicken might do after a few shots of tequila.

"I, um . . ." I shifted my arms restlessly over my stomach, and Marx watched my nervous behavior without comment. "I can pay you for letting me stay here if—"

"No. What do you like on your pizza?"

I blinked at the abrupt change of subject. How had we gotten from me paying him to pizza toppings? Did I miss the transition? "But—"

"Neither of us have eaten much today, and you threw up most of what you did eat in my trash can at the precinct, so what do you want on your pizza?"

Okay then. He didn't want to talk about money. "I'm not sure I can eat anything."

"Please try."

I puffed out a defeated breath and dropped onto the edge of the mattress. "Mushrooms and pineapple."

He arched an eyebrow. "Fungus and fruit . . . on your pizza."

"Yeah," I replied with uncertainty. Was there something weird about that?

"Do you want me to see if they have *broccoli* too?"

"Well, what do you put on your pizza?"

"Meat," he answered before pushing away from the doorway and walking back down the hall into the kitchen. Meat. Well, that was precise.

I sighed and rummaged through my bag. I pulled out a picture frame and stared at the portrait of my family. I had spent most of my life unaware of who my family was, and when Marx finally tracked them down, he discovered I was the only member of my family left alive.

They had been murdered a few months before I turned ten, and the trauma of that night had forced me to forget the first nine years of my life. The man who killed them had come after me in October. If he hadn't, I might never have regained the memories I now cherished.

"Oh, Gin-Gin." I stared at my twin sister's innocent face. We might have been identical, but we'd been so very different. Complications at birth had left her permanently innocent and unaware of the evils in the world.

I missed her the most.

I set the picture on the side table where I usually kept it at home. I never went a night without looking at their faces. I knew it was probably irrational, but I was so afraid I would forget them again.

I pulled out my pajamas and toiletries next, and my gaze drifted to the open bathroom door across the hall. I wanted to wash away the slimy layer of bad memories on my skin, but I hesitated at the idea of showering here.

I set my clothes on the bed and crossed the hall to scope out the unfamiliar bathroom. It was an elongated space that was probably three times the size of my matchbook-sized bathroom and, aside from the wooden floorboards and cream cabinetry, there wasn't a trace of color. Even the shower curtain was white.

His bathroom was as boring as his car. I thought about snooping through the cabinets and drawers, but I doubted I would find anything more interesting than tweezers and cotton balls. Maybe some dental floss. I set my purple toothbrush and tube of Crest on the counter, adding a splash of color.

I checked the security of the door, and another wave of anxiety washed through me when I realized the lock didn't work.

"Um . . . is there a trick to this lock or . . ."

Marx's voice drifted from the kitchen. "It's broken and I haven't gotten around to fixin' it."

I'd been afraid of that. I shot the shower a longing look. I desperately wanted to feel clean, but with my emotions so frayed, being undressed and vulnerable with no lock on the door would probably catapult me into a panic attack.

I tried to decide whether or not it was worth the risk as I paced the narrow hall between the rooms. The floorboards creaking beneath my footsteps had to be driving Marx up a wall, but he didn't comment.

I wondered if it was strange for him to have another person in his apartment. Of course, for all I knew, he had women over regularly.

Oh, I hope not, or that might get super awkward.

I heard the sound of plates clanking on the counter and then Marx appeared at the end of the hall. "If you wanna take a shower, I can stay in the livin' room until you're done. I won't come anywhere near the bathroom."

I chewed on my bottom lip as I considered it. "You promise?"

He smiled. "I promise."

I puffed out a breath. "Okay."

I padded back into the bedroom to gather my things and then closed myself in the bathroom.

I showered quickly, reminding myself each time panic began to crawl beneath my skin that Marx wasn't like Collin. He would never take advantage of my vulnerability or invade my personal space.

When I finally emerged from the bathroom in my pajamas and fuzzy green slippers, the pizza had already arrived.

"Feel better?" Marx asked as he placed a slice of lukewarm pizza on a plate for me.

I slid onto one of the stools tucked beneath the overhanging countertop and stared at the unappetizing food. "A little." I picked at the toppings without eating them.

Marx leaned on the counter across from me. "Are you gonna be okay tonight?"

I popped a piece of pineapple into my mouth and shrugged. "Sure." I swallowed, and the chunk of fruit slid down my throat and landed in the pit of my stomach like a rock.

"Would you tell me if you weren't?" he asked. When I gave him a noncommittal smile, he sighed. "I thought not."

I tried a few more bites of pizza, if only because I felt guilty that he'd bought it, but it didn't set well in my stomach. I pushed the plate back across the counter and stood. "Thank you for the pizza, but I think I'm just gonna go to bed." Not that I expected to be able to sleep.

Worry darkened Marx's eyes. "Okay."

I tapped my fingers on the counter, hesitating before leaving. "I'm sorry for putting you in this position. I realize it's probably inconvenient and—"

"You're welcome to stay here anytime and for as long as you want."

I parted my lips to question that statement, then decided we were both too tired. "Thanks."

"If you need anythin' tonight, please wake me up. Even if you just wanna talk."

I nodded, even though I had no intention of waking him unless the building was on fire, and started toward the spare bedroom. I paused again when another thought occurred to me. "I'm sorry if I wake you tonight. Sometimes I pace when I'm . . . anxious."

He smiled. "I've noticed."

Right . . .

I had spent five minutes pacing the length of his hallway while debating whether or not to shower. I probably looked like a loon when I did things like that.

I interlaced my fingers and twisted them in front of my stomach, nerves making me restless. "Well, good night, I guess."

"Sleep well."

I retreated into the spare bedroom and closed the door, locking it behind me. I dropped back against it and sank to the floor, squeezing my eyes shut.

God, please give me the strength not to run. Running is so much easier than fighting, but I'm so weary of running. Give me the courage to stand in the face of my fears. Amen.

8

My eyes fluttered open, and I stilled when I saw a faint strip of light glowing beneath the bedroom door. My fingers curled around the blanket in tight fists as I watched that strip of light for a shadow—his shadow.

For a long moment, I forgot how to breathe, but then the nightmares that had haunted my sleep gradually faded away and I exhaled a quiet, tremulous breath. I was safe here. I sat up slowly and combed my fingers through my sweat-dampened hair.

There was a time when I used to lie awake, staring at that pale strip of light with dreaded anticipation. My mind would tumble from one fear to the next: would I see his shadow move through the light—a sign that he was about to slip into the room—or would I fall asleep and wake up to his fingers around my throat?

But that had been another time and another place. I forced the unsettling memories away before they could grab hold and leave me shaking. I folded back the blanket and stood.

I rubbed at the goose bumps on my arms as I padded quietly across the wood floor in my bare feet and tucked my chilly toes into my slippers. It wasn't the temperature of the room that left me cold, but the memories.

Maybe some marshmallow hot chocolate would help warm me up. It would certainly make my taste buds happy.

I unlocked the door and pulled it inward just enough to peer into the hallway. There was no one out there. I stepped into the hall and paused when I noticed Marx's bedroom door standing wide open. I gripped the door frame and leaned into the inky blackness of his room, but he wasn't there.

Surely, he hadn't left in the middle of the night.

Curious, I moved as quietly as I could down the hall. I found a pair of socked feet—big, socked feet—sticking over the end of the couch. Marx lay on his back with a file splayed open on his chest, sound asleep. He must have fallen asleep while working.

Relaxation smoothed away the fine wrinkles around his eyes and mouth, leaving him looking younger and peaceful. I smiled. I had never seen him peaceful before. The closest he'd come to that around me was vaguely amused.

I tiptoed around him to turn off the lamp so it didn't shine under my door. He didn't stir when the light went out.

I meandered to the window that overlooked the street and pried open the blinds with two fingers. Apart from the quiet beat of a neighbor's music, the night was calm. It was a stark contrast to the restlessness and uncertainty of my spirit.

In moments like this, I craved the comfort of my father's endless imagination. He had been able to dispel any fear with a hug and a story. The spooky shadows on the bedroom wall at night were just shadows of fairies dancing in the moonlight. Tornados were just the result of God sneezing, and I used to wonder if He had really bad allergies. He sneezed on Kansas a lot.

If my dad were alive, I wondered what he would say to dispel *this* fear. Maybe he would just hold me and tell me everything would be all right.

I glanced over my shoulder at Marx as his words from yesterday evening drifted through my mind: *It's gonna be okay. I'll take care of it.* I might not have my dad, but I had the next best thing—a grouchy, protective, Southern detective.

I smiled, looked up toward Heaven, and whispered, "Thank you."

I was about to let the blinds fall shut when movement caught my eye. Something near the building. I stretched up onto the tips of my toes to get a better angle.

Two men lingered near a parked car. The color of the car was distorted by the orange haze of the street lights, but given the shape and parking spot along the curb, I was pretty sure it was Marx's car.

I frowned as I tried to figure out what they were doing. It was four in the morning, so I doubted they were just washing his car windows. I looked back at Marx and started to call his name, then thought better of it. He had to be up in about two hours, and I didn't want to bother him.

When I returned my attention to the street, there was no one there.

Where . . .

I pressed my nose to the glass, but I couldn't see where the mysterious figures had gone.

My gaze drifted to the front door, and I considered going down to take a quick peek—both to make sure they hadn't done anything to Marx's car and to make sure my sleep-deprived, nightmare-riddled brain wasn't imagining things.

Fear stabbed through me at the possibility of finding Collin outside, then quickly gave way to fury. I had been jumping at every shadow since he showed up outside my apartment, which was exactly what he wanted.

He would be thrilled to know that I was too terrified to step outside alone. That in itself made me want to throw open the door and march downstairs. I was not a coward, and I wouldn't let him turn me into one.

I crept past the couch and grabbed my jacket from the hook by the door. I double-checked the pocket for my pepper spray before slipping it on over my nightclothes and zipping it up. It wouldn't hurt to poke my head out and see what, if anything, was happening.

I turned the dead bolt, wincing at the faint click that sounded like an explosion in the silence. I barely cracked the door before a hand wrapped around my upper arm, scaring me so badly that I screamed and nearly jumped out of my slippers.

"Sorry," Marx said, immediately snatching his hand back. "I'm sorry. I didn't mean to grab you. My brain isn't exactly firin' on all cylinders right now."

I pressed my back flat against the now closed door as I panted and waited for my heart rate to return to normal.

Marx rubbed his bleary eyes with his fingers and asked, "What were you doin'?"

I suddenly realized he had his gun in his other hand. "Were you gonna shoot me?"

"No, I wasn't gonna shoot you." He set his gun on the side table next to the door and folded his arms. "Now answer my question. What were you doin'?"

"I wasn't running away."

"I didn't figure you were runnin' away in slippers."

I looked down at my slippered feet. That was a pretty good point actually. When I lifted my gaze back to his, his expression suggested he was still waiting for an explanation.

"I was . . . just gonna check out the street really quick."

His brows dipped down over his eyes. "You are not goin' outside in the middle of the night by yourself."

The disapproval in his tone only made me more determined. I tried very hard to look taller and more imposing, which was probably undermined by my fuzzy green slippers and candy-colored pajama pants. "Believe it or not, I did manage to get by on my own for ten years. I can handle ten seconds on a dark sidewalk."

He frowned. "Are you tryin' to prove to me or yourself that you're not afraid? Because you don't have to prove anythin' to me, and you have every right to be afraid."

I bristled. "Stop doing that."

"You're not that hard to read."

"How did you even know I was leaving?"

"It's been a while since I've had somebody else in my apartment overnight, so when I heard tiny sneaky feet passin' the couch, it woke me. Now, do you mind explainin' what's so interestin' about the street at four in the mornin' that you felt the need to risk your safety by goin' out there?"

I folded my arms and squared my shoulders. "You're welcome to come with me and find out."

His eyes narrowed. "Fine. But you stay behind me."

I gave him a little salute. "Yes, sir."

His eyes narrowed even further. "Are you mockin' me?"

When I only smiled, he shook his head and muttered under his breath. He pulled on his jacket and a pair of shoes that rested along the wall. I didn't bother putting shoes on. My slippers were warm enough.

I followed him out of the apartment and down the steps. The front door of the building squeaked on its hinges when Marx pushed it open, and bitter cold air splashed over us.

The sound of a metal can clanged on the pavement as two figures broke away from Marx's car and bolted down the street.

"Hey!" Marx shouted. He bounded down the steps after them with his gun raised, but stopped in the middle of the street when the two men disappeared into an alley.

He lowered his weapon and stalked back to his car, the street lights highlighting the irritation on his face.

"Why didn't you go after them?"

"Because it's the middle of the night and I don't have backup. And I'm not leavin' you standin' out here alone." He pointed a finger at me and added, "And I am very frustrated with you, by the way. You were gonna come out here by yourself rather than wakin' me up, which I specifically asked you to do. You could've gotten yourself seriously hurt."

I clenched my teeth against an argument. He might be right, but I had no intention of ever admitting that.

He circled his car, inspecting it for damage while I huddled by the front door, shivering from the cold and trying to keep my teeth from chattering.

From where I stood, I could see the message spray-painted across the hood in large, black letters: BACK OFF. And the vandals had left the can of spray paint lying on the sidewalk.

As he came back around the front, Marx grumbled, "Why do people always gotta mess with my car?"

"It's worse than the spray paint?"

"They slashed my rear tires. Apparently they don't want me goin' anywhere while I'm *backin' off*." He stopped in front of the car and glared at the bold message on the hood. "Does this strike you as somethin' Collin would do?"

"Yes, but . . . there were two men. He would've been alone," I explained. At least I thought he would've come alone.

Marx grimaced. "All right. Back inside before your toes freeze off. I'm gonna call it in and get CSU down here to take a look." He followed me back into the building.

9

Sam was one of the responding officers. He sat, taking notes, on the opposite arm of the couch from where I was curled up. Unfortunately, there weren't many details for Marx and me to impart.

"Are you sure neither of you saw any faces?" he asked. "Were they wearing masks?"

"I'm not even sure they had heads," I replied irritably.

The corner of Sam's mouth quirked up. "So, in other words, stop asking?" He closed his notebook. "Okay. Are we sure this wasn't Collin? Could he be upset that Holly's staying here?"

"Holly doesn't think so," Marx said, but his tone implied that he wasn't so certain. He was reclining back against the wall beside the door, a cloud of bitter anger hanging around him. He loved his car, and someone had just defaced it . . . again.

The last time that happened, it was when he drove me to Maine to visit Izzy, the woman who had rescued me the night my family died. The killer hadn't wanted me in Maine, and he followed us to the hotel and vented his rage on Marx's car.

Of course, after that he had driven Marx off the road in Kansas and left his car on life support. If this was my fault too, I was going to have to find a way to pay him back for all the repairs.

"I haven't had a chance to track down where he's staying or what he's been up to, but I'll make it a priority when I get off," Sam said.

Collin was extremely skilled when it came to technology, which was why I had tried so hard to live beneath the radar, and if he didn't want to be found, I doubted they would be able to track him down.

"You know," Sam began. "If your informant was executed for talking to you, this could have nothing to do with Collin and everything to do with your case. Maybe the same people are sending you a message to back off."

"I considered that."

I looked between them, concerned. "And if you don't listen to the message?"

"Then I expect they'll try to force me to listen."

My arms tightened reflexively around the pillow I was hugging. "You mean they'll hurt you?"

"I guess we'll find out, because I have no intention of backin' off. Three kids overdosed on this drug, my informant was executed before he could give me the rest of the details, and then they touched my car."

"You should have a mechanic go over it before you try to drive it," Sam suggested. "Just to make sure they didn't damage anything important."

"Like the break line?" Marx asked sourly. "That wouldn't be cliché at all."

I flinched when something thumped on the outside of the apartment door, then realized it was someone knocking. Sam stood slowly, and Marx grabbed his gun off the side table before moving to the door and looking through the peephole.

He sighed and returned the gun to the table before opening the door. "Jordan," he greeted without enthusiasm.

I couldn't see Jordan's face from where I sat, but the brown leather jacket he always wore and his confident, relaxed posture gave him away.

"Are you gonna invite me in?" he asked, and I heard the lilt of amusement in his voice.

"I haven't decided yet."

"That's okay, take your time. I'll just hang out here in the hallway at . . ."—he lifted his wrist to glance at his watch—"six thirty in the morning. Because that's not weird."

"Why are you here?"

"I went to see Holly this morning. She's usually getting ready for her morning run about now, but she wasn't home. She still hasn't given me her number, so I couldn't call her, and you didn't answer your phone. Jace is apparently in a coma at this time of the morning because I stopped by to see if she knew where Holly was, but the only sound coming from inside her apartment is the silence of the dead. And I knocked. Loudly."

"She's not a morning person," Sam explained.

"Why do you need to see Holly?" Marx asked. "Self-defense trainin' isn't until tomorrow."

"Since when am I not allowed to see Holly?" Jordan asked, suspicion and impatience deepening his voice. "Something's going on. Holly's not home, you're dodging my phone calls, and there's a forensics team analyzing your car on the street."

"My car has nothin' to do with Holly."

"Where is she, Marx?" he demanded, growing agitated. He and Marx had butted heads from the moment they met in Kansas, and there was a moment of tension between them before Jordan asked, "Is she okay?"

Marx exhaled loudly and opened the door wider, revealing me in the living room. It took Jordan a second to absorb the fact that I was curled up in the corner of Marx's couch in my pajamas.

"Hey," he finally said, and he slid both men a questioning glance before walking into the apartment without invitation.

"Sure, come on in," Marx grumbled after the fact, slamming the door.

"Hey," I replied softly, curling my body a little tighter around the pillow as he approached. He stopped on the other side of the coffee table, allowing me that physical boundary.

"Since you're not one for slumber parties, I assume something happened. What's going on?" he asked. "Does this have something to do with the guy I saw lurking around your apartment this morning?"

Silence descended over the room.

"What guy?" Marx finally asked.

Jordan shrugged. "Didn't get a name. Dark hair, pale blue eyes, about my height. Called me Wyatt Earp. Either he knows I'm a sheriff and thinks he's funny, or he's had a serious break from reality. I'm banking on the latter. I told him to leave when I saw him loitering."

Marx pulled a picture from his wallet on the side table and handed it to Jordan. "Is this him?"

Jordan only needed to glance at the picture before confirming, "Yep, that's the guy."

When he offered the picture back, Marx said, "Keep it. I have more."

Jordan's forehead creased as he studied the picture more closely. "Who is he?"

Marx and Sam shared a look, seeming to come to some kind of silent agreement, before Marx turned to me.

He drew in a deep breath, as if to physically brace himself for an argument. "Holly, I think—"

"No," I cut him off, anticipating the suggestion he was about to make.

Sam's eyebrows drew together, and though he didn't say it, I could see his disapproval of my *illogical response*—as he would call it—etched into the frown lines of his face. "Collin isn't going anywhere, Holly. If he shows up while you're with Jordan, and you haven't filled him in, he's gonna be blindsided. You need to . . . ."

I glared at him until he snapped his mouth shut. I didn't want him knowing about Collin either, but that hadn't been my choice. This was my choice.

"Why don't you give us a minute, Sam," Marx suggested.

"Sure. I'll just get started on finding out who vandalized your car." He packed up his things, then let himself out.

Marx walked over to the couch and crouched down behind it, folding his arms over the back of it as he met my eyes. "Sweetheart—"

"I don't want him to know."

"Why?" he asked, his voice gentle. "Because you're afraid of what he'll think of you?"

Unexpected tears stung my eyes, and I averted my gaze. I didn't want Jordan to look at me with that knowledge in his eyes. "Please don't make this decision for me."

81

"I wouldn't do that to you. But for your sake and for the sake of everybody determined to keep you safe, I'm askin' you to at least consider tellin' him."

Jordan knew very little about Collin because he was a subject I actively avoided. All he knew was that Collin was the name of the man who called and upset me on my birthday.

I looked at Jordan and felt the words tangle up in my throat. I shook my head and jerked my eyes back to Marx. "I can't."

I expected to see disappointment in his face, but there was only understanding. "That's okay." He brushed a strand of hair from my cheek so unexpectedly that I barely had time to register what he was doing before his hand was gone. "Do you mind if I tell him what I know?"

I tightened my arms around the pillow tucked against my stomach. Marx knew only a little of my past, but it was probably enough for a detective to put the pieces together.

He waited patiently while I wrestled with the decision. Jordan would find out my history eventually, either from Marx or from Collin's cruel taunting, and maybe it was better just to get it over with.

I nodded in agreement.

"You don't have to be here while we talk," he said. "You can wait in your bedroom if you want."

He was probably worried I would throw up all over his nice leather couch if I overheard their conversation. That was a very good possibility; I felt nauseous already, and all they had said was Collin's name.

The pillow tumbled back to the couch as I stood. I wrapped my arms around my stomach and tried to keep my shoulders straight as I retreated into the spare bedroom, closing the door behind me.

I heard Marx sigh as I started to pace the length of the small room. "How much do you know about Holly's life after she disappeared from Stony Brooke?"

"Only what she's told me," Jordan replied.

"So not much, then."

"No, she doesn't really talk about it. I get an insight here and there about her younger years, but if I try to ask her for details about anything later, she just shuts down and stops talking."

"Well, there's a good reason for that. And his name is Collin Wells. When Holly was fourteen . . ."

I pressed my hands over my ears to muffle his voice. Maybe someday the pain wouldn't be so raw that talking about my past, even thinking about it, made me lose my stomach.

I tried to focus my mind on something other than the conversation going on in the living room as I paced the too-small room.

What month was it?

February. What was good about February? Discounted chocolates after Valentine's Day, the smell of flower bouquets in almost every store. Spring was just around the corner, and there would be fresh flowers everywhere in a beautiful rainbow of colors.

Beautiful.

My mind snagged on that word and took me back to the bookstore in my hometown where a sheriff with sparkling blue eyes peered at me between the books and called me beautiful.

That illusion was about to be shattered, and whatever beauty Jordan had once seen when he looked at me would be gone. Something deep inside of me cracked a little under the weight of that heartbreaking realization.

I released a trembling breath. *Focus. Spring. Flowers.*

Spring was my favorite time of year. The air was cool and fresh, and there was something peaceful and invigorating about the rebirth of nature.

A memory of hunting Easter eggs in the woods with Gin and Jordan swept over me. It had been a day of laughter and joy, and no small amount of sugary sweets. Peeps—sugar-covered marshmallows in those cute little shapes.

Amazing.

Gin and I used to split the bunny Peeps. Literally. We would each grab an end and pull until the sticky deliciousness split in two.

The memory brought a smile to my lips, swiftly followed by a sense of longing.

I missed her so much.

Raised voices pulled my attention to the door. It sounded like they were arguing. I felt rather than heard the violent thump that sent vibrations through the floorboards beneath me.

What were they doing?

Marx's voice snapped through the apartment loudly enough for me to hear it through my hands. "Jordan!" A door slammed a minute later, sending another wave of vibrations through my slippers and into my toes.

I uncovered my ears and watched the door warily, half expecting something or someone to come crashing through it. I blinked at the quiet tap on the outside of it a moment later.

I hesitated before pulling it inward a few inches. Marx stood alone in the hall. His carefully vague expression made my heart twist painfully in my chest.

"He left, didn't he?" I asked.

That was the door I heard slam. I exhaled a slow, steady breath; I wouldn't cry. Jordan's reaction was nothing more than I had expected. I'd had a feeling he would leave when he realized I could never offer him anything more than strained friendship.

I tucked my hair behind my ears and straightened my spine. "That's okay," I forced out. "I didn't really expect him to wanna stay after you told him."

"Holly—" Marx began, stepping aside to let me through the doorway.

"Don't worry about it." My voice was raw despite my effort to hide it. Although I had expected Jordan to leave, it still left an ache of disappointment in my chest.

"He didn't leave because of you, sweetheart. I told him to take a walk and cool off," Marx explained.

"What do you mean cool . . ." I trailed off at the end of the hall when I noticed the shards of wood that had once been a side table littered across the floor. "What happened to your table?"

He came to survey the mess with me and let out a sigh. "Jordan happened to my table."

"And the wall?" I asked, my gaze sliding to the hole in the plaster.

"That was the table."

My eyebrows lifted in surprise. "He threw the table into the wall?"

"Mmm hmm. Apparently my car bein' vandalized wasn't bad enough for one day. He had to assassinate my side table."

"Why would he . . ."

"Why do you think?" When I just stared at the hole in the wall, at a loss for an explanation, he said, "Because he cares about you whether you think it's possible for somebody to care about you or not."

I lifted startled eyes to his.

I had never told anyone I felt that way, but he had an irritating habit of reading me. He offered me a sad, knowing smile before continuing his explanation.

"All this time he's been wonderin' why you're so on edge around him, why his touch can send you into a panic. Of all the possibilities he imagined, none of them even came close to the truth. When I told him you were tortured by your foster brother, and that the man he ran into outside of your apartment is *that* foster brother, he . . . didn't take it well."

I swallowed and looked at the remnants of his anger lying in pieces on the floor. Okay, maybe he had reacted a little more strongly than I expected.

"But . . . that doesn't make sense. He barely knows me." And I knew that was my fault. I deliberately kept him at arm's length because it made me feel safer.

"You were his best friend, Holly, and he's spent the past several months *gettin'* to know you. Don't begrudge him his anger for the childhood friend he loved and the young woman he cares about."

I chewed on that as I stepped carefully around the bits of strewn table and knelt down to clean up the mess. Jordan and I *had* loved each other as children; we had been practically inseparable.

But things were different now.

I was different now.

The front door crept inward, and Jordan filled the opening. My fingers stilled on a sliver of tabletop, and I straightened apprehensively.

He cleared his throat and said quietly, "I'm sorry about the mess." Although the apology was directed at Marx, his gaze lingered on me.

"It's fine," Marx said, but his tone clearly suggested it wasn't. "I'll give you two a minute." He walked into the kitchen and started rummaging through the refrigerator.

Jordan closed the door behind him and leaned back against it. Silence hung between us, and I searched his face, taking in his tightly pressed lips and the tears that shimmered in his eyes.

He drew in a breath. "Holly, I—"

"You made this mess. You should help clean it up."

There really wasn't all that much to clean up, but I pretended to be *very* busy when he sat down on the floor across from me.

For a moment, he remained motionless, and then he scooped some of the small pieces of plaster into a pile. "In all fairness, no single man's apartment should be this neat. It goes against some sort of man code."

A quiet, indignant snort issued from the kitchen. Apparently Marx disagreed.

"So you were just adding character to the space?" I asked.

He gave a subdued shrug. "The hole in the wall gives it a masculine air."

"Actually, it just looks like he has rage issues and punches holes in the wall when he's grouchy."

"I wouldn't say rage. Anger, maybe. Hurt, shock," he corrected, and I knew we were no longer talking about Marx.

86

I had expected the news to catch him off guard, disgust him, maybe even upset him—not to the point of throwing a table—but I had never expected it to hurt him.

He rested his hand on the opposite end of the table leg I had a hold of, and my heartbeat quickened.

"I'm sorry, Holly," he said, his voice heavy with pain and regret.

I snatched my hand back and scooted away from him, barely managing to squeeze out a response. "You don't have to apologize to me. It wasn't my table."

"I'm not talking about the table. I don't care about the table."

I tucked my hands between my thighs and stared at the floor. "I don't wanna talk about the other things."

The noises of breakfast being prepared in the kitchen abruptly quieted, and I knew Marx was listening to make sure Jordan didn't press me for details.

"Okay," Jordan agreed reluctantly. He shifted, drawing up a knee and draping an arm over it as he toyed with a piece of wood. "But can we talk about something related to the *other things*?"

I hesitated, wary. "Like what?"

"Like why you were so afraid for me to know. Marx knows, Sam knows, but you didn't want me to. Why?"

I hadn't wanted anyone to know. I had done my best to forget, but the truth never truly went away. "I thought, if you knew, you might leave and not come back."

And I hadn't wanted him to leave. Maybe that was selfish. But he reminded me of home, of another life, and of Gin.

"Why would you think that?"

I pointedly avoided looking at him as I tried to explain. "Because . . . because now you know I'm . . ." *Irreparably damaged? Tainted?* "That I can't . . ." Shame choked my voice, and I felt the pressure of tears building behind my eyes again. I bit down on my trembling lower lip and looked out the far window.

"Holly, what happened, what was . . . done to you doesn't make you any less beautiful of a person. That's on him, not on you. And it doesn't affect the way I see you."

I blinked fiercely. I was not going to cry.

How could it not affect the way he saw me? I wasn't whole anymore. My spirit was scarred and fractured, and each time Collin hurt me, I felt another little piece of it crumble away like dried clay.

Clay can be remolded.

The thought came out of nowhere, and I was still pondering it when Jordan said, "Knowing the truth gives me a better understanding of why you guard yourself the way you do."

I rubbed at my damp nose with my sleeve and dragged my eyes back to his.

"And I want you to understand that just because I think you're beautiful, it doesn't mean I'm gonna pressure you or,"—he paused, seeming to struggle with his words—"Force you into a relationship or situation you don't want. You don't have to be afraid to be alone with me."

I lifted my chin. "I'm not afraid."

The right side of his mouth quirked up in amusement. "Well, even if you were, hypothetically, you wouldn't have to worry. We both know Marx would shoot me if I did anything to hurt you or make you uncomfortable."

"Yes, I would," came from the kitchen.

"So why are you still here? I mean, if not for . . ." I drew my knees into my chest and wrapped my arms around them. "You know, a *relationship*."

"I'm here because I want a chance to know you, to spend time with you."

That answer didn't really allay my fears, so I waited to see if he had anything more to add.

"I promise I'm not asking for intimacy," he continued. "And I'm not asking to be your boyfriend. Just . . . let me be your friend who happens to be a guy."

I wanted to believe him, but in my experience, men didn't do *just friends*. They inevitably wanted something more than I wanted to give.

Jordan had told me once before that he was only interested in being my friend, but sometimes I caught him looking at me in a way that set off sparklers of anxiety in my stomach. It felt too similar to the way other men had looked at me before, and I didn't like it.

My doubt must have been visible on my face, because he said, "I swear, Holly. Just friends. The only way it would ever go further than friendship is if you want it to."

I missed the innocent, trusting bond we had shared as children, that unbreakable friendship, and I wanted to believe we could have it back.

"How does that work exactly?" I asked, and then added for clarification, "Friendship with you, I mean. What is that supposed to look like?"

I couldn't see us tearing through leaf piles and playing catch like we did when we were children.

"Whatever you want it to look like."

What *I* wanted it to look like? The only true friend I'd had in the past eighteen years was Jace, so I had a pretty limited knowledge when it came to types of friendships. "So . . . you're offering to be one of the girls?"

"If that's what it takes to spend time with you, yes."

"What about shopping?"

I caught the flicker of male dismay before he could conceal it from his face. "If you wanna go shopping, then . . . we'll . . . go shopping."

I loathed shopping, but I might drag him to a few stores just to see how long he could hold out under the pressure.

"How about baking? Can you bake?"

He gave me a crooked smile. "I'm better at the eating part, but I'm sure I can follow a recipe."

Ha! Following a recipe wasn't as easy as it sounded. I had tried.

I tugged at my lower lip with my teeth, considering the friendship he was offering. I wanted it so badly, which meant I needed to take the chance despite the insecurities and doubts gnawing at me.

"What if . . ." I hesitated before letting the rest of the words tumble out awkwardly. "If I wanna go for a run?"

He shrugged. "I'm always up for a run."

"Good. I wanna go for a run," I announced before I could chicken out. I stood and brushed the drywall dust from my hands.

He rose slowly, one eyebrow cocked in surprise. "Just the two of us?"

Apart from that brief time in Kansas when I needed his help to find Marx, we hadn't been alone together since we were kids.

I straightened my shoulders and said, "If that's okay with you."

Jordan grinned. "I have no objections."

Well, that made one of us.

My mind was firing out objections so quickly that I barely had time to consider one before the next one slammed into me.

I decided it would be a good idea to remind him of the ground rules. "Just because I'm *tentatively* agreeing to spend time with you . . . alone . . . doesn't mean you get to cross the border whenever you want."

He grinned and held up his hands. "Four feet at all times."

I narrowed my eyes at him. "Good. Because I carry my pepper spray . . . at all times."

He laughed. "I remember. If I pick you up and carry you, drag you, or touch you, I get sprayed in the face."

Oh yeah, I had made that threat back in Kansas.

"That sounds about right," I agreed, and his grin broadened. He probably didn't think I was serious, but I was. "I'm gonna go change now."

"And then you're gonna eat breakfast!" Marx shouted before I could escape into the spare bedroom.

I backtracked to the kitchen. "But I'm—"

"Not hungry. Yes, I know. It's becomin' a pattern with you, but you need fuel to jog." He looked at Jordan. "You too, since you're goin' with her."

One of Jordan's blond eyebrows crept up. "Yes, Dad."

Marx gave him a look that would've made me want to shrink between the floorboards. "Don't ever call me that."

I retreated into the spare room and locked the door before sinking onto the edge of the bed. The past twenty-four hours had been an emotional roller coaster. I was looking forward to a run to help burn off the excess anxiety Collin's visit had left churning inside me.

"Does she always lock the door?" I heard Jordan ask quietly from the kitchen.

"Sometimes people who've been through what she has need a little added security to help them remember what it feels like to be safe. If a lock helps . . ."

I turned my attention to getting ready. It was freezing outside, so I layered a few long-sleeved T-shirts and sweatshirts, picking my purple "Lettuce is for bunnies. Give me chocolate" hoodie to go on top.

I paused with my hand on the doorknob when I heard low, serious tones coming from the kitchen. I caught Marx mid-sentence, but it was obvious who he was talking about.

"You cross paths with him on the street, you need to keep your head."

"I'm not gonna lose any sleep over punching him in the face," Jordan replied.

"Jordan—"

"After what he did to her, you can't honestly expect me just to let him walk away if I see him again."

Marx sighed. "I understand where you're comin' from. It infuriates me that the monster who hurt her is walkin' around free. The fact that he's here with the intention of hurtin' her again, and I can't touch him, is almost enough to make me throw the rule book out the window and him right after it. But as temptin' as it is to go after him for what he did to her, it's not worth it."

91

"Yeah, I don't think we're gonna agree on that point."

"Keepin' Holly safe and makin' sure she feels safe so she doesn't try to run is more important than teachin' him a lesson, Jordan. If you wanna protect her, then keep your focus where it needs to be."

I forced myself to twist the doorknob and leave the quiet security of the bedroom. I padded soundlessly into the kitchen.

"He's . . ." Jordan bit off whatever else he intended to say when he saw me, but I caught the anger in his expression before he masked it.

"Have a seat, sweet pea," Marx suggested, with a nod to the vacant stool farthest from Jordan.

I narrowed my eyes at him as I walked to the stool. "I am not a pea."

"I don't think she's all that sweet either," Jordan teased halfheartedly.

"Not as sweet as sugar," I said, sliding on to my stool. I hadn't called Marx that since the killer—since Edward—drugged me and left me high as a kite. I knew it freaked him out. "Ain't that right, *sugar*?"

Marx pointed a spatula at me. "That's enough out of you, young lady. Haven't you ever heard not to antagonize the cook?"

"You won't do anything to my food. You like me too much," I said, grinning.

He smiled as he set a plate of pancakes, hash browns, and scrambled eggs in front of me. "You're lucky that's true."

The pancakes and hash browns had a suspicious prepackaged quality to them, but it was the thought that counted.

"So what are you gonna do today? Aside from cook breakfast," I asked him as I poked at my rubbery pancakes.

"I have a homicide to investigate."

10

Jordan and I jogged through the park until we were both too worn out to stagger another step. I could barely stand, but the freedom of running left me feeling recharged and determined to face the day.

I stared up at the winter trees and panted, trying to catch my breath. Jordan dropped back against a tree and tugged at the collar of his sweatshirt, letting the cold winter air breathe over his sweaty skin.

When I looked over at him, he grinned, all charming dimples. "You realize we have to jog back now."

"It's only three miles."

His blond eyebrows drew together. "Only? We already jogged nine. Do you have an off switch?"

I smirked at him. "Wimping out?"

A sparkle of challenge in his eyes preceded his declaration, "If you get too tired on the way back, I'll gladly give you a piggyback ride to the car."

"Ha, I just plan on leaving you behind if you get too tired."

"Well, I didn't expect you to carry me, but you could at least throw me a bone and pretend to pass out on the path next to me."

I smiled and shook my head as I started the long trek back to the car at a leisurely walk. Jordan fell in step beside me but afforded me the space I needed.

"You're faster than Sam," I said.

"A fact I fully intend to rub in his face."

He was faster than me too, but I wasn't admitting that out loud. "Do you jog a lot at home? In Kansas, I mean."

"Every morning. I try to encourage my deputies to exercise regularly too. Being fit is important in law enforcement. Nobody feels very confident in a cop who looks like he just ate his way through Dunkin' Donuts."

I laughed. "Probably doesn't help that Oma is always baking you guys cookies."

Oma was his grandmother, and she was a baking addict. She baked cookies the size of softballs, and they were mouthwatering.

Jordan shook his head. "She won't be happy until we're all too fat to climb over a fence. I have to jog for an hour and kickbox for forty-five minutes every day around Christmas."

Christmas . . .

I remembered Christmas in Kansas. Immediately after opening gifts with our own families, Jordan and I would meet in the woods to exchange the gifts we had gotten each other.

And then we would go through our stockings, trading and sharing treats. Gin would come bouncing out in one of her new princess dresses thirty minutes later, sticky-faced from candy canes and mint chocolates.

The memory brought a smile to my lips.

A gust of cold air turned my sweat chilly, and I shivered. I didn't do well with the cold, and if we didn't pick up the pace, I was going to freeze.

"Did you catch your breath yet?" I asked with a glance his way.

He gave me a wry smile. "I've been waiting on you."

Liar.

We broke into a slow jog for the return trip. I could push myself harder, but surprisingly, I was enjoying the companionship during my run, and I wasn't ready to return to the car.

A half hour of blessedly lighthearted conversation passed between us before we reached the edge of the park.

"We should make this a daily ritual," Jordan suggested breathlessly. "Though I don't think I'm up for twelve miles every day."

"I thought you were *fit*," I teased.

Jordan laughed. "I am, but I'm built for speed, not endurance."

I slid onto the hood of his car to rest, something Marx would never let me do. He would freak out if I left shoe prints on the hood of his car. "Well, we can't run every day anyway, because you have to go home soon."

Jordan had only gone home once since my birthday, and I knew he had a job and a family. He was the sheriff of Stony Brooke. I didn't imagine that was a job he could do over the phone.

He unlocked the car and grabbed the bottle of water off the dashboard. He broke the seal and tossed it to me. "I had planned to go back next week, but . . ."

I caught the bottle, dropped it, and snatched it before it could roll off the hood. I heard Jordan's snort of amusement at my perpetual case of the butterfingers.

"But what? Don't you wanna go home?"

His expression clouded over, much like it had this morning after he spoke with Marx in the kitchen, and I knew what was troubling him.

"Don't stay because you're worried about me. I can take care of myself." I made a conscious effort not to be offended by the doubt that flashed through his eyes. "Okay, so I'm a little . . . slow in self-defense class."

He set his own water bottle on top of the car and gripped the edge of the roof as he leveled a concerned look at me. "You get hurt a lot, Holly."

"I'm not the one who got stabbed," I reminded him.

He had tracked Marx and me back to my childhood home this past autumn, where Edward was holding us captive, and he was stabbed during his attempt to rescue us.

"Yes, I got stabbed."

"And thrown around like a rag doll," I added, just to be sure we were keeping an accurate account.

He rolled his eyes. "Yes, but in my defense, that guy was clearly on steroids in the womb. And my point is, in the space of two months, you were attacked in the park, drugged, assaulted, abducted, and . . ."

Nearly sliced to ribbons by a serial killer.

I pressed a hand to my stomach as I remembered the knife slicing into me. The scars were a haunting reminder.

I cleared the uncomfortable emotions from my throat. "For the record, I didn't get hurt in the park." By the grace of God. "And the rest of that was one insane individual, so . . . that's . . . a really flawed argument."

"You're a trouble magnet."

"Yeah," I agreed, rubbing the bottle between my palms. "You should probably run away while you still can."

His lips thinned in a smile. "I'm not running away. Now that I found you, you're stuck with me. But my point is, I was hesitant to leave *before* Marx told me about Collin. Now, I—"

"Jordan you have a family and a job. Your parents and your town need you." It had been my town too, once upon a time, but I would never be able to live there again, not after everything that had happened. "I won't be the reason you lose your job or fall away from your family. I don't want that."

"If I leave you here with that . . ."—he curled his fingers into fists and blew out a breath—"that man, I'm not gonna be able to do anything but worry about you every day."

"Would you be less worried if I was a guy? I'm pretty sure I could pull off baggy jeans and a crooked baseball cap."

He didn't seem to appreciate my attempt at levity, because his troubled expression didn't change.

"I would still worry if you were a guy. Just . . . differently."

"Well, just don't think about it," I suggested, dropping my gaze to my worn sneakers. "That's what I try to do."

He hung his head and let out a breath laden with too many raw emotions. Maybe that had been the wrong thing to say.

Tension played across his broad shoulders and down his arms, and I knew he was wrestling with anger.

At least he doesn't have a table to throw.

It seemed strange that the boy I remembered—the one who hid behind me from snakes and spiders, knees practically knocking together—had grown into this strong man with a desire to protect.

It was also strange that he had followed in his father's footsteps. He had dreamed of being anything but a cop, but here he was, a sheriff. I wondered if the death of my family had changed that.

It had changed my dreams too. My dreams of helping animals like my mom did had given way to dreams of finding a forever home, and then to simply finding a place where I didn't have to be afraid anymore.

I wondered what Jordan would've done with his life if he hadn't spent it trying to solve the murder of my family. I bet he would've become a football player. The one that runs really fast with the ball.

I bounced my toes on the hood as the cold wind cut straight through my clothing and took my body heat with it. I hated winter almost as much as I hated autumn. I was ready for February to end.

Jordan finally pushed his body up straight and said, "What do you say we get you cozied up to a heater before you turn into an icy hood ornament?" His calm tone belied the raw emotions in his eyes.

"Heat," I said passionately.

"Just so happens my car has a heater. And heated seats. And I might be willing to share."

"Oh?" I asked, sliding off the hood of the car. "You would do that?"

"Only if you promise to keep your hands to yourself. I have boundaries, you know," he said, completely deadpan, and I laughed.

He walked around the car to open the passenger door, then closed it after I settled into the seat.

He slid behind the wheel. "So where to?" When I shrugged, he glanced at his watch. "We should probably swing by your apartment to get your things."

The breakfast discussion this morning had revolved around how best to keep me safe with Collin in the area. Marx had suggested I continue to stay with him until they figure out how to deal with the situation, but I had only packed a few changes of clothes.

He had also suggested that I avoid being alone, which meant someone with a gun would accompany me everywhere.

"Right," I sighed, slumping lower in my seat. As we pulled out of the parking space and headed in the direction of my apartment, I tried not to dwell on the fact that Collin might still be there.

When we pulled into a vacant space against the curb, Jordan climbed out first. He rested one hand on his gun and looked around, his demeanor suddenly sharp and watchful.

Nerves fluttered in the pit of my stomach as I looked at my apartment. Yesterday morning it would've been a welcome sight, but all I could think about this morning was Collin leaning against the front door: the taunting curl of his lips, the chilling sound of his voice, the way he looked at me, even from a distance.

I was so afraid he would step out from behind the building. *Don't be such a chicken.*

I straightened my spine and shrugged off as much fear as I could before starting up the sidewalk. Jordan hovered nearby as I fished the keys from my bag. My fingers shook so badly that it took me four tries to unlock the door.

I breathed a sigh of relief when the last dead bolt clicked open. I pushed open the door, and my fat cat, Jordan—whom I had subconsciously named after my childhood best friend—chortled and flopped on the floor at my feet like a dead opossum. I hefted him up with a grunt and cradled him in one arm. "Hi, Tubby."

Jordan stepped inside but remained by the open door. My apartment was small, and I suspected he was trying not to crowd me. If he stayed on the four-foot perimeter, we couldn't actually be in the same room.

It was a one-room apartment—two, if you considered the tiny bathroom a room—and the end of my couch was about two feet from the end of my bed. My bed rested in an alcove that was cordoned off by heavy purple drapes, giving the illusion of a bedroom.

"What all do you need to grab?" Jordan asked.

"Cat food," I said, dragging the small bag out from under the sink. "Litter." I tugged that out next. "And a few more pairs of clothes."

My apartment felt cold despite the electric heat, and it was only when I brushed aside the purple drapes that the full icy draft washed over me.

My cat tumbled out of my arms onto the mattress as I stared at the windows by the bed. They weren't broken and rimmed with jagged pieces of glass; the panes of glass were just . . . gone.

I crossed to the windows and peered out into the frozen flower bed. I wasn't sure what I expected to find, but there was no one standing there, and no evidence that anyone *had* stood there recently.

My mind went strangely blank, and for a moment, I couldn't think. But then the truth crept slowly over me, and my lungs constricted.

Collin had been inside my home.

Who else would bother breaking into an apartment, my apartment, that clearly had nothing worth stealing? I stepped back, bumping into the side of my bed.

What did he do? He did something.

Collin would've left me a little reminder of our history just to taunt me. I looked around my apartment, and then I noticed what I had missed when I opened the drapes and saw the windows. The rod above my bed, where my clothes normally hung, was empty.

My eyes fell to the small wooden box resting on my cardboard nightstand. I stretched out a shaking hand to lift the lid, praying that everything would be as I left it.

Seeing the bottom of the empty box was like a blow to the stomach, and it knocked the wind out of me. I pressed back against the wall and hugged myself as I fought the rising panic.

Collin enjoyed playing pranks on people, especially me. He had done it frequently when I lived with his family: hiding my clothes and towels while I was showering, stealing my undergarments, putting tacks or bugs under my blankets or in my shoes.

I forced myself to swallow the bile that crept across the back of my tongue as I remembered what happened the last time he took all my clothes, and slapped the lid of the box shut. I couldn't stand staring at its emptiness.

"Let's go," I said, snagging my cat and backing into the center of the apartment.

Jordan looked me over in confusion. "You didn't pack anything. What about changes of clothes?"

I shook my head. "I just wanna go."

His brows drew together. "You look pale. I mean, more so than usual. And you're trembling." He stepped away from the door and crossed the apartment to stand beside me.

The instant his gaze landed on the windows—which had been just beyond his sight from his position by the door—his hand fell back to rest on his gun, and he moved cautiously around the bed to investigate.

There was a note of tension in his voice as he stared through the farthest window frame. "I'm guessing Collin came back after I left this morning." He scanned the floor. "What happened to the glass?"

I looked at the floor. I had been too preoccupied with the empty window frames to realize that no glass had crunched beneath my feet. It was as if someone had shattered the windows, slipped inside, and then cleaned up after themselves.

Collin had taken the glass for a reason, and I was pretty sure I would find out why in a very unpleasant way.

"Who knows. Can we go now?" I asked.

"Holly, someone broke into your apartment. Probably Collin. We can't just leave."

"Yes, we can."

"We need to report it."

"No, we don't."

His gaze dropped to my feet. I hadn't noticed I was bouncing my right foot in an anxious rhythm until he brought it to my attention. I forced myself to stand still.

"What did he take besides the glass?" he asked. "Anything?"

My eyes skimmed the bare curtain rod and then drifted unwittingly to the wooden box. His gaze followed mine, and he opened the lid to peer inside. He paused for a moment and then reached into the box.

To my surprise, he pulled out a folded slip of paper I hadn't even noticed. He opened it carefully, touching only the corners, and frowned.

He looked at me as he repeated the message on the paper, his tone puzzled: "How does it feel?"

I tried to choke off the whimper of fear that crawled up my throat. *Terrifying. It felt terrifying.*

"How does what feel? What is this supposed to mean?" he asked. Marx must not have shared that awful detail with him when he summarized my history. "What was in the box?"

I dropped my gaze to the floor and hugged my cat tighter for comfort. Knowing Collin had slipped in and taken my jeans and sweaters was unnerving enough, but the fact that he'd taken my personal things made me feel humiliated and vulnerable.

"Holly, what did he take?"

"My clothes." I forced my eyes to his. "All of them."

It took him a moment to understand what I meant, and then I saw a glint of anger in his eyes. "Okay. I'm gonna call this in. Try not to touch anything." He replaced the note in the box and walked back toward the front door to place the call.

I sank down on my couch. My cat plopped and sprawled onto the cushions, and I curled in on myself, dropping my face into my knees.

Just breathe.

I tried to convince myself it wasn't worth getting upset over, that they were just pieces of clothing I could replace. But I couldn't shake the sick feeling in my stomach.

Deep breath. One, two, three, four. And exhale.

Jordan ended his call a few minutes later, and I heard his shoes scuffing the cement as he crossed the room to stand in front of me. "You okay?"

"Fine," I muttered into my knees.

"I know you wanna leave, but the police are on the way, along with CSU, so we need to hang out for a bit."

I lifted my head. "Please don't tell Marx. He'll—"

"Worry? He has a right to worry. Collin broke into your apartment and took your clothes. *I'm* worried." He tapped his phone against his palm as he watched me with a small, tense line between his eyebrows. "Has he ever done anything like this before?"

I fidgeted uncomfortably, not wanting to share those stories. "He's never really been good at respecting a girl's boundaries."

"Yeah, so I've heard," he said, his words low and clipped with anger. He pulled out one of the folding metal chairs from my kitchen table and sat down to face me. "Marx said your placement with the Wells family lasted eleven months."

I nodded.

He seemed to struggle with something before finally asking, "Why didn't you run away? Why didn't you ask for help?"

I leveled a smoldering glare at him. "You think I didn't?"

His shoulders tensed. "I only know what Marx shared with me."

I sighed and slumped down on the couch, hiding behind my knees. I didn't want to talk about this.

"What happened?" he asked.

I picked at the lint on my running pants as I tried to work up the nerve to answer. "You know those stories you hear about women being held captive for days, months, sometimes years in some madman's basement?"

"Yeah."

"I spent eleven months of my life like that. Except my prison walls were constructed by threats and fear."

Sometimes my prison was more physical than that, like a box, but those moments were temporary.

"I was the oldest foster child the Wells family had ever taken in, but there were three younger kids." Their tiny faces materialized in my mind. Sweet, innocent babies. "Nathaniel, Nat, was the youngest. He had just turned six, and he hovered around me like a little butterfly. Michael—he was the little artist, and Cassie was only a few weeks older than Nat, and she was . . . so shy but sweet."

"You loved them," Jordan said, as if he had heard something in my voice I wasn't even aware I had shared.

I had held them when they cried, tucked them in at night, and I had loved them when everyone else in their lives had abandoned them.

"I did," I admitted. But I hadn't been able to protect them. "It didn't take Collin long to figure that out. I wasn't as easy to control as they were. I resisted and fought him at every opportunity."

"So he used them against you."

I nodded. "You asked me why I didn't run away. I did once. I don't think Collin's parents even noticed I was gone—they were too wrapped up in themselves—but Collin reported me missing."

My ever-dutiful foster brother.

The thought was laughable, but the memories weighed too heavily on me for laughter.

"The police picked me up. I tried to convince the officer not to take me back. I told him what was happening in that house, but he didn't believe me. I didn't have any proof."

Collin had been so careful when he hurt us, especially the younger kids. He rarely left marks, and if he did, he fabricated a story about an accident just in case anyone asked.

Jordan hesitated for a moment before asking, "What about a hospital? I mean, they could've done an exam if—"

"I didn't wanna be touched."

He let out a slow, tense breath and stood from his chair. He mounted his hands on his hips and tapped his fingers against his belt. "What happened when the officer didn't believe you? He took you back?"

"He told me that, as a foster child, I should be thankful a family was willing to open their home to me, that I had a safe place to sleep at night." If only he had known the irony of that statement. "And then he escorted me right back to the front door."

103

Jordan leaned on the back of my kitchen chair, gripping it tightly. "What happened then?"

"Collin . . . he made me . . . watch while he punished the other kids for my escape attempt." Unexpected tears slipped down my cheeks, and I brushed them away. "I didn't try to run away again after that."

"His parents? They didn't listen? They didn't care?"

The small laugh that bubbled out of me was tinged with bitterness. "Their perfect son would never do such a thing."

"What about your caseworker? You had a caseworker, right?"

"I had a weekly phone call with her, sometimes visits. I tried to tell her over the phone what was happening, but Collin took the phone from me and hung it up. And then he . . ." I tightened my arms around my stomach and tried not to shiver at the memory. "He broke one of Nat's fingers in front of me. He told me if I ever tried to tell what was happening, he would break one of their bones for every word I spoke. And then he made me call her back and tell her everything was fine."

Jordan's hands tightened on the chair, and the flimsy metal groaned. "So you didn't tell her he was hurting you."

I stared at my knees. "I didn't tell anyone after that. I never even spoke his name aloud." It had almost become an irrational fear—like chanting "Bloody Mary" three times in front of a mirror—that speaking Collin's name would somehow make the monster appear.

I caught a flash of movement through the open door, and fear had me reaching for the box cutter I'd hidden between the cushions of the couch. I popped out the blade.

Jordan lifted an eyebrow at the sharp tool poised in my hand.

"What?" I snapped defensively.

After Collin's disconcerting phone call on my birthday, I had stashed potential weapons all over. I had no intention of being helpless if he broke into my apartment to hurt me again.

"Remind me to get you a pocketknife for Christmas," Jordan said. He strode to the door and peered out. "It's just the police."

I relaxed a fraction and retracted the blade before setting the box cutter down on the cushion next to me.

A uniformed officer and a member of the Crime Scene Unit descended the steps onto my patio. "Thanks for coming, guys." Jordan invited them in with a wave of his hand.

They photographed my apartment and collected any slivers of glass they could find along with my wooden box to process them for trace evidence. They bagged the note Collin had left, but I knew they wouldn't find his fingerprints on it.

I stared intently at my knees as Jordan gave a statement to the officer. I refused to speak to him on the matter. Twenty minutes later, my apartment was cleared and the officers left with little to show for their efforts.

We swung by Jace's apartment to drop off my cat, and she agreed to watch my "tiny whale," as she called him, under the condition that I attended her next sled hockey game so I could watch her "wipe the floor with Warren."

She even told me I could bring along "the sheriff," who was standing right next to me and apparently, as far as she was concerned, had no name. She appreciated that he had saved my life in Kansas, but I wondered if a tiny part of her worried that he might replace her as my best friend.

I begrudgingly agreed to her terms and dropped my plump cat into her apartment before we left. He took off across her dining room, making enough noise for an entire stampede.

We pulled into a vacant spot in front of Marx's apartment fifteen minutes later. A tense silence hung in the car, and irritation prickled beneath my skin when Jordan glanced at me for what felt like the tenth time.

"I'm pretty sure I've mentioned I don't like to be watched," I reminded him.

"I'm just making sure you're okay. I thought you might be upset."

"I'm fine."

"You're not fine."

I cast a heated glare his way as I flung off the seat belt and opened the car door. "Don't tell me how I'm feeling."

He let out a heavy breath and pressed his forehead to the steering wheel. I slammed the car door and started toward the building.

The apartment door wasn't locked when I reached the second floor, either because Marx forgot, which was unlikely, or because he was expecting me back soon. I knocked, then opened the door and popped my head inside.

"Hello?" I called out.

"You don't have to knock, Holly." Marx's voice carried down the hall into the living room.

Jordan, who had taken the steps two at a time to catch up with me, followed me inside and closed the door behind him.

The television was tuned to a news station, and my attention was drawn to the portrait in the top right corner of the screen. Even months later, his face still chilled me.

"Investigators are still trying to link the string of deaths across the country to suspected serial killer Edward Moss Billings," a female reporter explained. "The FBI refuses to comment on the progress of this investigation, and the local detective responsible for uncovering the series of connected deaths remains behind the scenes. The young woman who was abducted by Edward Billings just this November still remains unnamed, but sources say she may be . . ."

The screen suddenly winked out, and I turned to see Marx standing in the kitchen with the remote.

"I'm surprised you don't have reporters crawling up the side of your building for a comment," I said.

"They'll figure out my name eventually." He set the remote on the counter. "My concern is them figurin' out *your* name."

I didn't even want to think about that. I nodded toward the screwdriver in his hand. "What did you break?"

"I didn't break anythin'. I just finished puttin' a lock on the bathroom door."

I walked to the bathroom door to inspect his handiwork. He had changed the entire door handle, and it now had a secure dead bolt on the inside.

I felt the pressure of tears in my throat. I would never have asked him to do this, but I knew why he had; he wanted me to feel safe when I showered here. The tears made their way to my eyes, and I tried to blink them back. What was wrong with me today?

Marx frowned. "Sweetheart, it's just a lock." He cast Jordan a questioning look.

"Collin paid her apartment a visit before we got there."

Marx's face hardened, and he set his tools on the counter. "We'll talk in the livin' room. Holly, there's somethin' in your room for you."

Wondering what he could have left in the spare bedroom, I went to check. I cracked open the door and gasped. "Riley!"

The German shepherd lay on a massive dog pillow with a bandage around his middle. His tail thumped the floor excitedly, and he lifted his head.

"Hi," I said to him, sinking to my knees beside him. His tongue lolled out, and he moved his head into my lap so I could rub behind his ears. "How's my little hero?"

I hugged his head, needing the comfort, and he didn't seem to mind. I heard Jordan shout good-bye to me a moment before Marx appeared in the bedroom doorway.

"I picked him up this mornin'," he said. "I'm tryin' to track down his owner, but in the meantime, I thought the two of you could keep each other company."

"I like that idea." I rubbed Riley's neck and planted a kiss on the top of his fuzzy head. I wanted to squeeze him with love, but he had a lot of healing to do before I could squeeze him. "Do we know how he got shot?"

Marx crouched down beside me and patted Riley's back. "Probably tryin' to protect somebody."

I hoped he had at least succeeded. I kissed him again. "You're such a good dog."

"Maybe he'll help you to feel a little safer." The glimmer of worry in his eyes told me Jordan had shared more than the details of the break-in. He had probably relayed the information I shared with him about my foster home. "We'll go to the store and get you some new clothes tomorrow."

I pursed my lips and nodded.

"Thank you. For this. For everything," I said. "I can, um, pay you for his vet bills and for the lock on the bathroom door."

I rummaged through my bag for money and pulled out a few crumpled twenties. It wasn't enough, but it was a start. I held them out to him.

He gave me a look. "It's cute that you think I'm gonna take that."

"Please."

"I don't want your money. Even if it wasn't in a state of complete anarchy."

I sighed and dropped the handful of bills to my lap. I tried to smooth them out over my knee, but the wrinkles were permanent.

I didn't understand Marx. He was the only person I knew who seemed to do things without expecting something in return. Everyone wanted something, even if it wasn't owed to them.

Even Jace had demanded something in return for watching my cat, and she was my friend.

Deciding the money was a lost, crinkled cause, I crammed it back into the side pocket of my bag and folded my arms. "If you won't let me pay you, then . . . I'll clean."

"Yourself? Because I know you're not suggestin' my apartment's dirty."

My mouth opened, and I floundered for a response. "Um . . . no?"

He lifted an eyebrow.

I tried to scrounge up a less offensive alternative. "What about cooking? I could make you dinner so you have something to

108

eat when you get off work after a long day. Or maybe breakfast so—"

"Holly," he said on a soft sigh. "I realize that you're used to people wantin' somethin' from you, but I don't want anythin' from you."

My shoulders slumped in confusion. "But I have to pay you back somehow."

"No, you don't. You stayin' here isn't some grave inconvenience. I don't need you to cook me food or clean my house, and I certainly don't need your money. You're my guest."

"But I—"

"Quit arguin' with me."

I snapped my mouth shut, at a loss for words.

"And try to get some rest," he suggested. He gave Riley's head one last parting pat before standing and moving to the door.

"But we're not done talking about the money thing."

"Yes, we are." He pulled the door shut on any argument I might have offered.

I lay down on the floor next to Riley and propped my head up on an arm. A yawn snuck up on me as I ran my fingers lazily through his fur. It was barely evening, but I had been awake since a little after three in the morning, and I was exhausted. I hugged Riley's neck gently and fell asleep on the floor next to my protective companion.

11

The next few days passed by quietly, and I could feel some of my anxiety ebbing. I stood in front of Marx's living room window with a mug of hot tea as I watched the snow fall.

I wasn't fond of winter, but there was a certain majestic beauty to the feathery snowflakes that fluttered down from the sky. The view beyond the snowflakes could've been nicer, but I supposed there were worse things too look at than run-down, graffiti-covered buildings.

I heard the quiet click of the coffeepot and glanced into the kitchen to see the last few droplets splash into the pot of dark liquid. I thought I would try my hand at making it again. I couldn't figure out how I could possibly make something that was already disgusting more disgusting, but apparently I had managed it at the precinct.

This pot looked less . . . sludgy.

I discarded my mug of tea on the peninsula next to my letter—well, my blank page that had aspirations of one day being a letter—and walked into the kitchen. Riley followed at my heels, his nails clicking on the floorboards. I poured a mug of coffee and set it next to my tea.

The pictures on the hallway wall across from the kitchen caught my attention, and I smirked as a mischievous idea blossomed in my mind.

Marx had chastised me yesterday for "tiptoein' around the apartment like a mouse"—apparently my attempts not to be bothersome *bothered* him—so I was going to make my presence known.

I was starting to realize just how much of a neat freak he was. Everything in his apartment had a specific place. When I put my toothpaste in the wrong spot, he moved it into the toothbrush cup holder on the bathroom counter without a word.

His kitchen sink was always empty because he washed the dishes the moment he was done with them, dried them, and put them back in the cupboard or drawer. And apparently the glasses had to be right-side up on the shelf. Upside-down, right-side up, tipped over—I didn't really care as long as they didn't roll off the shelf and conk me on the head.

His bathroom towel cupboard was also ridiculously tidy. It made me wonder if he organized his socks by color too.

I looked both ways down the hallway and then stepped forward to tilt all three of the pictures on the wall just enough that a neat freak might notice.

I glanced down at Riley, who sat beside me and rested one paw on my foot. "If he asks who did it, I'm blaming you." Riley cocked his head at me, and I smiled as I scratched him behind the ear.

Then I hurried to the peninsula and slid onto my stool to pretend complete innocence.

I tapped my eraser on the blank page of my letter as I tried to scrounge up something to say to my second—albeit not quite— mother, Izzy, but my mind came up blank. She had been kind to me for the two years I stayed with her, and she had tried to help when she learned that the man who killed my family had come after me a second time. But she was also serving a sentence for murder and drug trafficking.

Dear Izzy,

I couldn't tell her about the latest upheaval in my life, and I certainly couldn't tell her I was staying with Marx. She had hated him the moment she learned he was a cop, and I didn't think she would digest that turn of events very well.

Marx stopped in the hallway on his way to the kitchen, took a step back, and examined the slightly crooked pictures on the wall. "What in the . . ."

111

I pressed a hand to my mouth to smother a laugh. He readjusted the pictures with a puzzled frown and then gave them an odd look before walking into the kitchen.

"I made you coffee," I said. I grabbed the mug and hopped off the stool to carry it over to him.

He took the mug from me cautiously, and his brow furrowed as he peered into it. "Why is it whenever you make me a drink there's somethin' floatin' in it?"

I leaned forward to take a second look at the brown liquid and frowned in confusion. "I don't see anything."

"First it was marshmallows in my chocolate milk, and now this."

"What do you mean? It's just coffee."

"Oh, it's coffee. And coffee grounds. Did you use a filter?"

"Mmm . . . I might have forgotten that part."

His lips pressed together as he resisted the urge to laugh. He set the mug down on the peninsula and said very gently, "Maybe you should consider stickin' with hot chocolate."

I puffed out a breath and slid back onto my stool.

"It's not the end of the world, Holly. Don't look so disappointed."

"I'm gonna get it right," I told him. "I'll try again tomorrow."

Marx just shook his head, smiling. He dropped the file he had carried out of the bedroom onto the peninsula before turning to the refrigerator. "What are you workin' on over there?"

I closed my notebook. I knew how he felt about Izzy, and it was a subject that always seemed to rile his inner cop. "Just writing a letter."

He exhaled audibly as he fetched a jar of grape jelly from the refrigerator and closed the door. "To Isabel Lane?" When I fidgeted on my stool, he said, "Holly, you don't have to write to her."

"Yeah, well, I promised. And I keep my promises."

He leaned back against the counter with his arms folded. The look on his face made me brace myself for a lecture. "You don't owe that woman anythin'."

"Like it or not, she and Paul saved my life that night. If they hadn't come along, the killer would've caught me."

"Come along," he said evenly. "You mean when they hit you with their car, neglected to take you to a hospital, threw you in the back of their drug-filled caravan, and then drove you halfway across the country?"

I scowled at him. "Yes." I bounced the eraser end of my pencil off the countertop in agitation. "Izzy's alone. She doesn't have anyone in her life now that Paul is dead, and—"

He raised a hand to cut me off. "I will not feel sorry for a woman who abducted a nine-year-old girl."

"They were nice to me."

"It doesn't matter if they were nice to you. You were a child. They could've beaten you every other day and you still would've loved and trusted them. It's called Stockholm syndrome."

"I do not have that."

His eyes rolled heavenward as if I tested his patience. "Fine, don't call it that. You feel the way you do, and I can't change that. But I don't agree with it, and in my opinion, she doesn't deserve to have you in her life."

"You've never heard of forgiveness?"

"I don't think she deserves to be forgiven. She's a killer, a kidnapper, and a drug dealer."

"She didn't pull the trigger."

"That doesn't matter, Holly. She knew what happened and kept it to herself, which makes her just as guilty as the man who did pull the trigger."

"But—"

"There are some wrongs in this world that just shouldn't be forgiven."

"That's not true."

Marx rubbed at the tension between his eyebrows and sighed. "Let's not argue before I've had my coffee. It isn't a fair fight." He turned away from me and started preparing his breakfast.

I stared at the blank letter that stubbornly refused to write itself as I mulled over Marx's words. Was he right?

I could forgive a lot of things, but there were some people—some cruelties—that felt . . . unforgivable.

Edward had murdered my family, and even though he was dead, I didn't think I could ever forgive him. And Collin . . . if he asked, would God simply forgive and forget every despicable thing he'd done? If he sought God before his last breath, would I spend an eternity in Heaven with the man who hurt me?

The thought turned my stomach, and I closed the notebook. My heart suddenly felt too cold and hard for forgiveness, and I had nothing to say to Izzy.

I looked around, seeking a distraction, and my eyes landed on the file resting on the countertop. I knew I shouldn't do it, but it was just so tempting.

I lifted the cover and peeked inside. There were photos of the area surrounding the scene where Marx's informant was found. I snooped through the pages with interest. There were pictures of three teenagers—presumably the ones who had overdosed—and a man with a teardrop tattoo under his left eye. There was a sticky note on the picture with Marx's writing on it.

I squinted to try to make out the words: "'Teardrop' connected to Ruiz's death? Mother overheard phone call between them. Former drug affiliation. Part of new drug ring?"

"Holly!" Marx snapped, slapping the folder shut abruptly enough to make me flinch. He pulled it out from under my fingers.

"Sorry."

"Don't give me sorry," he scolded, dropping the file on the counter beyond my reach. "We both know you'd do it again." He gave me a stern look when I decided to say nothing rather than lie. I would definitely do it again.

"I was just—"

"Curious? My informant was murdered for what he knew, Holly. I don't want you anywhere near anythin' or anyone involved with this case. So keep your curious little nose out of it."

I lifted my chin. "My nose is not little."

"It may have escaped your notice, but everythin' about you is little. You're pint-sized."

I scowled at his back as he turned away to finish his breakfast. I was not pint-sized. I was almost average, except for three or four inches of height. "I'm putting coffee grounds in your coffee every morning," I threatened grumpily.

He chuckled as he spread jelly over his toast. He took a bite of it and swallowed before asking, "You ready?"

"Can I drive on the road today?" I asked, hopping off the stool. "I only hit one cone last time."

He opened the front door for me as he said, "Oh, well, if you're only gonna hit one pedestrian on the road, then sure, why not?"

I crinkled my nose at his sarcasm, and we walked downstairs to the car. I didn't get to drive on the road. It took me four attempts before I managed to complete the maneuverability course without running something over.

"Next time can I drive on the road?"

Marx gave me an uncertain glance from behind the wheel as we headed for self-defense training. "We'll see."

I huffed and looked out the window, my eyes snagging on a familiar street sign. It was the street where Ruiz had been gunned down. "Did you talk to that lady I told you about?"

"I tried. She slammed the door in my face. In fact, I spent the past few days knockin' on doors. Nobody's talkin' except Ruiz's mom, and she doesn't have much to say."

"Maybe I should try. I'm not a cop."

He looked at me as if I had just suggested skydiving without a parachute. "You want me to drop you off in gang territory, without a police escort, so you can go into random people's houses and ask them questions about a murder on their street? Have you lost your mind?"

115

"Well, it sounds bad when you say it that way."

His phone started to ring, and he grabbed it off the dashboard. "Trust me, there's no better way to say it. It only gets worse from there." A thoughtful crease formed between his eyebrows when he glimpsed the caller ID. "Shannon?" he said by way of greeting.

He frowned when the call abruptly disconnected. He snapped his phone shut and was about to toss it back onto the dashboard when it started to ring again. I saw the name Shannon flash across the screen.

"Who's Shannon?" I asked.

"My ex-wife."

"The woman you're keeping the ring on for?" He was divorced, but he never removed his wedding ring because he still loved the woman he had made his vows to.

He gave me a quelling look and answered the phone. "Hello?" The thoughtful expression on his face gradually deepened to concern when the other end of the line offered nothing but static. "Shannon, can you hear me?" Nothing. "Shannon."

I stiffened in my seat when a deep male voice rumbled through the phone loudly enough for me to hear, "You were warned."

The call disconnected.

Marx's expression turned dangerously flat, and he whipped the car around on the road so sharply that it left me scrambling for something to hold onto. He turned on a flashing light and sped down the road at nauseating speeds.

"I have a possible home invasion at 344 Chestnut Avenue. I'm en route now. Send backup," he commanded into his car radio.

He tossed his phone to me without warning, and I dropped it in my lap before managing to get a solid grip on it.

"Try callin' her number back," he instructed. When it took me a moment to process his request, he snapped, "Call her, Holly!"

I flinched at the anger in his voice and called back the most recent number. I vibrated anxiously in my seat as I waited for someone to answer. The phone rang several times on the other end and then rolled over to the answering machine.

"Keep tryin'," he said when I gave him a questioning look. "That's her home phone. Try her cell phone."

I scrolled through his contacts to find Shannon's Cell and hit send. We made another sharp turn, and I almost dropped the phone again. I threw a hand to the window to brace myself.

The call went to voice mail. I tried twice more to no avail before we skidded to a stop in front of a house that rested at the top of a hill.

I pressed a hand to my queasy stomach and handed his phone back. "No answer."

He took it from me and got out of the car. He drew his sidearm and then hesitated when he looked at me. I assumed he was going to tell me to stay in the car, but then his gaze flickered over the street warily.

"Come on," he said, gesturing me out of the car. At my puzzled look, he explained, "I'm not leavin' you in the car alone. Not with Collin lookin' for an opportunity to get to you."

Fear twisted my insides, and I scrambled out of the car and to his side in an instant.

"You stay with me and behind me," he instructed firmly. "Do you understand? Do not—"

"Wander off. Yes, I know."

I followed him up the steps to the front stoop of the blue two-story house. It had beautiful, expansive windows all across the front. His ex-wife must have made decent money.

The front door hung just a little off-kilter on one hinge, and Marx shouldered his way through it.

God, please let Shannon be okay. Please don't let Marx lose the woman he loves.

He stepped into the house with his gun angled downward. I cast a nervous look over the street before following him into the unlit foyer of the house.

Glass crunched beneath my shoe, and I hesitated. A vase had fallen from the overturned table and lay shattered across the wooden floor. I stepped over the puddle of water and crushed flowers that looked days past their expiration date.

Marx swept into the room on the left, and I paused in the doorway to absorb the breathtaking destruction. It looked as though a tornado had ripped through the house and left only the walls standing.

The furniture had been split open with a blade, the picture frames knocked from the walls, and the blue drapes were hanging crookedly over splintered blinds.

I picked up a picture frame and shook away the broken slivers of glass. It was a snapshot of Marx standing under a flower-draped arbor with his arms around a dark-haired woman. It couldn't have been taken more than four or five years ago; I could see the touch of gray at his temples.

He looked happy.

He swept past me and into the kitchen. "With me, Holly," he whispered, but it made his demand no less sharp.

I hesitated with the picture—it seemed wrong to put it back on the floor—and then set it gently on the mangled arm of the couch before scampering after him.

The kitchen was even worse than the living room; the cupboard doors, which hadn't been completely ripped off, sagged, revealing bare shelves. Every dish was shattered on the floor, and every ounce of food was strewn and crushed.

I stepped over a smashed box of Corn Flakes cereal and picked up a calendar from the wreckage. There was a colored key in the top right corner: pink for *worked out*, green for *ate breakfast*, blue for *took some me-time*. There were three colored slashes across most of the days. Some only had two—apparently she struggled to have "me-time" on a regular basis—except for the past three days. They were completely blank.

I flipped back to the month of January. Every day had been filled in the same way; Shannon was a consistent person. Why had she left the past three days blank?

I brought the calendar with me as I trailed behind Marx back into the foyer and up the steps. He took the steps sideways with his back to the wall, and angled the gun upward toward the landing.

"Shannon!" he called out.

I almost tripped up the steps when my foot slid on a magazine that was half covered by a towel. I managed not to fall on my face, but it certainly made my heartbeat stagger. I glared at the magazine and then continued up the staircase, trying to be more mindful of where I stepped.

"Holly, you have your pepper spray?" Marx asked as we stepped onto the second floor.

I slid my hand into my pocket and wrapped my fingers around the canister. "Yes." The feel of it didn't give me much confidence. The last time I sprayed someone with pepper spray, it had only fueled his anger.

"Good. Anybody comes out of these rooms that isn't me or a black-haired woman, use it."

My palms began to sweat at the mere thought of someone leaping out at us. What would they do? Would they run, or do to us what they had done to the house?

I tiptoed into the master bedroom on Marx's heels. He hesitated at the sight of the shredded mattress. This was probably the home he had shared with his wife, and it had to be hard for him to see it this way.

Someone had taken a great deal of time in tearing this place apart. Either that or there had been several people working in tandem. But why reduce it to such ruin? What was the point?

I walked to the bedside and looked down, brushing aside the down feathers from the pillows that floated into the air at my approach. I nudged aside the edge of a blanket.

"Marx."

He came to my side instantly. There was a picture on the mattress, but it had been ripped down the center, leaving only him with a disembodied feminine hand on his arm. A pile of colored confetti lay beside it, and I pushed a few of the pieces together, reconstructing a woman's face. It was the woman from the photograph downstairs: Shannon.

119

The muscles in Marx's jaw flexed with fury. "Come on. We have a few more rooms to check."

We made it to the threshold of the room when a noise came from downstairs, and Marx stopped unexpectedly. I collided with him and staggered backwards, groping at the edge of the dresser to keep from falling.

He pressed a finger to his lips and pointed toward the closet. He wanted me to hide while he checked on the noise downstairs? I shook my head and pulled out the pepper spray. I could help.

His face clouded with frustration and impatience, and he hissed quietly, "Get in the closet, Holly, and stay there."

I opened my mouth to object, but the look on his face made me reconsider. I shoved my pepper spray back into my pocket and picked my way through the debris toward the closet.

I pushed apart some clothes and hunkered down against the wall. I heard Marx's quiet footsteps as he crept from the room and down the steps.

I listened for any more mysterious sounds from downstairs, but the house had fallen silent again. Maybe there was no one in the house at all, and something had just fallen. Maybe the picture I'd left on the arm of the couch had slipped onto the floor.

I liked that possibility better than the alternative. As I waited for some signal from Marx that it was safe to come out, I let my eyes wander over the contents of the closet.

Shannon had almost as many clothes as Jace, and they ranged from expensive suits to beautiful gowns. It was like a shopping mall in her house. She probably only had to do laundry once a year.

I caught a familiar scent as I turned my head, and realized I was crouched by a suit jacket that smelled like Marx. Interesting. She had kept something of his.

Tired of waiting, I sat down and pulled the calendar into my lap to study it. I couldn't help but wonder if Shannon hadn't marked the past three days because she'd already been taken. But then, why would they wait three days to call Marx and let him know they had her?

Maybe it hadn't been three days. Maybe she just hadn't felt well the past few days, so she left the calendar blank. Maybe they had taken her just before Marx received the phone call, but something felt off about that scenario too.

Come on, Holly, think like a criminal.

I strained my brain to put the pieces together. The only reason I would spend this much time and effort destroying the home would be to make a statement, and the only reason to make a statement would be because—

The quiet creak of a floorboard in the hall brought my thoughts to a screeching halt. I held perfectly still, listening. Fear ballooned in my stomach when I heard the muffled crunch of a footstep in the debris scattered across the bedroom floor.

I was pretty sure Marx would've said something so he didn't frighten me, but I didn't dare move from my hiding place to see if it was him. I caught a glimpse of a reflection in the mirror across the room and bit down on my lips to keep a gasp from escaping.

It was the man from the photograph; the man with the teardrop tattoo.

12

"I think he'll get the message this time. We should go," Teardrop suggested, with a cursory glance around the room.

"He brought that girl with him again," a second man said. I couldn't see him from my hiding place, but there was a trace of a Hispanic accent.

"So what? What does she matter?"

"Because she must be important. A daughter maybe?"

"He ain't got no daughter," Teardrop said. "Just an ex-wife and that redneck family of his down south."

My heart fluttered with fear when Teardrop stepped toward the closet. I tried to conceal myself behind the large suit jacket and prayed he wouldn't see me.

He stepped inside and looked around. He shoved aside the hanging clothes with a hand, and everything on the rack jostled.

I tried not to move.

"Maybe they're a thing, then. He's obviously got some kinda somethin' for her. I wanna know what," the second man insisted.

"She don't matter. Let's go before he comes back."

The familiar sound of water drops erupted in the closet. I patted my coat pockets frantically in search of my phone, but it was too late. I froze with my fingers wrapped around it and locked eyes with Teardrop.

Crap.

"Would you look at that? She been hidin' in the closet the whole time we was talkin'," he grunted in disbelief. "Whatchu hidin' for, sweet thing?"

Another figure shifted, and I caught sight of an almond-colored arm reflected in the mirror. "Get her out. I wanna know who she is."

Teardrop shrugged and stepped forward. Frantic, I released my phone and grabbed one of the shoes scattered across the closet floor and chucked it at him. He ducked, and it hit the wall.

He swore and tried to swat the next one out of the air, but it thumped against his broad chest. Shannon had a lot of shoes, and I flung them one after the other at him. I had terrible aim, and some of the shoes missed him entirely, but others pounded into his face and chest.

"Stop it, you crazy—" Another shoe thumped him in the stomach, and his last word left on a grunt.

He glared at me as he straightened, and I could practically see the fury rolling off him. I groped in my pocket for my pepper spray when he started toward me again.

"Tear!" the second man hissed, the urgency in his voice drawing his friend up short. "We gotta go. He's comin' up the steps."

I huddled between the clothes, breathing hard, as I aimed my pepper spray at the man looming above me. I wasn't sure I could hit him in the face from this angle, but if he came any closer, I was going to try.

His fingers flexed in and out of a fist. "Crazy chick," he muttered under his breath, before quickly retreating.

I snatched up another shoe to throw if he came back, and waited to see what would happen next. I could hear them moving through the room. They weren't bothering to be quiet now.

The bedroom window squeaked as it was pushed up, and I heard them scramble out of it one at a time. Two muffled thumps announced their feet hitting the ground.

"Holly!" Marx called as he rushed into the room.

"Window! They went out the window!"

I stumbled to my feet and out of the closet just in time for Marx to shove me to the floor and out of the path of the bullet that zipped through the open window. It sank into the bedroom wall.

"Don't move," he instructed. He climbed off me and edged along the wall back to the window. He leaned out carefully with his gun at the ready, but the two men must have been gone, because he swore quietly under his breath and returned to my side. "You all right? Did they hurt you?"

123

"I'm okay," I said a little breathlessly as I lifted my head off the floor. I pushed myself to my hands and knees and sat back on my legs, gaping at the bullet hole in the wall.

That had been too close for comfort.

Marx offered his hand to help me up, and I noticed blood seeping through the sleeve of his shirt. "You're hurt," I gasped, climbing to my feet.

He turned his arm and glanced at it without concern. He wiggled a finger through a hole in the material, and with a sinking feeling in my stomach I realized what had happened. My eyes darted to the bullet in the wall and then back to his arm.

"They shot you!"

"It's just a scratch," he said dismissively.

"Tha . . . you . . . no," I sputtered as I followed him out of the room. "If that were my arm, you—"

"Would take you to the hospital."

"But it's—"

"Not your arm and it's just a scratch."

I pinched my lips together in frustration as I stomped after him, down the steps and toward the approaching sirens. "We're going to the hospital."

He turned to face me on the stairs, and I caught myself before my foot could land on the next step down. I settled two steps above him, which gave me a few inches on him, folded my arms, and scowled.

"Very intimidatin'," he said with obvious sarcasm. "But you can't carry me to the hospital, Holly, and I have the car keys." He dangled them in front of me to emphasize his point. When I bristled angrily, he added, "I promise I'll get it looked at, but all I wanna do at the moment is figure out what happened to my wife."

I deflated with a puff of breath and followed him outside to meet the cops who had just arrived. I remained on the stoop with two officers and specific orders not to move an inch—so of course I had to move at least two on principle—while Marx walked through the house with the other officer.

* * *

IT WAS EARLY AFTERNOON BEFORE we made it to the precinct. It was much busier during the day, and I trailed silently behind Marx, trying to be invisible.

Before Marx, I had never much cared for cops. Not because I had a criminal history—though I had broken a few laws while living on the street—but because they had never been the heroes so many people painted them to be. The heroes I had needed them to be.

My grudge had faded to a dull dislike and lingering distrust of anyone in uniform, with the exception of Sam and Marx. Maybe someday that would fade away too.

"Rick," a vaguely familiar voice called out. A tall man approaching sixty with snow-white hair stormed out of the office with the plaque on the door that read Captain McNera.

He had a round face and belly and a presence about him that reminded me of an intensely strict military grandfather who might threaten to snap a ruler between your shoulder blades if you didn't sit up straight in your chair.

Seeing him again made me a little edgy. I had met him in December, shortly after Marx and I returned from Kansas, when he "requested" a face-to-face meeting to discuss the details of our encounter with Edward Billings. We had both been in the early stages of recovery from our injuries, but that hadn't softened his questioning. Marx had done his best to redirect the questions away from me.

Now he looked flushed with concern as he stopped beside Marx's desk. I had never heard anyone call Marx Rick before. I knew his first name was Richard, but it still sounded odd.

"You were shot?" he demanded.

"Just a scratch," Marx repeated in flat tones as he tucked his gun into his desk drawer.

"Get it checked out. How's Shannon?"

Marx slammed the drawer a little too hard as he said with barely controlled rage, "She's missin'."

"Missing?" Captain McNera asked with widening eyes. "You mean you think someone took her?"

Marx planted both hands on his desk and leaned, his distress visible in the way he held his body. "I don't know, Matt. She wasn't there, and she's not answerin' her cell. That phone call came from her house, and the man said I had been warned. I think somebody went after her because of me."

"What have you done lately that might have made someone angry?"

"I'm just workin' my case."

"I'm pretty sure your case is the problem," I offered. The way their attention suddenly shifted to me made me regret opening my mouth.

Captain McNera cocked his head in thought as he looked at me. I saw the spark of recognition in his eyes a moment before he said, "Holly, right? The young woman with the stalker."

Well, there was a way to be remembered.

He offered his hand to me, and I glanced at it before replying coldly, "You tried to have me arrested."

"I'm sorry, I don't recall."

"When you thought I was withholding information about a murderer's identity. I wasn't, but you wanted Marx to arrest me anyway." I had been withholding Collin's name at the time, not Edward's.

"Ah. I'm sorry about that. It wasn't personal."

I narrowed my eyes at him. "You mean it wasn't personal to you. I would take being arrested pretty personally."

"Holly," Marx said in warning, and I folded my arms unhappily.

Captain McNera dropped his hand, and a smile taunted his lips as he glanced at Marx. "I don't think she likes me very much."

"Holly isn't one to hide her feelin's about a person," Marx explained. "So no, she doesn't like you. Why are you so certain Shannon's disappearance has somethin' to do with my case, Holly?"

I stepped toward his desk and reached for the case folder. When he didn't scold me for touching it, I opened it and pulled out the picture of the man with the teardrop tattoo. I set it on top of the pile. "He was there with another guy."

Marx straightened. "You're sure?"

"I hit him in the face with a few high heels when he found me in the closet. So yes, I'm pretty sure." I stepped back from the desk and added, "He said he thinks you'll get the message this time."

Captain McNera's lips tightened into a thin white line. "Well, he shouldn't be too hard to find. We'll see if some of the boys on the night shift can pick him up. What about the second man? Did either of you get a good look at him?"

Marx shook his head. "No. Holly?"

I lifted one shoulder in uncertainty. "I didn't see his face, but he said, 'he brought the girl with him again'."

Marx frowned. "Again?"

"You need to be careful, Marx," Captain McNera said sternly, and if the tone hadn't been enough to convey the reprimand, the use of his last name probably was. They seemed to be walking a thin line between friendship and chain of command. "If she's right and the vandalism and Shannon's disappearance are connected to the case you're working, her simply knowing what's going on could put her life in danger."

"I'm aware of that, sir. But Holly's an unstoppable force when you don't want her to know somethin'."

Captain McNera looked at me and said with a polite smile, "Why don't you give us a minute, kiddo. There are some sweets in the break room."

Kiddo? He might have been thirty or so years older than me, but I was far from a kid. I glanced at Marx, and he nodded with a tight-lipped expression. Apparently I was being dismissed so the "grown-ups" could talk. Nice. I didn't suppose stomping my foot and refusing to leave would help my case any.

I sighed and started off toward the break room, but I kept my pace slow so I could catch some of their conversation.

"Look, Rick, as your superior, your personal life is none of my business, but as your friend I gotta ask, is there something going on between the two of you?"

Marx hesitated. "I'm not sure I follow."

"The two of you shared a difficult experience in Kansas. It's only natural to bond after something like that, and she's a very attractive girl."

"I'm almost twenty years older than her, Matt," Marx said with audible outrage.

"I was ten years older than my wife when we started dating. It's not that unusual."

"Holly is younger than your youngest daughter. You know me better than that."

"You're letting her stay with you. Overnight. She was at your apartment in her pajamas the night your car was vandalized. I do read the reports, Rick, and the men do talk."

"You've known me longer than any of these men, so I would think my word would carry a bit more weight."

"So you're not sleeping with her?"

"No," Marx gritted through his teeth, at the same moment I thought, *Ew.* "I care about Holly, but why she's stayin' with me is nobody's business."

"Okay. Just . . . be careful. I don't wanna see you get hurt because you've gotten too attached."

I walked into the small break room and meandered over to the box of doughnuts on the table. I could go for a doughnut. Something with sprinkles.

My phone went off again, and I pulled it from my pocket to look at the screen. I didn't recognize the caller, but it was the same number that had called when I was hiding in the closet.

I debated whether or not to answer and then decided it couldn't hurt. "Hello?" I greeted. I lifted the lid of the doughnut box and surveyed my options.

Sprinkles, sprinkles . . . ooh, chocolate sprinkles.

"Someone didn't come home last night. Or any of the nights before that," Collin's taunting voice said through the phone. Fear weakened my knees, and I gripped the edge of the table for support. "What ever have you been up to, Holly?"

I breathed into the phone, but I couldn't bring myself to speak. Fear sent a river of frantic thoughts flowing through my mind: *What does he want? Is he here? Can he see me? Is he watching?*

I looked through the vertical blinds into the squad room at Marx. He was still talking to Captain McNera. My gaze swept over the faces in the room, but I didn't recognize any of them.

"Holly," Collin said in a singsong voice, drawing my full attention back to him. "You're too scared to speak, aren't you?" He laughed in that way that always made my body tense with apprehension. "Does the sound of my voice make you shiver in anticipation of pain? Do you start thinking about all the times I held you down and—"

I snapped the phone shut and dropped it on the table, backing away from it until I bumped into the counter. I slid into the corner, as far from the phone as I could get without leaving the room, and watched it warily.

Collin might be obscenely limber, but it wasn't as if he could crawl through the phone and attack me. And yet . . .

I cringed into the corner when the phone went off again. The sound stopped abruptly before the phone could roll over to voice mail. It went off again. Stopped. Went off again. Stopped.

He was toying with me.

I held my breath, waiting, but the next sound I heard was the chirp of an incoming text message.

Somehow, I made myself move forward and pick up my phone, but I lifted it as if it were a venomous snake that might whip around and sink its fangs into me. I opened it to read the message from the same unknown number:

*Have a donut for me. Something with those
sprinkles you love so much.*

He *was* watching. I moved stiffly to the window that
overlooked the parking lot and peered through the open blinds.

Where was he?

"Hey," a deep male voice said from behind me.

I jumped in surprise and barely swallowed a scream as I
whirled to see who had spoken.

Sam paused in the doorway with a frown. "Sorry," he said
slowly, and there was a question in his voice. "I didn't mean to
startle you."

I gripped my phone tightly between both hands as I stared
at him. My heartbeat slowed gradually, and the flood of fear his
sudden presence had unleashed drained away. He wasn't Collin.
Collin couldn't attack me in a police station.

Safe. I'm safe.

Sam stepped into the small room with deliberate slowness
as he watched me. He didn't say anything as he followed the edge
of the room to the coffeepot, but he was clearly trying to work out
the reason behind my extreme reaction to him.

"Why . . ." I glanced at the clock on the wall, noting the
afternoon hour, and tried to wipe all traces of fear from my voice.
"Why are you here? Shouldn't you be sleeping?"

He poured coffee into a mug. "I don't sleep fourteen hours
a day, Holly. This is my morning. And I'm here to talk to Marx
about something." He tipped the mug to his lips as he turned
around, then paused. "You didn't make this, did you?"

If I weren't concentrating on not freaking out, I would've
scowled at the indirect insult. But all I could manage was a slow
blink.

He took a tentative sip, braced for battery acid, and
swallowed with a grunt of approval. "Guess not." His dark eyes
studied me while he sipped his coffee. "Why do you look like you're
gonna faint?"

"I don't look like I'm gonna faint."

"You do. You're paler than water, and you're jumpier than usual, which I didn't think was possible."

My eyes fell to the phone clasped between my hands. I kept expecting it to ring or alert me to another message, but it remained silent. "It's possible to block a phone number, right?"

"Usually. Depends on the carrier and sometimes the type of phone."

I wouldn't be able to figure it out. I hadn't even been able to figure out how to change my ringtone when Jace had switched it to some screaming, obnoxious voice. Technology was a challenge.

"Would you . . ."

He held out his hand before I even finished the question. I strode forward and plopped my phone into his hand. "Which number?" he asked, scrolling through the screen.

"The recent one."

A faint line formed between his eyebrows, and his eyes flickered to my face. "They called four times in two minutes, and sent a text." It wasn't a question, so I didn't offer a response. "Doughnuts," he read aloud, and then his gaze slid to the box of doughnuts on the table.

He set down his coffee and strode past me to the window where he'd found me standing when he came in. He pushed apart the blinds and peered down into the parking lot. "Holly, are these calls and texts from Collin?" His tone sounded disinterested, but he looked at me expectantly when I didn't answer. When I nodded mutely, he said, "You should tell Marx."

"He has enough on his mind right now without me adding to it."

"That doesn't matter. You need to tell him." He punched a few more buttons on my flip phone. "Is this a pay-as-you-go device?" At my nod, he said, "I'm not sure you can block a number on one of these. It's not a service all pay-as-you-go carriers offer, but you'll need to call them and find out."

"I was hoping there was a magic button."

A brief smile crossed his lips. "Unfortunately, no. Your best option is to call and ask about blocking the number, and if they can't, memorize the number he's calling from or add it to your contact list so it comes up under his name and you know not to answer." He handed my phone back to me. "Even then, he can call from a different number you won't recognize. I know when an unknown number calls, you're probably tempted to answer just to see who it is, but don't. More than likely it's him."

His words sparked an idea in my mind, and I murmured, "Unknown number." Shannon. I started out of the room, then realized I'd forgotten something, and stopped. I looked back at Sam and gestured with my phone. "Thanks . . . for trying."

"Sure."

I squeezed my phone tightly in my hand to keep my fingers from shaking as I walked back into the squad room.

"I've known Shannon almost as long as I've known you," Captain McNera was saying as I approached. "She's a smart woman. If she had any indication that someone was in her house, she would've gotten out."

"I know she's a smart woman, Matt. She's a lawyer, and she was always light-years smarter than me. But I need more than that before I'll be certain she's okay. I need to find her."

Captain McNera clapped him on the back and said reassuringly, "You will, Rick. *We* will. Shannon's my friend too."

Marx was sitting on the edge of his desk with his arms folded when I stopped in front of him. He lifted his gaze from the floor to my face, and his eyebrows drew together with concern.

"What's the matter, Holly?"

"Can we talk?" I asked, trying to keep my voice level despite my lingering anxiety.

I glanced at Captain McNera, who was regarding me with interest. When he caught my gaze, he offered me a small smile and announced, "I'll be in my office if you need me."

"Thanks, Matt," Marx replied automatically, and tipped his head toward the chair the captain vacated.

I perched on the edge of it. "It's about Shannon."

Marx sighed. "Now isn't the time to ask me about how much I love her or why I still haven't taken off my ring, Holly."

"But I—"

"I'm not in the mood for personal questions."

Anger bubbled up inside of me. I was so tired of people interrupting me because they either assumed they knew what I had to say or they didn't care. "Do you think you can listen to me without interrupting for two minutes?" I snapped impatiently.

Marx blinked in surprise and then said, "Okay. I'm listenin'."

"What if Shannon isn't missing? Maybe she just left," I began. When Marx opened his mouth to say something, I glared at him and he clamped it shut again. I pulled Shannon's calendar from my bag and set it on his desk. "This is her calendar."

"You took it from the crime scene?" he asked in disbelief, keeping his voice low.

I hesitated for a moment before saying, "I plead the amendment that says I don't have to answer that."

Marx tried not to smile as he clarified, "The fifth."

"Yeah, that one. Hey!" I protested when he pulled a napkin from his drawer and used it to pluck the calendar from my hands.

"You can't touch evidence, Holly."

I wiggled my fingers. "But I already touched it, so can I just—"

"No."

I puffed out an irritated breath and dropped my hands into my lap. "Then could *you* turn it to February, please?"

He didn't look thrilled, but he used the napkin to flip the calendar month. "Happy?"

"Yes. So back to my point. Shannon kept a very strict schedule. The calendar is blank for the past three days, which means whatever happened to her probably happened three days ago. If they took her then, why wait until today to call you? And if they took her today, where was she when we got there? Because they were still there."

And then there were the dead flowers that any woman would've thrown away days ago had she been home to do so. Which brought me to my next point.

"I think they came to take her today, but she wasn't home. I think she left a few days ago. There were no suitcases in her closet, and I assume a woman with her means probably has some nice luggage, so she probably went on a trip. And when they realized they couldn't take her, they did the next best thing to scare you— they destroyed the home you shared with her."

"There are a lot of holes in your theory, Holly. The first of which is, you're basin' your entire theory on a calendar. Second, if she left of her own accord, why isn't she answerin' her phone?"

I looked down at my phone as I tried to think of a gentle way to tell him. "Because maybe . . . she saw your caller ID and is deliberately choosing not to answer."

I chanced a look at his face, but it was carefully blank. If she was just ducking his calls, then she was safe, but that would also mean the woman he loved was deliberately avoiding him.

I offered him my phone. "Maybe she'll answer an unknown number."

He took it silently and flipped it open. It took him a moment to decide to dial the number and send it through. I watched his face as he held the phone to his ear and waited. I knew the moment she answered, because I glimpsed the relief and heartache in his eyes before he closed them.

13

Marx rolled his sleeve down over the thin white bandage wrapped around his upper arm as he listened to Sam.

"The condition Collin has is called CIP—Congenital Insensitivity to Pain. It's an incredibly rare condition and not a lot is known about it. But apparently life expectancy isn't the greatest. Someone with this condition could have internal bleeding and feel nothing, an infected wound and not even know it if they didn't see it or smell it. They're not expected to make it to adulthood."

"He's thirty-two," Marx said. "So unfortunately, he made it."

"Yeah. This condition paired with a violent psychotic personality," Sam began. "Well, I can't say I'm surprised he hurts people. I am surprised he hasn't killed anyone though."

"That we know of," Marx said. "What about a criminal record? Is there anythin' he *has* been caught for?"

"Other than one disorderly conduct citation where he had a verbal disagreement with a cop when he was eighteen, he has no criminal record. Not even a sealed juvi record."

I could've told them they weren't going to find any criminal history for Collin. He was too intelligent to get caught.

"What kind of disorderly conduct?" Marx asked.

"A cop pulled him over for rolling through a stop sign." He paused before adding, "The cop was black."

Marx snorted. "And Collin's a racist. He probably couldn't help but make some kind of offensive racial remark. Too bad the cop didn't shoot him."

Sam dropped a file on the desk. "This was all I could find on him. And it's just basics like school records, travel history, traffic violations, financials. Thanks to some interesting maneuvering in the stock market, he's not lacking for money. That's probably why he's able to follow Holly across the country without needing to work. But the guy's clean."

Marx grimaced as he picked up the file and flipped it open. "The man tortured children, Sam. He's far from clean."

"I just mean that legally speaking, he could walk into this room right now and we couldn't touch him. There's no evidence that he's done anything illegal."

Marx's jaw clenched in anger, and he slapped the file on the desk. "How does a man who does the things he does manage to avoid consequences?"

"Because he covers his tracks really well, or because the kids he hurt are afraid to confront him," Sam said.

They were absolutely afraid to confront Collin. So was I.

"I realize that, Sam. It was a rhetorical question."

"Oh." Sam folded his arms over his broad chest. "He hasn't done anything in New York that we can arrest him for. At least nothing that's been connected to him."

Marx rubbed the back of his neck. "Well, I won't just sit here and wait for him to come after Holly again."

"I can talk to Sully, see if he can dig deeper than I could, but without a warrant, we're gonna hit a brick wall."

Marx sighed. "Okay. Let's see how far he can get before that wall comes up. Any idea where he's stayin' yet?"

Sam shook his head. "The guy's a ghost, but our contacts on the street know to call if they see him."

"What about the break-in at Holly's apartment? Did the lab find any evidence?"

"I checked in with them about an hour ago. There were no usable prints on the note left in the box, even though we all know Collin wrote it, and all of the prints on the box are too small to be Collin's. They're likely Holly's. And they couldn't tell anything from the few glass shards they recovered. I checked around, but no one saw anything."

Marx sighed irritably. "So even when we do find him, we have nothin' to arrest him for."

"Have we given any thought to an order of protection? Holly can request a family court order of protection against him if she feels threatened. Maybe you can talk to Shannon."

I cocked my head. "What does Shannon have to do with Collin?"

"She's the district attorney for the county," Marx explained. Pain shadowed his eyes when he spoke about his wife, but he blinked it away. "I'll talk to her and see if she thinks we have a case, but since Collin hasn't done anythin' the court might consider a viable threat, we might have a harder time gettin' a protection order."

"He called on her birthday and clearly indicated that he was watching her," Sam said. "He showed up outside her apartment, and he called her five times today and sent her a text that also suggested he was watching."

"He what?" Marx demanded, his attention snapping to me. "And I'm just hearin' about this now?"

I couldn't tell if the anger in his voice was directed toward Collin for calling or toward me for keeping it from him. I skewered Sam with a glare, but he just arched an eyebrow at me that silently communicated, "I told you to tell him."

"When did he call?" Marx asked.

"Once in the closet at Shannon's house and then while you were talking to Captain McNera," I said. "But I only answered once."

His voice sounded tightly controlled as he asked, "What did he say? Did he threaten you?"

I shifted my feet. I wasn't about to share what he had said; it made me feel weak, and I didn't want them to see me that way.

He looked at Sam.

Sam shrugged. "I came in after the phone calls. I just know she was scared."

"Holly," Marx pressed impatiently. "Now isn't the time for secrets. Tell me what he said."

"No! I don't wanna talk about it and that's my decision. You can't push me into another one." I turned and walked quickly toward the bathroom.

I slammed my hands into the door and slipped into the quiet space where neither of them could follow. Dropping back against the wall, I closed my eyes and let out a weary sigh. I didn't understand why God was letting this happen. Why did He allow this man to keep finding me and hurting me?

"Why won't You just make him stop?" I pleaded, opening my eyes and staring up toward heaven.

Even as I asked the question, I knew the answer. God worked through other people, and if Collin was going to be stopped, it would be because God lead human hands to do it. Unfortunately, He didn't just drop giant balls of burning hail on people who deserved it anymore.

Maybe Marx and Sam were the human hands meant to protect me. I had met Marx for a reason, and I had trusted him even when I knew better than to trust a man. God wanted him in my life, even if I had initially resisted.

Lord, I wish I understood Your plans. You said You have plans to prosper us and not to harm us, and I just wanna understand.

I sighed and pushed away from the wall, walking to the sink to run cool water over my wrists. It was one of the many small coping skills my therapist had taught me; it helped to cool the body and ease my nerves.

When I felt calm enough to leave the bathroom, I found Sam and Marx conferring around a mobile whiteboard. Circled at the top of the board was the word Overseer. Other bubbles branched out, trickling down the board, including Rafe "Teardrop" Malone and, at the lowest level, three names I didn't recognize.

"So how many victims so far?" Sam asked, perching on the edge of a desk.

Marx drew a number in the corner of the board and circled it, then said aloud, "Eight."

Eight? The last I heard there had only been three. The number was growing quickly. Marx glanced at the notebook in his hand and then proceeded to write the names of the victims beneath the number in his hideously illegible script.

"What are their conditions?"

"Five dead, one on life support, one soon to be released from the hospital, and one went home," Marx explained, denoting their conditions with single letters next to their names: D, H, and R. D for deceased, H for hospital, R . . . I wasn't sure about that one. Released, maybe?

"So how do we know the drug that's killing these kids is coming from the same source?"

Marx capped his marker and stepped back to look at the board. There was too little information on it. "Because the heroin is contaminated with fentanyl. Fentanyl, as you know, is cheap when locally made, and because it's eighty to a hundred times more potent than morphine, it makes for a faster, more euphoric high when mixed with heroin."

"So, in other words, the users are getting more bang for their buck, but it's costing the suppliers less to make it," Sam supposed. "Smart, except for the part where it's killing their consumers."

"I somehow doubt they care about the little people." Marx tapped the marker against his palm in agitation as he tried to piece together a puzzle that was missing ninety percent of its pieces.

"Probably not. But I'm sure the kids who sold to their friends at school care that they're dead." He gestured to the three unfamiliar names at the bottom of the list. Ah, the secondary dealers: the ones who bought from the drug dealer and then distributed to their friends. "I assume you interviewed them already. What did they have to say?"

"None of them are talkin'. They're afraid if they divulge the name of their supplier they'll end up dead."

"Well, it's a good possibility." Sam folded his arms and frowned at the whiteboard. "So where do we go from here?"

"Accordin' to Tear's record, he has former gang affiliations, but I didn't see anythin' recent. It's likely whatever gang he's involved with is behind the drug distribution."

"It's not a gang," I said from across the room, drawing their attention.

I tucked my cold fingers into the back pockets of my jeans and crossed the room to join them. I scooted onto the vacant desk across from Sam and waited, but neither of them asked about the phone calls again.

"I'm sorry for my temper," Marx said. "I didn't mean to come across as angry or impatient with you." He grabbed a bottle of cold chocolate milk from his desk and offered it to me.

"You're apologizing with chocolate milk?" I asked, taking it. I wasn't one to turn down chocolate anything.

"The vendin' machine's out of M&M's, so yes. And I don't want you in the middle of this case. I told you that before when you were snoopin' through my file."

"I'm already in the middle of this case." I tried to twist the cap off the bottle, but it didn't budge. *Seriously?* "Even if I wasn't staying with you, I saw Tear's face at the scene of a crime, and I heard him and his partner suggest that it wasn't the first time they tried to put a stop to your investigation. If they decide I'm a problem, it's not gonna have anything to do with this discussion."

"She has a point," Sam agreed.

"You're not helpin'," Marx grumbled in his direction.

I tried one more time to open the bottle and then gave it a frustrated look before setting it aside. I wasn't getting into a struggling match with a bottle cap tonight. "Please just let me help with this case."

I needed the distraction. I wanted to think about anything but Collin.

Marx leaned forward and twisted the cap off the chocolate milk for me. "I appreciate that you wanna help, but you're not a cop, and you're not a drug dealer turned informant, so there's not really much you can do."

"I lived with drug traffickers," I reminded him, glaring at the bottle cap that had popped right off for him. "And I overheard their *grown-up* discussions more than once, so I'm not exactly clueless about the wonderful world of illegal substances."

"You were nine. Overhearin' conversations doesn't make you an expert in criminal behavior."

A small spark of interest lit Sam's eyes, but his voice sounded as flat as usual. "You lived with drug traffickers? Why have I never heard this story?"

"It's a complicated story," Marx answered vaguely.

"They hit me with their car when I was nine and decided to take me home," I explained.

Sam frowned. "Like you were a stray puppy? They just . . . hit you with their car and decided, 'Hey, she doesn't have any ID tags, let's keep her'?"

"Pretty much," I said before taking a delicious, chocolaty sip of milk. I smacked my lips thoughtfully. "Needs marshmallows."

Marx smiled. "I guess you'll just have to make do without."

"So about your drug dealers. I—"

"Did you ever have access to the drugs?" Sam interrupted, apparently curious now.

I sighed impatiently and looked at him. "Once, and only because I was playing where I wasn't supposed to."

"What happened?"

"I thought all packages should have pretty decorations, so I sort of, um . . . bedazzled them," I admitted reluctantly.

Sam coughed a laugh. He had a sister; he knew what bedazzling meant. Marx, on the other hand, gaped at me in confusion before asking, "You did what?"

"She means she stuck shiny beads on everything," Sam explained after clearing the remnants of laughter from his throat.

Marx blinked before saying slowly, "You stuck shiny beads on the bags of heroin?"

"Yep." And Paul had been so angry that he was speechless. He'd also taken my bedazzler away and thrown it into the woods where he knew I was too afraid to go after it. "Now can we focus?"

Marx relented. "Why do you think it's not gang related?"

"Gangs are racially segregated, right? Tear is white, and this guy," I said, pointing at the question mark representing the mysterious man who had been working with Tear, "had a faint

Hispanic accent and he definitely had the coloring. I saw his arm in the mirror."

A thin line of interest formed between Marx's eyebrows. "You're sure?" At my nod, he and Sam exchanged a look.

"You think Tear is an enforcer?" Sam asked.

"If it's not a gang, then yes. Which means this guy"—Marx pointed to the question mark I had indicated—"is also an enforcer, and we don't know who he is yet." He scribbled something beneath it.

"Titanic?" I wondered aloud.

"Hispanic," he corrected.

"Maybe you should let Sam write on the board, because that looks like a sinking ship."

He pursed his lips and offered the marker to me. "His writin' is worse than mine. If it's so bad, you write it."

I shrugged and hopped off the desk to take the marker. I walked over to the board and erased his Hispanic Titanic and rewrote it. I put a little smiley face at the end of it just because.

"If it's not gang related, that's both good and bad for us," Marx said. "Good because their loyalty to their employer won't be nearly as strong as one gang member's loyalty to another. Bad because if our drug entrepreneur is hirin' his help, then he doesn't have a shortage of applicants."

"So even if we catch Tear and his partner, he'll just hire more," Sam supposed.

"Exactly. Our best chance is to catch one of them and get them to roll for a reduced sentence."

"If they're organized well, each level is only going to know the next person up the chain. The street dealer will have the name of his supplier, but probably not who his supplier receives the merchandise from."

"Then we'll work our way up the chain, startin' with Tear."

"You know we should hand this case off to narcotics."

"I have six dead bodies. If narcotics wants this case, they can fight me for it."

"Seriously?" a male voice asked from behind me, surprising me so much that I almost dropped the bottle of chocolate milk on the floor. I twisted around to look at the person who had spat that single word with such exasperation.

Jordan stood there with his arms crossed and a disgruntled expression that looked out of place on his usually relaxed face. "I called everyone in this room when no one showed up to self-defense training. Guess how many people answered."

"We've been a little busy," Marx informed him almost dismissively.

"I sent you a text," Sam replied.

"Training was at 11:30, Sam. You responded fifteen minutes ago to a message I sent at five after twelve, which is only . . ." Jordan glanced at his watch. "Five and a half hours late."

Sam shrugged.

I pulled my phone from my pocket and turned it back on. Two missed calls and a text from Jordan popped up on the screen. "Sorry," I breathed guiltily. I had finally given him my number, and when he tried to use it, my phone was turned off.

"Why was your phone off?" Marx demanded with a note of disapproval. "You need to keep it on and charged at all times, Holly."

I bristled indignantly. "Why? Because I'm a woman and the only way I can protect myself is to call a man to do it for me?"

Silence met my angry question. Sam opened his mouth to say something that would probably only fuel the sudden anger that had welled up inside of me, but Marx held up a hand to cut him off.

"That isn't what I meant, Holly." He folded his arms and frowned. "Nobody in this room thinks that. I don't know what Collin said to you when he called, but you are not weak or incapable."

I shifted uncomfortably on the desk and looked down at my phone. I wasn't so sure about that. Collin had reminded me just how weak and incapable I was by referencing *all the times* he'd held me down and . . . hurt me. A strong person would've been able to stop him. A capable person would've been able to keep him from ever doing it again.

I wasn't that person.

Marx leaned forward to capture my downcast gaze. "You're not weak and incapable, sweetheart. If you were, you wouldn't have survived this long. You hear me?"

I forced a nod.

"Good," he said, straightening. "And just to be clear, I would recommend everybody in this room keep their phone on and charged. Not just you. It has nothin' to do with you bein' a girl. But your sadistic foster brother does tend to make me a bit more concerned."

"Which was what I was gonna say before I was so rudely censored," Sam said, with an irritated flick of his eyes toward Marx.

I puffed out a breath and hunched my shoulders. "Sorry. I didn't mean to snap. I do appreciate you guys."

"We know," Marx said. "Given everythin' that's happenin', you're allowed to feel a little stressed out. Just please don't turn your phone off."

I hadn't planned to turn it off, but Sam's warning that there might not be a way to block Collin from calling made me anxious. I didn't think I had the nerves to deal with that right now.

"I think I'm gonna take a walk," I said, sliding off the desk. I needed some fresh air and open space.

"I'll go with her," Jordan volunteered before Marx could warn me not to go outside alone.

"Be careful with her, Jordan. He was on the premises today," Marx said.

Jordan glanced at me, then nodded at Marx. We left the squad room for a breath of fresh wintery air.

14

Dear Izzy,

I encountered the strangest thing today: a box of Lucky Mallows cereal with no marshmallows. How does that even happen? Somebody had one job: add marshmallows, and they failed.

I sighed and scratched out my ridiculous attempt at a letter as I frowned at the box of cereal on the counter. I had poured out the entire box of cereal into a large bowl, and there hadn't even been a fragment of a marshmallow.

"That is so weird."

I suspected foul play.

I dropped my pen, unable to think of anything meaningful to say to Izzy, and walked into the kitchen to find something else to eat. Maybe I would make breakfast for Marx before he got up and did whatever he did on Saturdays.

He had been unusually quiet the past few days after learning his ex-wife had been avoiding his phone calls. The heartache I had glimpsed in his eyes that day at the precinct lingered in my memory. I knew the pain of longing for unattainable love.

I blew out a heavy breath and opened the refrigerator, determined not to trip and fall down that rabbit hole of bad memories.

I tapped my lips with a finger as I considered the options. Maybe bacon and eggs would cheer him up. My breakfast-making skills were usually limited to pouring cereal into a bowl, but how hard could it be?

I gathered the items from the refrigerator and plopped them onto the counter. I read the directions on the back of the package of bacon. *Heat skillet, spread out strips of bacon, and cook to desired crispness.* That didn't sound so hard.

I hummed quietly as I danced around Riley in the kitchen. He had decided that lying directly under my feet was a splendid idea, and I kept tripping over him.

He watched longingly as I placed raw bacon into the skillet. "I'm not so sure bacon is good for you." I dropped a piece on the floor for him, and he scarfed it down before lifting his imploring eyes back to my face. "You didn't even taste that."

He licked his muzzle and gave a little snort of satisfaction.

I ignored his cuteness and plopped a few more strips of bacon into the skillet before turning it on high. I scrambled some eggs and poured them into another skillet.

A quiet creak of floorboards from outside the front door drew my attention. Marx's apartment building creaked and groaned like an old man's bones, and I wasn't used to it. I also wasn't used to the sound of feet shuffling down the hall at all hours. No one walked by my front door unless they intended to visit.

I had just decided to dismiss the noise as another of the residents walking down the hall, when a shadow shifted in the narrow strip of space below Marx's door. A deep, murmuring voice spoke just outside the apartment, and a tingle of warning crept up my spine.

Had Collin figured out that I was staying with Marx?

Nerves had me trading in the spatula for a meat tenderizer as I crept toward the door in my slippers.

I peered into the peephole, half-expecting to see those cold blue eyes from my nightmares—all the while hoping it was just the grouchy neighbor lady—but the warped, dark-skinned face on the other side of the door didn't belong to Collin or the elderly woman.

My death grip on the meat tenderizer relaxed, and I rested my forehead against the door in relief.

"You boys had better leave before I call the police," a woman said, her familiar voice colored by disapproval and brittle with age.

Boys? There was more than one man loitering in the hall?

"And buy some belts," she snapped. "They sell them at the store, right nearby pants that will actually fit you. The whole world doesn't need to see your underpants."

One of the men said something to her, but his voice was too low for me to catch the words through the door.

"Your mother should wash your mouth out with soap for using that kind of language!" she said a little louder. "You should be ashamed of yourself!"

Curious, I cracked the door to peer into the hall. I caught sight of black dreadlocks and a red bandanna disappearing down the steps.

My eyes drifted back to the rail-thin woman in her flower-printed robe, who stood in the doorway across the hall. The flowers were pink today. Yesterday they had been blue.

She huffed in disapproval and pressed a hand to the small of her back as she bent to pick up the paper. I hurried to get it for her.

"I can get my own paper," she groused. "I'm not dead yet."

I mutely offered the paper, and she snatched it with a scowl, looking like she wanted to swat me on the nose with it.

I stepped back beyond her reach and asked, "Is . . . everything okay?"

"Street hooligans. Always up to no good. I don't think that boy's washed his hair in ten years. And those clothes . . ." She shook her head.

"Were they bothering you?"

Marx could probably help with that. I imagine it could be handy to have a cop as a neighbor.

"Do you think I'd be standing out here in my house coat and slippers if they weren't bothering me? Of course they were bothering me. Stalking up and down the hall, loitering on the sidewalk, probably trying to spy or sell their marijuana." She said the word like mary-jew-anna, then fixed me with a look. "Do you do that marijuana?"

"No, ma'am."

147

She nodded, as if that were the correct answer. "I've seen you around here with Mr. Marx. Are you family?" When I shook my head, she frowned. "Cleaning lady? I've never seen a man with an apartment that spick-and-span, so I know he has a cleaner."

"I'm not his cleaner."

"Well, who are you then?"

I wanted to tell her it was none of her business, but I didn't want to upset the relationship Marx had with his neighbors.

"Holly."

She sniffed and narrowed her eyes. "Are you trying to burn the whole building down, Holly?"

I caught a faint whiff of smoke wafting through the open doorway. I drew in a sharp breath, and my gaze snapped back inside.

"Oh no . . ."

Smoke was pluming from the skillet of bacon. I dashed back inside, slamming and locking the door behind me.

I rushed into the kitchen and hopped over Riley to reach the stove. I pulled the skillet off the burner and waved an oven mitt over it to disperse the smoke and calm the volcanic grease eruptions.

I yelped and dropped the entire skillet on the floor when a horrendous wailing erupted in the apartment. I slapped my hands over my ears.

Marx rushed into the kitchen in his pajama pants and T-shirt. "Holly, what on earth are you doin'?" He maneuvered around me to turn off the burners and yank the eggs off the stove.

He stepped over Riley and the splattered bacon to open the kitchen window and then waved a towel under the smoke alarm on the ceiling.

When the shrill wailing finally subsided, I uncovered my ears and reluctantly admitted, "I was making you breakfast." I looked down at the burnt bacon on the kitchen floor and added sheepishly, "I hope you like your bacon extra crispy . . . and smoked."

He took in the mess on the floor, which Riley was happily helping to clean up, and released a frustrated sigh.

"I'll clean it up," I offered quickly.

"No. You and your fuzzy slippers get out of my kitchen before you catch my apartment on fire," he demanded, but there was no bite to his tone. "And take your dog."

"But I can—"

"Out," he said more firmly, and I clamped my mouth shut.

I grabbed Riley's collar and led him away from the temptation of bacon and around the peninsula. I plopped onto one of the stools and watched Marx clean up.

"I'm sorry I destroyed your kitchen," I said, hoping to soften whatever anger must be brewing beneath his calm exterior.

"You didn't destroy my kitchen."

"I made a mess."

He glanced at me as he set the skillet in the sink and filled it with water to soak. "That you did."

The foot I was bouncing nervously on the rung of the stool abruptly stilled at the complete lack of anger in his voice. That was it?

I burnt breakfast, filled his apartment with smoke, set off screeching alarms that startled him out of bed, and then dropped greasy bacon all over the floor. And "that you did" was his only reaction?

Cautiously, I asked, "You're not mad?"

"Did you do it on purpose?"

"No."

"Then no, I'm not mad. And it was very sweet of you to try to make me breakfast. Just . . . don't do it again."

"What if I promise not to burn anything next time?"

"I don't think that's a promise you can keep."

I sighed and dropped my chin into my hands. If I hadn't gotten distracted by the people in the hallway, I might not have burnt anything.

He gave me a small smile. "I know you're tryin' to make me feel better, but I'm fine."

149

I stared into his deep green eyes. He was doing his best to conceal the hurt from me, but I knew him well enough to recognize the changes in his behavior.

"By the way," he said as he returned the eggs to the refrigerator and pulled something out from beneath the tub of butter. He held up a twenty-dollar bill between his middle and index finger. "Stop it."

I raised my eyebrows innocently. "Stop what?"

"Don't give me *what*. You know what." He set the twenty on the counter and slid it toward me. "We talked about this. I don't want your money."

"Who says I put it there?"

"I don't make a habit of stashin' my money under the butter. I use a bank."

"Maybe Jordan put it there."

"Why would Jordan put money in my refrigerator? Or my Tupperware drawer? Or behind the stack of toilet paper rolls in the bathroom cupboard?"

"People do the strangest things."

"Holly," he said with a hint of impatience. He folded his arms and gave me a look that made me feel like he was demanding an explanation for the F on my latest report card.

How did he do that?

"You know most people would be happy if money magically appeared around their apartment," I said. "I would be."

"No, you wouldn't. Because that would mean somebody snuck into your apartment while you weren't there and left it."

Fair point. I would probably freak out and call him to come find out who broke into my apartment. "I'm using your water and electricity, and you won't let me buy groceries. And I'm eating . . . or burning all of your food."

"First of all, you eat like a bird, so you're not exactly breakin' the bank. Second of all, it's my house, which means I make the rules."

I folded my arms and straightened my spine. "I refuse to be a burden."

He frowned. "You're not a burden. I invited you into my home, and I know you know better than to entertain some silly notion that I feel obligated to have you here."

"I know that. But I need to contribute."

"You do," he said. "I sleep easier knowin' you're here with me instead of at your apartment where Collin can get to you. You bein' here gives me peace of mind."

I couldn't tell if he honestly meant it or if he was just trying to placate me.

"Now," he began, tapping the twenty-dollar bill with two fingers. "Did you hide any more of these?" When I pinched my lips together, he sighed, "Where?"

I lifted my chin. "I'm not telling."

He shook his head and smiled. "You're as stubborn as a brick wall." He left the twenty-dollar bill on the counter and prepared some toast for breakfast. "Are you spendin' the day with Jordan or do you wanna come to work with me? You're welcome to stay in the break room, but it might be a long day."

The break room? It was the size of a prison cell. I had no desire to spend twelve hours in that cramped space, and I was pretty sure Jordan had to be tired of shadowing me.

Someone knocked on the door before I had a chance to decide. Marx shook his head when I moved to answer it, and I sank back down on the stool as he strode into the living room and peered through the peephole. I was surprised to see Jordan standing on the other side of the door when he opened it.

Marx grimaced. "Speak of the devil."

Jordan arched a blond eyebrow at him. "I'm not sure whether to be insulted because he's the epitome of all evil or flattered because he was the best-looking angel."

Marx released a long-suffering sigh and stepped aside, widening the door. "Try not to get your big head stuck in my doorway."

Jordan grinned as he stepped inside. He blinked at the bacon smog and waved a hand through the smoky air. "Was there a fire?"

"Very nearly." Marx closed the door. "Holly made breakfast." He said that like it explained everything, and I scowled at him as he walked past me into the kitchen.

Jordan plopped on the stool farthest from where I was sitting, leaving the middle one open, and asked, "So what are your plans for the day?"

"Oh, um . . ." I looked between the two men with uncertainty before admitting, "I thought I might just stay here by myself and watch movies. Give you guys a break for the day."

"By yourself," Marx said slowly, frowning. His disapproving tone didn't bode well for my plans.

"With the door locked," I added.

"Collin has to know you haven't been home, and he saw you in my car. If he hasn't put it together yet, it's only a matter of time before he realizes you're stayin' with me. I don't want you here alone if he shows up at my door."

"So . . . I won't open the door. I'll stay away from the windows, and I promise I won't cook anything . . . unless it's in the microwave." When he started to shake his head, I said, "I just . . . need some time alone."

"It's not worth the risk." When I started to object to his objection, he spoke first. "You're not stayin' here by yourself. You know what he'll do to you if he manages to get you alone."

My stomach flipped over, and I shrank down on the stool at the terrifying thought.

Marx leaned on the counter and leveled a look at me. "What's this really about, Holly?"

"I told you already."

"I have no doubt that you would like some time alone, but that's not what this is about." At my perplexed frown, he explained, "Do you know what micro expressions are?"

"Um . . . I know micro machine cars are the tiny versions of real cars, so . . . the tiny versions of expressions?" I glanced at Jordan, who tried to conceal his smile. "Is that wrong?"

"No, that's right," Marx said. "When you try to be sneaky or deceptive, you have certain micro expressions."

I tried to make my face blank. I didn't like the idea of it doing things I didn't want it doing. "Like what?"

Jordan looked at me, and his eyes twinkled with amusement. "Your lips do this cute little twitching thing."

"They do not." I tucked my lips between my teeth self-consciously.

Marx smiled. "Yes, they do. Which is how I know you wantin' to stay here alone has absolutely nothin' to do with you wantin' alone time. This is about you feelin' like a burden again, isn't it?"

I cupped my hands over the bottom half of my face and said, "No."

Jordan laughed, and Marx just shook his head with a smile. "That just makes it more obvious, Holly."

I sighed and dropped my hands. "We're gonna have to go back to having conversations through doors so you can't read my face."

"You're stashin' money around my apartment because you feel guilty for eatin' my food, and now you're tryin' to avoid us because you feel like an inconvenience for needin' one of us to be with you at all times."

"Because that's exactly what I am."

He rubbed his forehead as if my reasoning gave him a headache. "You are in no way an inconvenience or a burden, Holly. I promise you that."

"It's not fair to either of you that you have to shuffle your schedules around so you can essentially babysit me every day."

Jordan crossed his arms and looked at Marx. "Well, I don't know about you, but I would much rather spend my time sitting in my bland motel room that smells like lemon cleaner, eating leftover pizza, and watching re-runs of *Family Guy* than spend my day with a pretty girl."

Marx's brows drew together. "I don't watch *Family Guy*."

"Yeah, but you're pushing fifty, so that's not really a surprise."

153

Marx gave Jordan a flat look. "It's a wonder I can't bring myself to like you."

I let out an exasperated breath. "I just thought maybe you would wanna do something without me tagging along. I'm monopolizing all of your guys' time, and that's not fair to you or the other people in your lives."

"Exactly who is it you think you're deprivin' of my company?" Marx asked. "My family lives in Georgia, there are very few people in this city I would call friends, and I work with two of the three."

Sam and Captain McNera, I assumed.

"Who's the third?" I wondered. Surely not Jordan. A few months ago I would've said Jacob, but he was nothing but a memory now.

Marx gave me a patient smile, and I felt abruptly awkward when I realized he considered me his third friend. "Oh."

"And I don't live here, so it's not like I have anybody to hang out with." Jordan shrugged.

I gave him a reproachful look. "You should be on your way home by now to see your family and do your job."

"Yeah, about that . . . I'm taking an extended leave of absence. And before you get angry with me," he said when I started to argue, "it's my life, and I've been with my family for twenty-eight years. This, right here"—he gestured between us—"I've been waiting eighteen years for this."

That brought my argument to an abrupt halt. I had forgotten how long he'd searched for me, and how long he'd waited for exactly this: spending time together.

"Sorry," I muttered, tucking my hands between my knees. "I didn't really think about it that way."

"I realize you didn't miss me like I did you all those years because of your memory loss, but if I didn't wanna be here, Holly, I wouldn't be." He stood up and shoved his hands into his jacket pockets. "Now, I'd like to play a game of pool. You up for that?"

"I don't know how to play pool."

"It's not that hard. I'll teach you."

Marx's phone rang, and he grabbed it off the counter to look at the caller before starting down the hall. "You two have fun." He paused briefly and looked back at me. "And Holly, if you get another call from an unknown number, don't answer it. Or just hand the phone to Jordan."

I nodded and then slid off the stool to change for our outing.

Jordan's assurance that pool wasn't hard apparently didn't apply to me, because I spent more time trying to figure out how to play the game than actually playing it.

I shifted my fingers on the pool stick, trying to find the right position. Why was holding a giant stick so complicated? I let the end of the stick thump on the floor between my feet and declared, "There's something wrong with my stick."

Jordan was making a polite effort not to laugh at me. "It's not the stick. Let me show you how to do it again."

He came closer and lined his stick up parallel to mine.

I tried to mimic the placement of his hands. "Okay, now what?"

"Now you draw it back slowly and aim at the white ball. Try to knock it into the others."

I did as he suggested, but the stick slipped and skipped off the green cloth of the table without ever touching the ball. I pinched my lips in concentration and tried again. I hit the ball the fourth time, but it went lopsided and rolled around the table without touching any of the others.

I dropped the pool stick back to the floor, feeling flustered. "What am I doing wrong?"

"It takes practice. I could show you how to do it better, but . . ." He leaned leisurely on his pool stick and smiled. "That would require me to trespass."

I pointed my pool stick at him threateningly. "Permission *not* granted."

He grinned, and it brought out his dimples. "That's okay. I just figured I would wait until no one was looking and then sneak across the border. Happens all the time."

"You wouldn't."

"While you're armed with a stick you could probably beat me over the head with? No."

"Maybe I would just kick your legs out from under you again."

"Yeah, sneaky ninja, that's never happening again." He recentered the white ball and lined up his shot. There was a loud crack as the balls connected and scattered across the table. "Your turn, my lady."

I glanced at the white ball in the middle of the table and then cast Jordan a questioning look. "And I'm supposed to hit that how?"

"However you can."

I walked around the table, considering my options, and Jordan moved around the table with me in order to stay on the four-foot perimeter. I took two steps forward, and he took two steps back.

I did it again, and he grinned as he retreated. "You're doing that on purpose."

"Mmmaybe." I took another slow, deliberate step toward him, and he laughed as he backed up.

"Keep that up and pretty soon we'll be dancing, and then I'm gonna be tempted to do things I shouldn't."

I gave him a wary but amused look as I stopped. "Such as?"

His eyes sparkled with mischief. "Keep stepping toward me and you'll find out." I took a step back instead, and he grinned wickedly. "Chicken."

I lifted my chin as I took another step back, bumping into the table. "I am not a chicken." I doubted he would actually follow through with whatever he was thinking, but I didn't want to chance it by stepping closer.

He remained where he was and nodded toward the table with that mischievous smile still tugging at his lips. "Take your shot before I take it for you."

I assessed my options and then hopped up onto the edge of the table. I raised the pool stick like I was about to spear a fish, and stabbed the white ball as hard as I could. It bounced and smacked into another ball. "Ha! I got one!" I shouted happily.

"Get off the table!" a man bellowed from behind the checkout counter.

I hopped down, and Jordan shook his head with a smile. "You're gonna get us thrown out."

"Don't worry, I won't let him get too rough with you when he tosses you into the street."

"Oh, well, if you're gonna be there to protect me, then I'm not worried."

It took us nearly an hour to finish our pool game. I managed to sink two of my balls into the holes by the time all of Jordan's were nestled tightly in the pockets. He waited patiently for me to finish with mine, but I surrendered halfway through, chucked the stick aside, and started rolling the stubborn balls into the pockets. That stupid stick just complicated matters.

"You are officially the worst pool player ever," Jordan informed me as we walked leisurely down the sidewalk.

"I blame the stick."

"Yeah, it's the inanimate object's fault."

"Precisely," I agreed. I tipped my head back to look up at the gray sky. Small snowflakes fluttered down from the swollen clouds, and I blinked as they landed on my eyelashes.

"You never have been good at anything sports related."

I didn't have many talents. Some people were gifted in many different areas, but I wasn't one of them. I was a fast runner, and I was a decent photographer. That pretty much concluded the list.

"I don't know," I said. "I could probably take some good pictures of sports players."

"You ever take pictures of things that aren't people?"

I caught a snowflake on my palm and smiled as it instantly melted. "Sometimes. I took a picture of a snowflake once. It's one of my favorites."

"If you have an album, I'd like to see it sometime."

I blinked in surprise. "Really?"

He gave me a half-amused, half-puzzled look. "Yeah, really."

I had a memory card full of photos of nature and architecture, but I had never shared them with anyone. No one had ever asked before. "Maybe I'll show them to you someday."

My phone chirped, and I pulled it out to check my messages. A picture from an unknown number loaded on the screen, and I jerked to a stop.

A little girl with chocolate-brown skin and black ringlets stood in front of a familiar building that no one should have been able to link to me. The caption of the picture read, "Such a sweet girl."

"Everything okay?" Jordan asked.

Another picture came through of eight-year-old Maya playing hopscotch on the sidewalk, accompanied by the message:

I do hope nothing happens to her while she's playing outside alone.

"No," fell beneath my breath.

I took off toward the building that was only two blocks away. I weaved through the busy street at a flat-out run.

"Holly, wait!" Jordan shouted.

He must have followed me across the road, because I heard blaring horns and screeching tires.

Lord, please don't let him hurt Maya.

I might not be able to prove it, but I knew Collin had sent these pictures, and he had no reservations about hurting children.

Jordan caught up to me quickly, dropping his speed to match mine. Relief almost brought me to my knees when we reached the retired fire station, and I saw Maya happily skipping through the chalk squares she had drawn on the sidewalk.

I looked around the area frantically, searching for Collin. My eyes landed on the exact place where he had taken the picture from—judging by the angle and lighting—but he was gone.

I offered my phone to Jordan as I scanned the fire escapes and small balconies of the surrounding buildings for any sign of him. "He was here."

I pointed to where Collin had been standing, and Jordan walked over to check out the area.

"Well he's not here now," he said.

A frown knitted his eyebrows together as he glanced at the side of the building and then away. I walked over to join him and froze when my eyes fell on the spot that had briefly drawn his attention.

Written across the brick siding with purple chalk that matched Maya's hopscotch squares were the words "Hello, Little Bird."

I felt a spasm of fear.

Collin called me Little Bird because his nearness left me frozen, trembling, and sucking in shallow, fluttering breaths like a "frightened little bird."

He knew I would come here, and this message was a cruel reminder that he could still reduce me to that terrified little creature.

I bent down without thinking and picked up the sliver of chalk Collin had probably used to write the message, and scratched at the words, my efforts growing more furious and frantic.

"Holly . . ."

I scratched until the chalk was reduced to a nub between my fingertips and the words were erased from existence, before dropping the chalk back to the pavement. I drew in a shivering breath and stepped back.

I caught the quiet concern in Jordan's eyes and felt abruptly self-conscious. I folded my arms over my stomach and tried not to tremble as I walked toward the old fire station.

If Collin had been close enough to Maya to steal a piece of her chalk, I needed to make sure she was all right. I crouched down to her level, and she paused, balancing precariously on one foot as she cocked her head at me.

"Hi, Maya. Do you remember me?"

She bobbed her head. "Holly. You used to tell me stories, and sometimes you braided my hair 'cause you did it better than mom. I would hug you but mom always said you don't like touches and I should always be p'lite and ask first."

159

I smiled through my worry. "I would love a Maya-hug."

A happy grin brightened her face, and she put her other foot down before throwing her arms around my neck. I hugged her back.

When she pulled away, she asked with wide, hopeful eyes, "Does this mean you're all better?"

My throat tightened. "I'm getting better."

A shadow stretched over us from behind. Maya looked up at Jordan, and I saw a flicker of fascination when she caught sight of his blue eyes.

Then her expression turned adorably serious, and her tiny black eyebrows pinched together. "You have pretty eyes but you're a stranger, and strangers are dangerous even if they have candy, so I can't talk to you."

I looked up at Jordan, whose lips twitched in amusement. He crouched down a few feet from me. "What if I'm a cop?"

She eyed him suspiciously. "You don't look like a cop. I think you're lying, and lying is bad. I don't talk to liars either."

Jordan pulled out his sheriff's badge and showed it to her. "I'm a sheriff."

She gasped. "Can I touch it?"

He almost laughed as he handed it to her.

She stared at it with wonder as she turned it every which way. "Rachel's husband says he's a cop, but I think he's a liar, and he's mean. I don't like him. Sometimes he comes over and yells, and sometimes he gets really mad 'cause Rachel won't come out, and he bangs on the door. Are you Holly's boyfriend? Mom says I can't have a boyfriend 'til I'm thirty."

I choked a little, and Jordan's expression blanked. It took him a moment to answer, "Well, I'm a boy and I'm Holly's friend."

"Okay," she said, thrusting out her small hand. "I'm Maya."

He shook her hand. "It's a pleasure to meet you, Miss Maya."

She giggled.

"Where's your mom?" I asked, looking around nervously.

"Inside. I'm supposed to knock when I'm done playing."

As if on cue, the fortified metal door creaked open and a middle-aged woman with mocha skin and guarded dark eyes stepped out. She wrapped a cardigan around herself and fixed her gaze on Jordan as she said calmly, "Maya, go inside and have a snack."

Maya tilted her head curiously. "But it's not snack time."

"You can have two this afternoon."

Her face lit up. "Fruit snacks?"

"That's fine."

Maya pumped a fist into the air as she cheered, "Yes!" She hurried inside, her small voice chanting musically, "Fruit snacks, fruit snacks, fruit snacks."

The woman closed the door after her daughter and folded her arms against the cold as she studied us, her gaze lingering suspiciously on the man who had just shaken her daughter's hand. "Can I help you with something?"

I stood slowly and rubbed my hands on my jeans. "Hi, Beth Anne."

Her gaze shifted to me, and she looked me over before recognition warmed her eyes. "Holly? My goodness. I didn't even recognize you. You've put on weight and you look healthy."

Jordan blinked. "You've put *on* weight?" He examined me critically, as if he couldn't figure out how I could possibly weigh less than I did now.

I had weighed about eighty pounds when I wandered by the building two years ago and started peeking through the windows. It had been a little over two weeks since my last brush with Collin, and I had moved from one abandoned building to the next, afraid that he would find me again if I stayed in one place for too long.

Most of what little food I found along the way hadn't stayed with me. My next panic attack would bring it all back up, and I had been too scared to keep returning to the same soup kitchens.

Beth Anne regarded Jordan with polite caution. "And who might you be?"

"This is Jordan. He's a friend," I explained.

"I see," she said. She gave him a courteous nod. "I would invite you in, but I'm sure you understand why I can't."

"I'm not sure I do actually," Jordan admitted.

"This is a women's shelter," she explained. "Your presence would make some of the women uncomfortable."

"Oh," Jordan said, glancing at me. There weren't any women's shelters in Stony Brooke, so this was probably the first time he had encountered one. His eyes swept over the building again, snagging briefly on the inconspicuous camera nestled between the cracks of the bricks and the newly added bars on the windows. "It looks like you've done a good job making it secure and discreet."

"That's the idea," she replied. "Some of these women just don't feel safe in the mixed company of homeless shelters, but some of them have spouses or significant others who want them back. It's best they don't know how to find them."

"And Holly lived here?"

She smiled at him but didn't answer. She had always been very adept at keeping people's secrets. Lives depended on it.

"She let me stay here for a while," I explained. "Helped me get my feet under me again. And then pulled a few strings with my former landlord to get me my apartment."

"How did you find this place?" Jordan asked.

"I don't actually know. I never came this far downtown before, but the police kicked me out of the building I was sleeping in and I just kept walking. I don't even know why I picked this building out of all the others, but something about it sent whispers of safety through me."

Beth Anne smiled warmly. "That was God, honey. There was definitely divine intervention involved. How else do you explain walking three miles from your usual haunts, and of all the abandoned-looking buildings to choose from, breaking into one that just happened to be a women's shelter?"

"You broke in?" Jordan asked in surprise.

I nodded at Beth Anne, giving her my silent consent to tell the story. "Threw a rock through one of the rear windows before we had bars. I found her in the pantry with her nose in a box of pastries. She was pretty scrawny, so I didn't really mind that she went after the food. Climbed back out the window and took off when she saw me."

"I'm surprised you didn't board up the window," he said.

"To be honest, I considered it, but I had a feeling I shouldn't. She came back the next night, and I was waiting for her with a box of those Little Debbie snack cakes. I got a good look at her, and I knew I needed to convince her to stay with us."

"Why?"

Beth Anne rubbed absently at her throat as she looked at me, probably remembering the condition I had been in. "She was . . . terrified. Banged up. Took me almost an hour to get her to calm down enough to stand still."

As Beth Anne told Jordan the story of how we met, the memories unfolded in my mind, taking me back to that chilly night.

I hadn't broken into the shelter with the intention of stealing. I had only wanted a safe place to curl up for the night. But when I crawled through the window and found myself in a pantry, I realized how hungry I was.

I never expected a woman to come into the room. I scrambled back out the window before she could call the police. The second night I came back, I did so with the intention of stealing.

But the woman was already there, offering me food. I thought it was a trap, and I was about to crawl back out the window, when she slid the box to me and took several steps back.

"It's not a trick. The food's yours," she said.

I grabbed the whole box of oatmeal cookies and hugged them to my chest. I wondered how long I could make them last.

She gestured to the shelf. "There's plenty more."

I glanced at the boxes of food hungrily, but I couldn't shake the nagging doubt that she had an ulterior motive.

Maybe she wanted to keep me here until the police came. They would arrest me for breaking in and stealing food, even though she was giving it to me.

Maybe she was a drug dealer or a criminal, and she wanted a favor in return for the food. Or maybe she was one of those female pimps, who sold other women by the hour. I had seen girls drawn into that life over the years.

"You're welcome to take the food and leave, but you don't have to go. We have beds, fresh clothes, hot food. You'll be safe here. No one will hurt you," she promised.

I waited for the strings that had to be attached to this too-good-to-be-true offer.

She looked me over, her expression pinched with concern. "Who hurt you, honey? Have you been to a doctor?" When I didn't answer, she offered, "I can take a look if . . ."

I stepped back quickly when she reached toward me, and she stilled, the remainder of her sentence hanging unspoken in the air between us. Very slowly, she lowered her arm. "My name's Beth Anne. What's yours?"

I glared at her distrustfully as I tried to rip open one of the oatmeal cookies. I couldn't manage it with three splinted fingers, so I used my teeth. If I could've shoved the whole thing in my mouth and swallowed, I would have just to ease the ache in my stomach, but I made myself chew. I was contemplating a second cookie before I finished swallowing the first one, when I noticed the doorknob behind the woman turn.

She was still issuing promises of safety when I grabbed two more boxes of pastries and disappeared out the window.

I came back the next night, surprised to find the window replaced but unlocked. I slipped inside and found a little box with a sandwich, an apple, a pastry, and a bottle of chocolate milk with a post-it note stuck to it that read "When you're ready, just knock."

The next night, after I ate the meal Beth Anne left for me, I approached the door I assumed connected the pantry to the main building and tried the handle. Locked. Two nights after that, I knocked.

"It took me a while to convince her that we were safe," Beth Anne continued, drawing me from my memories. "It was weeks before she said a word to me, to anyone. I didn't even know her name for the first month she stayed with us. If I hadn't heard her talking in her sleep one night, I might have thought she *couldn't* speak."

The first words I had spoken to her had been a question: "Why did you help me?" Anyone else would've called the police and had me arrested for breaking and entering, and theft, but she had shown me nothing but kindness.

She hadn't fit into my view of the world.

She had smiled at my question and said, "The Lord gives each of us a heart for something in this world, something we can change. Helping women who've been hurt is my heart, and I follow it."

She had changed my life. And it all started with Little Debbie snack cakes.

I looked up at Jordan. I thought I could see sadness in his eyes as Beth Anne described a young woman far more damaged and frightened than the woman he had come to know, but also a tiny flame of hope.

I wondered about that hope.

"She never did tell me her story," Beth Anne said. "But she was great with the kids and some of the other women who were having a difficult time. And she kept things interesting."

"Interesting how exactly?" Jordan asked.

"We took turns cooking. The normalcy and routine is good for healing. Thursday nights were her night to cook, and in the winter we all bundled up in anticipation of having to flee the premises or risk dying of smoke inhalation."

"I wasn't that bad," I disagreed.

She laughed softly. "God gifted Holly with a big heart and a resiliency I don't often see in my line of work, but when it came to equipping her with culinary skills . . . He forgot."

Jordan laughed, and I rolled my eyes. At least Marx wasn't here to overhear that. He would permanently ban me from his kitchen.

"And we're done storytelling," I decided.

Beth Anne smiled. "I'm happy to see you doing so well, Holly. And to see you in mixed company." Her gaze flickered back to Jordan briefly. "I've hoped and prayed you would heal and learn to trust again. But I am surprised to see you back here."

"I'm surprised to be here," I admitted. Collin shouldn't have known about this place. I shifted uneasily as I thought about the pictures of Maya and the implied threat in the second message. "Have you noticed any strange men lurking in the area?"

"Lurking?" she pondered aloud. "No. Just the usual. Although there was a man in January that did strike me as a bit odd. In fact, he was actually looking for you. Not sure how he found the shelter, but he said he was your brother."

January. He had looked for me here before he discovered where I was living. How had Collin even known about the shelter? How had he known I stayed here?

Jordan pulled his wallet from his back pocket and slipped a photo from inside the folds. "Is this him?"

Beth Anne studied the head shot of Collin. "It most certainly is. Handsome devil."

"Did he say anything else?"

"Not much," she said, her expression thoughtful. "Just that he hadn't seen her in two years and he was looking forward to a long reunion."

My heart staggered over itself in my chest, and I exhaled a long, slow breath to try to keep myself calm.

Beth Anne's gaze shifted to me when I didn't say anything. "Two years . . . just before you showed up at my shelter." Grim understanding suddenly crossed her face. "He's not your brother."

I shook my head.

She sighed. "He's the one, isn't he? The one you never talked about. The one who gave you nightmares."

Beth Anne had seen me at my worst: starving, emotionally raw, frightened of every shadow, and screaming in the middle of the night from unspeakable nightmares. There was no sense in trying to hide the truth from her.

I nodded.

166

"I knew something was wrong with him. I don't believe God ever forgets to give a baby a soul, but somewhere along the way, that man's soul shriveled up and died," she said regretfully.

"He's dangerous," Jordan told her. He pulled a card with his name and number on it from his wallet and handed it to her along with the photo. "If he comes back, call me, and it would probably be a good idea if Maya didn't play outside alone."

She accepted them without question. "We're good at taking care of ourselves, Mr. Jordan. Don't you worry about us. Holly, if you need a safe place to stay, we have room. You're always welcome."

If I set one foot inside that shelter, it would paint a bright red target on it. Collin would rip it apart brick by brick to get me out. I wouldn't put those women in any more danger than they already were, not even if it was my only place to hide.

I gave her a faint smile. "I appreciate that, Beth Anne, but I think I'm okay now." I cast another nervous look around the surrounding streets before saying to Jordan, "We should go."

"Holly," Beth Anne said, stepping forward and capturing my hands in hers before I could turn away. "I don't know why I feel like I should tell you this, but . . . sometimes life catches us by surprise and bad things, sometimes heart-crushing things, happen, and it's hard to get back up after that. But just remember that God is in the darkness with you, waiting to lead you out of it if only you take His hand. Know that you're loved, and you're never alone."

Something about her words, or maybe it was the unusual presence in her eyes as she spoke them, sent a shiver down my spine.

"Okay," I managed, before unlinking my hands from hers and stepping back. "Thanks." I started down the sidewalk but paused when I realized Jordan wasn't beside me.

Beth Anne had caught him by the arm. Her voice was quiet, but I heard the message she passed along to him. "You watch out for her. This man," she said, pointing to the picture, "he breaks bones. She still had broken fingers, and I'm pretty sure she was still nursing some broken ribs when she climbed through my window two years ago."

Tension rippled across Jordan's shoulders. I had a sinking feeling that if he and Collin were ever alone in a room together, someone would die. "I won't let anything happen to her," he said.

She nodded and released him. "Good man."

I braced myself for another uncomfortable interrogation as Jordan strode toward me, but all he said was, "You've come a long way from the woman she described."

I glanced over my shoulder at Beth Anne and smiled. "I had help."

15

We made one last stop after the women's shelter before Jordan took me back to Marx's apartment. I unlocked the door with the spare key Marx had given me and held the door open for him.

Jordan carried in a narrow side table to replace the one he had broken, and set it against the wall. He stepped back to take it in, and grinned mischievously. "You think he'll like it?"

"I think he's gonna shoot you," I said seriously. It was the most hideous table I had ever seen. There wasn't even an ugly enough word to describe it.

"You know CPR, right?" When I gave him a funny look, he shrugged with a wry smile. "Well, a guy can hope. I'll be in the hall until he gets home. I think he said about an hour."

"Oh, I um . . ." I tucked my hair behind my ears as I looked around the room. I was getting better with Jordan, at least in public places, but being alone with him behind closed doors still made my heart race and my palms sweat. I wished I could say it was because I found him attractive.

"It's okay, Holly. I don't mind the hallway. But I could use a pillow." He nodded to the couch I was standing beside.

I grabbed one of the fat pillows and tossed it at him. I almost took out a lamp with it, but he snatched it at the last second.

"Between the two of us, Marx isn't gonna have an apartment left by the end of the month," he commented. "And we really need to work on your aim. It's awful."

I crinkled my nose at him and threw another pillow. It nailed him in the back of the head as he turned to leave. That one landed perfectly. I heard him laughing as he pulled the door shut behind him.

I curled up on the couch with the copy of *The Wizard of Oz* Gin and I had shared, and continued reading it with Riley beside me. She and I never had the opportunity to reach the end of the book before she died, and I wanted to finish it for both of us.

The scratch of a key in the lock two hours later made me sit up a little straighter against the pillows. Marx stepped inside and I relaxed. "Hey," I greeted.

He gave me an interested look. "Did you banish Prince Charmin' to the hallway?"

I slid a bookmark between the pages and closed the book. "Nope, he banished himself. What's in the paper bag?"

"Spaghetti fixins," he said, his gaze shifting to my feet.

I abruptly realized I still had my shoes on, and my feet were on his leather couch. I lowered them slowly to the floor. "Can I help?" I asked, desperate to feel useful.

It must have shown on my face, because Marx opened his mouth to say something, closed it, and then sighed, "Don't blow up my kitchen."

He handed me the bag and stripped out of his jacket and shoes, placing them in their usual spot by the door. He glanced at the new side table, blinked, and then muttered, "What in the . . ."

It was a hot-pink-and-purple zebra-striped table we had found in the teenage girl's section of the store. Jordan had picked it out. Marx was speechless. When he looked my way, I ducked down behind the bag of groceries on the counter and laughed.

"Holly," he scolded, which only made me laugh harder. I pointed over the bag at the front door. I heard him rip it open and lean out into the hallway. "Jordan! Is this abominable piece of furniture your doin'?"

"You wanted me to replace it," he replied.

"This is not Africa. There will be no zebras in my livin' room. Remove it."

Jordan laughed as he came back into the apartment. He stood next to Marx and surveyed the table. "I think it adds a nice splash of color."

Marx grimaced. "It's loud, and it's stampedin' all over my senses. Who in their right mind would ever design somethin' that hideous?"

"Who said anything about them being in their right mind?" Jordan asked. "I'm almost positive there were drugs involved." He picked up the table and set it into the hallway before closing the door. "Now it can scream at your neighbors when they walk by."

Marx grumbled as he walked into the kitchen. He pointed a finger at me. "You quit your gigglin'. It's not funny."

I covered my mouth to hide my smile and silently handed him the box of spaghetti noodles. He filled a pot with water and set it on the stove. I started pulling groceries from the bag: sauce, cheese, meatballs, mushrooms . . .

"I thought you hated mushrooms."

"I do. But there's a certain young lady who's fond of them."

I smiled. There was a loaf of French bread in the bag too. "Out of curiosity, if I weren't here, what would you be eating tonight?"

"General Tsao's chicken and fried rice."

He didn't even hesitate. Somehow that didn't surprise me. I tossed the loaf of French bread to Jordan. "Would you cut that, please?"

"Jordan is not invited to dinner," Marx pointed out.

"So I shouldn't cut the bread then?" Jordan asked, pausing with a serrated knife over the loaf.

"Cut the bread, please," I insisted.

Jordan grinned smugly at Marx. "I think Holly wants me to stay for dinner."

"How unfortunate for you that it's my house."

I dragged one of the stools over beside the sink and plopped on it to wash the mushrooms. I was tired of being on my feet. Between pool and walking, Jordan and I had been on our feet all day.

"So how was your day?" I asked.

Marx slid a tray of meatballs into the oven. "Eventful."

When he offered nothing more, I prompted, "Meaning?"

He set a timer and then leaned back against the counter as he fixed me with a penetrating stare. "Why don't you tell me about your day." When I frowned at his displeased tone, he clarified, "I heard you received a few picture messages."

I shot Jordan a sharp look. "You told him?"

He at least had the decency to look guilty as he admitted, "Technically, I texted him." My anger must have radiated outward, because he quickly explained, "I had to, Holly. You're staying with Marx so he can keep you safe from Collin, which means he needs to know any time he contacts you or interferes with your life. How's he supposed to protect you if you're keeping things from him?"

"That wasn't your decision to make," I shot back.

"You didn't tell me about the phone calls or the text message at the precinct, and you weren't gonna tell me about the messages today," Marx said, and there was some emotion in his voice I couldn't quite identify. Hurt? Disappointment? "Why?"

I sighed and resumed scrubbing the mushrooms. "Because they're just pictures and phone calls. You have so much going on already with Shannon, this case, these people who are after you for working this case. I'm not gonna bother you with every little thing, especially when I can handle it myself."

Marx pursed his lips as he considered that, and I about fell off my stool from shock when he said, "Okay."

"O-okay?"

"If he calls you or sends you messages and you don't feel uncomfortable or afraid, then fine. But the moment it makes you feel threatened—"

"I'll tell you."

"Just so we're clear, if he says anythin' that even suggests he's watchin' you, that's a threat, and I expect you to tell me immediately."

I could hear the undercurrent of frustration in his voice, and I knew he must be thinking about the message Collin had sent while I was at the precinct. He had been watching me, and I had deliberately kept that fact from Marx.

I nodded in agreement and then asked, "So about your day . . . any luck on the case? Did you find Tear?"

"I did."

"And? Did he tell you anything?"

"No. He's dead," he answered with palpable anger. "I got a call this mornin' that he was found facedown in the gutter from a gunshot to the back of his head."

My brain struggled to reconcile that fact with the man I had just seen very much alive a few days ago. "When?"

"Looks like he was killed shortly after you got a good look at him at Shannon's house. My guess is that when we put word on the street that we were lookin' for him, he became a liability, and his employers had him executed."

"Somebody's cleaning up loose ends and trying to cut you off at the pass before you can dig any deeper," Jordan reasoned.

"Seems that way."

I sucked in a worried breath. "What about the kids who bought drugs from the street dealer? The ones you've been questioning? Are they gonna go after them next?"

Marx shook his head. "Doubtful, but I won't be surprised if I track down the dealer only to find a corpse."

"Please be careful," I pleaded. "They've already made it clear they don't want you investigating this case, and they're obviously not afraid to take lives."

"You do realize I'm a cop, right?"

"So that means I can't worry? Because I'm pretty sure I just read about a cop dying last week in a shooting."

"It means I know the risks, and I know how to take care of myself. I've been doin' it for twenty-five years. You don't need to worry so much."

I straightened. "Well, by your logic then, I've survived twenty-eight years, so you don't have to worry about anything happening to me either. Clearly, I'm an expert at surviving."

He gave me a thin smile. "There's a difference between survivin' and not gettin' hurt, and your track record for gettin' hurt leaves me plenty to be concerned about."

"He's got a point," Jordan agreed. "I'm pretty sure if we dropped you off in an empty parking lot all by yourself, you would manage to fall into a pothole or get hit by a parked car, if you didn't manage to get kidnapped first."

I hit him in the chest with a mushroom, and he laughed. Jerk.

"I appreciate your concern, and I promise I'll be extra careful," Marx assured me.

Despite his confidence that he would be okay, I worried for him over the next few days. I didn't think that worry would ebb until he either solved the case or dropped it, and knowing him, the latter was a foreign concept.

Jace sent me a text to remind me that her sled hockey game was today and she expected me to come. I texted her back:

Bringing the sheriff with me.

Jordan came by to pick me up in the early afternoon. I put on the last of my winter layers in the bathroom at the arena and then went to meet him outside the ice rink. I loved supporting Jace's sports, but I was allergic to the cold.

Sled hockey, aptly named because the handicapped players competed in sleds rather than skates, was my least favorite of her sports. Everyone looked the same in their protective gear, and I could never remember which number belonged to which player. And the hockey puck was so absurdly small that it was like trying to follow a speck of dust blowing in the breeze.

Jordan looked me over when I joined him outside the shatter-resistant barrier that would protect our teeth if a hockey puck went wild, and his lips twitched.

"Warm enough?" he asked, and I could hear the restrained amusement in his voice.

He was wearing his brown leather jacket, while I had donned the bright-red parka Jace had lent me for just such an occasion, gloves, and a large hat that covered my ears.

"I don't like the cold," I said, and the words left my mouth in a puff of steam.

"You look like the Michelin Man rolled in ketchup."

I narrowed my eyes at him. "Are you making fun of me?"

He shook his head with a fist against his mouth to hide his smile, but his eyes twinkled. "Not at all." He cleared his throat. "Do you wanna sit?"

He gestured to the freezing metal bleachers, and I shook my head. "My butt will go numb."

He lost it and laughed.

"Are you laughing at me?" I demanded. I would've put my hands on my hips to look fierce, but the parka was slippery and my hands perpetually sliding down my body would undermine my ferocity.

He coughed a little as he tried to regain his composure. "Do you wanna sit on my jacket?"

"No," I said firmly. "I wanna stand. Besides, you would freeze, and then I would feel guilty."

"I don't mind the cold," he reminded me. "You apparently do."

I resisted the juvenile urge to stick my tongue out at him. I turned to watch the players make their way out onto the ice.

"So is this a New York sport?" Jordan asked. "I've never seen anything like it before, and I was pretty sure I watched every sport in existence."

"It's part of the Adaptive Sports Program," I answered vaguely, squinting to try to pick Jace out of the players.

"Yeah, that tells me nothing."

I strained to remember the direct quote from the brochure. I wasn't great at explaining things. "A program to promote equality for handicapped athletes who are unable to compete in traditional athletic activities."

"So it's like traditional hockey, except with sleds."

"Um . . . I've never watched traditional hockey." I saw the black blur a split second before it slammed into the transparent barrier, and I braced for it.

Jordan ducked reflexively when the hockey puck slapped the barrier with a loud thwack. "Whoa," he exhaled, standing up straight and looking at me with wide eyes. "That was unexpected."

I smiled. "Yeah, he does that."

The culprit skated to the open doorway leading into the spectator area and leaned through it to see us. From the front, I could make out his dark hair and moss green eyes.

Wayne . . . something. I knew that wasn't right, but it was somewhere along those lines. Dang it, Jace had just said his name a week ago. William . . . Walter . . .

He waved a thickly gloved hand. "Hey, Holly!"

I gave him a small finger wave. "Hi, Philippians 4:13!" He had a habit of wearing his faith on his T-shirt, and more often than not, it was Philippians 4:13—*I can do all things through Christ who strengthens me.* It was the verse that carried me from one day to the next.

His face split into a wide smile. "Who's your jumpy friend?"

"Jordan," he introduced himself. "And you just caught me by surprise."

"Warren, but I'm fine with Philippians."

I blushed with embarrassment. I would remember his name one of these days.

Someone cut across the ice and nearly smashed into the side of Warren's sled before veering at the last second and parking beside him. Blue tips peeked out beneath the head gear, identifying Jace before she even turned her head my way.

She beamed at me from the ice and waved so excitedly that I was torn between laughter and shrinking down behind the wall so no one could see me.

"I beat his lap around the ice by three seconds," she declared. "He's getting slow in his old age."

I was a horrible judge of age, but I knew Jace was thirty. I supposed he could be a little older, but . . . probably not.

Warren rolled his eyes. "It's not the speed that matters. It's how you handle the puck, and I'm a wizard at puck handling." He looked at me and Jordan. "There's free skate after. You two should rent some skates and join us on the ice."

Jace snorted. "We would be picking Holly up the entire time. She has the coordination of a one-legged cat."

"There's an image," Jordan grinned at me.

176

Someone blew a whistle across the ice, and Warren and Jace issued quick good-byes before dashing away to rejoin the group. Another team skated out onto the ice, and Jordan watched with rapt attention as the frenzy for the puck began.

I couldn't follow it. They went left, then right, and then someone tried to take out the wall with their head. The wall won. Jace whipped down the rink and slapped the puck to Warren, and it vanished. I caught a faint blur of movement as it ricocheted back and forth between his hockey sticks, but that could've been my imagination.

"And they call this a sport," a chillingly familiar voice commented.

Terror trickled through me all the way to my toes, freezing me in place. My fingers tightened on the rail in front of me, and my eyes flickered across the barrier, searching out his faint reflection.

Collin stood several feet behind us.

I tried to breathe through the rapidly swelling panic, but even my lungs were frozen. If I kept gasping, they would probably crack and shatter like thin layers of ice.

God, I cried out silently. *Please . . .*

I didn't even know what I was begging for. I just wanted Collin gone. I wanted him to disappear in a puff of smoke like some kind of phantom. But he didn't.

With agonizing slowness, I managed to turn around. Having him behind me left me too vulnerable. My legs felt shaky, and I clung to the rail for support.

All the terrible things he had done to me came rushing back, and it was all I could do not to bolt out of the building or curl into a quivering ball on the floor.

Collin's ice-blue eyes laughed at me, and I knew he could see my fear. "What's the matter, Holly? You don't seem happy to see me, and I traveled all this way."

Jordan straightened at the sound of my name, and his attention shifted from the game to the man whose voice he hadn't recognized. Collin's face must have registered instantly, because his hand dropped to his gun and he stepped between us in the same breath.

"You need to leave," he said, and the cold, dangerous edge in his voice startled me. He was usually so warm.

Collin considered him with mild interest. "If it isn't the sheriff." His gaze locked with Jordan's, and he smiled wolfishly. "I'm going to guess, judging by the righteous anger in your eyes, that you have a little more information now than you did the other morning."

"You have no business being near her after what you've done."

"What I've done?" Collin's face twisted into a convincing imitation of confusion, but his tone was goading. "I'm not sure I know what you mean. Maybe you should elaborate. In great detail. I have plenty of time, and I do love the details."

Jordan's fingers tightened on his gun.

"Are you really going to shoot me in front of all the children?" Collin asked, clearly doubtful. When Jordan's fingers loosened on the gun, his lips spread into a smug grin. "I didn't think so. That's the trouble with you hero types—spineless."

"No, we just have a conscience."

"That's what I said." His tone suggested Jordan was dense. "In a standoff between you and me, *Wyatt*, I will always win, because I'm not shackled by your illogical moral code, or overburdened by a self-deprecating need to put others before myself."

"Moral codes keep this world in balance," Jordan replied curtly, his fingers flexing on his gun. I had no doubt he wanted this confrontation over as quickly as I did, but he had no legal grounds to remove or arrest Collin.

Collin could stand there until the arena closed if he wanted to, and no one could touch him.

"No. Moral codes are designed to protect the weak from the strong," he countered. "To provide them with a veneer of safety they haven't earned. Isn't that right, Holly?"

"Holly isn't weak," Jordan said with audibly strained patience. "But you know that. She stabbed you with a pair of scissors and shoved you down a flight of stairs. Or did you hit your head at the bottom and forget?"

Collin laughed, and it was a chilling sound that made my heart hammer against my rib cage. "Oh, I remember. I needed ten stitches, and it left an ugly scar." He tapped the place near his shoulder where I had stabbed him.

I had plunged the scissors in blindly, missing everything vital, but it had stunned him enough to give me a head start.

"And I would never say Holly is weak," Collin continued. "She has an internal strength that is frustratingly formidable. What is that, Holly? Where does that strength come from?"

I bit back my fear and forced out a single, trembling word. "Jesus."

"Jesus?" he asked in amusement. "Where was your Jesus two years ago when I found you in Pennsylvania? He certainly wasn't standing between us. I would've noticed that."

"Right beside me when I ran out the door and escaped." I was surprised by the sound of my own voice, because the strength to speak those words certainly hadn't come from me.

Something shifted in Collin's expression, and I glimpsed the evil lurking beneath his human skin. "Feeling brave behind the sheriff because you think he'll protect you?"

"I will protect her," Jordan practically growled.

Collin's charismatic mask slipped back over his face, and he cocked his head at Jordan. "You're like a loyal guard dog, aren't you? Driving away unwanted visitors outside her apartment, following along at her heels." Then something sparked in his eyes— a glimmer of understanding—and he laughed again. "Oh, you *like* her. How unfortunate for you. Tell me, what's it like to pine for a woman who won't even let you touch her?"

Collin left an opening for Jordan to respond, but he didn't.

"All this time you spend following her around, protecting her from harm, and she gives you nothing? That must grate on your ego. You could always just toss your inconvenient moral code out the window and take what you want. I mean, she's so,"—he gave my appearance a thoughtful perusal and made a distinctly male sound of appreciation in the back of his throat that turned my stomach—"sweet. It has to be tempting."

Jordan's fingers clenched, as if he were resisting the urge to hit him. Maybe Marx's words were echoing in his ears, making him reconsider. "No, it isn't *tempting*. Because what I want is to see her happy."

Collin gave him an incredulous look. "Because every man's first thought when he looks at an attractive woman is, *I hope she's happy*. Stop lying to yourself."

"You don't know anything about me."

"Of course I do. I know everything about Holly, and therefore everything about everyone she cares about. Sheriff Jordan Radcliffe of Stony Brooke, Kansas, childhood best friend . . . until she blocked you out of her mind for eighteen years. That had to sting. And then when you finally found her again, she wasn't quite right, was she?"

His cold eyes raked over me again. *Just breathe*, I told myself, trying to force the air in and out of my frozen lungs so I wouldn't pass out on the floor.

He pinched his thumb and index finger together as he said with obvious relish, "I think I broke her just a little."

Jordan stepped forward with his right hand curled into a fist, and I had a feeling he would've hit Collin if Jace's shrill voice hadn't startled him motionless.

"You!"

To my surprise, she wheeled around the outside of the rink in her uniform but without the protective gear. It was too early for the game to end, but she had gotten off the ice.

"Back off!" she said too loudly, pointing a finger at Collin. "I saw your picture; I know who you are. She doesn't want anything to do with you." She parked her wheelchair beside Jordan.

She didn't actually know anything about Collin; she didn't even know his name. I wasn't even sure how she recognized his face unless . . .

Sam.

I groaned inwardly. He had a picture of Collin, but he wasn't supposed to share any of the details with her. How much had he told her?

If I wasn't so frozen with terror, I might have fallen over in surprise when Warren came over, followed by another man in a wheelchair I had only seen on the ice. They made a human wall between me and Collin.

Collin's expression was a mixture of surprise and annoyance. "This is comical. A band of handicapables."

Warren planted himself beside Jace and glanced at me before saying to Collin, "Look, we don't want any trouble here. There are families with kids, and we're all just here to have a good time."

Collin's eyebrows arched. "Funny, so am I."

Jordan seemed unsure what to make of his backup, but he didn't object. He did, however, keep a hand on his gun in case Collin decided to become violent.

"Stop harassing my friend," Jace demanded.

"Yeah, maybe you should go," the second man suggested a little nervously.

Collin smiled, but he was clearly unhappy with their intrusion. He probably had an entire torturous conversation planned, and this wasn't a part of it. His eyes met mine, and I tried to stop shaking.

"I'm building you a box, Holly. Just for old times' sake," he whispered, just loudly enough for everyone to hear. I sucked in a sharp breath, and he grinned maliciously. "Sweet dreams."

"Creep," Jace muttered after he retreated, and there was a collective sigh of relief among the team members when he pushed open the doors and left the building. "Thanks for the backup, guys." Jace fist-bumped both of her teammates.

Warren paused before following his teammate back out onto the ice. "You okay, Holly?"

I nodded, still feeling a bit stunned. "Thanks."

Jace hugged me unexpectedly. It wasn't her usual hug that nearly knocked me off my feet; it was hesitant and tender, and it felt unusually comforting.

"How did you know?" I asked quietly.

She hesitated to answer. "Sam showed me his picture and told me to call him right away if I saw him. He didn't wanna tell me anything more than that, but I knew it had something to do with the person creeping around your apartment. So I bugged him about it until he told me it was the guy who called on your birthday, and that he might come looking for you. I knew he wasn't telling me everything—and I tried bribes—but I remembered how scared you were when he called. I memorized his face so I would recognize him if I saw him."

"Jace—"

"You're my best friend, Holly, and if anyone has a right to protect you, it's me."

My fingers ached as I unclenched the rail and wrapped my arms around her, hugging her back.

I was supposed to protect *her* from this piece of my life, not the other way around. How could I shield her from Collin's violence when she threw herself between us?

"We should probably go before he decides to come back," Jordan suggested. He still looked coiled for a fight.

Jace reluctantly released me and met my gaze. "I'm not sorry for snooping. I know how private you are, but I did what I had to do, so please don't be mad."

I wasn't angry with her, but I was so very worried she had just drawn too much attention to herself.

"Will you tell me about him sometime?" she asked. When I tensed, she added quickly, "Not tonight, but when you want. *If* you want." She didn't wait for an answer before looking at Jordan. "You better keep her safe or I'm gonna take out your ankles. I don't care if you have a gun and badge."

He gave her a brief smile. "Trust me, keeping her safe is at the top of my to-do list."

We left the rink and drove to Marx's apartment in silence. When we pulled up to the curb, I hurried up the steps and went into the apartment without waiting for Jordan. Marx was standing in the kitchen, and he blinked in surprise at my abrupt entrance.

"I'm gonna take a shower," I told him before he could say anything.

"You just showered before you left."

Jordan came inside and closed the door behind him. I grabbed my nightclothes from the spare bedroom and sequestered myself in the bathroom.

I heard Marx release an exasperated breath. "What did you do? She was fine when she left."

"Collin showed up at the rink."

I locked the bathroom door and slid the trash can and footstool in front of it just for added security, before turning on the water. I curled up in the bathtub under the spray of hot water and let myself cry quietly.

When Collin looked at me, I felt completely exposed. No matter how many layers of clothes I wore, everything from my innermost thoughts to the pores on my skin felt naked and vulnerable.

He destroyed any sense of security I had managed to scrape together, and I didn't know how to get it back.

The water ran cold before I managed to pull my frayed emotions together. I wrapped myself in layers of clothes, craving warmth and safety, and unbarricaded the bathroom door.

I hesitated when I found Riley curled up just outside of it. His head lifted, and he let out a low whine.

"He's been lyin' there the entire time you were in the bathroom."

My gaze shifted in the direction of Marx's soft-spoken voice. He was sitting on the hallway floor with his back resting against the spare room door. He looked tired, and there were creases of worry around his eyes.

"It's weird looking down at you," I said quietly.

A whisper of a smile crossed his lips. "It's just as weird lookin' up at you. Why don't you come down to my level?"

I lingered in the doorway for a moment before stepping out into the hall and sitting down against the wall opposite him. I drew my knees into my body and rested one hand on Riley's back. "I used all the hot water."

"I have this fascinatin' piece of equipment called a water heater. It makes more."

He studied me, probably noticing my pink nose, which betrayed tears that were long dry. I hoped he hadn't heard me crying in the shower.

"I'm sorry I wasn't there for you tonight," he said, and I could hear the regret in his voice.

I rubbed at my nose with my sleeve and looked at the floor. "It wouldn't have made a difference." Collin had come to frighten me, and Marx's presence wouldn't have changed that.

"Jordan told me what happened." He draped his arms over his knees and interlocked his fingers. "He said Collin made some pretty cruel comments."

If Jordan thought that visit was cruel, then he would be unpleasantly surprised when Collin decided to stop playing games.

"Have you talked with anybody about what happened in Pennsylvania or Maine?"

The question startled my defenses into place, and my voice came out sharp. "No. I don't want anyone else to know. I just wanna forget and move on."

"You can't just forget, Holly. You have to deal with it. There are counselors that can—"

"I'm not broken!" I shouted, coming to my feet. I could still hear Collin's words ringing in my ears, even over my own voice: *I think I broke her just a little.* "I don't need fixing."

Riley angled his body protectively between me and Marx, who stood slowly, hands held out in a soothing gesture.

"I didn't say you were broken, but whether you wanna admit it or not, you're hurtin', and him bein' here is bringin' it all back up." When I started to shake my head, he said gently,

"Sweetheart, I heard you cryin' in the bathroom. For nearly an hour. You came back and took a second shower immediately after seein' him because of how he makes you feel."

He made me feel filthy. No matter how hard I tried, I couldn't get him off my skin or out of my head. I couldn't scrub him away. The tears came without warning, and it made me angrier.

"I hate him," I admitted, my hands fisting at my sides. "I know that as a Christian I'm not supposed to hate people, but I hate him so much."

"I don't know much about God, but I doubt He's very fond of Collin at the moment either. At the very least I doubt He's fond of his choices." He regarded me for a moment before saying, "I don't expect you to confide in me, or Jordan, even Jace. But somebody, Holly. Talk to somebody."

"Why?" I asked bleakly, my voice thick with tears. "It's not gonna undo the things he's done. It's not gonna wipe away the memories or help me forgive myself for failing those other kids. And it won't give me back what he took." My voice broke as I swallowed a sob.

Marx let out a slow breath and blinked his eyes a few times as he stared at the ceiling.

"Can we not talk about this?" I pleaded, hugging myself. "There's no more hot water." And I would definitely want another shower if this conversation continued.

He cleared his throat and looked down at me with red-rimmed eyes. For a moment, I thought he might wrap me in a hug, but he must have suspected that was the last thing I wanted right now. He rubbed his face and sighed. "Why don't we make some brownies? I think we deserve a treat."

Confused, I asked, "You wanna bake brownies at ten o'clock at night?"

"I wanna eat brownies at ten o'clock at night, but the bakery's closed. So we're gonna have to make some ourselves."

"But . . . I'm a terrible cook. I'm almost as bad as Jace."

"I have a fire extinguisher."

"Do you even have brownie mix?"

"I do. I might even have some chocolate frostin'."

"You don't," I said, following him into the kitchen. "I ate it."

He paused to look at me. "Just the tub of frostin'?"

"Mmm hmm."

"Well, I have chocolate chips somewhere."

"I ate those too," I admitted with a sigh, and he laughed.

16

I couldn't sleep that night.

Every time my eyes slipped shut, Collin's face materialized against the insides of my eyelids, and old, terrifying memories crept through the darkness around me.

For the past hour, I had been staring at the blinking green light of the smoke alarm on the ceiling, counting every blink to distract myself.

I pondered another hot shower and a cup of chamomile tea, but I was honestly afraid to sleep. I folded back the blankets and slipped from bed.

I padded soundlessly into the living room in my slippers a little before one in the morning. Marx was sitting on the couch beside the lit lamp with a folder in his hands, and he looked up when I appeared at the other end of the couch.

"Hey, sweetheart," he greeted, with a pinch of concern between his eyebrows. "Everythin' okay?"

"Um, am I interrupting?" I didn't want to infringe on his space or personal time, but I wasn't in the mood to be alone.

It was a new and unusual sensation—craving the companionship of others over solitude—and I wasn't quite sure how to cope with it. I had always been more comfortable alone, especially when I was feeling vulnerable or afraid.

"Not at all," he said. He closed the file in his hands and set it on the coffee table. "Is somethin' on your mind?"

I curled up on the couch a few feet from him and rested my hands on my slippers. "I'm a woman. Isn't there always something on our minds?"

Amusement sparkled in his eyes. "From my understandin', there's about twenty things on your mind at any given time. It's a wonder you don't all suffer from ADD."

I smiled.

"If I had to guess, you're thinkin' about marshmallows and goin' for a run," he said, and I laughed. I usually did think about those two things.

"What do you think about?" I asked.

He leaned back against the couch and pondered my question. "I think about my cases a lot, about my family, about the women in my life."

"Like . . . girlfriend women? Are they still called *girl*friends when you're forty-something?"

He arched an eyebrow. "Is that your nice way of tellin' me I'm old?"

I smirked. "No?"

He chuckled. "Truthfully, I don't know. I haven't dated in a long time." He was quiet for a moment before asking, "Why the sudden interest in my thoughts?"

I gave a small shrug and stared at my slippers. I was interrupting his night because I was feeling insecure, and that was selfish. I should've just taken another shower. "Mmm, never mind." I unfolded my body and stood. "I'm sorry for bothering you."

"Holly." He leaned forward to catch me before I could slip away, and I flinched back the moment his fingertips brushed my wrist.

My reaction startled both of us. I hadn't meant to flinch, but after Collin's visit yesterday evening, every nerve in my body was raw with memories.

I folded my arms around my stomach. "I'm sorry. I'm not afraid of you. I just . . ."

"Don't wanna be touched," he finished when I didn't. "I know. I'm sorry I forgot." He studied me, as if he could see straight through me. "It's okay to not wanna be alone, Holly."

I fidgeted, unsure how to respond to that insight.

"And you're never a bother. So please don't ever think that." He gestured to the cushion, urging me to sit back down. "We don't have to talk."

"But I don't wanna *not* talk. Not talking is awkward. I just . . ." I rubbed my arm as I silently worked through my explanation. "Don't wanna talk about me."

I wanted to escape from the memories smothering my thoughts and plaguing my dreams.

"Can we talk about you?" I asked hopefully. I wanted to know more about the man God had dropped into my life that cold October night.

Both of his eyebrows lifted. "Me?" At my nod, he said, "Okay, but you might develop a sudden case of narcolepsy."

I smiled and sank back down onto the cushions. "Somehow I doubt you're as boring as your car and bathroom."

"There is nothin' borin' about my car. And what's wrong with my bathroom?"

"There's more color at a funeral."

He snorted indignantly, then begrudgingly admitted, "That's probably true. So what would you like to know?"

I drew my legs into my chest and wrapped my arms around them, considering. "Why did you become a cop?"

A hint of grief twisted the smile on his lips. "Why is it whenever you ask me a question, it's an uncomfortable one?"

I shrugged. "It's a gift."

I had asked him about his wife once, who had left him, about kids, which he wanted but couldn't have, and then I had asked him about his relationship with God, which was strained to the point that it scarcely existed. I didn't do it on purpose.

"When I turned eighteen, I left Georgia to join the army," he began.

I tried to imagine teenage Marx, with his intense green eyes and slightly crooked grin, in a military uniform. But he was permanently forty-seven in my head. "Can I see a picture?"

He got up to retrieve his wallet and indulge my request. He flipped through the photos tucked into the clear plastic sleeves of his wallet as he sat back down, settled on one, and then handed it to me.

"This ought to satisfy your girly curiosity."

189

There were three uniformed men standing in front of an American flag. A tall, fit man with vibrant green eyes and black hair stood in the center. The grin on his face was slightly cocky. He was unmistakable, even all those years ago.

I looked at Marx. "You were adorable."

He rolled his eyes and snatched his wallet back. "I had a big head and an even bigger attitude." He closed his wallet and set it out of my reach. "I was finishin' my four years and contemplatin' reenlistment when I got word that my friend Bryan had been murdered."

He leaned forward and pulled a folder from the small pile on the coffee table. He flipped it open and slipped a photo from beneath a paper clip. He handed it to me. I stared at the pale-skinned young man with a vibrant smile.

"He and his wife had just moved to New York City six months earlier. She was pregnant, and he was on his way to meet her at a prenatal appointment, but he was stabbed to death in the parkin' lot of the clinic."

The lingering sadness in his voice made my heart ache for him. "Did the cops catch the killer?"

He shook his head. "The detective assigned the case never could track down a solid lead. I joined the police force and worked my way up to detective. I still haven't been able to solve Bryan's murder." He took the photo from me and tucked it back into the file. "But I check into it every now and again, hopin' to find somethin' new."

I wished there was something I could do to help ease the pain I saw in his face when he looked at the photo. "I'm sorry you lost him."

He closed the file and returned it to the pile. "If he hadn't died, I doubt I would've become a cop."

"And then I would've had to deal with some detective with a boring New York accent that night in the park," I pointed out, hoping to lighten his mood.

He smiled. "I suppose you didn't expect Southern when I opened my mouth."

190

"Um, no. Definitely not."

"It seems we were both surprised, then."

Puzzled, I asked, "What surprised you?"

"I took one look at you sittin' on that curb, wrapped in a blanket, and thought you were a mousy little thing. I thought for sure when I asked you a question that you'd burst into tears. Then I approached you, and realized I was out of my element. I had no idea how to deal with you."

I grinned. "Really?"

"A six-foot, hundred-fifty-pound meth-head I can handle, but this practically five-foot-nothin' girl made me think twice about everythin' I said and did. I spent the entire night tryin' to figure you out."

"I thought detectives enjoyed a good mystery."

He laughed. "You're not just a mystery, Holly. You're an entire series of mysteries with no clues to help guide the way. It took me until the road trip to Maine just to figure out how to deal with you without puttin' you on the defensive."

I smiled down at my slippers.

"What's got you out of bed so late?" he asked.

I shrugged a shoulder. "Just restless, I guess."

"Anythin' I can help with?"

"No." I had showered, made and eaten brownies, written in my journal, and prayed, but I still couldn't shake Collin loose from my thoughts.

The corners of Marx's lips tipped down, and I knew I didn't need to explain it to him. He had already suspected the reason for my sleepless night. "Why don't we watch a movie? Somethin' light." He grabbed the throw blanket from the back of the couch and a pillow. "Here. Snuggle up."

I leaned away from him. "I'm . . . not cuddling with you."

He blinked and then laughed. "I meant in your corner of the couch, Holly. Not with me."

"Oh. Right." I flushed with embarrassment and accepted the items he held out to me. "Thanks."

I curled up on my end of the couch with the pillow and blanket, keeping about three-quarters of a cushion between us, and glanced at Marx.

Amusement still lingered on his lips as he flipped through the TV stations. He settled on an animated movie about a robot named WALL-E. It seemed like an odd choice for a gruff detective, and I lifted my eyebrows at him.

"Well, we're not gonna watch a horror film," he said at my curious expression. "We have enough nightmares to deal with. It's lighthearted and I think you'll like it."

"It's a cartoon. About a robot."

"I did in fact notice that," he said dryly. "But accordin' to the information guide, he's 'loveable.' If memory serves, he's also intensely awkward and he doesn't say much. Remind you of anyone?" He cast a pointed look my way.

I scrunched my nose at him. "I am not intensely awkward." Maybe I was a little awkward . . . occasionally.

It was two thirty in the morning before the movie ended. Marx was bleary-eyed and clearly exhausted, but he kept his head propped up on a fist. He looked at me when I sat up and pushed the blanket off.

"I'm gonna try to sleep again," I said.

"I reckon I should turn in too." He stood, stretched, and yawned. He took the blanket I left wadded up on the cushions when I stood, folded it into perfect alignment, draped it over the back of the couch, and smoothed the wrinkles out of it.

Really?

He caught me looking at him funny and asked, "What?"

I smirked. "Nothing." I walked around the back of the couch toward the spare room, paused, and then rumpled the perfectly arranged blanket.

"Holly!" He called after me in frustration. I scampered into the bedroom, snickering, and closed the door.

17

I stared at the empty space along the wall where I remembered leaving my shoes, and then turned in a slow, puzzled circle as I tried to spot them. My mother used to tell me when I couldn't find something that "it didn't just sprout legs and walk away." But apparently my shoes had done just that.

Marx came out of his room dressed for work and paused in front of the pictures on the hallway wall that were tipped just slightly in the opposite direction this time. He frowned at them and tilted his head.

"Funny how this never happened until a few weeks ago." He gave me a chiding look as he straightened them, and I widened my eyes in exaggerated innocence. "You're not as sweet and innocent as you appear, young lady."

I grinned. "Maybe the wall's just crooked."

"Because that's more probable than a mischievous little houseguest," he said with obvious sarcasm, but he was smiling when he walked into the kitchen to prepare his breakfast.

I laughed softly and looked under the stools. "Have you seen my sneakers? I can't find them."

"Where did you last have them?"

"I put them by the wall next to yours the night we had spaghetti."

"Mmm hmm. And before that?"

I frowned at the odd question. "They were on my feet."

"And where were your feet?"

"Um . . ."

"I'll give you a hint." He turned to face me and leaned against the counter with his plate of toast. "They were on my couch."

I parted my lips to say something and then remembered his warning the first night I stayed here: *yes, you can wear your shoes, but don't put them on my couch. If you do, they might just disappear the next time you take them off.*

My mouth dropped open. "You stole my shoes."

He smiled and took a bite of his toast.

I folded my arms and asked, "And how do I get them back?"

"You can have them back when you find them."

I puckered my bottom lip in a pout.

He narrowed his eyes at me. "Don't give me that cute face. It's not gonna get you your shoes back."

A knock on the front door drew our attention, and all levity vanished. Marx set his unfinished toast on the counter and walked to the door. He peered through the peephole and frowned.

When he unbolted the door and opened it, one hand rested on his gun. "Can I help you?" he demanded of the young man standing outside in the hallway.

The man smiled. "Are you Richard Marx?"

"That depends on who's askin'."

I gravitated toward him slowly, curious. The young man offered him a sealed envelope and then a clipboard. "Just the delivery guy. Please sign for your package."

Marx frowned as he accepted the envelope and signed the form. He handed the clipboard back and was already closing the door when the man said, "Have a nice day!"

He opened the envelope slowly after glancing at the return address, which was an unnamed PO box. He peered inside before pulling out the contents. There was a card inside with pink curly script that shouted, "Congratulations, it's a girl!"

A faint line appeared between his eyebrows as he flipped it open. Inside were the printed words that came with the card: "When she arrives, everything changes. The world grows brighter and every moment is more precious because she's a part of it."

Handwritten beneath that was a deliberately cruel message: "Since you can't have your own kids, it must be nice having Holly around to offset your inadequacies. Have a daddy-daughter dinner on me."

Marx's jaw clenched as he pulled two prepaid ticket stubs from inside the card. "Fried chicken dinner," he grumbled angrily. He shoved them back into the card and threw it on the couch before scrubbing a hand over his face in frustration.

"I'm so sorry," I said quietly.

I looked up into his eyes, sifting through the layers of emotions I saw there. Although he would never admit it, Collin's words had hurt him. He had always wanted kids, but his wife hadn't.

What had I even been thinking by accepting his invitation to stay here? I knew how dangerous Collin was, and I was putting him at risk. I waited for him to come to that realization too and ask me to leave.

When he didn't, I drew in a breath and asked reluctantly, "Should I get my things?" I hadn't even bothered unpacking my bag; it was still tucked into the closet with everything in it except my journal and family photo.

Marx frowned down at me. "Absolutely not."

"If I go, maybe—"

"You're stayin' right here where I can protect you."

His tone left no room for argument, and I pressed my lips together. I could've pushed, but I didn't—maybe because I was too terrified to face my foster brother on my own.

I flinched when someone pounded on the door again, and a mental flash of Collin standing in the hall with that antagonistic smirk on his face made me take a step back. Now that he knew I was staying here, I wouldn't be surprised if he dropped in for a visit.

Marx touched the top of my head with gentle reassurance before looking through the peephole. When his hand didn't grip his gun, I knew it wasn't Collin in the hall.

He opened the door, and Jordan's blond eyebrows crawled upward as he looked between us. "Usually you make me knock two or three times before you open the door. Does this mean I'm growing on you?"

"No," Marx said flatly.

Jordan shrugged and, assuming his welcome, stepped inside. "Morning, Holly."

195

"Hi."

Jordan cocked his head at my flat response, and his gaze slid from me to Marx questioningly. "Everything okay?"

"Collin sent me a card this mornin'," Marx explained as he closed and locked the door. "He knows she's stayin' with me."

Jordan's lips thinned. "What did the card say?"

"Nothin' that bears mentionin'. Just Collin bein' an irritation." Cruel was more like it.

I looked at Marx. "So am I coming to work with you, or . . ."

Marx grabbed his badge off the kitchen counter and clipped it to his belt as he considered it. "I have a lot of runnin' to do today. My student dealers are from three different schools, so I'm guessin' some of their extracurricular activities overlap, and my street dealer is in that overlap somewhere. I'm gonna go talk to them again and see what I can work out on the street."

"By yourself?" I asked with a pang of worry.

He smiled at me. "Yes, by myself. But I'll be wearin' a vest if it leads me to a dangerous neighborhood, and I'll have my radio to call for backup if I need it." When I parted my lips to speak, he said, "No, you can't come with me."

I snapped my mouth shut. How had he known I was going to ask that?

"You're not a cop," he pointed out, as if I needed the reminder. "And if you're on the street with me, I'm gonna be too worried about keepin' you safe to focus on my job."

"I kept myself safe on the streets for years." Mostly. And I had brushed elbows with the darker side of that life on more than one occasion. "I'm not some clueless girl you need to shield from the world."

Marx sighed. "I know that. But I also know you've seen and experienced more than your fair share of darkness in your life, and if it's possible to keep you from havin' to experience any more, then I intend to try."

I knew he had an innate desire to protect people he perceived as weaker or less capable, and I wasn't sure whether to be offended or touched that he was so determined to keep me safe.

The warmth and affection in his eyes robbed me of any indignation and left me feeling . . . confused and off balance. I wasn't used to people caring about me, and I had no idea how to respond. I chewed on my bottom lip and looked at the floor.

"She handles people caring about as well as she handles compliments," Jordan observed.

Marx grunted in amusement. "You mean how she gets all adorably awkward?"

I flushed with embarrassment. "Stop it."

"Her voice gets this little squeak," Jordan pointed out.

"My voice does not . . ." I trailed off when the octave of my voice came far too close to a squeak. I pursed my lips, feeling flustered.

"And she doesn't finish her sentences," Marx added with a small smile.

I drew in a breath and puffed it out. "I . . . really dislike both of you right now." I lifted my chin and strode past them into the spare bedroom to grab my boots.

Jordan's laughter floated after me. I shoved my feet into my ankle boots since I hadn't had a chance to find my sneakers yet, and wrapped a green scarf around my neck.

When I emerged from the room, Marx and Jordan were engaged in a hushed conversation. As usual, their voices fell away when I appeared, and I felt a rush of irritation.

Everyone was always so cautious about what they said in front of me.

"So you wanna go to a party?" Jordan asked, completely derailing my annoyance.

"What?"

"You know, beer, pizza, loud music." When I just blinked at him, he grinned. "Joking. Except about the pizza part. There may also be games, movies, and some popcorn."

197

My eyebrows came together. "Between the pizza, pasta, brownies, and more pizza, I'm starting to think you guys are conspiring to make me fat."

Marx nudged the cake pan on the counter toward me and suggested, "Have a brownie."

I smirked at his less than subtle confirmation of my theory. I picked a corner piece that had come out just a little too crispy but not quite burnt from our brownie baking adventure. I loved the crispy edges.

"Thanks," I smiled. I offered one to Jordan.

"Brownies for breakfast. Nice." He took a massive bite and chewed contentedly before swallowing. "Jace and Sam are gonna be there."

"Just the four of us?"

"Yep."

I nibbled on my brownie as I considered it. I needed to spend some time with Jace. We hadn't seen much of each other lately, and watching her on the ice from twenty feet away hardly counted. "Okay." I set the remainder of my unfinished brownie on the counter and looked up at Marx. "Please be careful out there today."

"I won't take any unnecessary chances. I promise. Have fun at your party."

I wasn't sure about this "party," especially since it was taking place during a time of day that Jace was probably still hibernating.

When I knocked on her apartment door, I expected one of two things: dead silence, or a wild-haired zombie in a wheelchair to drag open the door with an exaggerated groan.

To my astonishment, the door flew inward. Jace beamed when she saw me standing in the hall, her wild bed-hair tamed into smooth layers, and her blue eyes shockingly alert.

"Good morning, sunshine!" She grabbed my hand and practically dragged me into her apartment and into a hug.

"Squeezing," I choked out, and she released my waist with an apologetic grin. I inhaled and patted her shoulders awkwardly before stepping back. "Someone had their coffee this morning. And apparently steroids."

I was pretty sure she had cracked my spine.

"Sam brought me a French vanilla cappuccino with five shots of espresso," she said, grinning.

Oh, good grief.

I didn't notice Sam in the kitchen until he stood up from behind the open refrigerator door and said with what sounded like indifference, "Holly."

"Sam," I replied with a tense smile. I slid my hands into the back pockets of my jeans and returned my attention to Jace. "So you're kind of a spaz, then."

"Oh, totally," she agreed, with several dizzying bobs of her head. "I have a few sips left if you want them."

"That would probably send me into irrational fits of giggling for hours. I think it's safer for everyone if I pass."

"I might like to see that," Jordan admitted. He glanced both ways down the hall before stepping inside and locking the door behind him.

I smiled at him. "The last time that happened, I think it involved feet."

Jace sucked in a quick breath and said, "Don't you dare tell that story."

Jordan grinned. "I would love to hear that story sometime, but Sam and I have snacks to prepare."

"I can help prepare snacks," I offered.

"We actually wanna be able to eat them," Sam said evenly.

Ha-ha. I wasn't that bad.

"I offered to help too, but for some reason they want us out of the kitchen today," Jace said, with a puzzled shrug. "I'm a good cook too, but whatever."

Jace could catch a potato on fire in the microwave, but I decided not to mention that. Jordan strolled into the kitchen and punched Sam in the arm in some form of manly greeting as he grunted, "Hey."

Sam frowned and punched Jordan back a little harder, sending him stumbling. "Hey."

Jordan arched an eyebrow at him but didn't retaliate. "Did you check the grounds before I got here?"

"Yep, we're good."

I shrugged off my coat and curled up in the corner of Jace's couch with a pillow. Happiness filled me when I saw my fat cat, Jordan, gallop out of her bedroom toward the couch. He chirped at me in recognition.

Jace scooped him up and set him on the couch before plopping onto the cushion next to me. "Your cat is a beached whale. I'm putting him on a diet."

I hugged my chubby kitty and peppered the top of his head with kisses. "He's just huggable."

She gave me a look. "His fat rolls have fat rolls. And when he runs across my floor, the people below me think it's thunder."

I laughed. That was one benefit of living in a basement. There weren't any tenants beneath me to complain about the noise.

He wiggled free and stretched out across my feet, purring. It was like a fuzzy foot massage.

Jordan and Sam were chatting in the kitchen as they prepared the snacks. I heard Sam growl, "This morning was the third time I've gotten into my car to find that someone switched my radio to the Spanish-Mexican station."

"Like they physically got in your car and changed the station?" Jordan asked.

"Yeah, and I never see it happen. And just to make sure I understood it wasn't a glitch, they left this tied to my antenna this morning." Sam reached into his pocket and pulled out a tiny Mexican flag. "One of these days I'm gonna punch Collin in the face and relieve him of his teeth."

"Get in line," Jordan grunted.

Jace inhaled a breath to say something, then seemed to lose her nerve, which was unusual for her. She tended to just blurt things out without a filter. She tried again.

"So I know you don't like to talk about your past, but this Collin guy . . . is he like . . . an ex-boyfriend or something? Is he the reason you don't date? I mean he's obviously unhinged, so I completely understand if he put you off dating."

She looked at me expectantly.

How did I explain Collin to her without sending her into overprotective mode? "It's . . . complicated."

"I'm totally okay with the abridged version."

I shifted in my seat, and my cat gave a rumble of disapproval. "He was my foster brother, and he's"—a psychotic, sadistic lunatic—"overly interested in me."

Her face crinkled in what looked like disgust. "As in he has a crush on you?"

"I don't know that I would call it that."

"I know you're not biologically related, but . . . ew. There are just some boundaries you don't—"

"We're not talking about serious things, are we?" Jordan asked from the kitchen, and the look in his eyes when he met mine told me he had overheard our conversation. "Because we're supposed to be having fun."

"Fine," Jace said on a theatrical sigh. "But I mean, she's staying with Marx because of him, so that means he's dangerous, right?"

Sam walked into the living room and handed her a massive bowl of popcorn and a root beer. "Yes, he's dangerous," he said. "That's why you're supposed to call me immediately if you even think you see him in the area."

I gave him a grateful smile. I deeply appreciated that he was looking out for her. He returned my smile before fetching another bowl of popcorn from the kitchen.

He detoured to the window on his way back, pulled the sheer curtains aside with two fingers, and peered down into the front yard of the apartment property.

"Got the cards," Jordan announced. He walked quickly behind the couch and snitched a handful of popcorn from Jace's bowl.

She swatted at him, but his reflexes were faster.

He plopped into one of the wooden chairs on the other side of the coffee table. Sam handed me a bowl of popcorn and then sat down beside him.

Jordan shoved a hand into Sam's personal popcorn bowl and retrieved a fistful of buttery popcorn. "Thanks," he mumbled before popping it in his mouth.

Sam glowered at him. "Really?" He shoved the bowl at Jordan and then got up and went back into the kitchen. I heard the familiar crinkle of popcorn paper and then the hum of a microwave before he called out, "Holly, do you want a drink?"

"There's chocolate milk in the fridge and marshmallows in the cupboard," Jace called back before I could answer.

Sam appeared at the edge of the kitchen with a bemused frown. "What am I supposed to do with the marshmallows?"

"Holly likes marshmallows in her chocolate milk."

Sam arched an eyebrow at me. "I'm not even gonna comment on how weird that is." He disappeared back into the kitchen.

He returned a minute later with my drink and his new bowl of popcorn. He shot Jordan a warning glare as he sat down. "Take my popcorn and I'm gonna take a finger."

"Harsh," Jordan replied with a smile. He opened the box of cards and shuffled them. He licked his thumb and began to deal them around the table.

"I'm not touching that," Sam said when the card landed on the table in front of him.

Jordan paused for a beat. "Why not?"

"Because you licked it."

"I didn't lick it. I licked my thumb."

"And then you smeared it all over the card."

Jordan gave him a funny look. "And?"

"I'm eating," Sam explained. "I'm not gonna touch a card dripping with your spit and then use the same hand to put popcorn in my mouth."

"Dripping with my spit," Jordan repeated. "You mean like this?" He gave another exaggerated, slurping lick of his thumb, plucked a card from the top of the deck, and dropped it in front of Sam.

Ewww. I tried not to wrinkle my nose in disgust. Sam just got up from the table and walked away, muttering under his breath about unsanitary people.

"I take it Sam doesn't like germs?" I whispered to Jace.

"Nope. We can't even eat from the same bowl of chips and salsa when we go out for Mexican," she whispered. "And don't even get me started on buffets."

Jordan scooped Sam's cards back into the deck and redealt, minus the thumb licking. Sam eventually caved and brought a bottle of hand sanitizer over with him so he could join the game. He and Jordan bickered back and forth like brothers the entire time.

Sam slugged Jordan in the arm and nearly knocked him out of his chair for trying to steal another handful of popcorn.

Jordan laughed and then rubbed his arm. "Ow! What do you expect me to do? Take Holly's popcorn? That's a violation of the border laws."

"Go make your own," Sam suggested. "Or wimp out and beg her to share with you. She's an irrationally nice person. She might consider it."

I hugged my bowl of popcorn protectively closer.

"Yeah, I don't think she's gonna share with me. Besides, yours is closer."

Jordan made one last halfhearted attempt to steal Sam's popcorn, and then seemed to decide it would be less painful to make his own.

The pizza arrived a few hours later. Jordan paid the delivery man and opened the top box as he was kicking the door shut. He pulled out a slice of pepperoni and sausage. The molten hot cheese practically oozed off the crust into his mouth.

"Hot," he exhaled, blowing out steam. He shoved the pizza boxes at Sam and fumbled for the first cold drink he could find. He took a few deep gulps and then said, "Wow, that was hotter than I expected." He glanced down at Sam, who was giving him a flat look, and then back at the glass in his hand. "Oh, I'm sorry, was this yours? You want it back?"

"No," Sam gritted out. "You can keep it. I'll get another one."

Jace chewed on a fingernail as she observed their interaction. I tried not to smile, but Sam as a germaphobe was just kind of funny and unexpected.

"I'll get you another Pepsi," I offered, and I went to fetch him one. I grabbed a fresh glass and a cold can of pop from the refrigerator, but I paused at the threshold of the kitchen.

Jordan and Jace were laughing about something, and Sam was shaking his head with a small smile on his lips. Seeing their joy warmed me, and knowing I was somehow a part of it . . .

I had spent so much of my life living on the fringes of society, hiding from everyone who might be a threat, that I'd forgotten what it felt like to be included, to have a group of friends to just . . . laugh with.

It made me feel like I mattered.

Sam caught me watching them from the kitchen, and I flushed with embarrassment when he stood and walked over.

"You get lost?" he asked.

I smiled and offered the drink to him. "Nope."

He took it and cocked his head as he studied me. "In all the time I've known you, I don't think I've ever seen you this calm. You're usually jittery."

I tucked my fingers into the back pockets of my jeans and rocked on my toes. "It helps knowing I have Jace to protect me if anyone creepy shows up."

His lips quirked in a barely perceptible smile. "Yeah. I heard about the ice rink."

I knew he had. This entire "party" was designed to help me feel safe after Collin's visit had ripped open wounds that had barely begun to heal.

"Thank you," I said. "For helping me feel safe."

He studied me for a long moment and looked as if he might have something meaningful to say, then shrugged and grunted. "Sure." He stalked back into the living room, and I followed with a smirk.

Sam was a man of few words.

We spent the rest of the afternoon playing games and watching movies, and as the day progressed, I felt some of the knotted tension in my body begin to ease.

"You ready to head out?" Jordan asked when it was nearly dusk.

"Yep." I stood and stretched. Jace and I hugged good-bye, and I gave Sam a wave before opening the door to leave. I barely swallowed a scream when I found a man standing just on the other side.

Recognition slowly dawned, and my heart rate slowed. It was my landlord, frozen with his shoulders bunched in surprise and his fist raised to knock.

"Mr. Whittaker?"

"Ms. Cross," he squeezed out, going a shade paler. "I wasn't . . . expecting you . . . here."

I folded my arms and glared at him with suspicion. "You're not here to make an *arrangement* with my friend, are you? Because her boyfriend is a cop."

I hadn't thought it possible, but he paled even more.

"Holly, I'll take care of it," Sam said, brushing past a slightly confused Jordan. "Whittaker," he said with disdain. He stepped into the hall, forcing my landlord to retreat, and then closed the door.

"Who's that guy?" Jordan asked, throwing a thumb toward the door.

"The new landlord." Jace leaned forward on the couch and whispered, "Sam's been talking to the other tenants, and apparently Mr. Whittaker has been making some indecent propositions with some of the female tenants. Not me, but ones who have like no family and stuff. Sam confronted him, and now the guy's like all agreeable and stuff. Promising not to cause anymore trouble and whatnot."

Sam came back in and closed the door behind him, his expression tight.

"What's going on with this guy and his female tenants?" Jordan demanded, before anyone else could speak.

Sam glanced at me before answering, "There are three young women in this building without family in the area, aside from Holly, and when they couldn't pay the extra fee Mr. Whittaker threatened to impose for one reason or another, he offered them an alternative to eviction."

"What kind of alternative?" Jordan asked.

"A sexual arrangement. He also approached Holly."

"I . . . never said anything about . . . anything like that," I stammered uneasily.

Jordan's jaw tightened, and he leaned closer to whisper, "Your lips are twitching."

I bit down on my lips in frustration.

"I doubt you're the exception, Holly," Sam said. "Either Marx interrupted, or you just didn't tell him that part for fear Mr. Whittaker might mysteriously disappear."

I glared at him.

"I'll take that as confirmation."

Jordan cast me a worried look. "This guy doesn't have keys to your apartment, does he?"

I shook my head. "Just me." A fact about which I was immeasurably relieved. No more landlords sneaking in uninvited. "And I don't think he's gonna bother me again anyway. Marx listed himself as my next of kin on the information card, and Mr. Whittaker's afraid of him."

Sam grunted in amusement. "Not surprising."

"Why were you talking to Mr. Heebie-Jeebie anyway?" Jace asked, giving a theatrical shudder just to emphasize her point.

"We made an arrangement of our own."

Curious, I asked, "Does it include a bullet-point list of all the logical reasons he shouldn't creep on people?"

Sam gave me an unamused look, and I smirked. "No. I agreed not to make his life miserable so long as he doesn't harass his tenants, and he informs me of any unexpected male visitors or suspicious activity."

The look he shared with Jordan made my stomach flip over. Unexpected male visitors like Collin?

I tried to keep my voice even and strong, but it came out thin with fear. "He's here? Collin's here?" Was that why Mr. Whittaker had stopped by?

"Possibly," Sam replied. "Whittaker's supposed to call me if he sees him in the area, but since I was here, he decided to tell me in person." He turned his attention to Jordan. "I'm gonna do a quick check of the property, and then I'll escort you and Holly to your car."

I sank onto the arm of Jace's couch after Sam left and tried not to let Collin's potential nearness unravel my nerves. I felt Jace's arms come around my waist, and she pressed her face against my back.

"It's gonna be okay, Holly. He can't get to you here. Not with Sam and Jordan in the way. No guy in his right mind would try that."

I forced a nod, trying to believe her, but I wasn't sure the phrase "in his right mind" applied to Collin. When the doorknob turned a few minutes later, I stiffened with apprehension, but it was only Sam.

"We're clear. Let's go," he said.

Jordan gestured for me to go ahead of him, and we walked down the hall single file, with me in the middle. Even though I knew they wouldn't let Collin touch me, I couldn't keep my eyes from darting frantically over every visible inch of grass and sidewalk when we stepped outside.

My gaze landed on my apartment, and I felt a pang of longing. I missed my home and the sense of independence that came with living on my own and providing for myself.

Someday I'll get there again.

As we neared Jordan's car, I noticed something propped on the hood. It looked like a toy. Jordan slipped around me and walked to the front of his car.

A puzzled line formed between his eyebrows.

He picked up the item and showed it to us. It was a Sheriff Woody doll from *Toy Story*, and there was a small envelope attached to it.

"It's addressed to Wyatt," Jordan said with a grimace.

Sam folded his arms. "He leaves me a Mexican flag, and he leaves you a sheriff doll. The guy lacks creativity."

Jordan opened the envelope and pulled out a key card with a hotel symbol on it.

My breath caught. "Please tell me that's not the key card for your hotel room."

He pursed his lips and flipped the card to show us the room number written in black permanent marker. "That's my room number. I left the spare key card on the nightstand when I left the room this morning."

I stared at him. "He was in your hotel room?"

"Maybe. But the keys aren't labeled with numbers; they're programmed. So it's possible he just knows my room number and wrote it on a different card to prove he knows where I'm staying."

"He's trying to unnerve you," Sam said.

"And yet all he's managed to do is annoy me."

They both seemed unusually calm considering Collin might have been in Jordan's hotel room. At the very least, he knew exactly where Jordan was staying.

"What do we do?" I worried, looking between them.

Jordan unlocked the car and opened the passenger door. He tossed the doll and card into the backseat like they were no more important than crumpled burger wrappers, then stood back with his hand on the top of the door. "We take you back to Marx's place like we planned."

"But what about—"

"We'll take care of it," Sam said, but he offered no further details. "Good night, Holly."

I looked at Jordan to see if he would be willing to explain exactly how they intended to "take care of it," but he just smiled and said, "Your nose is turning pink. You should probably hop in and get out of the cold breeze."

Sighing, I climbed into the car, and he shut the door. He exchanged a few hushed words with Sam before climbing behind the wheel. Marx was just getting home when we arrived.

"You're still in one piece," I observed with relief.

He smiled as he unlocked the apartment door. "I told you I'd be fine." He looked over my head at Jordan, who lingered on the steps. "I'll call you later about self-defense trainin'. There are a few things I'd like to discuss with you."

Jordan's brow creased with cautious curiosity, but he said, "Sure."

"You're gonna be careful, right?" I asked. The possibility that Collin might have been inside his hotel room worried me.

He gave me a reassuring smile. "Sam's gonna come check the room with me just to make sure everything's fine, and then I'm gonna grab my stuff and find another place to stay."

"What happened?" Marx asked.

"Collin knows where I'm staying, and he may have been in my hotel room. He left a key card with my room number written on it, and a gift he no doubt finds poetically hilarious, on my car."

This taunting game Collin was playing with them was because of me, and I wished I could put an end to it. I was bringing nothing but trouble to their lives.

"Wipe that guilty look off your face, young lady," Marx said. "This isn't your fault."

I shot him a scowl that made the corner of his mouth lift in amusement. He couldn't tell me what to do with my face.

"The fact that he's targeting the three of you because of me makes it my fault," I explained. "He's my problem, and I should never have—"

"What?" Marx demanded, eyes narrowing. "Stayed?"

I folded my arms and looked away.

"Before we go any further with this conversation," he continued, "you should know that if you run, I will spend every moment tryin' to track you down before Collin does."

My eyes snapped back to him. "That's called stalking."

"Cops don't stalk; they pursue."

Jordan laughed behind me.

"Well, don't do that. Don't . . . pursue. If you spend all your time looking for me, you'll lose your job, and I don't want you to lose your job because of me."

"We're not gonna have to worry about it, because you're not runnin' away." He crossed his arms in a way that silently declared, "And that's final."

I glared at him.

"Just because Collin wants to hurt you, Holly, it doesn't mean everything he does in the pursuit of that goal is your fault," Jordan explained. "His decisions are his, and you're not responsible for them."

"You know, this whole you two being united against my point of view thing is really frustrating."

Jordan grinned, revealing his dimples. "Yeah, well, I never thought I'd agree with an old guy so much either."

Marx glowered at him. "Get out of my hallway."

"Oh, this is your hallway? Is your name on it?"

"Could you be more juvenile?"

"Probably." He tossed his car keys up and down in his hand. "But I'll behave because Holly's standing here."

What could that juvenile behavior be if he was reluctant to do it around me?

Jordan gave me a small bow and said, "Have a good night, my lady." He turned and disappeared down the steps, leaving an odd feeling in his wake: longing for him to stay or maybe just disappointment that he was leaving.

I wasn't sure, and I didn't know what to do with either, so I shoved them aside for later contemplation.

I followed Marx into the apartment. "So about my sneakers . . ."

"You mean the pair of sneakers that defiled my couch?" he asked as he secured the door. "I haven't seen them since they disappeared."

"Could you at least give me a hint?"

"Sure. They're not on my couch."

I sighed, dropped my bag on the couch, and started the hunt for my shoes. I searched the entire living room, kitchen, bathroom, and finally found myself in the spare bedroom.

I turned in a slow circle as I took in the room. Surely he wouldn't have hidden them in here. I checked the closet, the side table, and I was just crouching down to check beneath the bed when something shattered the bedroom window from the outside.

I screamed and threw up my arms to protect my face as glittering glass rained down on top of me.

18

"Holly!" Marx shouted as he rushed into the room. I heard a curse slip beneath his breath as he made his way to me. "You all right?"

"Yeah," I said shakily. "I'm okay." Shards of glass tinkled to the floor as I slowly lifted my head and looked around the room with wide eyes. Someone had just thrown a rock the size of a grapefruit through Marx's apartment window.

At least it hadn't put a hole in the wall.

Marx leaned out of the now empty window frame and looked down at the street with his gun in his hand. I stood and tried to shake the slivers of glass from my hair. I hissed in through my teeth when a piece of glass cut into my heel.

Marx's gaze darted to me and then to my socked feet surrounded by glass. He walked to the closet and grabbed a pair of shoes for me. "I'm gonna check the parkin' lot. Lock the door after I leave and stay away from the windows."

I slipped the flats on carefully and tiptoed through the glass as I followed him out of the room, bypassing Riley, who was standing in the hallway. "I wanna come with you."

"Absolutely not."

"But—"

"Holly." He pinned me with a look that made all arguments freeze in my throat. "Stay in this apartment, lock the door, and call Sam. Please."

I nodded, and then he was gone. I closed the door and locked it, hating that the only thing I could do was hide behind a locked door and call for help. I pulled my phone from my pocket and dialed Sam's number.

He answered on the third ring, his monotone greeting making me feel like an annoyance. "Yeah."

"Someone just threw a rock through Marx's window."

Sam paused for just a breath before asking, "Anybody hurt?"

I stopped in the doorway of the spare bedroom, taking in the broken glass, and blew out a breath. "Just the window."

"Where's Marx?"

"Outside."

"Where are you?"

"Inside."

"Doors locked?"

"Yes, Sam," I said, exasperation seeping into my tone. "I'm not an idiot."

"It's just a question, Holly. Don't get angry."

I pulled the phone away from my ear and glared at it, instantly angry. Riley tried to follow me into the spare bedroom as I looked around for something to clean up the glass with, but I held up a hand. "No, no, no. Stay."

The glass would shred his paws.

Sam cleared his throat. "Did you just tell me to stay? Because I'm coming over. I'll be there in about five minutes."

The call disconnected, and I blinked at my phone screen in confusion. He'd hung up without even saying goodbye. "Okay then, guess we're done talking." I snapped my phone shut and shoved it into my back pocket.

I looked down at the rock, noticing for the first time that there was a white piece of paper rubber-banded around it.

My toes felt suddenly cold.

The last mysterious note accompanied by a broken window had been from Collin. I reached down and picked up the rock, unwinding the rubber band with trembling fingers. I set the rock back on the floor and unfolded the note slowly, trying to work up the nerve to read it.

I opened the last fold to find a short message scrawled across the page in capital letters: BACK OFF OR SHE'S NEXT.

Relief, brief and powerful, swept over me when I realized the note wasn't from Collin—it was too similar to the message left on Marx's car—but concern followed quickly on its heels. The message might not be from Collin, but it was hardly a love poem.

Back off or she's next.

I looked at Riley uneasily. "I don't suppose you're secretly a girl." Riley cocked his head at me. "Yeah, I didn't think so." That left me as the only "she" in this apartment.

Unless they were talking about Shannon. They had already targeted her once.

A series of sharp thumps erupted in the living room a few minutes later, and I poked my head into the hall, giving the front door a wary look.

"Holly, open up," Marx shouted through the door.

The fear left me in a rush, and I walked to the door to let him in. He stalked inside, crossed the living room, and started yanking the drapes shut so ferociously that I thought he might rip the curtain rods right off the wall.

I stepped forward to help, and he snapped, "No. I don't want you anywhere near the windows. I couldn't find whoever threw that rock, and I don't want you gettin' hit if they decide to throw somethin' else."

I backed away and folded my arms, gripping the threatening note in one hand while he closed all the curtains. If someone decided to pitch another rock through the window, his drapes weren't going to stop it. But I decided not to mention that.

"After my car and Shannon's house, I doubt this was just bad luck," he said under his breath.

"It wasn't." I held out the note.

He took it and read the message briskly before asking, "Where did you get this?"

"Wrapped around the rock."

He leaned against the peninsula as he studied the message. He glanced at me, and I caught the glimmer of worry in his eyes.

Someone knocked on the door and Marx moved around me to open it. A young officer I had never seen before stood in the

214

hallway: tall and trim with one of those faces that reminded me of the boy bands Jace listened to.

"Daniel." Marx greeted him with a slight nod and stepped back to let him enter. "Where's Sam?"

"Hi, Detective. He's coming. He said something about a brick through a window?" He glanced around the apartment, his brown eyes slipping past me and then snapping back. He gave me an interested once-over that made me fidget. "Hi," he practically purred.

I glanced at Marx to see if he had caught the overly friendly note to his voice or if maybe I had imagined it. Judging by the faint line between his eyebrows, it hadn't been my imagination.

"I'm Danny," the newcomer announced, drawing my attention back to him. "Sam's new partner. Well, less new. It's been five months. You must be Holly."

His attention stuck to me like fly paper, and I just wanted to shake it off.

"Stop staring at her." Sam's voice preceded him through the doorway by only a second, and I caught Danny's slight flinch at the reprimand.

Sam pulled on a pair of gloves and passed between us without so much as a greeting. He followed the shards of glass scattered throughout the hallway back to the spare bedroom.

Danny cast me a sheepish look before turning and following Sam down the hall. He leaned into his partner and whispered, "You're embarrassing me."

"You're embarrassing yourself."

"I wasn't even staring at her. I was just . . ."

"Ogling?" Sam offered.

Danny let out a low grunt of frustration. "You weren't even in the room."

"I know you."

I thought I saw Danny's ears turn a shade pinker, but he didn't say anything more. He glanced at me one last time and then pulled on his own gloves in preparation for work.

Sam stopped him before he could enter the room and suggested, "Why don't you wait downstairs for CSU. Someone will need to show them where to go. Marx and I can handle this." When Danny shrugged and stripped the gloves back off without complaint, Sam narrowed his eyes suspiciously and added, "And don't hit on Holly."

Danny frowned. "Why do you even care? You're dating that wheelchair chick."

Sam gave him a flat look, but there was a glint of warning in his eyes. "That *wheelchair chick* is her best friend, which means Holly matters to me too. And she's unavailable, so keep your distance from her."

Sam disappeared into the room, and Marx held the front door open for Danny. I felt a flicker of sympathy for the man, who clearly appreciated being dismissed about as much as I did, but it was quickly overshadowed by relief when Marx closed the door after him.

Marx gave me an understanding smile, as if he knew I was relieved to no longer be the center of the man's attention, and then joined Sam in the spare room.

"Sounds like Holly's growin' on you," I heard Marx say quietly.

Sam sighed, as if that fact bothered him deeply. "Yeah."

"Is that a problem?"

"She reminds me of my sister. Now it's like having two sisters. You know what I wanted when I was a kid? A brother."

Marx chuckled.

A quiet tapping drew my attention back to the front door. "So are you single?" a voice whispered from the other side.

I blinked as my distracted brain tried to process the question. Was I really being hit on through a door?

Another quiet tap, and then the low voice asked, "Can you hear me?"

I stared at the door as I considered pretending I couldn't hear him. I didn't want to have this conversation. Maybe I could just sneak away and leave him talking to dead air. Would that be rude? I needed an etiquette check. I pulled out my phone and sent Jace a text:

> *What's the proper response when you're being hit on*
> *through a door? Is walking away and pretending you*
> *didn't hear them too rude?*

She responded a moment later:

> *Is he knocking?*
>
> *Yes,* I sent back.
>
> *When he knocks again, ask him who's there.*

I laughed out loud without meaning to and clapped a hand over my mouth. Silence fell on the other side of the door. So much for sneaking away and pretending I didn't hear him. Now he knew I was still standing here.

Another message came through from Jace:

> *Who's hitting on u thru a door? That's awkward. Is*
> *he 2 shy 2 do it in person?*

"Holly?" Danny called through the door.

I hesitated before saying, "Sorry, I'm on the phone." It wasn't a lie, and it brought another moment of blessed silence. I sent Jace a quick response, letting her know the "2 shy" guy was Sam's partner, then snapped my phone shut and tucked it into my back pocket.

I gave the door one last sympathetic look as I considered the man banished to the other side of it, and then retreated to the bathroom. I barely made it through the doorway before my phone alerted me to another text message from Jace:

> *DANNY!? He's such a player. He flirts with*
> *everyone. Sam's always trying 2 rein him in. If he*
> *asks u out say no.*

Did she actually think I would say yes? I ignored the text and rummaged through the drawers for something to help with the glass. I picked through my hair with a pair of tweezers, plucking out the larger pieces, and then used a comb to brush the rest into the sink.

I cleaned the small nicks on my body with peroxide and placed a bandaid on the heel of my right foot.

"Who do you think 'she' is?" Sam asked from the room across the hall. I glanced over to see him reading the note. "Do you think they mean Holly or Shannon?"

"I don't know," Marx admitted. "I asked Shannon to stay with her family until this case was resolved, but she was pretty upset about her house, so I don't know if she'll listen. But I can't decide if it was a coincidence or not that they threw the rock through Holly's window."

"Do they know she's staying with you?"

"They saw her come out of the buildin' with me the night they vandalized my car, and they've seen us together more than once."

"So there's a good chance they know she's staying here. But how did they know which room she was in?"

Marx rubbed a hand over the back of his neck as he admitted, "I don't know that either."

"Well, they clearly want you to back off before you compromise their business, but so far, they're not willing to kill you to do it," Sam said.

"Well, once they cross the line and kill a cop, it won't be just one determined detective they have to worry about. The NYPD will be out for revenge, and they don't want that kind of attention."

"So they're trying to intimidate you into backing off by threatening the people you care about."

Fury darkened Marx's face. "They're cowards, and I will not let them push me into a corner."

Sam glanced at the note again. "Well, then maybe you should remind Shannon of the danger if she comes back here, because my guess would be this note is for her. They went after her and she wasn't home, so they left her house as a message. Maybe this means they're gonna physically go after her next, and the fact that it came through Holly's window is just a coincidence."

"I'll try to get a hold of her again," Marx decided. "CSU should be here soon, though I doubt they'll find anythin' useful."

Sam handed the bagged note back to him. "Barring any disasters that I get called out to tonight, I'll see if I can track down a board to put over that window."

"I would appreciate that. But maybe . . . leave Daniel in the car. I think his attention makes Holly uncomfortable."

Sam sighed like a put-upon parent. "Kid's got the libido of a rabbit." He offered me a parting nod before letting himself out of the apartment.

I heard Danny the moment Sam stepped into the hall. "Tell me you were joking about the 'unavailable' thing, because she's hot, and I haven't had a date in days."

"I told you to go downstairs," Sam snapped.

Danny said something in response, and Sam argued back, their voices fading away down the hall.

Marx joined me in the bathroom. "Anythin' need stitches?"

I stiffened when he raised a hand to touch me. He paused, giving me a moment to adjust, and then brushed the hair back from my face.

He was gentle as he nudged my head left, then right so he could inspect the cuts from the glass. I could see anger in the tense line of his jaw, but none of it touched his voice. "Nothin' too deep, thankfully. How's your foot?"

I stepped back from him, ignoring the sharp pain in my heel. "It's fine."

"Did you clean it?"

"Yes."

Most of the cuts were superficial, but the one on my heel had needed some extra attention. It would probably scar, but then it would just blend in with the rest of the scars on the bottoms of my feet.

I wiggled my bare toes on the chilly floor, wishing I had a clean pair of socks or my slippers to hide my feet in. But they were in the spare room, surrounded by glass.

Marx ducked back into the bedroom and grabbed my slippers from the closet just as I was contemplating putting my flats back on, one of which was still a little damp with blood.

"Thanks," I said in surprise.

He dropped them onto the floor in front of me, and I slipped my feet into them gratefully.

"I'm not sure what time Sam will be back with that board, and it's gettin' late, so you're welcome to sleep in my room and I'll take the couch," Marx offered.

"I'll just watch movies or something until he comes back."

"It could be late."

I shrugged and then started to put away the first aid materials I had found beneath the bathroom sink.

"I'm sorry about this, Holly."

I met his eyes, pondering the regret in his voice. "About what?"

"I brought you here to keep you safe, and somebody just threw a rock through the window of the room you're stayin' in."

"I got you abducted and beaten up by a serial killer, and now my psychotic foster brother is mailing you free fried chicken dinner tickets. I'm not really sure a rock through the window compares."

He gave me a stern look. "Neither of those situations is your fault."

I tucked my hands into the back pockets of my jeans and returned his stern expression. "You didn't exactly throw a rock through your own window, unless you learned how to split yourself in two."

"Point taken."

He folded his arms and leaned in the doorway, his eyes staring through me as his mind drifted to someplace beyond the bathroom.

"Sam's not wrong," he finally said. "These people are targetin' those I care about to force me to back off this investigation. It's only a matter of time before they realize you're one of those people. If they haven't already."

I frowned. "We haven't even known each other that long."

"True," he conceded. "But I don't think that's gonna matter to them. Shannon and I have been divorced for two years, and they still went after her."

And I was staying with him . . .

"If there ever comes a time when I need to shoot somebody to keep you safe, I wanna be on the same page."

"You really think that might happen?"

"Let's hope not. But if we're ever in that situation, I need you to understand that I *will* shoot that person, and I need you to know *when* I'm gonna shoot that person so you can get out of the way."

"And I suppose you're not just gonna shout, 'Duck so I can shoot that guy.'"

The right corner of his mouth quirked up. "No, that wouldn't be a very good idea. It needs to be somethin' only you and I are aware of. A trigger word or phrase."

"Why do you call it a trigger word?"

"Because it means I'm about to pull the trigger."

Oh. That made sense. I gave it some thought and said with a slow smile, "As much as I like zebras."

Marx's eyebrows drew together. "I am not sayin' that ridiculous phrase."

"I like it. Reminds me of that table we picked out for you."

"No."

"Then you pick one. I'm gonna go watch a movie."

It took him a moment to realize he was blocking my only exit from the bathroom. He stepped back, and I slipped by him. "We have to agree on one."

"I like mine," I shouted back, and I heard him mumble something about hideous zebra tables.

Riley followed me into the living room. I perused the movie selections on Marx's shelf until I found something that looked funny and lighthearted: a film about two dogs and a cat lost in the wilderness. I might have seen it once when I was little, but I wasn't sure.

I put it into the DVD player and curled up on the couch. Riley stretched out along the front of the couch to keep me company, and I let one arm dangle over the edge so my fingers could play lazily in his fur.

His presence comforted me.

Evening quickly faded into the wee hours of the morning, and I yawned as exhaustion tugged at me. Sam hadn't returned with a board for the window yet, but I could already feel my mind beginning to drift.

The haunting dreams slithered into my mind before I even realized I was falling asleep.

Heart-wrenching sobs poured out of the shadows around me, and I spun in circles, trying to find the child who was crying out. Then *he* was there. His very presence seemed to suck the breath from my lungs, and no matter how deeply I gasped for air, I couldn't draw it in. Darkness closed in around me, trapping me, and I pounded my fists against it, trying to break free before it crushed me to death.

I finally managed to pull in a lungful of air just as I resigned myself to the fact that I was going to die this time, and my eyes snapped open. A dark shape loomed over me, and I felt the warmth of a hand on my shoulder. The breath I had just managed to capture left me in a scream.

I scrambled away, my movements frantic and clumsy. Something was tangled around my legs, and I landed hard on the floor. I crawled backwards until my back smacked against a wall.

"Holly," a Southern voice said gently. "It's just me. I'm gonna turn on a light."

I winced at the sudden flash of brightness and shielded my eyes. Marx's face came into focus through the halo of light, and I blinked at him, trying to orient myself. "Where . . ."

"You're in my apartment. You fell asleep on the couch."

I glanced at the couch, noticing the blanket that had tangled itself around my legs—I didn't remember having a blanket—and the pillow that still had a vague impression where my head had rested.

I remembered curling up to watch a movie, and fighting to stay awake until Sam could cover the window. I couldn't believe I had fallen asleep. I only ever slept behind locked doors.

Marx crouched slowly beside the couch so we were on the same level. I realized the reason for his slow, careful movements when Riley let out a low, warning growl from my left.

My scream had triggered his protective instincts, and he was focused on the only possible threat in the room. I touched his back gently and stroked his fur until his growls subsided.

"I'm sorry if I scared you," Marx said, keeping his voice quiet. "But you were cryin' in your sleep."

The questions shimmering in his eyes made my throat tighten against answers I didn't want to give, and I brushed at the wetness on my cheeks; I hadn't even noticed the silent tears.

"Are nightmares common for you?"

I rubbed my damp fingers on my jeans before wrapping my arms around my knees. "Everyone has nightmares."

"Not like that."

I pulled my lips between my teeth for a moment and drew in a slow, calming breath before speaking. "I've had them on and off since I was fourteen, but they've been worse lately."

We both knew why. Neither of us had to say Collin's name.

"Do you ever have nightmares?" I asked.

Marx lowered himself to his knees on the hardwood floor. "Sometimes I have a bad dream or two."

I somehow doubted he ever woke up screaming in the middle of the night.

"Sometimes dreams become a lot less scary if you share the weight of them with another person," he said.

I hugged my knees tighter. "I'm not sure my nightmares work that way."

"Because they're memories?"

After a moment, I nodded. "Nothing anyone says or does can change them, not even me. I know what's gonna happen, but it still happens."

"*What* happens?"

I dropped a hand to Riley's back, my fingers tightening in his fur, as the memories flooded through me. "A lot of things."

"Some of them I can guess, given what you've been through." He didn't share his theories aloud, and I was grateful for that. "But there's somethin' you kept sayin', somethin' about not bein' able to breathe, and beggin' somebody to let you out."

I squeezed my eyes shut. I hadn't realized I had spoken aloud in my sleep. I was afraid to imagine what else I might have said.

"What did he do, Holly?"

I opened my eyes, but I couldn't look at him. "I wasn't always afraid of small spaces. Gin and I used to play hide-and-seek in closets and in the nooks beneath the steps. I even hid in the cupboard under the bathroom sink once, but she couldn't find me, and I didn't want her to get discouraged, so I made some noise and then pretended to be surprised when she found me."

I smiled through my tears as I remembered the glee on her face.

Now, I would never be able to hide in a cupboard or a closet. I could barely use a bathroom stall without hyperventilating. I was afraid the space would collapse in on me and I wouldn't be able to get out.

"You told me once that your claustrophobia was a childhood fear," Marx recalled.

I swallowed. "Collin had a, um . . . a wooden box in the basement. An old gun chest that belonged to his dad, I think. It was too small for a person, but . . . I guess that was the appeal."

"He locked you in a box?" His voice was so tight with tension that I thought he might snap. "For how long?"

I stared hard at the cracks between the floorboards. "Hours. Sometimes days." After I ran away and the police brought me back, he had locked me in the box for two days as punishment.

"Days?" Marx asked, sounding horrified. "He just left you in there?"

"He would've let me out. If I begged. But the box was . . ." Tears choked my voice, and the words *better than the alternative* died in my throat. I couldn't go there if I wanted my stomach to stay where it belonged. "There was hardly enough room to breathe, and sometimes . . . I passed out. When I woke up, I would panic because I forgot where I was, and I would try to claw my way out."

I splayed my fingers in Riley's fur as I looked at them, remembering all the times I had to dig the splinters out from under my bloody fingernails.

"Sometimes I thought I was gonna go crazy waiting for him to get bored and let me out. And other times I thought maybe he wouldn't let me out at all, and I would just die in there."

"Oh, Holly," Marx exhaled. He lowered his head, his expression unreadable.

I hadn't meant to share so much, but once I began, the pain had just poured out of me.

Marx was quiet for a long moment, his gaze distant, but I could tell by the repeated clenching of his jaw that he was angry.

I drew in a breath to apologize—I should never have burdened him with my pain, especially when he already had so much to deal with—but somehow I knew an apology would only upset him more.

"What are you thinking about?" I asked instead, not entirely certain I wanted to know.

"Currently, I'm contemplatin' committin' a homicide," he said matter-of-factly, and I blinked.

"Um . . . won't that just . . . give you more work to do? Since you investigate homicides?" I replied tentatively.

He offered me a thin smile. "Probably. But it would be worth it to put that pathetic excuse of a man in the ground."

I swallowed hard at the intensity in his voice. Did he really care about me that much, or was I just seeing a cop's innate anger toward injustice?

He let out a tense breath and stood. "I'm gonna make us some hot chocolate. Why don't you get back on the couch under the blanket. It's a little chilly in here with that window uncovered."

And with that, the painful conversation was over. I sagged against the wall in relief and watched Marx prepare the hot chocolate.

When he was nearly finished, I pushed to my feet and moved to the couch, snuggling under the blanket for comfort and warmth. He handed me a mug before taking a seat on the far end of the couch.

"Sam didn't come back with a board to cover the window?" I asked, glancing at the spare room door. It was closed, but the wintery chill seemed to seep right through the wood.

"He did. But he got called to a robbery, and by the time he got here, you were sleepin', so I told him I would fix it later. I didn't wanna wake you."

"Oh."

"Quit worryin' about the window and drink your hot chocolate."

I smiled and looked down at the massive marshmallow bobbing on top of my hot chocolate. "This marshmallow's the size of a baseball."

"I think you're meant to set them on fire and use them as torches."

Ick. Burnt marshmallows. I took a sip and savored the sweetness that brought a little warmth back to my extremities.

Riley gave Marx a suspicious look and then came to lie down on the floor between us. He seemed to have adopted me quickly, and I felt a twinge of sadness at the knowledge that I couldn't keep him.

"I think I'm gonna stay up for a while," I said. The rest of the night most likely.

"Me too."

I frowned at him. "You don't have to do that. You can go back to bed."

"I'm not all that tired."

The dark circles under his eyes said otherwise. He kept me company for the next several hours despite my assurances that I was fine. Apparently he was in overprotective mode, and it would take a crane to remove him from the couch.

19

I was a twisted bundle of nerves when I walked into self-defense training with Marx later that morning.

He had mentioned on the way over that we were going to be working on breaking out of holds today. He wanted me to have at least a basic understanding in case Collin managed to corner me.

That news, combined with a night of sleep fragmented by nightmares, left me feeling like I might burst into irrational tears at any moment.

That wouldn't be embarrassing at all.

I paused in the doorway when I saw Sam and Jordan stumbling around in the center of the mat. Jordan had him in a frightening-looking headlock.

"Why is Sam here?" I asked.

"He's here as Jordan's demonstration partner. They're gonna show you how to escape each hold. And then you'll have a chance to try."

The thought of a man restraining me was almost enough to make me bolt out of the room. "Right," I replied as evenly as I could manage. "That . . . makes sense."

Sam tapped Jordan's arm, and Jordan released him with a satisfied grin. Sam cast him a disgruntled glare. "I hate you."

"You're just a sore loser," Jordan teased before grabbing a towel off the floor and wiping away the beads of sweat on his brow. His eyes shone with warmth as he came over to greet me. "Good morning, Holly."

"It's certainly morning," I agreed without enthusiasm. With as long as Marx and I had been up, it felt closer to evening.

Concern crossed Jordan's features as he studied my face. "Are these cuts from the window breaking?" He stretched a hand toward me, and I stepped back from him at the same moment he caught himself. "Sorry." He let his arm fall back to his side.

I had a few small cuts from the falling glass, mostly at the edge of my hairline, but they weren't worth worrying about.

"Sam filled you in on what happened last night?" Marx asked.

"Yeah, he did." Jordan glanced between us. "He said you weren't sure if the message was in regard to Holly or your ex-wife, but that it's somehow related to the case you're working."

"More than likely it was referrin' to Shannon," Marx said. "They've gone after her once already. I'd rather err on the side of caution, though, so I need you to pay extra attention when you're out in public with Holly. If these people target her in any way, I wanna know about it before they have a chance to make a move."

"Yeah, not a problem. But can we talk for a second?" Jordan nodded for Marx to follow him off to the side.

I remained where I was since I apparently wasn't invited to this conversation.

I barely heard Jordan's whispered admission from across the room. "I don't think this is a good idea."

"We already covered your feelin's on the matter," Marx replied, his voice as tired as he looked.

"You want me to teach her to break out of holds, but she flinches if I get too close to her. I don't wanna put her through this."

"Would you rather she be completely defenseless when Collin comes after her again?"

"You know I don't," Jordan snapped on a whisper. "But she's already nervous around me, and you're asking me to put her in positions that terrify her."

"Nobody said this was gonna be easy. It's gonna be scary and uncomfortable for her, and it's gonna take a lot of time and trust exercises before she's . . ."

"Hey," Sam said, snapping my attention away from the conversation. He draped a towel over the back of his neck as he approached.

"Hey."

"You look tired."

"Didn't really sleep well. Speaking of sleep, shouldn't *you* be sleeping?"

He frowned. "You know, your frequent misperception of my sleeping patterns makes me sound like a lazy sloth."

I smirked. "Not my intention."

He smiled faintly and pulled a bottle of purple Powerade from his bag. He offered it to me. "You shared a blue one with me last time. I figured it was my turn to bring the drinks."

"Thanks for not bringing fruit punch."

He grimaced. "I don't think I could ever drink that stuff again."

Since Edward drugged our fruit punch, even the smell of my once-favorite drink turned my stomach. I imagined it was the same for Sam.

He tipped the purple drink to his lips and gulped down half of it. Good grief. Apparently the experience hadn't taught him not to chug his drinks.

I took a small sip of mine and screwed the cap back on. "So why was Jordan squeezing your head when I came in?"

"Because he's an—"

"Sam," Marx interrupted, his voice carrying a warning. "There are ladies present."

Sam swallowed whatever word he'd intended to say. "What I meant to say was . . . he's a jerk."

"I was proving a point," Jordan said, returning to my side. At my questioning look, he explained, "That just because he's stronger than me. It doesn't necessarily mean he's gonna win."

"Just wait till I hit you next time," Sam replied.

"Yeah, that might hurt. But you'd have to catch me first, and I'm faster."

Sam grunted. "So you keep saying."

I smiled to myself as I slipped off my boots. Jordan was the faster of the two, and he *had* said he was going to rub it in. I stepped onto the mat in my colorful toe socks. They reminded me of Fruit Loops. I liked Fruit Loops.

Jordan's attention fell to my feet, and he grinned. "Rainbow socks, huh?"

I folded my arms over my stomach as I bounced on my toes. "Yep. I wasn't in the mood for my pink ones."

"They're cute." When I curled my toes under my feet, he laughed. "Seriously? I can't even compliment your socks without you getting bashful?"

I lifted my chin. "I am not bashful."

"Yeah, you are," he said, his amusement still lingering on his lips. "Are you ready to start training?"

I glanced past him at Marx, who had found a comfortable spot along the wall, before asking, "Um, how intense is this gonna be?"

"Not too physically intense, but . . . it will be hands-on."

I swallowed uneasily and forced my voice to sound nonchalant. "I know." I had no idea how I was going to make it through this lesson, but I was frightened enough of Collin to try. Determined—that sounded much better than frightened. I would stick with that one.

"Okay, well let's get started then." Jordan strode to the center of the mat and motioned for Sam to join him.

"If you try to put me in a headlock again, I'm gonna hurt you," Sam warned him.

"Play nice, gentlemen," Marx advised. "Let's not forget why we're here." He nodded toward me for emphasis.

Sam heaved a frustrated breath and extended his arm. "It's gonna be really hard not to flatten you when you grab my arm."

"Try to contain yourself," Jordan advised. "I wouldn't want you to pull a muscle in front of an audience." He wrapped his hand around Sam's forearm, but directed his next words toward me. "The thumb is the weakest part of an attacker's grip, so when you pull away, you're gonna wanna pull through their thumb."

Sam jerked his arm free with ridiculous ease and then returned it for Jordan to grip again.

"Obviously, Sam is a little stronger than the average woman, so—"

"A little?" Sam snapped indignantly.

"Fine. Marginally stronger," Jordan amended. "If a man grabs you, he's gonna have more upper body strength. You probably won't be able to just yank your arm away. If that's the case, wrap your other hand around your fist so you have the strength of both arms to pull through his thumb."

Sam fisted the hand of his restrained arm, folded his other hand around it, and then pulled through, breaking away from Jordan's grip.

"All right, rainbow toes, come give it a try," Jordan suggested, and Sam stepped aside so I could take his place.

My heart fluttered anxiously at the thought of him touching me, but I forced myself to walk across the mat.

Be brave . . .

"Hold out your arm for me," he instructed.

I hoped he wouldn't notice the fine tremor in my fingers as I extended my arm. He reached forward cautiously, as if trying not to startle a frightened rabbit, and wrapped warm fingers around my wrist.

He kept his body at a distance, giving me space to breathe.

I exhaled slowly. Somewhere in the back of my mind, a doubt whispered that this was a bad idea, that once I gave him permission to touch me, I couldn't take it back.

"Notice how my hands are big enough that my fingers fold around your wrist and reinforce my thumb?" he asked.

He wiggled his thumb for emphasis, and I saw the pucker between his brows as his thumb brushed over the band of nearly transparent scars on my wrist. He started to turn my wrist over to get a closer look, but I wrenched my arm back.

My sharp retreat startled an apology from him. "I'm sorry."

I tried to tug my sleeve down to cover the scars. I had a matching set on my left wrist—pale, permanent reminders of six horrifying hours—but my bracelet covered them.

Jordan looked like he wanted to ask about them, but he held out his hand instead. "Try again?"

I hesitated before holding out my arm. His hand closed gently over my wrist.

"You have small wrists, which means if I squeeze, it'll be a lot harder for you to pull free." When I drew in a breath to protest, he said, "Don't worry, I'm not gonna squeeze. We're just gonna practice the proper technique, so don't pull too hard. Go ahead and give it a try."

I mimicked the method I had seen Sam use the second time, and my arm came free without resistance.

"Good," Jordan said with a smile. "One more time just to make sure you have the motion down."

Again, he offered no resistance. I seriously doubted that if he wanted to hold on to me, this simple maneuver would help me escape.

"Okay," he said. "If an attacker can't drag you away, they'll probably try to incapacitate you so they can carry you away. You're small enough that it wouldn't be that hard to carry you. So Sam and I are gonna show you how to get out of a hold they might use."

I retreated to my previous spot on the mat to watch the demonstration.

Jordan wrapped an arm around Sam's throat and pulled him back against him. "Now, this can either be used to restrain someone or to render them unconscious."

Fear rippled through me.

I was intimately familiar with that position, and every ounce of pain and terror that came with it. One moment Sam was trapped as I had been so many times before, and the next he was free.

How . . . how had he done that?

"Okay, Holly, your turn," Jordan announced, and dread punched me in the stomach. I stared at him, breathless and unmoving.

He said something else, but my mind refused to process it. All I could think about was that arm around my throat, squeezing until my airway collapsed.

Marx appeared beside me, his expression pinched with concern. "Holly?"

233

"I c- . . . I c-can't."

I didn't realize my hand was hovering protectively over my throat until he wrapped gentle fingers around my wrist and pulled it away.

"Okay," he said.

I slipped my wrist from his grip and stepped back. "I don't wanna do this anymore. I can't . . . do this."

His insightful green eyes studied me. "Collin's done this to you before."

I shied away from the memories. "Edward—"

"Edward doesn't put this much fear in your eyes. I know the memories of what he did to you are uncomfortable, but I'm not lookin' at discomfort right now."

I hated being an open book to him.

"Look, sweetheart, I understand how you feel, but—"

"You understand how I feel?" I asked in disbelief, and an inexplicable rush of anger heated my voice. "Really? Were you afraid to sleep at night when you were a kid because you might wake up with someone's fingers wrapped around your throat? Did you have to see the delight in that person's eyes because they enjoyed watching you struggle for breath? Did they hold you down by the throat or restrain you while they . . . they . . . hurt you?"

He closed his eyes and let out a long, measured breath before opening them again. "Holly, I—"

"Exactly which part do you think you understand!"

A long beat of silence, broken only by the sound of my agitated breaths, stretched through the room.

"You're right, I don't understand what it feels like to go through that. I've never been hurt that way," Marx finally said, his voice so gentle and compassionate that it made my eyes burn. "What I meant was, I know you're scared and you don't like to be touched, but nobody in this room is gonna hurt you."

I followed his attention to the men across the room. Jordan had his fingers interlocked behind his head as he stared hard at the floor, and Sam was tapping his fingers on his biceps in a way that would've made me take a few steps back if I'd been standing any closer to him.

I was abruptly horrified by the realization that they had both heard me. I had completely forgotten about them in my momentary anger. I covered my face with my hands and groaned.

"Don't be embarrassed," Marx said.

Embarrassed? I had slid way beyond embarrassment and skidded straight into humiliation.

"I know your instinct is to avoid this situation at all costs, not to deliberately put yourself in it. But if Collin grabs you, would you rather know how to escape or just have to wait until he lets you go? If he intends to restrain you while he hurts you again, what are you gonna do?"

The possibility sent a tremor through me, and I lowered my hands to look at the doorway. I wanted to leave, but at the same time, I knew he had a valid point. I never wanted to feel that weak and vulnerable again.

"I don't know." I glanced at Jordan, taking in the strong arms that could hurt me so easily. The mere thought of them wrapped around me, trapping me, made my heart thump harder. "What if I can't get away? What if I want out, but I can't . . . ."

"Just say stop and everybody backs off."

I couldn't suppress the skepticism from my expression. In my experience, the word "stop" had about as much power as the word "abracadabra."

"You have my word, Holly," Marx said, reading my face. "Nobody's gonna force you to do anythin' you don't wanna do. If you wanna leave right now, I'll take you home."

I chewed on my lower lip as I considered my options. I might lose it and have a panic attack right there in front of everyone, but I would be angry with myself if I didn't at least try to learn how to protect myself.

"I'm gonna be right here with you the entire time," Marx said, solidifying my decision.

I swallowed and nearly choked on my own voice as I said, "Okay. I'll try." I wrestled with my pride before adding, "And I'm sorry I yelled at you."

I hadn't meant to raise my voice.

He gave me a warm smile that washed away my regret. "You, little Ms. Holly, have a bit of a temper when you get scared."

I smiled apologetically. "I know."

I rubbed at the goose bumps on my arms as I walked to the center of the mat. Jordan waited, letting me control the space between us.

"You sure you wanna do this?" he asked.

"No," I admitted honestly. This was quite possibly the last thing I wanted to be doing right now. I slid my attention to Sam, who was standing about five feet away. "Why are you hovering?"

"You know those social experiments where a guy manhandles a woman in public to see how many people will intervene on her behalf? There's always the one good Samaritan who body-slams the guy for crossing the line." He looked pointedly at Jordan. "I'm that guy."

Jordan arched an eyebrow. "Planning on body-slamming me?"

"Planning on crossing the line?"

Jordan gave him a halfhearted grin. "Not without permission. And Holly's very strict about the lines." Then his eyes narrowed. "You're just waiting for an excuse to get me back for that headlock, aren't you?"

Sam's lips spread into a small, tight smile. I wondered if he ever showed his teeth, or if smiling was always a reluctant gesture.

"Try to body-slam me and I'm gonna put you in a headlock on the ground and have Holly sit on your legs," Jordan warned.

"Except for the fact that I can lift her with one leg, that's almost intimidating."

Marx sighed. "The two of you have the attention span of children. Focus for five minutes."

The men put their joking aside, and Jordan slipped behind me. "I'm gonna be very gentle. And like Marx said, if you say stop, I'll release you and back away to the boundary. Okay?"

"Four feet?"

"Four feet."

I swallowed the nervous lump in my throat. "Okay."

"I'm gonna wrap my arm around your neck and I need you to grab my elbow, pivot your left leg behind mine as you bend down, turn your head, and duck out. Just like the demonstration."

I nodded.

The moment I felt his body press up against my back, I stiffened. He started to wrap an arm around me, but my insides clenched with fear.

"Stop," I said, jerking away from him.

He withdrew his arm and immediately backed four feet away. I pressed a hand to my stomach as I tried to calm my fluttering nerves.

"Take your time," Marx suggested, his tone encouraging. "It's gonna be uncomfortable, but you're perfectly safe."

I nodded and paced for a few minutes before I scrounged up the courage to try again. "Okay," I said, steeling myself for the unwanted physical contact.

Jordan approached slowly. "Same thing as last time, okay?" He waited for my nod and then stepped into the very personal space around me. "Try to concentrate."

He wrapped an arm loosely around my throat. My hands snapped to it immediately, desperate to pull it away.

"I'm not gonna hurt you. You have plenty of time to think."

Think. That seemed to be the last thing I was capable of doing as my instincts kicked in and screamed at me to escape by any means necessary.

"Stop. Please stop," I pleaded, gasping for air that my lungs couldn't find. "Stop, stop, stop."

Jordan released me, and I sank to a crouch, trying to suck in air. Why couldn't I control my body just long enough to get through this?

My lungs opened and sweet oxygen flooded through me, swiftly followed by frustration.

Marx crouched beside me. "You wanna take a break?"

"No," I said, more sharply than I intended.

"I know you're frustrated, but try to be patient with yourself."

I didn't want to be patient. I wanted my body to obey me. Why was that so hard?

I pushed to my feet and drew in a fortifying breath. I could do this. I *would* do this. I wouldn't let what Collin did to me control my life. This was just another hurdle in the healing process, and I was going to climb over it, no matter how many times I tripped along the way.

I rubbed my sweaty palms on my thighs and looked at Jordan. "Third time's the charm, right?"

He looked as uncomfortable as I felt, but he smiled. "Whenever you're ready, rainbow toes."

I marched over to my spot, and he joined me. With surprising gentleness, he pulled my braided hair back over my shoulder so it was out of the way.

"Don't be scared of me," he said softly, his tone pleading.

I couldn't promise that.

My heart thumped too hard as he locked an arm around my throat. I grabbed his forearm, wishing I had longer fingers that could close around it for a stronger grip. I wanted to rip it away.

I could feel the familiar panic unfurling in my stomach as I tried to escape, and his arm tightened around my throat.

"You're squeezing too tight," I tried to say, but my voice came out as a whimper.

I felt his hesitant breath against my back. "I'm not squeezing, Holly."

Was it fear that felt like a tightening band around my throat? My airway was collapsing. Tears skated across my eyes, and I could barely see Marx standing directly in my line of vision.

"Breathe, sweetheart. Breathe through it," Marx said. "You're okay."

I tried to ignore the persistent knock of memories, but they seeped through the cracks of my resolve and surrounded me, robbing me of my voice when I wanted to beg Jordan to stop.

The arm around my neck was cutting off my air. Fear turned my thoughts to liquid, and they slid away down the drain along with the droplets of water from the shower.

I tried to ease the pressure on my windpipe by holding my weight on the tips of my toes, but my feet slipped on the slick tile, and I choked.

I clawed frantically at his arm, but my fingertips slid uselessly from his damp skin.

"You're so entertaining when you're desperate," Collin taunted, a barely restrained laugh in his voice. "I'm tempted to just let you strangle yourself unconscious. But I think you're more fun when you're awake."

He lowered his arm a fraction, letting me find my feet, and I greedily sucked in oxygen while I had the chance.

He pulled me flush against him, and the solid feeling of his body against my back triggered a whole new panic—one that had nothing to do with too little air.

"No," I cried, shoving against his stomach with my hands and elbows, desperately trying to force his body away from mine. "Please."

He staggered back a step as I shoved hard against him, but he didn't fall. "Holly," he began, rebalancing both of us, and I heard Jordan's voice rather than the one I expected to hear. "It's okay. You're okay."

Jordan's voice shattered the terrifying memory, and I latched onto it, trying to ground myself.

It's not Collin, it's not Collin.

I could hear a woman crying—deep, gasping sobs—and it wasn't until I drew in a broken breath that I realized it was me.

"I told you this was a bad idea. She's terrified and she's panicking," Jordan said in a low voice. "I'm gonna let her go."

"Give her another minute," Marx suggested.

"Marx—"

"Let her do this, Jordan."

"You can only fight one thing at a time, Holly," a deep, even voice rang out from somewhere in the room. Everything blurred into smudges of color through my tears, and I couldn't separate him from what was probably the wall. "Fight the panic first, then your attacker."

Fight the panic first.

The idea drifted through the overwhelming fear and took root. If I could rein in the panic, I could focus on what I needed to do to escape.

But my thoughts felt like frantic birds; every time I tried to focus, another burst of fear sent them fluttering in every direction, and I couldn't seem to catch them.

I could feel the memories and the debilitating fear threatening to drag me back under, and I fought to concentrate on the present, on the differences between this moment and that one.

I could feel soft material beneath my fingers—a T-shirt maybe—and beneath that was the warmth of skin, and . . . my panic spiked as I realized I still had my hands pressed against a man's stomach, and *he* was pressed against my back.

I choked on a sob.

"It's just me, Holly. You're safe," Jordan whispered into my hair. His voice was rough with emotion, but it held none of the menace I expected to hear from a man with his arm around my throat. "I promise you're safe."

It's not . . . the same. I'm not there. He's not him. It's not—it's not the same.

I refused to let myself think about anything more than the T-shirt beneath my fingers. It was soft and smooth, like a workout T-shirt, and I could feel the edge of a design.

I drew in a breath, held it for four seconds, and exhaled.

My feet weren't bare, and they were planted firmly—toes to heels—on a soft, dry floor rather than slippery tile that left me desperately scrambling for balance.

I drew in another slow breath.

I wasn't trapped in that small space with Collin; I was in a large room with blue floors that smelled like rubber, sweat, and the faint aroma of Marx's cologne.

My breaths hiccupped as I trembled, but I could hear them slowly smoothing out as the panic receded.

"There we go," Marx said quietly. "Grab his elbow and pivot, Holly."

I did as he said, my technique unbalanced and shaky, but I finally managed to duck out of the arm that restrained my neck. I staggered back across the mat, putting as much space between me and the men in the room as physically possible.

I sank down in the corner, burying my face in my arms. I could feel Marx hovering nearby, but he didn't touch me as I fought to regain control of my body.

Realization hit me as the intense emotions slowly drained away: I had done it. I had broken out of the hold. A small bubble of pride swelled inside of me.

I wasn't helpless.

20

I lingered in the break room as I waited for Marx to return from his "bust." He had gotten word about where to find his street dealer, and I had watched as he and a few other officers strapped on bulletproof vests and inserted earpieces before heading out.

I was staring into the box of doughnuts, trying to decide which one I wanted, when a familiar voice said, "Hey, kiddo."

I stiffened and then turned to see Captain McNera standing in the doorway. He gave me a pleasant smile that made him no more likable. "Tough choice?" he asked as he stepped into the room. "Which ones are giving you the trouble?"

"Chocolate cake and blueberry," I replied tentatively.

He nodded. "Both good options. But I'm guessing you don't wanna eat both." When I shook my head, he said, "Tell ya what, cake doughnuts are my favorite and I like blueberry too. My blood is in need of a little sugar, so why don't we split them."

"Are you diabetic?"

"No, I just have a sweet tooth the size of the Atlantic. So what do you say?"

I wanted to say, "take a hike," but he'd been Marx's friend for a long time, so I tried to be civil. "Sure." I grabbed a plastic knife from one of the drawers and cut both doughnuts in half. I paused before grabbing the halves and putting them on a plate for him as I thought of Sam and his germ phobia. "Do you mind my fingers?"

"Not at all."

I placed his on a plate and held the plate out without moving toward him. He leaned forward and took it from me.

"I keep forgetting how shy you are," he admitted.

I licked the stickiness from my fingers as I retreated with my plate to the farthest wall. "Did you really come in here for a doughnut?"

He smiled. "No, young lady, I did not. Rick asked me to check in on you if he wasn't back in an hour." That didn't surprise me. "He said you've been having some issues with a man, and he's concerned about you being alone." At my displeased frown, he explained, "He didn't betray your confidence. That's all he told me."

He wasn't worried about Collin breaking into a police station and dragging me out; he was worried about me leaving the police station and getting myself into trouble.

"I never had a chance to thank you, Holly."

I nibbled on my doughnut. "Thank me for what?"

"Rick is an amazing cop, but after Shannon left him, he became a different person—always tired, angry, and distracted. He hardly ever smiled. It wasn't until he returned from Kansas with you that I noticed the change in him. He's happier. He smiles more, and to everyone's surprise, he even laughs from time to time. I'm pretty sure we have you to thank for that."

I shifted self-consciously. "I haven't done anything."

He smiled and lifted the doughnut to his lips as he explained, "You just have a way about you."

I wasn't really sure what that meant, so I decided to ignore it and focus on my doughnut. I worked on my blueberry half quietly, fully aware that he was still watching me.

"I realize that you and I didn't get off to a very good start," he said after a moment. "But I hope that if you continue to be a part of Rick's life, you can find it in yourself to forgive me."

"Are you guys close?"

"We've been friends since I transferred to this precinct twenty years ago. He and I were partners for a time."

"Who's his partner now?"

"Rick doesn't get along well with most people, so he generally works alone. I figured him for my job someday—he was the better cop—but he has a bit of a temper."

I smirked. I had seen that temper before, but he seemed able to control it better now. "He's a good man."

"Yes, he is." He studied me. "What is it between you two? I know he's not romantically interested in you, and I don't get that sense from you either."

I shrugged. "Just friends."

"Hmm." He looked thoughtful for a moment, then said, "Well, if you're ever having a doughnut dilemma, I'm just over there." He pointed to his office. "And I'm happy to share a doughnut with you anytime."

I forced a smile and then sank into one of the folding chairs after he left the room. I watched him through the glass as guilt gnawed at me. He was clearly trying to make amends, but he had made the terrifying situation last autumn even harder, and I would rather upchuck my doughnut than say the words "I forgive you."

I knew in my heart that it was wrong to hold a grudge.

Jesus offered us forgiveness whether we deserved it or not—no matter how many times we rejected Him, and no matter the depth of our sins. What right did we have to deny it to someone else who was seeking it? What right did I have?

I looked at my knapsack on the table as my thoughts turned to Izzy. Captain McNera wasn't the only one trying to make things right. Was I holding onto my pain and anger so tightly that I was withholding forgiveness?

I pulled my notebook from my bag and flipped it open to the unfinished letter. I stared at the nearly empty page, struggling to find the words to fill it.

I uncapped the pen, pressed it to the paper, and waited for the words of forgiveness to flow out of it. But what I began to write took an entirely different path:

> *Your face is the first one I remember after my family died. The first arms to hold me. It doesn't matter that you took me illegally. It doesn't matter that I only lived with you for two years, or that you were a criminal. You were all I had in this world to hold onto. And you abandoned me. You were the closest thing I had to a*

244

mother and you chose drugs over me. You left me alone.
And I hate you for that. I hate you because . . .

Because I had loved her.

I heard Marx's brusque voice coming from the squad room, and I set my notebook aside. My eyes widened when he strode in with his hand wrapped around the arm of a man in handcuffs. He shoved the man into the vacant chair beside his desk, and the man called him a few choice names.

"Next time, I'll aim higher," the man sneered. "You don't have a bulletproof helmet."

Marx stripped off his vest, laying it across his desk, and I caught the glint of metal embedded in it. My insides twisted. Was that a bullet?

"There's not gonna be a next time. Even if you manage to find yourself a lawyer without a conscience to get you off the drug charges, you shot a cop."

The drug dealer leaned forward in the chair and spat on Marx's shoe.

Marx arched an eyebrow and said dryly, "Charmin'." His head lifted when Captain McNera called him. He motioned an officer in uniform over and requested, "Take him down to bookin'. Make sure he gets his own cell. I don't want there to be any *accidents.*"

"Five star accommodations, huh?" the drug dealer asked as the female officer pulled him to his feet. "And a pretty escort." He looked her over and winked.

She ignored the comment and propelled him forward through the squad room. He looked around the room, and I had a bad feeling as his calculating eyes skimmed over the empty desks and then the few officers who were at the other end of the room.

Recognition lit his eyes when he saw me standing in the doorway of the break room, but I was certain I'd never seen him before. He stopped abruptly, and the female officer tried to force him back in step beside her.

"Walk," she demanded.

The man glanced back over his shoulder toward Marx and Captain McNera, who lingered outside of the captain's office to talk quietly, and then back at the officer escorting him. He sized her up quickly and then threw his shoulder into her hard enough to knock her off her feet.

He barged into the break room, and I scrambled back from him. His hands were still cuffed behind his back, but that didn't discourage him from trying to reach me as I skirted the edges of the room to avoid him. I had no idea what I had done to upset him. I hadn't even spoken to him.

"So you're it, huh?" he demanded.

My back smacked the wall, and I didn't have anywhere else to go. He opened his mouth to say something more as he closed the distance between us, but his words were lost when Marx wrapped a hand around the back of his neck and slammed his face down on the break room table.

I flinched at the harsh sound of the impact.

"You don't go near her. You don't talk to her," Marx growled in warning.

"A little jealous, Detective?" The man wheezed in amusement. "I would be too if that was my girl."

Marx tightened his hold on the back of the man's neck when he twisted in an effort to see me, and leaned down to growl, "You don't even look at her."

"Detective," the female officer protested, trying to pull his arm away from the man. "Let him up. I've got this."

Marx looked at me less than two feet away from where he had the man restrained, and then at the officer. Frustration laced his voice. "See that you do this time."

The woman's jaw hardened, but she only nodded and grabbed the man securely by his arms. Marx released him and stepped back, letting her take over.

"You can't hold me, Detective," the man said as he straightened. He ran his tongue over his split lip and then spat blood onto the carpet.

"We'll see about that."

The officer hauled the man out of the room, and I caught Marx's faint wince of pain as he braced an arm against his side for the barest instant.

"You were shot?" I asked.

He lowered his arm from his rib cage at my quiet question. "It's just a bruise. The vest took the brunt of the impact."

"It's not just a bruise."

"It's nothin' to worry about."

I crossed my arms and asked irritably, "Do I get to use that line the next time I get hurt and just don't wanna tell you about it?"

He grimaced. "You have a habit of turnin' things around on me, and I don't like it." He stared at my unwavering scowl and sighed. "It's a cracked rib or two. It tends to happen when you get shot in the vest at close range. I'll be good as new in a few weeks."

He wouldn't be good as new, but unfortunately there was nothing to do but wait.

"And no, if somebody hurts you, you don't ever get to tell me it's nothin' to worry about. I expect a name and detailed description so I can hunt them down and return the favor," he informed me. "Or at the very least, arrest them."

"Fine. I agree never to use that line if you agree to stop getting shot."

He smiled. "I'll do my best. I sent a message to Jordan. He'll be by in about an hour to pick you up."

"Why?"

"Because I have paperwork and an interrogation to do after my briefin' with McNera. I don't want you to be stuck in this room until midnight. And then there's the fact that you were almost attacked less than a minute ago."

"Maybe he just really wanted a doughnut."

Marx shot me an unamused look. "Whatever the reason, I'm not comfortable with you bein' here when I'm otherwise occupied."

"And yet, you want me to stay here while you're otherwise occupied for the next hour. Or are you wanting me to go outside and wait for Jordan on the curb?"

He frowned. "You know I don't want you waitin' on the curb. Stop bein' difficult, and don't get into any mischief."

"Wouldn't dream of it," I said, sliding onto the table beside the box of doughnuts.

"Mmm hmm. If I didn't know you, I might believe that. If you need me, I'll be in with McNera. Don't be afraid to knock."

Time seemed to drag by at a snail's pace until a familiar face I couldn't quite place passed by the break room window. He wasn't wearing a uniform, but no one gave him a second glance, so he was likely an off-duty cop.

I perked up with interest and suspicion when he stopped by Marx's desk. He glanced around the room before shifting a few folders. He tilted his head to read one of them. Now he was snooping.

I hopped off the table and walked quietly into the squad room. "What are you doing?" I asked from behind him, and the man jumped, startled.

He whirled around to see me, and I watched surprise and irritation flash across his face before recognition settled. His lips spread into a dazzling smile that probably made most women swoon.

I didn't even sway.

"Holly, hey. What are you doing here?"

I folded my arms and pointed out, "This isn't your desk, and those aren't your files."

"Yeah, I know. It's Marx's desk. Have you seen him? I was hoping to talk to him."

"I have seen him, and he's not in that folder."

His smile turned sheepish. "Yeah, I have a curiosity problem. Mom always told me I have a tendency to poke my nose where it doesn't belong."

That I could understand; I had the same problem. "He's in a meeting."

"Oh," he said, sounding a little disappointed. "I guess I'll just leave him a note. One of my buddies might have seen someone he's been looking for. Actually, maybe you can give him the message for me." He pulled a crumpled piece of paper from his jeans pocket and offered it to me.

I took it from him hesitantly and looked down at it. There was an address written on it. "What's the address for?"

"Now who's being curious and nosy?"

He leaned back against Marx's desk, and his eyes roved over me with enough interest to ignite a tiny spark of anxiety in the pit of my stomach.

I had seen that look before, and the memory of our first meeting stirred in my mind. It had been at Marx's apartment the night someone threw a rock through the window. He was Sam's partner: Dane? Daniel . . .

Danny.

"Green is a good color for you," he said. "Brings out your eyes."

I blinked at the unexpected compliment and then looked down at my sweater. It was a vibrant shade of grass green that accentuated my red hair.

Danny's lingering gaze, which I suspected had little to do with the shade of my sweater, made me deeply uncomfortable, and I folded my arms. "Where's Sam?"

I hoped he would walk in at any moment and tell his partner to move along. I didn't want to be rude, but I wasn't interested in anything this man had to offer.

"Probably sleeping." He cocked his head as he studied me. "You have stunning eyes, and I don't just mean the golden root-beer color, but the way they always look deep and mysterious, like there's an entire interesting world behind them. I'm curious about that."

"You should try to be less curious."

Pot, meet kettle.

The dismissiveness of my words didn't seem to register with him, because he just smiled. *Right* . . .

"I'll make sure Marx gets this," I said, holding up the note.

I started to turn and head back toward the break room when he pushed away from the desk. The casual movement brought him within inches of me, and I immediately back-stepped, bumping into the desk chair behind me.

"You know, I'm off tonight. You should come over for dinner," he said.

"Um . . ." I floundered for an excuse that would provide me with a polite exit from this conversation. I didn't want to hurt his feelings, especially since he was Sam's partner and I would have to see him on occasion. "I, um . . . I don't like cops."

Confusion furrowed his brow. "You're staying with Marx, and you don't seem to mind Sam."

Maybe I should've specified. "I don't *date* cops." Or anyone, but that wasn't a conversation I wanted to have with someone who was essentially a stranger.

He stepped toward me, sending my heart rate tripping. "I'm not a cop tonight. Just an average guy."

That made it sound like he was only interested in tonight. I swallowed the nervous lump in my throat and tried to back away discreetly. "I don't think so."

"It doesn't have to be a date. We could just grab a coffee, maybe go for a walk. I know a great coffee shop near Central Park."

"I'm . . . busy."

He frowned and glanced around the squad room. "Busy hanging out at the police department? There have to be more exciting things for an attractive woman to be doing. I'm heading out in a few minutes if you wanna join me, or I could pick you up later this evening."

He advanced another step, as if he didn't realize I was backing away from *him*. I wanted this conversation to be over. "I—" My blind retreat sent me straight into a solid, warm object, and a frightened squeak escaped my throat.

I stumbled over a man's large feet, nearly losing my balance, but gentle hands on my upper arms steadied me.

"She said no," a familiar voice said, and I looked up to realize that the person I was stomping all over was Jordan. He deliberately stepped aside to give me an escape route, and I took it, but he kept his eyes on Danny.

I retreated to the doorway of the break room.

Danny appraised Jordan in a challenging way, caught sight of the sheriff's badge on his waist, and frowned. "Let me guess. You're another one of the cops she supposedly doesn't like."

"I'm her friend, and I think she made it clear she's not interested in spending time with you."

"It didn't exactly sound that way to me."

"Maybe you should get your hearing checked," Jordan suggested. "Because I specifically heard 'I don't date cops' and 'I don't think so' in response to your offers."

Danny's eyes sparked with irritation. "We were having a private conversation."

"In the middle of the squad room? If she were interested in having a private conversation with you, you would be having it in *private*."

"What's your problem, man?"

"*My problem* is that she declined your offer and you should've let it drop. But you kept pushing until you made her uncomfortable."

"I wasn't pushing," Danny shot back. "And I didn't make her uncomfortable."

Jordan snorted. "She was backing away from you. As a cop, I would think you'd be better at reading body language."

Danny's face turned crimson. "What business is it of yours if I ask her out or not? You're not her boyfriend and she's not wearing a ring, so she's fair g—"

Jordan stepped forward, and Danny swallowed the rest of his words, a look of wariness crossing his features. They might be about the same height, but Jordan was more imposing.

"Fine, I get it," Danny said, throwing up his hands. "She's unavailable at the moment. Just . . . don't tell Sam I asked her out again."

"That's between you and Sam."

Danny heaved a defeated breath and cast me a slightly dejected look before leaving the squad room. I slumped against the door frame in relief.

I would've preferred to resolve the situation on my own, but things hadn't gone according to plan.

"Sorry if I stepped on your toes, but you looked like you wanted an exit," Jordan said as he strode over.

"I'm pretty sure I'm the one who stepped on *your* toes." Or rather, stumbled clumsily all over them.

He smiled. "I take it it's not the first time he asked you out."

"I ignored him last time." But that was a little harder to do face-to-face. "He's not creepy, just . . ."

"Persistent?" he asked, when I tried and failed to find the right word. "I can understand that."

Heat crept into my cheeks, and I ducked out of the doorway so he could join me in the room.

"You know, I think I almost had him convinced I wasn't interested before you stepped in."

"That's not how it looked from where I was standing," he said, lips quirking in amusement.

"Well . . . clearly you had a bad vantage point."

He laughed. "If it makes you feel better to think that, sure. I couldn't see a thing from across the room. Fifteen feet away. With a clear line of sight." He stripped off his jacket and tossed it on the table.

I gasped. "What happened to your arms?"

There were scratches all over his forearms, some of them deep enough that they had scabbed over. He glanced at them without concern. "I forgot to wear long sleeves during training."

Horrified, I asked, "I did that?" I had never meant to hurt him. I didn't even remember scratching at his arms. "I'm so sorry."

"They're just scratches." He shrugged and dropped into a chair. "Don't worry about it. I'll be sure to wear long sleeves next time."

Next time. My stomach flipped at the thought of enduring another of those frightening sessions, however necessary they may be.

"So can we talk about why you're avoiding me?" he asked, leaning forward in the chair.

"I'm not."

"You've come to work with Marx the past three days and hidden in this room instead of doing something with me, and when I send you a text, I get a one-word response—yes, no, fine. That constitutes avoidance, and it's been happening since self-defense training."

I fidgeted nervously under his probing gaze.

"Look, restraining you while you were terrified and crying isn't one of my fondest memories either, but please tell me you understand that I would never actually hurt you."

"Of course I know that. I just . . ." *Needed some space after that unsettling lesson. Lots and lots of nonconfusing, safe space.* "I'm not really sure . . . where exactly we stand on boundaries now. Because I can't . . . I mean I'm not comfortable with . . . that."

Understanding registered on his face. "You're afraid that since you gave me permission to touch you during training that the boundaries aren't there anymore."

It wasn't a question, but I nodded anyway. He sighed and ran a hand through his hair as he took a moment to pull his thoughts together.

"I probably should've addressed that earlier. Unless it's an emergency, I will never assume you're okay with me touching you. I will always ask before going hands-on during training. And outside of it, I will hover on the four-foot perimeter until you take pity on me and let me step closer."

Some of the heavy worry I'd been wrestling with the past few days lifted, and I breathed, "Okay."

Amusement sparkled in his eyes. "What exactly were you worried I would do without those boundaries? Hug you? Tickle you?"

I fixed him with a threatening glare. "Don't you ever try to tickle me."

He laughed. "Yeah, I'm pretty sure you would make me regret it. So what else is bothering you?" When I cast him a questioning look, he pointed out, "You keep fidgeting, which means you're still uncomfortable about something, and I'm pretty sure it's not the threat of tickling."

I tried to stand still. "What, are you taking lessons from Marx on how to read my thoughts now?"

"Just learning your mannerisms. So, what else?"

Embarrassed, I muttered, "I panicked during training and I . . . feel like an idiot."

His lips flattened into a thin line. "I figured it was something like that. You're not an idiot, and you have nothing to be embarrassed about or ashamed of. We put you in a position Collin put you in, and none of us expected that to go smoothly."

Well, it hadn't.

He hesitated before asking, "You had a flashback, didn't you? That last time I had my arm around you."

I rubbed at my arms and gave a reluctant nod. That horrifying memory of Collin had floated up and wrapped around me so tightly that it was all I could feel, hear, smell . . .

I had panic attacks unexpectedly, but flashbacks were rare. I deliberately avoided situations that might trigger them.

"Would talking about it help?" he asked.

I shook my head.

"Okay." We were both quiet for a moment before he asked, "Do you remember when we were kids and I came to see you the day after you broke my nose with a tree branch?"

"Yeah. Sorry about that, by the way."

He smiled. "I was so scared of you that I was shaking before and during. My granddad described his heart attack to me once, and I was so sure I was having one when I was walking through your backyard."

"You were not that scared."

"Oh, trust me, I was panicking the whole way. You broke my nose. I was envisioning what else you might break if I came within swinging range. But Dad insisted I had to apologize for making fun of your pigtails."

"I think I forgave you instead of breaking something else."

"Yeah, and I never even thought about picking on you again."

"I can't believe I scared you that badly."

"Not my proudest moment, but I'm not afraid to admit it. I walked on eggshells around you for quite a while, afraid you might randomly beat me up again."

A reluctant smile tugged at the corners of my lips.

"I guess the roles are reversed now," he said with a twinge of sadness. "You walk on eggshells around me because you're scared."

"Not because I'm afraid you're gonna beat me up or break my nose."

He smiled a little. "I always thought you had a cute nose. I would never do anything to hurt it."

I rubbed the tip of my nose self-consciously with my fingers, and he grinned. I thought about reminding him that I had my dad's nose, which meant he thought my dad had a cute nose.

Before I could say that, though, a frantic voice erupted outside of the break room, drawing both of us to the doorway in curiosity. A uniformed officer pounded on the captain's door, and it snapped inward to reveal Marx.

"What?" he demanded impatiently.

The officer inhaled and said in one long breath, "The drug dealer you just arrested and had escorted down to holding tried to hang himself in his cell."

"With what?" Marx shouted loudly enough to startle the entire room to silence.

"Somehow, he got his hands on a shoelace. Maybe we missed it when we booked him."

Marx pushed past him out of the office and demanded, "What's his condition?"

The officer hurried to keep pace with him. "Faint pulse, but he was blue and unconscious from lack of oxygen."

"Ambulance?"

"On the way."

I frowned up at Jordan, who watched Marx and the officer until they stepped into the stairwell.

"That guy was just up here bragging that the police couldn't hold him. Why would he try to kill himself an hour later?" I asked.

"Maybe he meant he wouldn't be alive for them to hold." At my skeptical look, he said, "Yeah, probably not what he meant."

"Maybe he had help hanging himself."

Jordan stared at me for a long, thoughtful moment before conceding. "Maybe, but that's not something you need to be in the middle of. Marx will figure it out."

"Well, what do we do?"

He grabbed his coat and shrugged it on. "We go out for a snack. You owe me an ice cream."

"Since when do I owe you an ice cream?"

"Since you bruised my ego."

"It's not my fault your ego's so fragile," I teased, grabbing my own coat. After one conflicted look in the direction Marx had gone, I followed Jordan out of the building.

21

We walked down a side street, weaving around a few patio dining areas that spilled out behind restaurants and cafés. I worked my way through a rocky road ice cream cone, and between the icy snack and the frigid air, I couldn't stop shivering.

"Cold?" Jordan asked after a long lick of his ice cream.

I let out a small, shivery laugh. "Yeah, aren't you? It's like f-fifteen d-degrees." I should've thought ahead and borrowed Jace's parka for this outing instead of wearing just my black wool jacket.

"Nope. I told you, I don't mind the cold. It's actually kind of refreshing." He glanced at me when I shivered again. "Here, hold this."

"W-w-what are you d-doing?" I asked, when he handed me his ice cream cone and started stripping out of his jacket.

"Giving you my coat," he said as he finished tugging it off. He plucked his ice cream cone out of my hand and offered me his coat.

I stepped back from him. "I don't w-want it. I d-don't n-need it."

The right corner of his mouth lifted despite his effort not to smile. "If you can say that again without your teeth chattering, I might believe you."

I lifted my chin defiantly and almost managed to repeat myself without my voice shivering from the cold. "I d-don't w-want it. Put it back on."

His brow furrowed as he studied me. "You know, you're the only woman I've ever had this problem with."

"What problem?" I asked, gripping my ice cream cone with both gloved hands and desperately wishing it was hot chocolate.

He dangled his coat in front of me for emphasis. "This. A woman refusing to accept my coat even though she's freezing."

"Offer your c-coat to a lot of w-women?"

He grinned. "Not the way you're thinking. A few ladies I dated. But also my mom and Oma. Accepting my coat doesn't make us a couple, and if you're refusing because you're afraid I'll get cold, I'll ask for it back if I start to shiver."

I bounced on my toes for warmth as I considered it. "You s-swear?"

"Occasionally."

I rolled my eyes and accepted the coat. It was still warm from his body heat, and I tugged it on over my other clothes. My gloved fingers fumbled with the zipper a few times before I managed to zip it up.

"Ice cream in F-F-February is a t-terrible idea," I said through chattering teeth.

He smiled as he continued eating his ice cream cone in nothing but jeans and a long-sleeve, dark-blue shirt. Not a shiver in sight. Jerk. "I'm kind of enjoying it."

I ate my ice cream down to the cone and threw the rest in the trash. I hated the cones; they tasted like Styrofoam.

Jordan stopped abruptly and caught my wrist when I would've continued walking. I staggered backwards off balance.

"Hey!" I objected. I tried to twist my arm free, but his fingers were wrapped all the way around my wrist and locked in place. "Jordan, let go!"

I looked up at him and stopped struggling when I noticed the intent expression on his face. I followed his gaze to a man leaning against the short black fence that enclosed the outdoor dining area ahead of us. His head was bald, and a tattoo of a serpent coiled around his neck and up onto his cheek.

It was the man from the crime scene where Marx's informant had been murdered. He was looking directly at us, and the intensity in his gaze was as unsettling as I remembered.

Jordan glanced left at a second man, who was leaning against the side of the building in the alley. Something about the man's black dreadlocks, barely restrained by a red bandanna, struck me as familiar.

"Jordan," I said, suddenly worried.

He turned around, pulling me with him, but stopped short when it brought us face-to-face with a third man who had one arm draped over the roof of a car and one hand resting on something tucked into the waistband of his loose jeans. The man's tongue flicked out to moisten the piercing on his lower lip, and he winked at me. Jordan's grip on my wrist tightened reflexively, but he was careful not to hurt me.

"What's happening?" I asked.

"I don't know," he muttered under his breath.

The bald man with the snake tattoo flicked his thumb over his nose in an obvious signal, and the other two men straightened and started walking toward us. They closed in around us, and fear crept up my spine.

Jordan's hand went to his gun, but as far as I could tell, none of them were holding a weapon. "Stay behind me," he said urgently. He backed me up against the nearest car and planted himself in front of me.

"What do they want?"

"I guess we're about to find out."

My pulse quickened as they closed in around us. That all-too-familiar trapped feeling sent my mind racing, desperately searching for an escape.

I looked around and noticed a few people watching, but the moment I met their gazes, their eyes skittered away. A few passersby glanced our way and then hastily retreated into the nearest building.

We were completely on our own.

The bald man stepped directly in front of Jordan and looked him over with a grunt that clearly communicated he wasn't impressed.

"Whatever the problem is, we can work it out," Jordan said in a reasonable voice.

The bald man looked around at his friends and then cocked his head as he asked, "So you're just gonna give me whatever I want?"

I drew in a sharp breath of surprise. I recognized his voice: this was the second man from Shannon's house. That put him at two of Marx's three crime scenes. And considering he knew I saw Tear at the house, I couldn't help but wonder if he was the one who put the bullet in the back of his head.

"That depends on what you want." Jordan's voice conveyed nothing but calm, but he kept a hand on his gun.

He was trying to resolve the situation peacefully, but knowing what I did now, I doubted anything he said would make a difference.

The man leaned a little to the right to look at me, and my breath caught at the glitter of violence in his eyes. "Maybe I want the girl."

A muscle in Jordan's jaw ticked, and his fingers flexed on his gun. "You would pick the one thing . . ." *That I'm not willing to part with*, his tone suggested.

"Tell you what. Let's make a deal," the bald man suggested. He rubbed his hands together eagerly. "Leave while you can still walk, and we don't got a problem."

I tensed. They would just let Jordan walk away if he agreed to leave me behind?

He wouldn't just abandon me, would he? He had faced down a knife-wielding giant for me armed with nothing but a screwdriver a few months ago, and he had sounded so opposed to handing me over.

But that was before they threatened him.

The bald man lifted the front of his shirt just enough to reveal the handle of the gun in his waistband and nodded to the side. "Take a walk, amigo."

"Yeah, that's not happening," Jordan said, his voice as tight with nerves as my stomach.

The bald man grinned. "I guess that means you ain't gonna just give her to us?" He was shorter than Jordan by at least two inches, but that did nothing to diminish his confidence as he stepped forward. "You the boyfriend?"

"Does it matter?"

"Not to me. But it might to her when I put a bullet between your eyes," the bald man said with a shrug.

"Jordan," I began, my voice shaking. I didn't want him to get shot because of me. He pushed me back with an arm when I inched forward.

"What's your problem?" he asked the man in a low voice.

The bald man nodded to me. "That skinny little ginger behind your back is my problem."

Anger tightened Jordan's shoulders. "She didn't do anything to you."

"Maybe she did, maybe she didn't. Ain't really any of your business, boyfriend. Funny thing, though . . . I seen her with another guy more than once. She been steppin' out on you." He watched Jordan as if he expected him to lash out in jealousy or rage.

He must have been talking about Marx. He had seen us together at least twice.

I glanced at the man on my left when he moved subtly closer. His tongue slipped out to moisten his pierced lower lip, and I realized he was watching me rather than Jordan.

My heart thumped faster.

Jordan must have noticed the man's movement too, because he wrapped his left arm around me protectively but never took his eyes off the leader.

"If you guys are just looking for someone to terrorize, there are easier targets," he said.

"Maybe we like a little challenge," the bald man grinned.

"If you're looking for a challenge, try sports. She's off limits."

"Not to me and mine." The man took another fearless step forward.

Jordan's arm tightened around me. "No one's touching her."

"Oh yeah? Who's gonna stop us?" He shoved Jordan hard, knocking both of us backwards. I yelped as the force slammed me into the car, pinning me between it and Jordan's body. "In case you forgot how to count, amigo, there's three of us and one of you."

261

Jordan straightened and placed one hand on the car, which was all that kept his body from slamming me up against the rear door again when the man shoved him a second time.

"Maybe I'll just drop you right here—leave you bleedin' on the sidewalk—and take her anyway."

Jordan was a hairsbreadth from losing his temper. I was flush against his back, and I could feel the bunching of his muscles beneath my hands.

"Last chance," the bald man said. "I'm takin' your girl one way or another. You just gotta decide whether or not you're still gonna be breathing when I do."

The other two men moved in a foot, and I all but clutched at Jordan's T-shirt for security.

"It ain't like we gonna hurt her," the man with the bandanna commented, and a low unsettling chuckle passed between the men.

I swallowed the frightened whimper that tried to escape, and kept my posture straight despite their efforts to intimidate us. I didn't want to give them the satisfaction of knowing I was afraid.

"Jordan, maybe you should just go and . . . get help," I suggested softly. I desperately didn't want him to leave me, but I also didn't want him to get himself killed trying to protect me.

"I'm gonna pretend you didn't just say that," he grumbled back, sounding offended by the suggestion.

The bald man spread his arms theatrically. "So . . . I take it we don't have a deal?"

Jordan didn't budge. "No."

"Brave but stupid. Get the girl."

The other two men started forward. Jordan punched the bald man unexpectedly and sent him stumbling back a few steps. He had his gun drawn and aimed at his head before the man even had a chance to regain his balance.

The other two men jerked to a stop and drew their guns in a far clumsier, slower manner, pointing them at Jordan.

Fear gripped me, squeezing the breath from my lungs. I barely heard the sound of windows slamming shut and people scrambling out of their café chairs over the violent pounding of my heart in my ears.

The bald man swiped the trickle of blood from his nose with a thumb and blinked at Jordan through watery eyes. "Now you're dead."

"Your boys can shoot me, but I *will* take you down with me," Jordan said evenly. It wasn't a threat—Jordan didn't often issue threats—it was a promise.

"And leave your girl all alone with these two?" The bald man sneered as he sniffed and wiped at his nose. "They'll take her apart."

Jordan's resolve didn't even flicker. "She's a fast runner. She'll make it."

I would never leave him here on the sidewalk if he had been shot, but I thought it probably best to keep that fact to myself for the moment.

"You willing to die for her?" the bald man asked with a confident tilt of his chin.

"Absolutely," Jordan said without hesitation. "Are you?"
Oh, please nobody die.

The bald man must have seen the sincerity in his eyes because he hesitated. He might be willing to sacrifice the lives of his men, but sacrificing his own life apparently gave him pause. He sniffed and demanded, "You're gonna deliver a message for me."

"I'm listening."

"I want that cop she's so cozy with—the detective—to step off. This is his last warning. He thinks he ain't got nothin' to lose, but that fine little thing right there . . ."

Jordan's shoulders tightened when the man gestured in my direction, and he shifted the angle of his body to shield me.

"Might just disappear if he don't back off. If he keeps tryin' to take what's mine, I'm gonna take what's his, and he ain't never gonna find her."

"I'll pass the message along," Jordan said.

"You do that." The man looked Jordan over again as he took a few steps back, as if he were still considering his chances. A

263

jerk of his chin had the other two men retreating with him. "You better hope he cares about you, ginger, or we're comin' back to pay you a visit, and you won't like it."

Jordan kept his gun trained on the three retreating men until they disappeared down one of the alleyways. His shoulders relaxed a fraction, and he lowered his gun. He turned around to find me practically standing on his heels. "You okay?"

I folded my arms over my stomach and stepped back into my comfort zone a few feet away. "I'm not the one who got shoved twice and physically threatened. I should be asking you that."

Jordan released a tense breath, and I could tell the encounter had left him shaken. "It's not the first time I've been shoved or threatened. I'm fine."

I didn't agree with that logic at all.

I had a feeling if I'd been on the receiving end of the shove rather than him, even though I've been pushed around before, he wouldn't be as nonchalant about it. But bringing that up would only upset him more.

"Come on. We need to talk to Marx," he said.

When we arrived back at the precinct, Marx was leaning against his desk with a file in his hands and a phone tucked between his shoulder and ear.

"Because he's my suspect," he said with agitation. "What do you mean I need to..." He listened for a long moment before grimacing and slamming the phone back into the cradle. He rubbed his tense forehead.

"Was that about the guy who spit on your shoe?" I asked, announcing our presence.

Marx looked up at me, frowned, and then shifted his disapproving frown to Jordan. "I asked you to take her somewhere else."

"I did," Jordan replied curtly. He shoved aside a stack of files on the vacant desk across from Marx and sat down. "We need to talk about your case."

Marx cocked an eyebrow. "It may have escaped your notice, but you don't actually work here."

"Your case is stirring up trouble."

"I'm aware of that. This case is the reason my car was vandalized and Shannon's house was broken into. You're not tellin' me anythin' I don't already know."

"We just had a run-in downtown."

Marx narrowed his eyes as he glanced between us. "Define run-in."

"It's not as urgent as it sounds. We can talk about it later after you sort out your drug dealer thing. And it was really more like an intense conversation," I explained, and Jordan shot me a frustrated look.

We had bickered the entire drive over about whether or not to bother Marx with this right now amidst everything else he had going on. No one had been hurt, and we were safe for the moment.

"Holly, considerin' you could get mugged in an alley and brush it off with your I've-had-worse-days attitude, I think I'd like to hear the explanation from Jordan," Marx said.

I tried not to be offended.

"Three men cornered us on the sidewalk, all armed," Jordan said.

Marx flicked me an equally frustrated glance. "A conversation, Holly?" I hadn't said there weren't guns involved. I scowled at his reproachful look. "What did they want?"

"Holly."

Marx's shoulders stiffened. "Come again?"

"They were there for Holly," Jordan explained. "They gave me the opportunity to walk away so they could take her without a fight. When I didn't, they tried to go through me to get to her."

Marx's gaze snapped to me. "Are you okay? Did they hurt you?" He scanned me for injuries that weren't there.

"I'm fine. They just wanted me to pass along a message."

"It doesn't take three armed men to intimidate somebody into passin' along a message, Holly. One will usually do," Marx replied with a hint of anger in his voice.

"They want you to back off this case. The leader said if you don't stop trying to take what's his, he's gonna take what's yours, and he was referring to Holly. He said if you don't heed the warning, he's coming back for her, and he implied that he would hurt her," Jordan explained.

Marx's face became dangerously flat; even his voice sounded flat, but I could see the sparkle of fury in his eyes. "I wanna know every word that was said, and everythin' that happened."

Jordan relayed every detail of the standoff on the sidewalk, and when he finished, Marx looked as though he might explode. I considered stepping out of the room and letting him vent, because I knew he would do his best to contain his anger while I was present.

"So what are you gonna do?" Jordan asked.

Marx tapped his fingers on his biceps in an agitated rhythm. "Well, I'm not gonna give them what they want, if that's what you're askin'."

"You're gonna keep investigating despite the threat to her safety?"

"Jordan, if I bend to their will out of fear for her safety, what kind of message do you think that's gonna send? Word spreads quickly on the street, and anybody I investigate in the future will know that all they have to do to halt my investigation is to target her. It will only increase the amount of danger she's in if I let them know she's my weakness." At my sudden, indrawn breath, he glanced at me and clarified, "I mean that in a good way, sweetheart."

There was a good way to mean that?

Jordan sighed. "So what do we do then? I managed to hold three of them off because I had a gun on the leader, and he wasn't willing to die. What if they come back with reinforcements?"

Marx looked at me, and I glimpsed the uncertainty in his face. He wanted to protect me, but he also didn't want to drop his case. "I need you to stay here until we figure this out."

I didn't want to stay here, but I also didn't want to risk Jordan's life because he felt compelled to protect me despite unreasonable odds, so I simply nodded.

Jordan arched a blond eyebrow at me. "That was awfully agreeable of you. Are you planning a secret escape?"

I crinkled my nose at him. "No."

"Should we barricade the doors?"

"Stop it."

"Post security guards by all the exits?"

I resisted the urge to throw something at him just to shut him up. "I'm not gonna sneak out!"

"I'd rather you both stay on the premises for the time bein'," Marx interjected. "I'm gonna have you both look at some mug shots and see if you can identify any of the men who approached you on the sidewalk. If we can find them, then maybe we can end this."

"We've seen the leader before," I said. "It was the guy from the first crime scene where your informant died—the one with the snake tattoo."

Marx shuffled through the folders on his desk and pulled one out. "I had the crime scene photographer take pictures of the bystanders at Ruiz's scene." He flipped through the pictures until he found the one he was looking for, and then held it up for me to see. "This guy?"

His finger pointed to the man with the snake tattoo in the background of the photo.

"Yep."

"His name is Miguel Martinez, also known as Snake. For obvious reasons. He has a rap sheet a mile long, includin' just about every offense imaginable."

"Sounds like a great guy," Jordan muttered sarcastically under his breath.

"He was also the second guy from Shannon's house. I recognized his voice," I said. "He knew I saw Tear. Do you think he killed him?"

"Probably." Marx stood and taped the picture of Snake to the whiteboard next to Tear's picture, filing him under enforcer. "He probably killed Ruiz too, considerin' he was at the scene. And that's the first place he noticed you."

He held up a second, slightly blurry photo that captured the eerie way Snake had been watching me that afternoon on the sidewalk, and Jordan took it from him.

"Why is he looking at her like that?"

"He was probably tryin' to figure out how she was connected to me. See that guilty look on her face in the picture?"

"Yeah, like she just got caught with her hand in the cookie jar."

I rolled my eyes. "That would never happen. I would just take the whole cookie jar."

"She was supposed to stay in the car," Marx continued. "But I spotted her in the crowd and she waved at me, which drew his attention to her. Then he saw us together at Shannon's house. Somebody, I don't know if it was him, probably got a look at her the night they vandalized my car."

"The guy who came into the break room," I began. "He .. . seemed to recognize me too, but I don't think I've ever seen him before."

He sat back on his desk and frowned pensively. "Okay, let's focus on figurin' out who the other two men were. The rest can wait."

He stood, and Jordan and I followed him into a side room with a large rectangular table. He pulled out a chair for me, and I settled into it. My eyes widened when he thumped a few heavy binders onto the table.

"Whoa," I said, drawing the word out as I took in the binders. "Haven't you guys heard of digital albums?"

"Says the girl who can't change her own ringtone," Marx replied dryly. "And yes, we have digital files as well, but these are all the known gang members and drug dealers we have a record of in the city."

I dragged one of the binders toward me before remembering I was supposed to pass along another message, this one far less sinister. I pulled the crumpled note from my pocket and offered it to him.

"I was supposed to give you this. It's from Sam's partner."

A thoughtful crease formed between his eyebrows as he took it. "When was Daniel here?"

"While you were in a meeting with McNera."

"He stopped by to ask Holly out again," Jordan mumbled as he flipped through a binder. I shot him an exasperated look that he probably didn't even see.

Marx arched an eyebrow at me. "And you said . . ."

"Doesn't matter."

I could hear the smile in Jordan's voice as he continued flipping through the pictures. "She said she doesn't like cops."

Marx's lips twitched. "Probably not your best argument given that you spend all of your free time with cops."

"Can we just drop it?"

"Would you like me to have a talk with Daniel about his advances?"

Yes, yes, I would, because my attempts are failing miserably. "No," I sighed. "I can handle it myself."

"I think I scared him off for a while," Jordan announced, finally looking up. "I doubt he'll try again anytime soon."

Marx seemed to consider that. "Okay." He looked at me. "Did he leave a message with this address?" When I shook my head, he said, "I'll give him a call, then. I have a few things to take care of, but I'll be around if you need me."

He ruffled my hair with a hand, and I ducked, covering my head as I snapped, "Quit that."

He laughed as he strode out of the room, and I glared after him as I tried to fix my rumpled hair.

22

I puffed out a frustrated breath and slammed the last binder shut. Hundreds of photos had yielded only one possible result, and the photo had been taken years ago.

"Anything?" I asked Jordan.

"No. The closest is probably the guy you picked out." He lifted the picture and flipped it over to read the name. "Darnell Walt."

Bandanna guy.

It was hard to say for sure—because I had only glimpsed the man's hair and red bandanna—but I thought Darnell might have been the man I saw retreating down the steps of Marx's apartment building the morning I burnt breakfast. *Someone* had been lurking outside Marx's door before the old woman scared them off.

I pushed back from the table and stood. "I need to stretch my legs."

"Want company?"

"If you don't mind, I'd like a little time to myself," I admitted, hoping it wouldn't hurt his feelings. I appreciated all that they were doing to protect me, but I was starting to feel like I couldn't breathe.

"Feeling a little crowded?" he asked, with a perceptive smile.

I smiled back. "Maybe a little."

"Completely understandable. I'm gonna grab a bite to eat and some coffee. You want a snack or anything?"

"I'm good. Thanks." I left the room and pulled out my cell phone to check the message I had received while we were engrossed in the mug shots. The pinch of tension in me relaxed when I realized it was from Jace and not another unknown number.

Collin had been noticeably absent from my life since the ice rink—no texts, calls, *or* unwanted visits—and that made me suspicious. He was plotting something.

270

The text was a picture message from Jace, and I smiled to myself when a pair of hot-pink lace-up heels loaded on the screen with the caption:

> *Saw these and thought of you.*
> *Never*, I wrote back.

Another picture message came through, and the pair of green slippers that were designed to look like ferocious alligators made me laugh.

> *These?* 😊

I bit the corner of my lip and grinned as I typed:

> *Do those come in Sam's size? Because it would be funny to see his face.*
> *No* 😔, she replied, *I already checked.*

I paused midreply when I strolled past an office and overheard a man explaining, "I don't know what's wrong with the camera down there. It's been in and out for weeks, and I put in a request to have it checked out, but someone's dragging their feet."

"I processed Banks, and he did not have a shoelace," the female cop from earlier protested. "Someone had to have given one to him or gave him a hand in hanging himself. And you're telling me the camera just happened to be out."

"Yes, that's what I'm saying."

She released an agitated breath. "Then you tell Mr. Snippy that, because I would rather not. He already thinks I'm incompetent."

"You're not incompetent, Jill."

"Well, I know that, but the only suspect he managed to round up on this drug case is now dead, and it looks like I screwed up."

So the drug dealer was dead, and the officer who processed him didn't believe he had killed himself any more than I did. Something strange was going on, and it made my nose tingle with curiosity; I wanted to go poke it somewhere and see what I could find out.

"Eavesdropping again?" a dry voice asked from behind me, startling my phone right out of my hands.

I turned around to find Sam bending down to retrieve it off the floor. He arched an eyebrow at the open text message. "Alligator slippers?"

I snatched my phone back from him and snapped, "Don't sneak up on me."

"I didn't sneak. You're just jumpy."

That was probably true, so I tucked my attitude away along with my phone and asked, "What are you doing here?"

"I work here." He was in his uniform, and I glanced at the clock on the wall. It was already time for his night shift. "What are *you* doing here this late?"

"Apparently I'm under arrest." House arrest, or rather precinct arrest. That's what they called it when you weren't allowed to leave the premises, right?

His thick black eyebrows knitted together. "What?"

"It's a long story. I'm sure Marx will fill you in." I stepped around him and strode back in the direction I had come from. I could go for one of two things right now: solitude or some sneaky secret information about the case.

The sound of Marx's voice inside the captain's office as I passed by brought me up short. I leaned against the door and listened to the conversation. It wasn't that I didn't realize eavesdropping was a sign of poor manners, but I was tired of being left out of the loop because everyone thought I needed to be protected.

"A picture of her among his personal effects that were removed durin' processin'," Marx was saying.

"Taking a picture of a woman on the street is not a crime, Rick," Captain McNera said calmly.

"This picture wasn't taken on the street; it was taken by our crime scene photographer at my crime scene. How does a drug dealer have access to those photos?"

272

There was a long pause before Captain McNera mumbled angrily, "He doesn't. We need to talk to our crime scene photographer."

"She's on her way in now."

"If the men who attempted to abduct Holly today went straight for her, that means they knew what she looked like before hand. Her picture could've been distributed to any number of these people."

When Marx spoke again, there was a note of desperation in his voice. "What do I do, Matt? How do I protect her?"

I had never heard him sound so uncertain before, and it worried me. Marx took everything in stride with confidence, but the voice filtering through the door sounded rattled.

"You can't."

His grim prediction dropped a veil of uneasy silence over the room, and I pressed my ear flush against the door, listening for even the smallest sound.

Captain McNera spoke first. "The very fact that you care about this girl and wanna do everything you can to protect her is the reason she's in danger. I understand that she means a great deal to you, but you're endangering her life."

"Then what am I supposed to do?"

"The way I see it, there are two options. One, hand the case off to another detective. That will remove their attention from you and the girl."

"Her name is Holly," Marx said curtly. "And I have never handed off a case. I'm not gonna start now just because they think they can threaten me and the people I care about. And shiftin' this case to another detective will only put them and the people they love in danger."

"I thought you might say that, which brings us to option two. Protective custody until this case is resolved."

I drew back from the door in confusion. Protective custody? What on earth did that mean? It sounded like he wanted to lock me in a cell for my own "protection."

"Protective custody," Marx repeated back, his tone laced with disbelief. "You want me to place her in the care of people she doesn't know or trust and expect her to be okay with that?"

"They're US marshals, Rick. They'll take good care of her."

"I don't doubt that. But you don't understand Holly. She won't take kindly to bein' locked away somewhere with strangers. In fact, I'm pretty sure she'll flat out say no."

"Convince her. She listens to you."

Marx snorted. "Holly doesn't listen to anybody. You do remember last fall when I tried to place officers inside her home to protect her from her stalker."

I had refused with emphasis.

Captain McNera sighed. "We don't have any other choice, Rick. If you're that worried about her well-being, hand off the case. Ricardo's worked a number of narcotics cases. He has the experience."

"Experience, yes. Brains, no. I wouldn't trust him to solve this case even if there was a yellow brick road leadin' to the supplier's front porch."

"If you think you can get these guys off the street, then do it, and do it quickly before anyone else gets hurt. But convince her to go into protective custody. You've seen what they do to their own people. They won't hesitate to hurt her just because she's a girl."

Another moment of silence, and then I heard the creak of a chair as Marx stood. "I'll talk to her and let you know what we decide."

The door to the office glided inward, and I leveled a determined look at Marx as I said, "No."

He sighed and hung his head. He stepped out and closed the door behind him. "Let's talk somewhere a little more private."

He gestured to the break room, and I folded my arms unhappily as I stalked into the room with him on my heels. He closed the door behind us.

"I understand why you don't like the idea of protective custody, but we at least need to discuss it," he said. "It's the best way to keep you safe for the time bein'."

"Who are the US marshals?"

"US marshals specialize in a lot of difficult tasks, one of which is keepin' people hidden and safe for extended periods of time. No one will be allowed to know where you are or how to contact you."

Shocked, it took me a moment to respond. "I won't be able to talk to any of you?"

He shook his head. "It's safer if you don't."

"For how long?"

"I don't know. It could be days, weeks, or even months."

A small inner voice whispered that he just wanted me out of the way, that by staying I was hindering not only his job but his life. Regardless of what he said to my face, I was a burden and he wanted me gone.

I tried to smother the voice, but it continued to whisper through my mind, giving strength to my doubts and insecurities.

"I'm sorry if I made your investigation more difficult or caused you any more stress. I didn't mean to."

Marx frowned and opened his mouth to say something, but I wasn't finished.

"And you don't need to call in the marshals. I know how to disappear on my own."

I could catch a bus tonight, which would be safer than spending the night at home and leaving in the morning. I tried to open the door to leave, but Marx put a hand on it to hold it in place.

"Holly," he began, a hint of exasperation in his voice. "I don't want you to disappear. I just want you to be safe until I can wrap up this case, and then the marshals will bring you back. This is a temporary situation."

Sam rapped a knuckle on the door and then popped his head in. "Hey. Danny and I are about to head out, but I wanted to make sure everything's okay before we do."

"No," Marx grunted. "It's not okay. Come in."

Sam frowned and then stepped inside. "Does this have something to do with Holly saying she was under arrest?"

"She's not under arrest, but I do need her to reconsider protective custody."

"Why does she need protective custody? I thought we decided the note wrapped around the rock was referring to Shannon."

"We were wrong," Marx said. "My drug dealer went after her in the break room this mornin', and we found her picture on him. And when she went out with Jordan this afternoon, three men tried to grab her off the sidewalk."

Sam absorbed that with a slow blink and then slid his gaze to me. "You're holding it together pretty well, considering."

Was I supposed to freak out and hide under the break room table? I gave him a frustrated look. "I've had worse days."

He grimaced. "Yeah, I guess you have." He folded his arms and looked at Marx. "So what's the plan? Put her into protective custody until you get these guys off the streets?"

"Except she won't go."

Sam lifted an eyebrow. "You had to see that coming."

"Of course I saw that comin'. I'm not blind."

"Well, you can't force her. She just needs to understand that the guys who tried to grab her today are enforcers, which means no matter how many of them you shoot or arrest, they'll just keep coming. And if your attention is split between protecting her and doing your job, it's gonna take you longer to solve the case, which will give them more opportunity to grab her."

Not if they couldn't find me.

"Also, the longer it takes you to solve this case, the more kids are gonna die from exposure to the contaminated drug." Sam glanced at me and shrugged. "Ultimately, it's her decision."

I glared at him.

"I know this is gonna be hard for you, but it's just for a short time," Marx said.

"I can't. I can't stay with these people. You . . . you know why." I gave him a beseeching look, desperate for him to understand without me having to put it into words.

"I know. And I will do everythin' I can to ensure that at least one of the marshals is a woman and that all of them understand and respect your boundaries."

I folded my arms and gripped my elbows. "And you know how I feel about cops. The only ones I trust are you, Jordan, and . . . Sam."

Sam grunted, "Well, at least I made the short list."

"Please trust me on this, Holly," Marx pleaded. "In order for me to do my job and get this drug off the street, I need to know that you're safe, and this is the only way."

I didn't want to go into protective custody, but I also didn't want innocent kids to keep dying because Marx's focus was split between protecting me and solving this case.

"You realize that most of the time when you say, 'Trust me,' things don't exactly go as planned," I reminded him.

"You'll be fine. I promise," he assured me.

I puffed out a breath and stared down at the floor. "Fine. I'll try protective custody. But if they creep me out, I'm leaving, even if I have to hitchhike."

Sam blinked. "You wouldn't." He had lectured me about the dangers of hitchhiking a few months ago when I was prepared to go to Kansas alone.

"I'd rather you just steal a phone and call me. I'll come get you," Marx said.

Jordan opened the break room door and stepped halfway inside, his expression cautiously curious. "Did I not get the group text that we were having a secret meeting?"

Marx's lips pinched in that way that I was coming to realize meant he was dreading what he had to do next. "Holly, why don't you give Jordan and me a minute. We need to talk."

I glanced between them and then ducked out of the room when Jordan stepped aside. Sam followed me out into the squad room, and I heard Jordan ask, "What exactly do we need to talk about?" before Sam pulled the door shut.

I watched through the window, frowning as their calm conversation abruptly escalated into an angry confrontation. Jordan's normally relaxed voice rose as he gestured toward me through the glass.

"No! I just got her back. I'm not letting you stuff her into some hole for an undetermined length of time where I can't see her or talk to her!"

"You need to calm down," Marx shot back. "Take a breath."

Sam folded his arms and watched the display with interest. "I had a feeling that decision wouldn't go over too well with him."

"Don't tell me to take a breath! You're the reason she's in danger. Drop the case or hand it off to someone else!"

I took a wary step back from the window when Jordan leaned forward and gripped the back of a folding chair. Sam arched a curious eyebrow, and I explained, "Sometimes he throws things when he gets angry."

Sam took a deliberate step back with me. Marx and Jordan bickered in circles for nearly ten minutes, but thankfully no chairs came flying through the window.

I tuned them out as I looked up at Sam. "You're not gonna tell Jace about the thing on the sidewalk, right?"

He gave me a look reserved for the mentally deranged. "She hyperventilates when you're five minutes late. I'm not about to tell her three men tried to grab you off the sidewalk this afternoon."

I breathed a sigh of relief. "At least we agree on something."

23

I rubbed my sweaty palms on my jeans as I paced from one end of the squad room to the other. Marx had said someone from the US marshals would be by shortly to take me into "custody."

"You're gonna wear a hole in the floor," he said, watching my nervous behavior.

"They're not gonna handcuff me, are they?" I worried.

"No, they're not gonna handcuff you," he sighed. "You're not a criminal."

Well, that was a relief.

"Are you gonna mail my letter?"

His lips flattened. "I promised I would whether I agree with you writin' to that woman or not."

After stressing for weeks over what to say, I had finally finished my letter to Izzy. It was brief, but it said the only things that mattered:

I forgive you.
Love, Holly

It still hurt that she had chosen her drug-dealing career over me, but I wasn't angry with her anymore.

And despite the prickle of bitterness I felt toward God when I thought about how easily he might forgive Collin, I couldn't let that stop me from doing what I knew was right. It wasn't for me to decide who or what God forgave; I could only decide who I would extend that grace to, and I had chosen to extend it to Izzy.

"Izzy's not a bad person, you know," I told Marx.

"That's debatable. But I'm less concerned with her bein' a bad person than I am with the bad company she kept. If she crossed anybody or owes anybody from her past money, I don't want them findin' their way to you."

"If that were the case, wouldn't they have gone after her or

279

Paul long before now?" When his expression turned grim, I stopped pacing. "What?"

He started to speak, but then the stairwell door opened, and a tall woman entered the room. Her pale-blonde hair was swept up into a ponytail that swayed like a pendulum behind her as she moved, and her gray eyes took in the squad room in one perceptive sweep.

A taller man with bright-red hair filed through the doorway behind her, and a second man with midnight-black hair and a stocky frame that left him just an inch or so shorter than the woman followed up the rear of the group.

I gravitated toward Marx, who straightened from the desk he'd been leaning against. Jordan stood and folded his arms as the group approached us.

The woman's gaze glided over each of us and then settled on me. "Considering you're the only woman in the room surrounded by testosterone, I'm gonna guess you're Holly."

I looked up at her and felt absurdly short. She was almost, if not exactly, as tall as Marx. It made me long for a pair of those silly shoes Jace was always buying me so I could at least be average height.

"I'm Deputy Marshal Melbourne," the woman said in a voice that commanded attention. "But you can call me Kristen. The gentleman to my left is Mike, and the fellow on my right with the wild hair is Jefferson."

Jefferson inclined his head. "Ma'am."

Kristen's attention slid over Jordan, who was grimacing, and landed on Marx. She extended her hand. "I assume you're the detective who requested this detail."

"I am," Marx confirmed, shaking her hand briskly. "I understand this is an unusual situation, given she's not a material witness."

"I spoke with your captain and he briefed me on the situation. You're working to bring down a narcotics ring, and Holly's in the cross fire." She arched an eyebrow as if to ask, *Did I miss anything?*

"Essentially, yes."

She nodded. "You're right, it's not a case we would ordinarily take—this kind of thing is usually done in-house—but your captain called in a favor. Apparently he has friends in high places."

"I appreciate it. I need her someplace safe until I can wrap everythin' up with a nice little bow."

"I think we can manage that. We arranged a safe house, and we're ready to move out when we're done here."

This whole situation made me sound ridiculously important. I was just an unemployed woman who lived in a basement with her cat, for crying out loud.

"There are a few things I would like to discuss with the three of you before you head out," Marx said. "If you wouldn't mind joinin' me in the conference room."

"Of course," Kristen agreed.

The four of them disappeared into a small side room and closed the door. If they were supposed to safeguard *me*, why wasn't I invited to the discussion?

"Marx is probably just briefing them," Jordan said, as if he knew what I was thinking.

"Briefing them on what?"

"Probably on the challenge they just agreed to."

"What challenge?"

Amusement eased some of the worry in his expression, and it took me a moment to realize why he was smiling at me.

I bristled. "I'm not a challenge."

One of his eyebrows lifted. "I seem to remember you being exactly that the first time I tried to protect you. You stole my car keys and then tried to steal my car."

I folded my arms and lifted my chin, refusing to take the blame. "With good reason." Marx had been missing, and Jordan had refused to help me look for him. So I had decided to look for him myself, even if I had to steal a sheriff's car to do it.

"I'll concede that point. But when we found Marx's car in the ditch, all I asked was that you stay in my car with the doors locked for your own protection. Not only did you get out of my car, but then you wandered into the woods alone and got abducted by a serial killer."

"I . . . that was . . ." I huffed in frustration. "I need a doughnut." I stalked off toward the break room.

"Don't you mean a quarter of a doughnut?" he teased, trailing behind me. "Because you never actually eat the whole thing."

I lifted the lid of the pastry box to scope out my options. There weren't many good ones left.

Jordan rested a hip on the table beside me. "Are you gonna be okay with these people?"

"I'm not gonna wander into the woods alone or steal any cars while in their custody, if that's what you're worried about. I mean, unless something goes wrong."

He glanced at the conference room door across the squad room. "Yeah, the 'something going wrong' part is what worries me."

I plopped my doughnut on a plate and closed the box. "You don't trust them?"

"Do you?"

I glanced across the squad room at the conference room door. "I don't know. But Marx does." I looked down at my doughnut and then up at Jordan. "Want half?"

He grinned. "I told you you weren't gonna eat the whole thing. But no. I'm more of a bear claw kind of guy."

Hmm. I was pretty sure I hadn't seen Captain McNera leave for the night, and he would split a cake doughnut with me. I grabbed a plastic knife and cut half off for him. "Be right back," I said, walking out of the room.

"Where are you going?"

"To make amends."

"With a doughnut?"

I knocked on the outside of the captain's door. I heard him clear his throat and say, "Come in."

He was seated behind his desk as I expected, but his eyes

were puffy, as if he had been crying recently. He returned a photograph of his family—a wife and two grown daughters—to his desk and gave me a polite smile that I recognized for what it was: a fragile cover.

"I can come back later," I said, turning to leave.

"Nonsense. Please come in." He gestured toward one of the guest chairs on the opposite side of his desk.

I hesitated and then decided to step inside. "If it's not too nosy to ask, is everything okay? You seem upset."

"Just a little bad news in the family," he replied. He settled his forearms on the desk and clasped his hands together. "What can I do for you?"

I ignored the chair he offered and stepped forward to set the doughnut on his desk before retreating again. "You said cake doughnuts are your favorite."

He smiled, and there was a glimmer of warmth in it this time. "They are. Thank you for remembering. And for sharing with me."

"Sure." I wanted to say more, but I wasn't sure how to go about it. "I know it's none of my business, but you mentioned that there's some kind of bad news in your family. I could, um . . ." I chewed on my lip as I tried to work up the nerve. "I could say a prayer. I mean, if you want."

A deep furrow formed between his eyebrows. "That's very thoughtful, but I don't believe in God."

"Oh." I didn't really know how else to respond to that blunt statement.

"Even if God does exist, I'm not sure He cares about my problems," he added, almost as an afterthought.

"So when your daughters had struggles growing up, you didn't care?"

He frowned. "Of course I cared. They're my children. They're a part of me." At my small smile, he sighed. "I see where you're going with that, but my wife has already tried. I prefer to resolve my own problems."

"So it's something you can fix on your own?"

He cleared his throat and said dismissively, "Thank you for the doughnut, Holly."

I nodded but paused before leaving. I had come here to say more than that. "I forgive you, by the way, for . . . trying to have me arrested in October."

Regret flickered through his eyes. "You're a sweet kid, Holly, and I truly am sorry."

"I'm not a huge fan of this whole protective custody thing, but I'm not surprised." I kept my tone light and teasing as I said, "You seem to have a lot of bad ideas."

He chuckled softly. "My wife would agree."

"You said Marx is your friend. Take care of him while I'm gone. Don't let him get hurt."

"He's in good hands."

I smiled and tugged the door shut behind me after I left. Jordan was waiting beside Marx's desk with a troubled expression. He seemed to be struggling with the idea of protective custody as much as I was.

"Did you make your amends?" he asked.

"I think so."

I started toward him when the side room door opened and Kristen exited with her team.

"We should get going, Holly," she said, stopping in front of us. "I'll send Jefferson with Marx to collect your personal belongings, and he'll rendezvous with us at the safe house."

Jordan straightened. "I wanna go with her."

Kristen appraised him. "Are you a federal marshal in disguise? Because that's the only way you're gonna be a part of my operation."

Jordan glared at her. "No, I'm not, but I—"

Kristen raised a hand to cut him off. "I've met my fair share of friends and significant others who have difficulty accepting the strict guidelines of this program, and I can respect your feelings, but don't do anything that's gonna force me to arrest you." She returned her attention to me. "Are you ready, Holly?"

Now that it was actually time to leave with these people, I

wanted to back out. But I knew that wasn't an option. I nodded reluctantly. "I guess so."

"Mike will drive and I'm gonna sit in the back with you," Kristen explained, tossing the car keys to her partner.

"You're letting me drive?" Mike asked in surprise. "Is there an asteroid speeding toward earth that's gonna kill us before we reach the car? Because every time I ask to drive, you shut me down."

Kristen smirked at him. "Don't get used to it." Turning back to me, she said, "We'll need you to leave any electronic or tracking devices here, including any fitness bands and your cell phone."

I pulled my cell phone from my pocket and stared at it. The thought of being completely disconnected from the people I cared about didn't set well with me. I released an uneasy breath and held my phone out to Marx.

He opened his hand, and I dropped it into his palm. I pulled out my apartment keys and slipped off the spares, placing them next to my phone in his hand.

"Are you sure?" he asked in surprise.

He knew how important the security of my home was to me, and that I had never before trusted anyone enough to give them keys to my apartment.

My landlord Stanley had violated my trust and made copies, and it had allowed an intruder into my home. When Marx had my locks changed, he had given me both sets of keys and left it to me to decide what to do with the spares.

"I trust you. And I want you to have them." I doubted he would need them, but I was glad he had them.

I was pretty sure I saw an unusual shine in his eyes as he closed his fingers over my phone and keys, but it was hard to tell. "I'll resolve this case as quickly as I can, and then you can come home."

He looked like he wanted to hug me, but he left that decision to me as well. I wasn't quite ready for such drastic displays of affection, so I simply nodded.

I looked at Jordan, who was struggling not to let his anger and worry shine through his expression. I wished there was something I could say to make him feel better about this situation.

But the truth was, I had to stay in hiding for however long it took Marx to resolve this case, which could be a long time if his leads kept dying.

"So . . ." I began, tucking my hands into the back pockets of my jeans, "maybe when I get back, we can go get *two* scoops of rocky road, but minus the creepy guys on the sidewalk, and maybe someplace with a heater."

His gaze slid past me to the marshals, worry in his eyes. "Yeah, we can do that."

I had a feeling he was concerned that something would go wrong and, for one reason or another, I wouldn't come back.

I drew in a breath of courage and took a step closer to him, crossing over the invisible four-foot boundary between us. He shifted against the desk, seeming unsure whether or not he should move away.

I stretched out a hand, hesitated as anxiety clenched low in my stomach, and then wrapped my fingers around his for the briefest instant.

I had allowed him to touch me during training, but this was the first time I had willingly touched him since we were children.

"I'm coming back," I assured him, giving his fingers a gentle squeeze.

I pulled my hand back before he could do anything more than blink in surprise. My actions surprised both of us. But if his instincts were better than mine and something did go wrong at the safe house, I wanted him to have this memory—a moment of physical connection between us that didn't involve me being afraid of him.

"Try not to beat up on Sam too much while I'm gone," I said. "I know you can't tell from his face, but he has feelings. And tell him bye for me." He hadn't been able to stay because he had to go out on patrol with his partner. "And give Jace a hug for me. Or . . . a high five or something."

286

"Holly," Kristen prompted, and I reluctantly pulled my eyes from Jordan to look at her. She gestured for me to follow them.

I nodded and then whispered to Jordan, "Good-bye."

He swallowed visibly, and resolve filtered into his eyes. "Not good-bye. You're coming back, remember?"

I forced a smile. "See you later, then."

I fell in step behind Mike as we left the squad room. The drive to the safe house took several hours, and if I wasn't mistaken, we passed by certain buildings more than once.

We eventually pulled onto a narrow road straddled by trees, and I sat up straighter in my seat. Maybe I should've mentioned that I wasn't fond of wooded areas. The road dead-ended at a two-story house, and Mike parked the car near the front stoop.

He climbed out and opened my door. "Welcome to your home away from home, Holly."

I slid slowly off the seat and stared at the house. There were motion-activated lights mounted on the siding, and I was pretty sure I spotted a camera tucked up under the gutter. It reminded me vaguely of hiding at the shelter again.

"I'm gonna park the SUV around back and then I'll meet the two of you inside," Mike announced.

Kristen strode around the vehicle to join me, and slung a bag over her shoulder as she cocked her head at the house. "Not too bad, right? Has a nice bathroom and comfortable beds. The kitchen is stocked with everything we'll need for a while."

"Does it have chocolate?"

She offered a restrained smile that did little to brighten her serious features. "Let's find out."

I followed her up the front steps and into the foyer of the house, my gaze wandering over the unfamiliar interior. "How many entrances are there?"

Her gray eyes glinted with thoughtful curiosity. "Most people say exits instead of entrances when they're already inside. They're typically more concerned with how they can get out rather than how someone else can get in."

Apparently I was going to have to be careful with what I

said around her, because she was going to analyze my every word like some sort of therapist. Just what I wanted: another shrink.

"Marx mentioned that you have an unwanted admirer. I assume that's where that anxiety stems from."

"I'm not anxious," I snapped.

"Defensive too. He's a sore subject, I guess." She dropped her bag onto the chair beside the door. "Well, the good news is, he won't be able to find you here either. And if by some chance he manages it, and he's a threat, he would be dead before he reached the doorknob."

I blinked at her in astonishment. "You just shoot people who try to get in?"

"We have procedures, but we're not playing games with your life, Holly. We have no intention of handcuffing a threat who manages to breach safe house security. Cliché as it sounds, we prefer to shoot first and ask questions later if it reaches that point."

I didn't agree with that approach. It sounded like senseless bloodshed. "It's hard to get answers from dead people."

Kristen arched an amused eyebrow. "Not really. It just requires a bit of patience because there's a pretty big lag time between asking a question and getting an answer, but a few hours of research and investigating usually tells us everything we need to know."

"Seems to me that asking first would be faster and a bit more helpful."

"In an ideal world where the villains monologue about their dirty deeds and illegal crimes, sure. But this is reality, and most of these guys clam up the instant they realize they've lost."

"I guess that makes sense," I conceded.

"I respect human life too, Holly, but sometimes you just have to draw a line. You may not have to as a civilian, but we do. Trust us to know what we're doing. And as far as entrances go, you don't need to worry about them. They'll be covered by my people. The only door you need to worry about is the one that leads to your safe room." She nodded toward the steps. "If you'll follow me."

A long hallway stretched in both directions at the top of the steps, and I glanced at the four closed doors.

"You're gonna be on the far left," she explained, leading me to the room in question. She opened the door and swung it inward. "It's an average room, but it has an extra lock and shatterproof windows."

"Shatterproof windows?" I asked as I stepped inside. The room was plain, with few pieces of furniture and no decorations. "So, if they make it through the door, I'm basically screwed because there's no escape."

Kristen arched an eyebrow at my tone. I knew I was being snippy. "There are three lines of human defense between you and any potential intruder. Then there's the front door and this door with an added lever lock." She tapped on the door with her knuckles.

I tipped my head back to look at the lock she mentioned and frowned. It looked like something you would find on the stall door of a public restroom, which didn't exactly scream secure, and then there was the added bonus of it being at the top of the door.

Maybe if I stood on my tiptoes I could poke it with my middle fingertip.

"All doors on this floor will remain locked, except yours, so if anyone does manage to enter the house, they won't know which room you're hiding in," Kristen said. She nodded for me to follow her back into the hall.

I gave the lock at the top of the door one last unfriendly look before leaving the room. "So how many exits are there again?"

Kristen surrendered to a smile. "There are three doors in and out of the house: one through the garage—which will be sealed—one at the front of the house, and one at the rear. I'll walk you around."

She walked with purpose, every step brisk and efficient, and I found myself scampering on occasion to keep up with her. We toured through the various rooms of the house, and I tried to keep it all straight in my mind. I hadn't tried to memorize an entire house since I was seventeen.

I had committed every inch of my last foster family's home

to memory, planning my hiding places and escape routes. In the end, none of it had mattered. My foster mother had let Collin waltz right through the front door under the guise of my math tutor.

I had come back from school to find him sitting in the living room with her, calmly discussing my school grades with a genial smile on his face.

The memory made me shudder.

"Everything all right?" Kristen asked, regarding me with interest.

"Fine." I forced my memories to the recesses of my mind and reminded myself that this situation was vastly different. These people wouldn't let the enemy waltz through the front door, and if by chance he did make it inside, God would see me through it.

Right, God? No matter what happens, You'll get me through this . . . at least mostly intact.

"Tell me something about yourself, Holly," Kristen said, drawing me from my silent prayer.

That was a rather broad request. "Um . . . I wear a size 6 shoe." There. That would teach her to be less abstract in her questions.

She laughed as we descended the steps. "Well, as fascinating as that is, I was aiming for something a little deeper than your shoe size."

"You should be more specific because the next deeply personal fact I was gonna share is that I despise the color yellow."

She grunted in what might have been amusement. "Now you're just oversharing. Dial it back a little."

I smiled.

"Marx gave me the highlights, but I'm interested to know a little more about you. Like what makes you *you*?"

"Does anybody ever actually know how to answer that question?"

"No, I guess not. How about this, what are you passionate about?"

I thought about it for a moment. "Jesus, my camera, my friends . . ." *Marshmallows.* But I kept that last thought to myself.

"You're a photographer?"

"On occasion. I don't have the talent to create, but I can at least preserve what's already been created by taking a picture of it."

"That's an interesting way to think about it."

"What about you?" I wondered. "You must be passionate about the law to wanna do this job."

"I'm passionate about the people I'm protecting, not about the laws I'm upholding while doing it."

"What made you wanna be a marshal?" I asked, following her into the kitchen.

"A culmination of things," she said. She opened one of the cupboards and pulled out a chocolate bar, tossing it over the island counter to me. "Dark chocolate to replenish the soul."

I almost caught it but wound up picking it up off the floor from between my feet. "Such as?"

She ripped open her own chocolate bar and bit off the corner before saying, "I think it's an extremely important and dangerous job, but it needs to be done and I'm capable of doing it. It feels like I'm making a difference."

"When did you realize you wanted to do this job?"

Some deep emotion shadowed her eyes, and she looked down at the floor. "When I was eight. I was taken into witness protection until I could testify against the person I saw murder someone. The agents saved my life, and I knew that someday I wanted to do the same for some other little girl."

Cautiously, I asked, "What about your family? Did they go with you?"

Her intense gray eyes stared at me, and I saw them harden as she resolved not to discuss it. "I'm gonna see what's taking Mike so long. You wait here."

She stalked out of the kitchen, and I felt a pang of regret for causing her pain. Talking about my family was difficult too, but they had been brutally murdered. I wondered what it was about her family that still haunted her.

I turned to gaze absently through the French glass doors into the trees. Movement caught my eye, and I twisted around to see the source of the reflection.

Jefferson walked through the kitchen, his soft steps at odds with his muscular frame. His red hair and the dusting of vibrant freckles across his cheeks and the bridge of his nose added an element of boyishness to his features, but I still tensed instinctively in response to his presence.

He smiled warmly as he stopped by the table and dropped a duffle bag onto it. "Here are your belongings from Detective Marx's apartment. He also gave me this to pass along. He called it your survival kit." He set a second duffle on the table. "I checked it over. No electronic devices or trackers. It's clean, so you can open it privately."

Privately, I silently scoffed. He had already gone through everything. There was no such thing as privacy.

I exhaled and let the undeserved bitterness float away on the air before saying, "Thank you for bringing my things."

He smiled and inclined his head before leaving the room. I plopped into one of the chairs and unzipped the "survival kit." It was stuffed full of miscellaneous items: the picture of my family, my journal, three packs of Swiss rolls, my bag of M&M's with all of the yellow and brown removed, my Bible, and a Ziploc bag of Lucky Mallows marshmallows.

There was a sticky note on the bag with a message:

I thought you might like these back. Maybe you'll think twice the next time you feel the urge to tip the pictures on my wall.

I laughed softly to myself. I pulled out the remaining objects in the bag: a brand-new sketchbook with charcoal and pastels.

Tears welled in my eyes. Marx knew how much I would struggle with this situation, and he was trying to make it easier for me. I opened the sketchbook to find a note written on the first page in Marx's messy script:

I was saving these for a special occasion, but since I won't get to see you for a while, I wanted you to have them. You're going to have a lot of time on your hands to work on your sketches. Maybe you can improve your butterflies so they don't look like they've been through a blender.

I laughed through the veil of tears as I remembered the first time he had seen and insulted one of my sketches.

I know that the next few weeks and possibly months may be hard and a little scary, but you will get through it. I'm not sure how I'll adjust to my kitchen no longer smelling like smoke without you here to burn things, but I guess I'll manage. Try not to send the safe house up in a blaze of flames. I warned them about your cooking.

"Jerk." I laughed. He was the one who overcooked the brownies.

Don't take any chances, and as much as it may go against your nature, listen to the marshals. Their only job is to keep you safe, so try not to fight them on every decision. I want you back in one piece.
~Marx~

24

Kristen brushed aside the drapes in the living room to peer out into the darkness. "Are you always this edgy?" she asked.

She let the curtain drift shut and fixed her curious gray eyes on me as I paced the length of the room. She glanced down at her watch and added, "In about ten minutes you'll have been pacing for two straight hours."

She was timing me? I frowned at her and popped a blue M&M into my mouth from the bag of candy Marx had provided.

She folded her arms. "Look, Holly, I know you're nervous, but everything's gonna be fine."

"I'm not nervous for me." I paused and then, because I tried not to lie, amended, "Okay, maybe a little, but what about Marx? He's not gonna stop, and if these people can't get to me, what are they gonna do next? They've already shot at him twice."

Kristen sat down on the arm of the couch. "He means a lot to you."

I tossed a candy up and down in my palm as I regarded her. "Maybe."

"You know, I read a little about him in an FBI case file. He and an unnamed civilian woman cracked open the serial killer case—the man suspected of killing fifty-one people across several states. The FBI is still trying to put all the pieces together."

"There was a Kansas sheriff involved too," I said, correcting her misunderstanding of events. "He actually put the pieces together long before Marx got involved."

Her lips spread into a knowing grin. "I had a feeling you were that civilian woman." When I shot her a wary look, she held up her hands in mock surrender. "Your secret's safe with me. But I am curious. Why all the secrecy? You could be famous for your part in such a large unveiling. Fan mail, supporters, interviews, talk shows. Maybe a book with your name in the title."

That sounded like a nightmare. "I never wanted any of that."

Her eyes followed my dizzying turns as I reached one wall and turned on my heel to propel myself back in the other direction. "From you, I actually believe that."

"How many deaths have they linked to the killer?" I wondered.

"They reviewed the evidence and materials provided to them, but so far they've only officially connected six of the seventeen families to Edward Billings, yours included. They have a lot more work to do. I'm surprised your detective didn't insist on being a part of the investigations."

"He's not much for media attention either."

"Or he wanted to focus on more important things," she countered, giving me an interested look. "The moment I stepped into the precinct, I got the sense that Marx is unusually protective of you considering there's no relation between you, and he didn't hand you over into my care lightly."

"I guess you better do a good job then," I half teased.

"Oh, I intend to. Failure is not in my vocabulary. Unless we're talking about college statistics courses. Those were my arch nemesis."

I smiled a little. Somehow knowing that this woman, who seemed confident and perfect in every way, had failed at something made her feel more approachable. I failed at just about everything; I was pretty sure it was just a part of my genetic code.

"As far as Marx is concerned, I wouldn't worry," she suggested. "He strikes me as a very capable cop. He's not some novice running around cluelessly on the street with a gun."

"Did you miss the part where I mentioned that they shot at him twice? And hit him both times."

"Well, it's a good thing men don't mind scars like we do," she replied with a shrug. "We all excel at something, and for him, being a cop is it. He might walk away from this mess with a few more scars, but records show he *will* walk away."

I had to trust that he would or I was going to drive myself crazy. "What do you excel at?"

"Well, if you ask my foster brother, my greatest skill is my poker face because I always beat him at cards."

Her foster brother. So something *had* happened to her family. I decided not to ask for fear it would make her uncomfortable again.

"But I'm also an excellent marksman," she continued. "I can shoot the wings off a fly from down the street with the right weapon. At everything else, I would say I'm fair to moderate."

"A fly, huh?"

A smile flickered across her lips and then vanished as she pressed her finger to the ear piece that must have been a radio. "Repeat that?" She paused to listen, and concern creased her face as she stood.

"What's the matter?" I worried.

"We have a trespasser." She strode out of the living room toward the foyer but stopped with a hand on the front door when I tried to follow her. "I need you to stay inside until I verify whether or not the trespasser is a threat," she said.

"But I wanna come with you."

"I don't think that would be wise."

"I'm not known for my wise decisions."

She quirked a small smile at that. "So I've heard. Marx did brief me on the challenges you would present."

I folded my arms and met her eyes with stubborn determination. "I'm going with you."

"For example," she said with a trace of frustration and amusement in her voice. "Just please stay behind me." She opened the door and stepped on to the front porch.

I peered around her to see the shadowy figure lying face down in the grass between Jefferson and Mike with his hands behind his back.

Jefferson tossed something to Kristen and metal glinted in the security lights. "He's got a badge."

Kristen caught the badge and turned it over in her hands thoughtfully. "And he thinks it's a free pass to do whatever he wants. Nice, but being a member of law enforcement doesn't give him a right to muck up my operation."

I tried to descend the steps to see if the prone figure was someone I knew, but Kristen blocked me with an arm.

"Easy there," she said. "Let me check him out first. You stay on the steps." She strode across the lawn toward the three men and crouched down in front of the prone figure. "How does that grass taste, sheriff?"

Sheriff? I descended one of the steps and strained to see the man on the ground without venturing into the grass. Mike and Jefferson both shook their heads at me, which made me want to step into the grass even more.

"You are a sheriff, right? Or did you buy this badge in the toy department?" Kristen asked. "We'll call it in just to be sure, not that it will make much difference."

The man grumbled something that I couldn't hear.

Kristen stood and stepped back. "Get him on his feet."

Jefferson and Mike pulled the man to his feet, and the motion sensor lights illuminated his features. Blond hair, a handsome face, and eyes narrowed in indignation.

Jordan. How had he gotten here? How had he even known where I was? I didn't even know where I was.

"I wanna see Holly," he insisted.

"I heard you the first time, but your wants really aren't my concern," she replied without sympathy.

I hopped down the last two steps and crossed the lawn to join them. Jefferson regarded my approach with uncertainty, while Mike just said, "Kris . . ."

Kristen immediately put herself between me and Jordan, but I maneuvered around her.

"What are you doing here, Jordan?" I asked.

She raised an eyebrow at me. "You know him?"

"Yeah, he's a friend."

She sized Jordan up with a swift glance and then grunted. "Right, the irritable one from the precinct. I thought he looked vaguely familiar." She nodded toward the house. "Take him inside. The *friend* and I are going to have a talk."

Mike took Jordan by the elbow and led him up to the house, while Jefferson followed behind like a watchful shadow.

Kristen turned to me. "You still have your belongings packed?"

"Yeah, why?"

"Because we may need to move to a new location. It depends on just how reckless your friend was. Come on, let's get you inside."

I walked back into the house to find Jordan seated in a chair in the kitchen, his arms still behind his back. Mike was giving him a distrustful glare.

"You look a little put out there, big guy," Jordan said with a satisfied smirk.

Lines of irritation formed around Mike's eyes. "You've got no business being smug after we took you down without a fight."

"I let you take me down. How else was I supposed to get inside to see Holly?"

Kristen grabbed a kitchen chair and dropped it in front of Jordan. She sat down, her knees almost brushing his as she faced him. Apparently she didn't have much of a personal bubble.

"How did you find us?" she asked, an unmistakable chill creeping into her voice.

"I followed the redhead," he answered simply, with a nod toward the man standing behind him.

Kristen's eyes flicked to Jefferson, whose brows drew together. He shook his head.

"We're very adept at spotting a tail," Kristen informed Jordan.

"I'm very adept at not being spotted."

She narrowed her eyes at him. "Prove it. What route did he take?"

Jordan sighed and started listing off road names and directions in a bored voice. The more he described the trip, the deeper Jefferson's frown became.

Kristen held up a hand to cut him off. "I've heard enough." She stood and paced around the table, looking contemplative.

Jordan glanced at Jefferson. "That fourth loop was completely unnecessary. Nobody was following you . . . except me."

"What did he have on him?" Kristen demanded as she looked between her team members.

"A gun and a cell phone, but the phone was off. No GPS tracking." Mike set the phone on the counter along with Jordan's gun.

Kristen picked up his phone and turned it over thoughtfully. "Did you use a GPS device that can be remotely accessed?"

"Like I said, I followed the redhead. So unless he qualifies as a GPS . . ." He shrugged.

"Did you tell anyone where you were going?"

"No."

"Is there a chance you were followed?"

Jordan gave her a flat look.

"Do you realize how much danger you put her in by coming here?" Kristen demanded, some of her irritation shining through her calm exterior.

"I would never do anything to endanger Holly, including leaving her with people she doesn't know or trust."

Kristen dropped his phone on the counter and folded her arms. "So let me get this straight. You don't trust us to protect her, so you risked giving away her location so *you* could protect her? You have a very convoluted method of ensuring her safety."

"I have a vested interest in her safety. As far as I know, she's nothing but a job to you."

Kristen tapped her foot as she glared at him. "Jefferson, check his car for any form of tracking device that he may or may not be aware of. I want to know within five minutes whether or not we need to move Holly."

Jefferson nodded and ducked out of the room without a word.

"I'm gonna take another walk around the perimeter," Mike announced. "If you're good here." He nodded specifically toward Jordan, and there was a glimmer of concern in his eyes.

Kristen smiled, and it was warmer than I had expected. "I can handle him. Let me know if you find any more uninvited guests lurking in the trees."

Mike returned her smile and left.

"So are you gonna uncuff me?" Jordan asked.

"No," Kristen said flatly. "You're under arrest for interfering with a federal case."

"Well, you can't exactly throw me in jail. You would either have to call the police to come pick me up, which would betray the safe house location, or have one of your guys transport me, which would leave Holly poorly protected. I don't think you're willing to do either."

"Make yourself comfortable, smart guy, because you're gonna be in that chair a while."

She walked over to the glass doors to look into the trees around the back of the house.

"Hey," Jordan said as I approached. "You doing okay?"

I smiled as I folded myself into one of the chairs. "I'm not the one who was just shoved facedown in the dirt."

He squinted his eyes. "You know, I've noticed that you almost never answer that question. You always manage to deflect it back to me."

I widened my eyes innocently.

He lowered his head and laughed. "Right. You're fine."

"Aren't I always?"

"Yeah, even when you're not."

He shifted in his chair, grimacing a little as he struggled to find a comfortable position, and I caught a glimpse of his bound wrists.

There was something utterly terrifying about being restrained and helpless. I remembered that feeling with unsettling clarity.

I didn't realize I was rubbing at the scars on my wrists until Jordan asked, "Are you all right?"

My eyes drifted to his, and the warm compassion that pooled in them momentarily froze me. I moved my hands to my lap beneath the table and forced a smile. "I'm fine."

He searched my face. "You don't look fine."

I pressed my lips together as I considered whether or not to share my thoughts with him. "Just thinking about . . ." I gestured to his handcuffed wrists.

Something changed in his expression, and he readjusted in his chair so the handcuffs were no longer visible. "About what happened with Edward?"

"No," I said, surprised. I hadn't been thinking about Edward at all.

"Collin?" he asked, studying me. "Did he use handcuffs when he"—my shoulders stiffened in anticipation of his next word, and he seemed to reconsider—"when he attacked you two years ago?"

My eyes fell to the table. "I don't wanna talk about that night, okay?"

Silence fell between us, and I felt a twinge of guilt. He was trying so hard to rebuild our friendship, but every time he asked me an uncomfortable question, I refused to answer, and it felt like I was pushing him back a step.

I drew in a shaky breath, hesitated, and then whispered, "He used zip ties." I swallowed the bile on the back of my tongue. "It took me six hours to finally get free."

When I looked up, Jordan's expression was clouded with pain and regret. "I'm sorry."

His sympathy made me uncomfortable, and I looked away again.

He slumped back in the chair. "I wish I could've been there to keep you safe. Not just that night, but . . . every time he hurt you."

Was that why he was here now? Because he regretted not being there to protect me then? I wasn't sure how I was supposed to feel about that.

I drew in a quick breath and said, "I'm gonna grab a snack. Do you want something?"

"Only if you're willing to feed it to me."

I paused at the unsettling thought and then slipped out of the chair before the conversation could descend any further into awkwardness. I walked to the counter to grab an apple.

"Copy, thanks. Keep me updated," Kristen said before dropping the two fingers she had pressed to the earpiece.

"Well? Does this mean we're not leaving?" I asked as I plucked an apple from the bowl.

"Not at the moment," she said, glancing over her shoulder at us. "The car's clean, but we still don't know if he was followed. Stay away from the windows and doors, and don't go anywhere in the house alone until Mike radios back that the grounds are secure."

I rummaged through the refrigerator for something Jordan could have. I pulled out a juice box. It wasn't food, but it was something. I popped the straw into the box and set it on the table in front of him as I curled back up in my chair with my apple.

He arched an eyebrow at me. "A juice box, huh? I haven't had one of these since grade school."

"Is that a complaint?"

"Nope," he smiled, leaned down, and took a sip. He grimaced as he swallowed. "Grape."

"Oh, I forgot you were never a fan of grape."

"Grape is a thousand times better than cherry. Cherry tastes like cough syrup."

I scrunched my nose at that remark. "I happen to like cherry."

He grinned. "Yeah, I know."

I rolled the apple between my hands. I had no desire to eat it; I had just needed a reason to get up from the table. "You shouldn't have come," I finally said. "Now you're in trouble with the federal government."

"I wasn't just gonna sit on my hands when I knew your life was in danger."

"Sitting with your hands in cuffs is better?"

"If it means I'm here with you, then yeah. No question."

I sighed. "It's not your job to protect me, Jordan. It never was. Not when we were kids, not when Collin . . ." I let that thought trail off as I shied away from the memories. "And not now. The last thing I want is you risking your life or your freedom out of some misguided sense of obligation or guilt."

Jordan was shaking his head before I even finished speaking. "My being here has nothing to do with obligation or guilt, Holly. I just got you back a few months ago, and I'm not about to let something happen to you."

I looked down at my apple and picked at the shiny skin with a fingernail, leaving small crescent marks across the surface.

I didn't understand why he cared so much; the little girl he once loved no longer existed. She died years ago. I was a completely different person, one with a history full of land mines.

"I can't be the girl you remember," I said. "The childhood friend you're still trying to protect. I wish I could be, but I'll never be that carefree, trusting girl who was afraid of nothing." I looked up to meet his eyes. "She's gone. So if you're hoping to get *that* person back, then—"

"She's not gone," he cut in. "*You're* not gone. You adapted to survive terrible circumstances, but you didn't lose yourself." After a moment, he added carefully, "And Collin didn't destroy you."

I closed my eyes to hold back the unexpected tears.

"Despite eighteen years and all the challenges you've faced, I still see the compassionate heart of the girl who was my best friend. You have that same determined fire that got us into so much trouble, and you still crinkle your nose when you disagree with something. And your attitude still outweighs you by fifty pounds."

That sparked a laugh and sent the tears spilling over. I wiped them away.

He smiled. "Everything about the girl I knew is still there. I just have eighteen years of catching up to do."

I tucked my lips between my teeth as I absorbed his words. "Thank you," I said quietly.

"For what?"

"For . . . caring, I guess."

One side of his mouth curled in amusement. "You realize you don't actually have to thank me for that."

I shrugged and stared awkwardly at the table. "It takes some getting used to, and I'm . . . trying. It means a lot that you care despite the fact that I keep almost getting you killed."

"That's not exactly how I remember it. More like trouble keeps finding you, and I happen to be there."

Happen to be there? Really?

"You have a very strange idea of . . ." I bit off my words when Kristen stiffened by the glass doors, her attention fixing on something outside.

She drew her gun and backed away slowly as she touched her earpiece. "I have a possible intruder on the south side of the property."

Jordan straightened. "What?"

"Holly, this is that moment we discussed," Kristen announced as she flipped off the kitchen light, leaving the inside of the house murky with darkness, while the outside glowed with security lights.

Fear threaded through me. I grabbed Jordan's phone off the counter in case I needed to call for help and whispered, "We have to go. Upstairs."

Jordan stood and moved with me, putting himself between me and the glass doors despite the fact that he was unarmed and bound.

"Stop that," I scolded. "They have no intention of killing me. We'd both be safer if I was standing in front of you."

"Yeah, I don't like that plan."

When Kristen snapped her gun up, he shoved me into the wall with his shoulder. I heard the gunshot a split second before the glass shattered.

A man outside the window lurched forward with his gun still raised, and then tumbled down the slope onto the lawn.

25

Kristen crept forward across the broken glass to check the gunman who had landed facedown on the ground. She nudged him over onto his back while keeping her gun trained on him.

She studied his face for a moment and then her hand went to the earpiece. "We're compromised," she said in a low voice. "Keep an eye on the trees, gentlemen. They're probably crawling."

She took her own advice: backing through the doorway with her weapon fixed on the trees. She cast Jordan a venomous glare as she passed him. "We need to move. Now." She all but dragged me out of the kitchen and into the hallway.

"Who was that guy?" I asked.

She moved down the hallway ahead of me on light toes, and I strove to tread with equal softness between her and Jordan.

"Darnell, the enforcer you identified as one of your attempted kidnappers. If he's here, the rest aren't far behind," she answered without looking back at me. Her attention was fully focused on the hallway ahead of us.

Fear sparked in my chest, and I looked up at Jordan. He drew in an uneasy breath and said, "It's gonna be okay." But I saw the glitter of fear in his eyes.

"That wasn't very convincing," I murmured back, and he pressed his lips together. He was unarmed and handcuffed; he was completely defenseless if the enforcers breached the house.

"Uncuff me and let me have my gun. I can help."

"You're the reason we're in this mess. I'm not doing you any favors." She pressed a hand to her earpiece and asked quietly, "How's my perimeter looking, guys?"

She paused to listen and then winced when the sound of gunshots crackled through the earpiece loudly enough for us to hear. Jordan and I turned back toward the shots that echoed off the trees around the back of the house.

Kristen readjusted her earpiece and called out, "Mike. Jefferson."

Glass shattered somewhere in front of us, and Kristen returned both hands to her gun as she stilled, listening. A quiet thump announced someone crawling through a window, followed by the soft crunch of footsteps.

They were inside the house.

Kristen inched forward to the edge of the hallway. She jerked back abruptly, and plaster exploded an inch from her face as a bullet bit through the corner of the wall.

"Back up," she instructed, and Jordan and I shuffled backwards.

Kristen leaned forward a fraction and snapped back to avoid a second bullet. It sank into the wall adjacent to us. If it hadn't, I wouldn't have seen the shadow stretching into the hall from the kitchen.

Someone was behind us.

I wasn't sure if it was one of Kristen's people or one of the intruders.

"Kristen," I whispered urgently.

Her attention shifted to me and then slid past me to the shadow just as a man stepped into the hallway. It definitely wasn't one of her people.

I saw the glint of his gun a split second before she barked, "Down!"

I clamped my hands over my ears and dropped to a crouch next to Jordan a second before she fired. He curled his body over me protectively, and fear stabbed my heart when I heard the gunman squeeze off a single wild shot before collapsing.

"Jordan," I gasped, afraid he'd been hit.

"I'm fine." I felt rather than heard the rumble of his words from his chest as I huddled against him. I uncurled just in time to see the first shooter plow into Kristen from behind and take her to the floor. Her gun skidded across the living room floor and disappeared beneath the couch.

She rolled around on the floor with the man in a tangle of jerking limbs before he managed to twist on top of her. I saw the confusion register in his expression the moment he saw her face.

"You're not the one I'm looking for."

"Yeah, I hear that a lot," she muttered.

When he pointed his gun at her head, she grabbed his arm, wrapped a leg around his neck, and flipped him onto his back. She jerked his arm, and he let out a howl of pain as something snapped. The gun dropped from his fingers.

The man kicked up at her, and she released his arm as she rolled out of the way. He staggered to his feet as her rolling retreat brought her gracefully to hers.

Jordan sat down and quickly maneuvered his bound arms under his legs so that his hands were in front of him. "I'm going for the gun," he whispered to me. "Stay down." He slunk carefully down the hall toward the dead intruder.

I crouched there, unsure what to do. I watched Kristen dip beneath her opponent's brutal swing and then land a kick to his midsection that knocked him back. I wished I knew how to fight like that.

I was so focused on the scuffle that I didn't see the third man until it was too late. He came around the corner and caught me by the arm before I could do anything more than suck in a frightened breath.

"Jordan!" I screamed, fighting to break free as the man wrenched me toward him.

Jordan's head snapped up from the body in the hallway, and he shot to his feet, bringing his gun up to aim at the man who was trying to drag me from the room.

My captor, who was scarcely taller than I was, hauled me in front of him as a shield, and Jordan hesitated. I cringed as pain shattered my eardrums when the man pulled the trigger. Jordan dove into the kitchen.

I twisted violently as the man dragged me through the living room and into the foyer. He snapped something at me, but the ringing in my ears drowned out his voice. I got the message, though, when he shifted his grip to my waist and picked me up: stop slowing me down. He carried me through the foyer toward the open front door.

I planted my feet against the frame. I was not going out that door.

I kicked off with every ounce of force my legs could muster, and sent both of us tumbling to the floor. I landed on top of him, and he let out a breathless cough.

Before I could scramble off him, he rolled, and I let out a frantic shriek as his weight pressed me into the floorboards. I clawed for the gun that had slipped from his fingers on impact, but it was out of reach.

Then his weight was suddenly gone. I rolled over and looked up just in time to see Jordan wrap an arm around the man's neck and squeeze. The man flailed, gasping for breath.

I stared into his frightened eyes and swallowed. I had been in that position before with Collin, and I could empathize. After what felt like agonizingly long minutes but was probably only seconds, the man went limp. Jordan dropped him carelessly onto the floor as Kristen came in. She looked a little unsteady on her feet, but she was still in one piece.

"Okay," she exhaled. "I know when to give in." She pulled a small silver key from her pocket and tossed it to Jordan.

"Thanks." He uncuffed himself and rolled the unconscious man over onto his face before handcuffing his wrists together. "How'd your guy fare?"

She grimaced. "He won't be needing any handcuffs." She offered a hand to me and pulled me to my feet with a small wince. She must have been hurt, but I didn't see any obvious injuries. "You all right?"

"Fine, thanks."

"Good." Her eyes flicked to the figure lying on the front stoop, and she froze.

I couldn't see the man's face from where I stood, but I recognized the uniform. It was one of her people. She crossed the foyer and crouched along the inside wall.

She pressed two fingers to the neck of the motionless male figure, and I saw the fine mist of tears that collected in her eyes before she blinked.

"Good-bye, Mike," she whispered, and I heard the anguish in her voice. She kissed two fingers and pressed them to his lips.

She collected his radio earpiece, gun, and cuffs before rising. "Let's go." She tossed the earpiece to Jordan. "I assume the offer to help still stands."

Jordan nodded once as he pressed the earpiece into his right ear.

"Good. I'm at least one man down, so I appreciate the backup."

The lights overhead abruptly went out, and I heard a curse slip from Kristen's lips. She stepped closer to me, and I saw the silhouette of her gun as she angled it toward the open front door.

"You got her?" she asked.

I didn't understand the question, but Jordan answered. "Yeah, I got her." He started up the steps, which were awash with shadows from the exterior lights. "Come on, Holly."

I hesitated, confused. "Kristen, aren't you coming?"

"No. Get to the safe room and call for help."

"But . . . what about you? What are you gonna do?"

"What I do best. Shoot the wings off flies." She gave me a gentle, backwards shove toward the steps and whispered with urgency, "Now go."

Jordan caught my arm and started pulling me up the steps before I could decide what to do. I stumbled before righting myself.

We sprinted down the hallway toward my designated safe room. The sound of male voices rising up from the lower level drew me up short on the threshold, and I turned to look back.

Kristen was going to get herself killed. I didn't care how good of a shot she was or how mind-boggling her self-defense skills were, she was only one person.

Jordan stepped between me and the stairwell, as if he intended to physically block me from running back down the steps.

"She knows what she's doing. Going back down there won't help her."

The male voices grew louder, and I reluctantly retreated into the small bedroom.

Jordan closed the door soundlessly behind us and locked it. I pointed to the sliding lock I couldn't reach at the top of the door, and he slid that into place too.

I pulled his cell phone from my back pocket and sat down against the far wall. The glow of the screen was almost blinding in the darkness when it powered on, but then it turned black.

Did I break it?

I turned the smartphone over in my hands, trying to turn it back on. Where were all the buttons?

Jordan reached over and pressed a fingertip to the screen. The phone came to life with a simple touch. It was one of those phones with the virtual buttons. That was dumb. My phone had real buttons.

He brought up a text message box for Marx, and I typed a brief message:

It's Holly. Bad guys are in safe house. Help.

I wanted so badly to hear his voice, to feel the small measure of comfort it would bring me, but it wasn't worth the risk.

I glanced at Jordan and saw a frown darken his face. He cocked his head, as if he were listening to something. Someone must have been speaking into the earpiece.

"What?" I whispered.

He pulled the earpiece out of his ear and handed it to me. I tucked it into my ear and stiffened at the familiar voice that spoke.

"And I know there's one more of you. You're outnumbered five to one, but you don't have to die. We just want the girl."

Snake—the leader of the group who had come for me on the sidewalk. A sinking sense of dread filled my stomach as I looked at Jordan. He had humiliated the man during their last altercation, and I had no doubt Snake would kill him if he had the chance.

A text message flashed across the screen of the phone:

Where are you? Are you okay? How many of
them are there?

I had no idea where I was. I strained to remember any details that might help him find us, but nothing came to mind. I handed the phone to Jordan, and he read the message. He had recounted nearly the entire route that Jefferson had taken to get here. He could tell Marx how to find us.

After he texted the directions, he looked at me and mouthed, "How many do you think there are?"

I held up five fingers and then pointed to the earpiece. He stared at me, and I saw that faint sparkle of fear in his eyes again. We were severely outnumbered.

"We ain't gonna hurt her." Snake's voice crackled through the radio. "Just bring her out and nobody else has to get hurt."

I thought about Mike lying dead on the stoop, and the tears in Kristen's eyes. He had been more than a coworker to her, and he had died trying to protect me. Jefferson was probably dead. I didn't want anyone else to die for me.

My life wasn't worth that.

I looked at the door, considering whether or not to hand myself over to prevent more bloodshed.

My insides shivered at the thought of being taken by Snake and his men. I had no idea what they would do to me.

But Marx would drop the investigation, and then he would be safe. Jordan would be safe. I looked at him—my friend—and knew I couldn't risk his life. There were too many men, and he would never survive a confrontation.

"Come out, little mouse!" a man bellowed from somewhere closer than the bottom of the steps. Jordan's head snapped up, eyes locking on the door. "Come on out and no one else has to die!"

My heart thumped against my ribs. I started to stand, but Jordan caught my forearm and pulled me back down.

He shook his head—he wouldn't let me leave this room—and if I fought him, it would draw them here, and he would die anyway.

"Please," I mouthed silently.

He shook his head again, his expression uncompromising. There was nothing I could say or do to change his mind, so I relaxed back against the wall.

His eyes narrowed suspiciously at my easy compliance, but he released my arm. He gestured for me to give him the earpiece back, and angled the phone toward me. There was a new message from Marx:

> On my way, and there are three squad cars en-route. Stay put. And don't let Holly do anything reckless.

I frowned at that last comment. I wasn't reckless. When was I ever—

Several more gunshots echoed through the night, and I flinched. If Kristen was the only one still alive out there, then it had to be her they were shooting at. Or was she shooting at them?

I was tempted to peek through the window to see what was happening, but that probably qualified as reckless. Someone might see me, and that would give away our hiding place.

Jordan typed something but didn't send it through. He handed me the phone so I could read and answer the question:

> You okay?
> Fine. Just a little nervous.

His playful reply brought a small smile to my lips:

> Chicken.
> Not a chicken. Don't make me kick you in the shin.

He arched an eyebrow and replied with,

> bring it on, sneaky ninja.

"She's here somewhere," an unfamiliar male voice announced from the hallway, and my breath caught.

I typed on the phone as I angled it toward Jordan:

> *You should hide in the closet. They don't know*
> *you're here.*

He shook his head, and I wanted to yell at him that it wasn't his job to protect me. My fingers fumbled on the fancy touch screen as I tried to type quickly.

> *If you hide in the closet, you can catch them by*
> *surprise when they—*

A loud crack down the hall made my fingers freeze on the keyboard. It sounded like wood snapping. I didn't need to finish the sentence because they had just finished it for me.

Jordan looked conflicted by my suggestion. I knew he would rather shield me with his body, but they would shoot him the moment they saw him. They wanted me alive.

He took the phone from me and wrote:

> *If something goes wrong, remember our self-*
> *defense training. And don't be afraid to bite . .*
> *. hard.*

He stood soundlessly and moved to the closet, concealing himself behind the sliding door. I sent Marx a quick message:

> *They're coming. Calling you. Don't speak.*

If something went wrong like Jordan feared, I wanted Marx to know exactly what had happened, but I didn't want them to know he was listening. If they took me, maybe they would give something away that would help him find me. I caught his quick reply before I called him and turned off the screen:

> *Ok. I'll be there soon.*

"Empty," a man announced.

Another loud crack, but this one was closer. They were kicking down doors one by one to check the rooms. I heard the third one give way, and then the doorknob to my room jiggled. My heart skipped in terror, and I slid the phone into my back pocket as I came to my feet.

Something slammed against the door, and I flinched. Grumbling curses arose as the door held firm, and then something slammed into it again. It splintered under the impact and flew open, crashing into the dresser nearest to it.

I hugged the wall as a man shoved his way into the room. His irritation gave way to delight when his eyes landed on me. "Well, look what we have here," he said, his tongue flicking out to lick his pierced lower lip.

The man with the serpent tattoo on his face stepped into the room after him. Snake's eyes slithered over me in amusement. "I told you we'd pay you another visit, ginger, and I said you wasn't gonna like it."

26

My heart thundered in my ears as I slid along the wall to avoid the man with the pierced lip. The way he looked at me made my throat constrict in fear.

"Stay away from me."

The gun twitched eagerly in his hand. I had thought they wanted me alive, but he looked very much like he had other ideas about that.

"We need her breathing," Snake reminded his partner, sounding bored.

Pierce—for lack of a better name—hesitated and then moistened his lower lip again. "You're mine later."

He reached forward to grab me and then swayed suddenly as a gunshot cut through the room. I watched the shocked expression slide off his face as blood blossomed on his chest, and then he collapsed in a heap on the floor.

Snake let out a string of curses and immediately ducked out of the room. The bullet Jordan had meant for him splintered the empty dresser along the wall.

"Holly, get down," Jordan demanded. He slid out of the closet and crept slowly toward the doorway. "And stay here."

I hunkered down in the closet. It wasn't the rapid pop of gunfire that made my heart race, but the unbearable stretches of silence in between.

I knew it only took one bullet to end a life, and I prayed that every stretch of silence didn't mean one of them had hit Jordan.

When it was quiet for too long, anxiety and worry drove me from my hiding place. I peered out into the empty hallway before creeping along the wall toward the stairwell. I peered around the corner, and my heart twisted in my chest at the sight below.

Jordan lay unmoving at the bottom of the steps. A figure crouched over him, but it wasn't Snake. I must have made a noise, because the man stood and whirled around, snapping his gun up in my direction.

I froze, and so did he.

The security lights filtering through the open doorway illuminated half of his face. I had only met him twice before, but I recognized Sam's partner, and relief swept through me. Help had arrived.

"Danny?" I called out.

He lowered his gun instantly. "Holly, is that you?"

"Is it safe to come down?" I was pretty sure the body lying on the floor next to Jordan was Snake, but it was too dark to be certain.

He looked around. "Yeah, for the moment."

I darted down the steps toward Jordan. I hesitated when I had to step over the man Jordan had choked unconscious and handcuffed. He wasn't unconscious anymore. He was dead.

Had one of his own people shot him in the head? I was almost positive Kristen wouldn't do something like that, and I knew Jordan wouldn't.

I sank to my knees beside Jordan and scanned him for injuries. It was too dark to tell if he'd been shot.

"Jordan." I shook him, but he didn't stir. "Jordan, please wake up." When Danny crouched down on the other side of him, I demanded, "What happened?"

"I don't know. I came in when I heard the gunshots, and he was already on the floor." He glanced at Snake, who was lying a few feet away. "That guy was about to put a bullet in his head."

I shook Jordan again.

"Holly," Danny said, wrapping a gentle hand around my wrist. "We need to go. More of these guys are gonna crawl out of the woodwork. We have to get you someplace safe."

I jerked my arm away from him. "No. No, I'm not leaving him."

"He's got a strong pulse. He's gonna be fine."

"You can't be sure of that. If more of these people come and he's just lying here unable to defend himself, they'll . . ."

I got my first good look at Danny when I lifted my head to argue with him, and my words fell away. He was dressed in jeans and a light jacket with sneakers.

"Where's your uniform?"

"At home," he said simply. "I was on a plainclothes assignment when I heard the call over the radio."

Suspicion threaded through me, but it took me a moment to realize why. "No, you weren't. Sam couldn't stay and say good-bye to me because he had to go out on patrol with you. I saw you leave the precinct with him in your uniform."

I stood slowly and took a small, wary step back from him.

"Yes, but then we were called back in because I was needed for a discreet assignment, which is why I drove an unmarked car instead of the squad car, and I'm wearing plain clothes instead of my uniform, which would kinda stand out," he explained as he stood.

He slid his gun into its holster and held out his hands in a pacifying gesture so similar to the one Sam had used with me at the warehouse that it gave me pause.

"Look, I get that you've been through a lot and you're probably not sure who to trust right now, but I'm Sam's partner, Holly. You know he doesn't trust many people, but he trusts me with his life every day. So please trust me to take you someplace safe. We can call Marx on the way to let him know you're okay."

I knew that if Sam trusted him, I could probably trust him with my life, but my instincts rebelled at that thought. "No," I finally decided. "I'm not leaving Jordan."

A flicker of frustration crossed his face. "You have to be a stubborn snot about everything, don't you?"

His words and the icy tone of voice startled me. He reached out and snatched my wrist in a painful grip, yanking me toward him.

"Hey!"

"We're leaving, whether you like it or not."

"Let go of me!"

I tried to tug my wrist free, and when his fingers only tightened, I fisted my imprisoned hand, grabbed it, and thrust

318

through his thumb the way Jordan and Sam had taught me. He was as surprised as I was when I stumbled away from him.

I hadn't actually expected that to work.

We stared at each other for a fraction of a second, uncertainty hanging between us like a visible thread, before I came to my senses. I darted into the den that doubled as an office, and he chased after me.

I screamed when he tackled me into one of the upholstered chairs. It toppled backwards, spilling us into a tangled heap on the floor. I thrashed wildly, trying to escape, and I heard his grunt of pain as my elbow connected with his stomach.

I scrambled to my hands and knees, but he gripped a fistful of my hair and ripped me back down when I tried to stand. I let out a squeak of surprised pain.

"Don't make this harder than it has to be, Holly," he advised, sounding a little breathless. "It won't go well for you." He stood and pulled me to my feet by my hair.

What little bit of self-defense training I received had been from a cop. How was I supposed to use it to defend myself against another cop? I clawed at his hand, trying to free myself.

"Quit struggling," he demanded, twisting his hand in my hair until I winced. "You're only gonna hurt yourself."

I threw another elbow into his stomach, and he grunted out of anger more than pain.

"Knock it off."

"Let go!" I cried out as he dragged me back toward the foyer. He stumbled over my feet, which I intentionally put in his path to trip him.

"I said stop struggling!"

With one hand still tangled in my hair, he slammed my head into the nearest door frame. Pain splintered through my skull, and a wave of dizziness swept over me.

I didn't remember sliding to the floor, but that's where I found myself in the next instant—back flat against the wall with something warm and wet dripping down my forehead into my eyes.

I blinked at the blurry figure who crouched in front of me.

"Great," he exhaled, rubbing a hand over his face. "Now he's gonna be ticked. All this could've been so much easier if you just would've gone to dinner with me. But no, you had to be difficult, forcing me to make other arrangements."

I didn't understand, and it must have shown in my expression, because he explained, "You didn't really think that meeting on the sidewalk with Snake and his guys was a coincidence, did you? You weren't coming with me willingly, and I couldn't exactly kidnap you from the precinct."

He pulled his handcuffs from his belt and grabbed my right wrist, dragging it away from my forehead.

Fresh fear cut through my foggy thoughts when I realized his intentions, and I tried to jerk away from him. He snapped the cuff onto my wrist with minimal effort, and the feeling of it against my skin sent tendrils of panic through me. I couldn't be restrained and helpless again.

"No," I pleaded. "Please . . ."

"I'm not gonna hurt you," he said, then paused, seeming to remember it was a bit late for that promise, and amended, "Again. I'm not gonna hurt you again as long as you cooperate with me."

"Please no handcuffs," I begged, tears burning across my vision. I tucked my left arm behind me, trying to keep it away from him. "I'll cooperate."

He sighed in irritation and wrestled my arm out from behind my back. "Somehow I doubt that." He snapped the cuff into place.

The nearly overwhelming fear squeezed my lungs. "Please take them off." I twisted my wrists frantically, trying to wrench free.

"You're afraid of handcuffs but you're friends with three cops? That's gotta be an irony," he mused, and then added mockingly, "But you don't like cops, you don't *date* cops. I think you're a stuck-up little liar."

Tears threatened to spill over, and I had to fight them back. If I didn't focus my mind on something other than the metal around my wrists, I was going to have a panic attack.

"You did something to Jordan, didn't you?"

Danny glanced over his shoulder at Jordan's motionless body. "I probably should've just shot him. I really don't like that guy. He's always getting in the way. But I just clipped him on the back of the head with my gun. He'll have a headache, but he'll be fine." He looked me over and asked, "You have a phone or weapon on you?"

I pressed my lips together and shook my head.

His eyes narrowed suspiciously, and his gaze slid back to Jordan. "I wouldn't put it past him to have given you a phone or a knife, and I'm not about to be tracked, maced, or stabbed."

He reached for my legs, and my heart leaped into my throat. "What are you doing?" I protested anxiously, pulling my knees into my chest.

"Frisking you for weapons or a phone. Sit still and it'll be quick and painless."

I shook my head. "No."

"What happened to 'I'll cooperate'?" he asked with a sneer.

"I don't want you touching me. Ever."

His jaw hardened, and I knew I must have wounded his pride. Not only did I not want him running his hands all over my body, I didn't want him finding the phone in my back pocket. I needed that connection to Marx.

I gasped when he grabbed my ankle and wrenched up my pant leg. He searched inside the top of my sock and then did the same with my other leg. I kicked at him, but he batted my foot aside.

He shot me an impatient glare. "Keep it up and we're gonna do this with you facedown on the floor and my knee in your back."

When his hands moved up my legs, I screamed and tried to squirm away from him. He slapped a hand over my mouth and looked around nervously. Was there still someone on the premises that worried him? Was Kristen still unaccounted for?

"Do that again and I'll gag you," he said.

I sank my teeth into his pinky, and he jerked his hand back with a yelp of pain. I spat the taste of his blood from my mouth.

"You bit me, you little . . ." He drew back a hand to hit me, and I ducked my head between my arms. He must have changed his mind at the last second, because the blow never landed. "You're lucky I don't hit girls."

He grabbed the chain of the handcuffs and yanked me to my feet by my wrists. I clenched my teeth against a whimper of pain.

"I don't have time to fight with you on this. I'll just have to pull off the road and frisk you later before we get to our destination."

He gripped my waist instead of my arm this time, apparently determined not to let me wrench free again. I squirmed and tried to peel his fingers away, but he only dug them in deeper, drawing another wince of pain from me.

"And if you pull any more of that biting and kicking crap on the way to the car, I'm gonna put a bullet in pretty boy's head. Understand?"

My eyes snapped to Jordan's motionless body, and I remembered the venom in Danny's earlier statement: "I probably should've just shot him." I wouldn't give him a reason.

"You know, it's a shame it had to work out this way," he said, his suddenly flirtatious tone at odds with the way he roughly dragged me toward the door. "We could've had a nice evening together."

Sure . . . right up until you knocked me out and stuffed me into the trunk of your car.

"We could've had a delicious homemade meal, maybe a little dessert." His gaze swept over me, and I recognized the unsettling hunger I had seen in his eyes at the precinct. It made my stomach lurch with dread.

"The plan was flawless," he continued. "A little something in your drink to help you relax for the road trip, and you would've just fallen asleep. From there, all it would've taken was a convincing story about your abduction by thugs that I unfortunately couldn't save you from. None of this had to happen."

I locked my legs as he tried to walk me out the front door. He lifted me up just enough to carry me over the threshold and down the steps.

"Out of curiosity, where did I go wrong with the dinner thing? Too forward?" He paused, but I didn't answer. "Another guy? It can't be that I'm not your type. I'm a cop and I'm a good-looking guy. And I know I'm charming."

Was he serious right now? He wanted to know why I had rejected him?

"Or do you think you're too good for me?" Old bitterness tainted the question, and I could see it in his eyes when he glared down at me. "Is that it? You think you're better than me?"

He squeezed my waist tightly when I didn't answer, and I bit back a pained whimper.

"I don't usually date guys who slam my head into walls," I said, trying to loosen his viciously tight grip across my stomach.

"That was your fault. I tried to make this easier on you, but you don't like the easy way. You're lucky I'm not like these guys." He gestured to the body of one of the enforcers we stepped over. "They would've hit you back and then some, so why don't you show a little appreciation."

Appreciation, I scoffed silently. He was trying to abduct me. "How did you even find me? I thought safe houses were supposed to be—"

"Safe?" he said with amusement. "No place is ever truly safe, Holly. All it took was one very small tracker hidden on the underside of the marshals' car while they were in the precinct parking lot. Led us right to you. They think they're so much smarter than the rest of us."

So it hadn't been Jordan who led them here. Danny was responsible for the bodies scattered across the lawn and inside the house.

"People died because of you."

"No, they died because of you," he shot back. "If you'd accepted my invitation when I offered it, all of these people would still be alive."

The thought made me sick. Could I have prevented all of this if I had simply agreed to have dinner with him? If I had just gone willingly?

"Where are you taking me?"

"A place you'll probably be a while, since Marx doesn't know when to back off."

"You don't have to do this. Let me talk to him, and maybe I can get him to drop the case," I pleaded.

"He won't drop the case. I know Marx. Unless he has a good incentive—like the well-being of someone he cares about—he doesn't back down."

They were going to hold me over his head to ensure he backed off the investigation. For how long? Would they even keep me alive, or just kill me and lead Marx to believe there was still hope?

I dug in my heels as we approached the car, trying to slow Danny down and buy myself a few more minutes.

He yanked me forward impatiently. "Come on, Holly, don't make me hurt you again."

"Like you care."

"I do. I don't *want* to hurt you, but I'll do what needs to be done."

"And the others?"

He shrugged a shoulder. "I'll do what I can to keep them in check while I'm around, but I have a pretty busy job, so all I can promise is that they won't kill you."

Fear trickled down to my toes. "And you're okay with that? Aren't you supposed to be one of the good guys?"

He looked down at me. "I am one of the good guys. I put my life on the line for people who don't deserve it every day, and do you think I get rewarded for it? No. I get a measly paycheck, hate from half the community, and criticism from the other. No gratitude."

I tried to pull away from him, and he crushed me tighter against him. "Stop it." He popped the trunk of his car, and I redoubled my efforts to escape. I couldn't go into that cramped, dark space.

He wrapped both arms around my waist and hoisted me up to stuff me into the trunk. I planted my feet on the car and pushed back as I screamed for help, hoping someone would hear me.

"Why can't you just . . ."—he grunted in frustration—"go in the trunk!" He shoved harder, and I pushed back.

I was not going in that trunk without a fight. He was going to have to knock me out to get me in there, which unfortunately I didn't think he would lose any sleep over.

"It's a short trip. I promise."

A maroon car sped into the drive and skidded to a stop in front of Danny's vehicle, blocking him in. Danny swore and jerked me back from the car. He wrapped an arm around my body, gripping my shoulder and holding me flush against him. My breath caught when I felt the metal barrel of the gun press against my temple.

Marx stepped out of the car and snapped his gun up in one fluid movement. "What are you doin', Daniel?"

Jordan staggered out of the house with one hand pressed to the back of his head and the other gripping his gun. He looked pale and dazed. Confusion flashed across his face when he saw Danny holding a gun to my head.

"Stop!" Danny barked when Marx inched forward. He jammed the gun into my temple, and shivers of fear flowed through me.

Marx stilled. "You don't wanna hurt her, Daniel. She's just an innocent girl. Let her go."

Danny laughed. "I'm not an idiot, Marx. The moment I let her go, you and Mr. Overprotective here are gonna fill me full of holes."

Jordan seemed to have shaken off his lingering confusion and disorientation, and he had his gun trained on Danny.

"Nobody has to die today," Marx said.

"Oh, plenty of people died today. There's a house full of dead people. I don't plan on being one of them. Let me and Holly get in my car and drive off, and I promise she gets to live."

Marx's jaw tightened. "I'm not lettin' you take her."

"Then we have a problem, because I'm not letting her go so you can shoot me."

"I could shoot you right now if I wanted to, Daniel," Marx said, keeping his voice level.

Danny squeezed me tighter against his body. "I doubt you would risk that. You care about her too much."

"You're nearly six feet tall. You chose a barely-five-foot hostage," Marx pointed out. "I could shoot you in the head between one breath and the next."

Danny shifted nervously. "You won't do it. You could hit her accidentally, and I don't think you could live with yourself if you kill her."

"Can you?"

"I can live with a lot for the right amount of money."

"Money. That's what this is about?" Marx asked with disgust. "That's why you have a gun to that girl's head?"

I swallowed uncomfortably when Danny's arm tightened across my body.

"No, I have a gun to her head because you have a gun to *my* head," Danny sneered. "Is this the part where you offer to put your gun down if I put my gun down?"

"I'm not puttin' my gun down." Marx's eyes captured mine briefly and then shifted back to Danny's. "Because as much as I like zebras . . ."

I missed whatever lay at the end of that sentence, because my mind flashed back to the moment in the bathroom of Marx's apartment when he told me we needed a "trigger word" so that we both knew he was about to pull the trigger, and he was waiting for me to duck.

Danny was speaking when my mind returned to the present. "Never pictured you as a zebra print kind of guy, M—"

I followed every step of the escape maneuver I had practiced with Jordan, and I was still silently praying it would work when I slipped free of Danny's grip and hit the ground, a second before a series of gunshots rang out.

Danny crumpled behind me, and I scrambled through the gravel driveway to put distance between us.

Jordan kicked the gun from Danny's hand and rolled the gasping man onto his stomach to cuff his wrists behind his back.

I had seen a man die from gunshot wounds before, but that didn't make watching it a second time any easier. I could hear the wet rattle of Danny's breathing as his lungs filled with blood.

Marx holstered his gun, then slipped his hands under my arms and hefted me to my feet. My legs folded beneath me as my head swam with dizziness, but he caught me and propped me up against his car.

"Get them off. Please," I pleaded, thrusting my wrists toward him. He pulled a small key from his pocket and unhooked the handcuffs.

"You're okay now," he said soothingly.

Okay . . .

Danny had been prepared to shoot me, and there was a house full of dead bodies, lives snuffed out over money. Over me. I was anything but okay. I stared at the man barely clinging to life as my mind tried to process it all.

Marx brushed the hair back from my face. "Who hurt you?"

I touched my forehead with trembling fingers and stared at the slick redness that coated them as I pulled them away. A mixture of shock and amusement colored my response. "Would you believe me if I said I bumped into a door?"

His expression darkened. "Did Daniel help you bump into that door?"

I gave him a shaky smile. "Technically it was a door frame."

He released a tense breath. "We'll get it looked at, but right now we need to move. There could be more of them on the way."

How could there possibly be more?

He turned to Jordan. "I need you to stay here. Backup will be here any minute, and they need to know what happened."

Jordan's gaze shifted to me as he stood, and then he looked back at Marx. "I'm not—"

"I need to get her somewhere safe. Now. I don't have time to argue with you."

"Kristen," I said, with sudden worry. "She's still here somewhere and she might be hurt. Jordan . . ."

He gritted his teeth before saying, "I'll find her."

Marx settled me into the passenger seat of his car and then slid behind the wheel. I caught Jordan's worried gaze as we peeled out of the driveway and onto the back road.

27

"Where are we going?" I asked as we drove down an unfamiliar street.

Marx glanced in the rearview mirror, and his eyes narrowed at the headlights that appeared out of the darkness behind us.

He slowed to twenty miles per hour, and one hand fell to rest on his gun as the vehicle closed the distance between us.

I gripped the handle on the passenger side as I twisted around in my seat. The headlights pressed in on the rear of the car, and I could feel Marx's tension. Could this be more of the enforcers he had mentioned?

I held my breath as the headlights gave way to a truck. It swerved over the line to our left, and then cut in front of us. It sped up and disappeared down the road.

Marx's fingers relaxed on the steering wheel. "The only safe place I can think of at the moment," he finally said, in answer to my question.

"But if they've been following us for the past month, studying our movements, they're gonna know every place we can think of."

"I haven't been here in the past month." He returned both hands to the steering wheel. "I haven't been here since summer, and I don't know where else to go."

"Where?"

"Matt's house."

He was taking me to Captain McNera's house? I thought about the man who had been in tears due to some bad news in the family the last time I'd seen him. "I don't think we should go there. What if they follow us? Won't that put him and his family in danger?"

"You let me worry about that."

A few minutes later, we pulled into the driveway of a two-story house set back from the road. I followed Marx up the front steps onto a wraparound porch and sank weak-kneed into a chair that rested against the railing.

He pounded on the frame of the screen door with the side of his fist. "Matt!" He waited a beat before pounding and calling for his friend again.

I bent forward, resting my head on my knees. It felt like there was a thunderstorm booming around between my ears, and I couldn't seem to shake off the dizziness.

"How's your head?" Marx asked.

I offered him a thumbs-up and heard him sigh. He pounded on the door again, but he didn't shout this time. My head was grateful for that.

I looked up when I heard a dead bolt snap, and the front door wrenched inward. A shadowed figure filled the opening, and fear gripped me when my eyes snagged on the gun aimed at Marx's chest through the screen door.

There was a beat of breath-stealing uncertainty before the gun lowered and Captain McNera exhaled, "Holy mother of . . ." He flipped on the light just inside the door, and the dull yellow glow illuminated his tired, lined face. "Do you have any idea what time it is, Rick?"

"I'm sorry, sir, but we have a problem," Marx said. "The safe house was breached."

Captain McNera blinked, his sluggish mind apparently struggling to come to terms with that news at one a.m. "When?"

"About an hour ago."

"Casualties?"

Marx nodded but didn't elaborate. "Can we discuss the details inside?"

"Right, of course." Captain McNera opened the screen door to invite him in. "Helen's at some kind of women's retreat with the church, so we can talk freely in the kitchen. I'll make some coffee."

Marx helped me to my feet despite my assurances that I was fine, and I saw Captain McNera's eyes widen a fraction in surprise. He hadn't noticed me sitting there in the dark.

"I got her out," Marx explained.

"When you said the safe house was breached, I thought the worst," he admitted. He placed a gentle hand on my shoulder, and I stiffened at the unexpected contact. "I'm glad you're okay, kiddo."

He gestured us inside, and Marx led me into the kitchen. He pulled out a chair at the table and demanded, "Sit before you fall over."

I plopped into the chair with a half-hearted protest. "I'm not gonna fall over. I'm fine." Aside from the pain ricocheting around inside my skull, which I wasn't about to admit to.

"You're a bad liar." He opened a drawer and pulled out a washcloth as if he were in his own kitchen, then held it under the faucet.

"I didn't see any suspicious vehicles in my driveway," Captain McNera said as he strode into the kitchen. "Any chance you were followed?"

"I'd like to think not, but there's always a chance," Marx admitted reluctantly. He drew up a chair in front of me and sat down. "Let's see how bad it is." He brushed my hair aside and dabbed gently around the gash on my forehead.

"What happened to your head?" Captain McNera asked, his expression pinched with concern. He must have just noticed the blood trickling down my face. I had tried to wipe it away—it was all over the sleeves of my purple T-shirt—but it continued to flow.

"Daniel got a little rough," Marx explained irritably.

Captain McNera frowned. "Daniel who?"

Marx sighed, and I caught the glimmer of conflicting emotions in his eyes before he said, "Maybe we should just start from the beginnin'."

"I think that would be a good idea."

"I got a text from Holly that the enforcers had breached the house, so I called for backup and immediately headed to the address she provided."

Captain McNera's gaze shifted to me. "No one was supposed to know where you were. How did they find you?"

"Danny . . ." I swallowed as I thought about how this news might impact Sam. "Sam's partner was working with them. He put a tracker on the marshals' car."

Disbelief and something that might have been righteous indignation brightened Captain McNera's cheeks. "That's a very serious accusation, Holly."

"I realize that."

"You can't just accuse one of my officers of conspiring with drug dealers without proof. Maybe you misunderstood the situation."

Anger boiled to the surface, making my voice sharp. "I didn't misunderstand."

"I heard the entire conversation between them, sir. Holly called me and put the phone in her back pocket, and I heard his confession. When I got there, he had her handcuffed and was tryin' to force her into the trunk of his car," Marx explained. "When that didn't work, he put a gun to her head."

Captain McNera paled. "Put a gun to her . . ." His gaze shifted to me, and he just stared at me, shocked, before gesturing to his forehead. "That's from the gun?"

"No," Marx said before I could speak. "That's from the door frame he slammed her head into when he got angry."

I watched fury chase away all other emotion on Captain McNera's face. "How could I have misjudged him so completely? I thought he was a good officer. I thought—"

"It's not your fault," Marx interrupted.

"Of course it's my fault. I'm his commanding officer. I should've seen it." He rubbed at his face as if it might help him make sense of things.

"Nobody saw it. Sam was his partner and he had no idea that Daniel was involved with this."

Captain McNera's anger drained away, and he looked abruptly tired. "That's not gonna be an easy conversation."

"No, it won't, but I'll be there if you want."

Captain McNera nodded as he pushed away from the counter. "I would appreciate that. I know you and Sam are close.

I'm gonna grab the first aid kit out of the hall closet so we can take care of that head wound, and then we'll figure out what to do next."

Marx stood and rinsed the bloodstained rag out in the sink as Captain McNera left the room. "I think you might need stitches."

I touched at the gash with light fingers and hissed in a breath.

"Don't touch it," he chided, returning with a clean washcloth. "You're gonna get it infected."

"It's just a scratch."

He gave me a flat look. He had said that same thing to me the first time he'd been shot, and apparently he didn't like having it flung back at him. "It is not a scratch. Now hold still."

He reached to push my hair back out of my face so he could continue cleaning the wound, but I brushed his hand aside. "Stop fussing. I'm fine."

"I will fuss if I wanna fuss."

"I'm perfectly capable of tending to my own injuries," I pointed out. I had done it plenty of times before. I held out my hand for the washcloth.

"You're gonna be stubborn about this, aren't you?"

"Apparently I'm a stubborn snot about everything," I said, motioning for him to hand over the cloth.

He grimaced. "I heard that comment. That man knows nothin' about you."

"So I'm not a stubborn snot?"

He almost smiled. "Stubborn? Frequently. A snot? Never. He was just angry that you weren't gullible." He placed the washcloth in my hand. "The bathroom is through the livin' room and down the hall if you need a mirror. Second door on your left."

"Thanks." I took the washcloth with me as I wandered through the tastefully decorated living room toward the bathroom. I paused when I heard Captain McNera's low, angry voice coming from the hallway.

"Rick is at my house with the girl. Come get her, and try not to screw it up like Danny did. We don't need any more casualties." He paused as if he were listening and then said, "I know it puts me in the middle of it, but there's no other way. Say you followed them, and make sure no one suspects my involvement. A bump on the head ought to do."

The meaning behind his words washed over me and carried away my breath. I retraced the conversation in my mind, desperately searching for any other possible meaning, but I came to the same shocking conclusion each time: Captain McNera was the person behind the attack at the safe house. Danny had been working for *him* when he put the tracker under the marshals' car.

I backed away, retreating into the kitchen, where Marx was brewing a pot of coffee. My eyes met his, and I froze.

God, how do I tell him that his best friend betrayed him?

There were so few people in this city he considered friends, and he had known Captain McNera for twenty years. They had been partners on the police force.

"Holly, what's the matter?" he asked.

I opened my mouth to answer, but the truth caught in my throat. He might consider me a friend, but he'd known Captain McNera for so much longer. What if he didn't believe me?

"Holly?"

"I . . . overheard Captain McNera on the phone." I licked my lips and forced the rest of the words out. "He called someone to . . . to come get me, and told them not to screw it up like Danny did."

An uncomfortable silence followed my announcement. When Marx finally spoke, his voice was taught with anger. "What exactly are you sayin', Holly?"

I bit my bottom lip as tears pooled in my eyes. *God, I don't wanna break his heart.* "He told them . . . to make it look like they followed us, and to make sure no one suspects he's involved."

Doubt and confusion played across his face. He shook his head in silent denial even as I saw the beginnings of questions in his eyes. He stepped back from me and rubbed a hand over his face.

"I'm sorry."

He held up a hand to silence me as he visibly struggled with the news. I swallowed the lump of regret in my throat, and my eyes flitted to the back door. If he chose not to believe me, I would need to slip away before Captain McNera's people came for me.

"I found this on the living room floor."

My spine stiffened at Captain McNera's voice, and I turned to see him walking casually into the kitchen, the damp rag I'd been carrying to the bathroom draped across his palm.

I hadn't even realized I'd dropped it.

He offered it to me, but I stepped back from him, retreating slowly until my back touched the flower-patterned wall. His expression turned questioning, and then he looked at Marx, who was regarding his longtime friend with uncertainty.

Captain McNera sighed, and weariness crept over him, rounding his shoulders, darkening the circles beneath his eyes, and deepening the grooves in his heavily lined face until he seemed to have aged ten years between heartbeats.

"I wish you hadn't heard that phone conversation, Holly."

Marx's eyebrows knitted together. "Tell me it's not true. Tell me you didn't have anythin' to do with any of this."

He set the first aid kit he had brought with him on the counter, and tossed the rag on top of it. "I can't do that, Rick."

He drew the gun he'd had with him when he opened the front door, and Marx snapped his weapon up in the same instant.

Marx was completely exposed in the middle of the kitchen; he had no vest to protect him this time, and it was a trained officer at the other end of the weapon aimed at his chest.

"Matt," he gritted out, and I could hear the pain and fear in his voice. He was holding his best friend at gunpoint, and he wanted more than anything not to have to take that shot. "Put it down. You don't have to do this."

Captain McNera gave him a threadbare smile. "I'm not some unstable suspect who doesn't know what they're doing, Rick. You can't talk me down. I know what I've done, and I know exactly what I'm doing now."

"So this entire time, this entire case—everythin' that's gone wrong—was because of you," Marx realized. "You had my informant killed to cover up your operation because you knew I planned to track him down and get the rest of the information. And Tear—"

"He was a liability. Holly identified him."

"And the dealer I brought in? Did you have him killed so I couldn't question him?"

A memory surfaced in my mind. "Danny was there when he wasn't supposed to be, and he would've known the cameras weren't working right. He killed him, didn't he?"

Captain McNera's lips puckered as if he had just tasted something sour. "Danny was a mistake. I knew it the moment you brought me the picture of Holly you found on the dealer. I don't know what he was thinking using a crime scene photo of her that only our department had access to."

"And the cop you wanted me to hand the case off to— Ricardo—I assume he's the one who's on his way here now," Marx said. When Captain McNera didn't answer, Marx demanded, "Why?" I could hear the weight of his grief and anger in that single word.

"For my family. I need them to be taken care of."

"For your family?" Marx asked in disbelief. "What about my family, Matt!"

Captain McNera shook his head. "I would never have hurt Shannon. I care about her too."

"You sent your bulldogs into her home."

"It was just supposed to scare you off the case."

A muscle in Marx's jaw flexed. "And Holly?"

Captain McNera frowned. "She's not family."

"She's family to me!" Marx shouted, and I cringed at the volume of his voice. "And don't pretend you didn't know. You sent them after her *because* you know."

Captain McNera's lips whitened as he pressed them together. He didn't deny it.

"Is that why you asked me about my relationship with her? So you could figure out if you could use her against me? Did you send that drug dealer after her in the precinct so you could gauge how much I care for her?"

Regret flickered across Captain McNera's face. "You reacted like a father protecting his little girl. I didn't expect that, and I almost . . . reconsidered."

"But you decided to take her anyway. What was the plan? Hold her over my head so you could keep me from movin' forward with the case until you decided to bow out?"

"You didn't give me a choice."

"There's always a choice."

"I knew it was only a matter of time when you called me about your informant's information. You never could look the other way. Holly was my last chance to discourage you from ruining everything. I took precautions for her safety. They were never gonna hurt her."

"Never gonna . . ." Marx trailed off in disbelief. "Look at her, Matt. She didn't do that to herself!"

Captain McNera glanced at the gash on my forehead. "They weren't supposed to—"

"You're not that naive. Even if Daniel hadn't lost his temper, you hired thugs. Did you really think they wouldn't hurt her, or did you just decide that the benefits outweighed the risks?"

"If you had just backed off, she wouldn't be hurt at all."

Fury and pain warred for control on Marx's face. "Twenty years, Matt. We've been friends for twenty years. When exactly did you switch sides? When did it become okay to sell drugs to kids, murder people, and abduct innocent girls just to keep your secrets?"

"You don't understand, Rick."

"No, I don't." His voice shook with rage. "You betrayed our friendship. You betrayed everythin' we stand for. And for what? A more lucrative retirement plan? How much did your morals cost, Matt?"

"Don't judge me!" Captain McNera yelled, and the gun vibrated with anger in his hand. "Don't pretend you've done everything by the book."

"There's a big difference between grayin' a few lines to catch a criminal and breakin' the law. I never crossed that line. Don't demonize me to soothe your conscience."

Tears welled in Captain McNera's eyes. "You're right. I crossed a few lines that I regret crossing, but there's nothing I can do about that now."

Marx shook his head. "I don't understand what happened, Matt. You were a good cop. You helped a lot of people."

"And what do I have to show for it? More bills than I can afford, a house in foreclosure because I can't pay the mortgage. I've learned a lot in my years on the force, but mostly I learned that criminals can make in a day what I make in a year."

"You knew that goin' into it, but you wanted to make the world a better place."

"I was a foolish kid full of unrealistic expectations and impossible hopes. The world will never be a better place, because the people who work hard, who spend their lives trying to make a difference, are the ones who never win. We deserve a chance. Our families deserve a chance."

"Spare me the propaganda, Matt," Marx said curtly. "I've heard it all before from every dirty cop I've arrested and every low-life criminal with a sense of entitlement."

Captain McNera sighed. "It doesn't matter. None of it matters now. I can't change what I've done. I can't fix this."

Marx clenched his teeth as if he desperately wanted to keep the words from escaping. "No. You can't. But nobody else has to get hurt."

"You could just look the other way for once, for the sake of our friendship."

"I can't do that. You know I can't do that. Just put the gun down and we'll talk. We can work with the DA to get you a deal, somethin'—"

"I'm dying, Rick."

His words seemed to echo in the silence that followed.

"Unless that sentence is two months or less, it won't matter anyway. Doctors gave me two more months at most. Inoperable brain tumor."

338

Moisture gathered in Marx's eyes, and he looked like he might double over from the excruciating impact of that news, but he kept his spine straight.

The conversation with Captain McNera in his office came back to me: he had been crying while looking at a photo of his daughters, and he had explained it away by saying "bad news in the family."

I understood now.

Death for someone who didn't believe in God meant eternal separation from the people he loved. It was an end. He was losing his family, and all of this—every terrible decision, every life lost—had been to provide for them when he was no longer here to do it. That didn't make it right, but I felt a pang of sorrow for him.

"Why didn't you tell me?" Marx choked out.

"They would've forced me out, citing that my judgment might be impaired, and I need the money. I can't let Helen lose the house. I can't leave her with all of my unpaid medical bills." Captain McNera wiped at the tears on his face with the back of one hand while keeping the gun trained on Marx. "Let this go, Rick. Let me die at home with my family."

Marx visibly wrestled with that decision. It took him a moment to find his voice. "You could've come to me for help, but you made your choice."

Captain McNera grunted as if he had expected nothing less. "I won't go to jail, Rick. I won't see that look of shame in my family's eyes."

I looked at Marx in alarm. Had he heard the unspoken threat in those words?

"You've always been an amazing cop and a better friend than I ever deserved. I'm sorry for putting you through all of this, but I want you to know that I never intended for you to get hurt."

Captain McNera slowly lifted his gun to his temple.

"Don't do this, Matt," Marx pleaded.

"Please don't," I said, stepping forward.

"Holly," Marx snapped.

I knew he wanted me to stay out of harm's way, but I couldn't just cower by the wall and do nothing while a man took his own life. The pain of his suicide would ripple through the lives of everyone around him, especially Marx.

"Don't do this to your family, to your friends. If you kill yourself, you're murdering a little piece of everyone who has ever loved you, everyone who has ever cared about you. You're hurting them in a way they may never recover from. Please . . ."

Captain McNera looked at me through a haze of tears.

"If you care about them at all, don't deprive them of loving you for two more months. Even if there are bars in between, bars are better than nothing but memories."

Captain McNera smiled sadly and shifted his eyes back to Marx. "I see why you love her." To my surprise, he looked back at me. "You're a sweet kid, Holly, but there's no hope to be had here."

Sweat beaded across his brow as his finger flexed on the trigger.

"There's always hope," I said, tears brimming in my eyes. "You can see your family again. Death doesn't have to be a final good-bye. Just a . . . a 'see you later.' Please just—"

"I don't believe in an afterlife, Holly. There is no God, no heavenly gate, no eternal life with the people we love. There's only a grave. We're all just . . . nothing but dust." Fresh tears dampened his cheeks, and the gun wavered at his temple. "I truly am sorry for this." He lowered the gun and then angled it in my direction.

Dread slammed into me.

"Matt!" Marx shouted, stepping forward. "Don't make me do this!"

I flattened myself against the wall.

"Forgive me," Captain McNera said, his words catching on a sob as he leveled the gun at my chest.

I braced for the searing pain of a bullet, but the only pain I felt was the quiet breaking of my heart when I saw Captain McNera fall.

Marx kicked the gun away from his friend's hand and crouched down to press two fingers to his neck. His face was a mask of pain as he closed his eyes. He had killed his friend of twenty years to save my life.

I parted my lips to say something, but there was nothing to say. I wouldn't thank him for killing his friend to save me, and saying I was sorry fell so short in this moment.

He stood and walked to the wall. He stared at it for a long time, seeming petrified by his pain; then he clenched his fingers into a fist and hit the wall, denting the plaster. He hit it again before dropping back against it and sliding to the floor.

He covered his tear-stained face with a bloody hand, and his shoulders shook as he cried silently.

Seeing this man, who was always brave and strong, crumple under the weight of grief was heartbreaking.

I crossed the kitchen and sank to the floor beside him. There were no words to soothe this wound, so I wrapped my arms around his shoulders and rested my head against his, holding him while he cried as he had once held me.

28

We sat on the edge of the ambulance as forensic specialists crawled over the scene with what looked like half the police force.

I picked at the temporary bandage the EMT had placed over the gash on my forehead, and glanced over at Marx.

His expression was numb as he handed his gun off to one of the forensic specialists. The woman bagged it and muttered her thanks before departing.

"Why did they take your gun?" I asked.

His eyes tracked the black body bag that was carried down the porch steps and loaded into the back of a coroner's van. "Because I . . . discharged my weapon."

Because he had shot someone.

A man I didn't recognize strode toward us, and Marx straightened his shoulders. "Lieutenant," he greeted somberly.

The man's expression was grim. He glanced at me and then said to Marx, "Let's talk privately." He nodded to the left, and Marx stood and followed him across the yard.

As I watched the police through the window of the house, I couldn't help but feel sorrow for the woman who would come home to find her husband dead and her family broken.

"Holly," a deep voice said, and I looked over to see Sam standing a few feet from me. Even in the darkness, I could see the pain in his eyes.

I slid down from the ambulance. "Hey."

"You should sit back down."

"I'm fine."

"You have a head injury." I could hear the undercurrent of anger in his voice. Apparently someone had filled him in that his partner was the reason for my head injury.

"Danny?" I asked.

He shook his head. "I just came from the safe house. He died on the way to the hospital."

"I'm sorry."

He gave me a small, tight smile. "Me too. The Danny I knew would never have done something like that. And he would never have . . ." He gestured to my head and grimaced. "I guess I didn't really know him at all."

"People make mistakes."

His expression hardened. "That wasn't a mistake, Holly. It was a conscious decision. It wasn't like he just forgot to make note of something in a report. He didn't accidentally murder people and cover it up. And he definitely didn't *accidentally* try to stuff you in his trunk before putting a gun to your head."

I pulled my lips between my teeth and looked away. There was no arguing with that.

"I knew he fixated on you from the moment he saw you. I just thought he was interested in you. I didn't realize he was targeting you."

"That's not your fault."

"He was my partner."

"That doesn't make you responsible for his decisions."

"I should've known something was off."

I had a feeling that nothing I said would lift the mantle of misplaced guilt from his shoulders, so I decided to change the subject.

"Were there any survivors besides Jordan?"

"Two of the marshals survived. The guy, Jefferson, was in critical condition, and Kristen was unconscious from blood loss. But she should be fine. Jordan's still there answering questions."

I breathed a sigh of relief and sat back down on the back of the ambulance. Too many people had died over me today, and it left a heavy stone of guilt and sorrow in my chest somewhere in the vicinity of my heart.

"How's Marx doing?" Sam asked.

I glanced over at the spot in the yard where the lieutenant and Marx spoke. "He just killed his best friend."

343

Sam's gaze followed mine. "Yeah." He drew in a deep breath that seemed to fortify him, and said, "I'm gonna get back to work. I just wanted to make sure you were okay."

I was pretty sure that my bump on the head was the least of the wounds sustained tonight. There was a faint sheen of tears in Sam's eyes, but knowing him, he would never let them fall. "Do you, um . . . need a hug?"

He cocked his head. "That's quite an offer coming from you. But no, I'm fine. I'll see you later." He walked away to confer with another officer.

Marx returned a few minutes later and sat back down beside me.

"What now?" I asked.

"I have to go to the hospital to have a few blood tests done to prove that I wasn't under the influence of anythin' that might have impaired my judgment. And I'm officially on administrative leave until they sort everythin' out. Then I have a mandatory meetin' with the department shrink to decide whether or not I can return to duty." He stared down at his badge as if he were suddenly questioning everything. "If I even wanna return to duty."

I stretched out a hand and touched the badge. He looked at me questioningly, but let me take it from him. I tucked it into his jacket pocket. "You're an amazing detective."

He gave me a fragile smile and wrapped a gentle arm around me. It took me a moment to relax, but then I let him pull me into a side hug.

"Thank you, Holly."

"For what?"

"Just for bein' you." He pressed a startling but gentle kiss into my hair, and my heart twisted a little at the memory of my dad doing that same thing when he tucked me into bed every night. "How's your head?"

"Dented. How's your heart?"

He paused before admitting, "Broken."

"I have duct tape somewhere. I'll fix it."

I could hear the faint smile in his voice as he said, "Of that I have no doubt." He rested his head on top of mine, and we sat together in silence as the night passed away in a sea of flashing lights.

Epilogue

Black lights ignited the pale colors in the bowling alley, and I lifted my camera to capture Jace leaning her head on Sam's shoulder with a contented smile on her face. Her smile was even brighter under the black lights, and it warmed me to see my friend so happy.

I moved on to capture Sam's sister, Evey, who had joined us for the evening. She was tall and willowy with raven-black hair and eyes as black as inkwells.

It took me a while to detect the subtle notes of anxiety beneath her poise. Every now and then she tugged at the hem of her shirt as she glanced around the room, presumably searching the faces for someone.

My camera landed on Marx next, and a twinge of pain cut through my heart. It had been two weeks since he killed his best friend, and I could see the anguish of that moment in every line of his body.

He had been cleared of any wrongdoing for shooting Sam's partner, Danny, and the captain, but he was still struggling to come to terms with it. There was an ongoing investigation into the officers under Captain McNera's leadership, but I had overheard that at least one had been arrested.

The drug ring was in a state of collapse, but the success had come at too great a cost.

Marx noticed my attention and offered me a small smile that didn't reach his eyes. I smiled back and gave him a little finger-wave.

I let my camera rest around my neck on the strap and pulled my cell phone from my pocket. I typed out a quick text to someone I thought might be able to help Marx through his grief better than I could.

"Funny thing about black lights . . . really pale things glow," Jordan commented, startling me as I hit the send button. "You're practically bioluminescent."

I smirked. "I'm not that pale." Though I was a bit brighter than anyone else in our group. My gaze skipped back to Marx as I tucked my phone back into my pocket. "Do you think he blames me?"

"Blames you for what?"

I looked up at him. "Because he had to kill Captain McNera to save my life."

"No. If he blames anyone other than McNera, it's himself for being so blind to what was happening. He'll be okay. He just needs some time."

I sighed. It hurt watching him in so much pain and not being able to comfort him. "Yeah, I guess so."

"You pick out a ball yet?"

I surveyed the long rows of various bowling balls and shook my head.

"You kinda need a ball to bowl."

I lifted my chin. "Yes, I know. Just because I haven't been bowling in . . ."—I mentally calculated the length of time—"nineteen years doesn't mean I've forgotten that I can't just chuck random things down the aisle to knock out the pins."

He grinned. "It's called a lane, not an aisle."

I rolled my eyes at him, and he laughed. I walked away to find a ball. I spotted a pretty purple one and plucked it from the shelf. I carried it over to the table where Marx was seated.

"I found my ball," I declared, thumping it onto the table.

Marx crawled out of the quiet place in his mind where he'd been hiding and blinked at the ball. "Why am I not surprised that you chose purple?"

I rotated the ball to slip my fingers into the large holes. They were a little big, but I could manage it. "Are your ribs feeling any better?"

He had been shot while pursuing a suspect in the case a couple of weeks ago, and while the bulletproof vest had saved his life, the impact had bruised and cracked a few of his ribs. Bowling wouldn't exactly help matters.

"My ribs are fine," he sighed. "Quit worryin'."

347

"I'll worry if I wanna worry," I teased. If he could fuss over a gash on my head, then I could worry over his cracked ribs. And there was nothing he could do about it.

A faint smile touched his lips as he shook his head. He reached up and tugged on the rim of my sparkly hat. "You keepin' that on all night?"

The gash on my head was healing fine, and the doctors said it shouldn't leave a noticeable scar, but at the moment it was very noticeable, and it made me self-conscious. "Yep."

"You might get hot," he pointed out, and I shrugged.

Jordan came up beside me and frowned. "Uh, Holly, that ball is sixteen pounds."

"Yeah," I said, casting him an uncertain look. "Is that an unlucky number or something?"

Jordan and Marx exchanged a look, and Marx sat up straighter in his chair as he pointed out, "It's a fairly heavy ball for somebody your size."

I hugged the ball to me. "Sixteen pounds isn't that heavy."

"It is when you're throwing it repeatedly," Jordan explained. He lifted his own ball—a blue one with shiny flecks that reminded me of his eyes. "Mine is sixteen pounds."

Sam thumped his ball on the table behind Marx. "Given your height, weight, and limited upper-body strength, you should consider an eight-pound ball."

Jordan arched a blond eyebrow. "Now you're just asking to be put in a headlock."

"Obviously, I meant Holly," Sam said with a disgruntled look toward Jordan.

"Wait, why obviously me?" I demanded indignantly. Was I the only person in the room he considered to have limited upper-body strength?

"Tread carefully, Sam," Marx advised. "That ball's gonna hurt if she chucks it at your head."

"I'm just stating facts. It's not like she's unaware of her dimensions." He said that like I had some sort of impairment.

Jordan gave him a look that I couldn't quite interpret, and asked, "Why are you so attuned to Holly's dimensions?"

Sam narrowed his eyes. "Don't go there."

"Go where?" I asked in confusion. "What am I missing?"

"Just let them work it out," Marx suggested.

"Work what out?"

Jordan and Sam muttered to each other as they walked away, and the tension between them abruptly diffused as Jordan gave Sam a light, playful shove, and Sam shoved him back, nearly knocking him over a table.

"Did that situation make sense to you?" I asked with a glance at Marx.

"Mmm hmm," he replied with a small smile, and his tone implied that he had no intention of sharing more than that.

"I'm not that short," I informed him, my tone daring him to disagree. "There's nothing wrong with my dimensions."

His smile widened, almost touching his eyes, but he didn't disagree.

Good.

I turned my attention to Jace. She popped her wheelchair up onto the platform and rolled forward with her ball in her lap. One of the bowling attendants approached her and asked, "Would you like me to put up the bumpers, Miss?"

Oh boy.

Sam just stared at the man, seeming uncertain whether or not his girlfriend had just been insulted. Jace straightened her spine and asked in a saccharine voice, "Why would I need bumpers?"

The attendant hesitated at her tone of voice, probably sensing dangerous waters ahead. "Because you're . . . I mean . . . you know." He gestured to her wheelchair.

I covered my face with a hand. I didn't want to watch him die.

"Totally fantastic?" Jace suggested.

"Um . . . because you're . . . in a wheelchair. I just thought . . ."

349

"Out of curiosity, what do my legs have to do with me rolling a ball with my hand?" She wiggled her very functional fingers at him. "It's not like I'm playing kickball."

I splayed my fingers to sneak a peek at the attendant's face. He looked as if he had swallowed a wasp and couldn't spit it out. He turned crimson, ducked his head, and walked quickly away.

Jace rolled her eyes and wheeled up to the lane. She drew her arm back and released the ball. It rolled gracefully down the lane, and the pins exploded in every direction, leaving none standing.

"Ha!" she declared triumphantly. Sam high-fived her as she rolled off the platform. "Bumpers . . ."

"Your turn, Holly," Marx said.

"Oh, really?" I asked, perking up.

"Ladies first."

I carried my ball onto the platform and looked down at the colorful shoe-print stickers that laid out the path to the lane. Seriously? Did people actually get lost from point A to point B? Maybe they just accidentally veered at the last second and threw the ball down the wrong lane.

I followed the footprints to the edge of the lane and paused. How hard could this be? I did it when I was little with my family. I hefted the ball up, bracing it with my left hand—okay, it was a little heavy after holding it all this time—and tried to aim it toward the middle pin.

I threw it, and it landed with a shocking thud that sounded like an anvil dropping. I flinched and stood there to watch it roll lazily down the lane and into the gutter.

Hmm. Apparently I did that wrong.

When I spun on my heel to go back to the tables, there was complete silence. Jordan was scratching his head and looking around the room, Marx was making a valiant effort not to laugh, and Sam just looked stunned.

Jace grinned, "That was awesome."

Marx cleared his throat quietly and said, "You're supposed to roll the ball, Holly, not chuck it."

I frowned. "It rolled."

"Into the gutter," Sam muttered under his breath.

I shot him a glare.

"You get to go again, Holly," Jace pointed out.

The machine regurgitated my purple ball, and I picked it up. I cradled it against my stomach as I walked back to the lane. *Roll it, don't chuck it. Roll it . . .*

I gripped the ball and swung my arm, trying to figure out how I was supposed to do that without the thunderous thump. My arm was getting tired. I needed to do some strength training or something.

I took a deep breath, braced myself, and let the ball go. I felt the violent impact beneath my feet before the ball rolled lopsidedly into the gutter.

Marx had a hand over his face when I turned around and his shoulders shook with silent laughter. Jordan strolled up to take his turn, and he smiled at me.

"You really struggle with rolling balls into things, and you don't even have to fight with a pool stick this time."

I scrunched my nose at him and stepped off the platform. Jace high-fived me anyway as I walked past her.

Sam shook his head. "That was awful. Are you good at anything?"

Jace backhanded him in the stomach, and he grunted in surprise. "She's my friend. Be nice."

"I was just joking. Mostly," he replied.

I went to sit by Marx. I slid onto the tabletop, because I hated their twisty, springy chairs, and sighed. "I suck at this game."

"You only had one turn."

Jordan rolled the ball with expert precision, and it practically floated down the lane before cracking into the pins and taking them out. I slid a slightly flustered look Marx's way and said, "So did he."

"It takes practice."

"Are you good at bowling?"

He puckered his lips in thought. "I don't know. I haven't gone since Shannon and I went before the divorce. I suppose I did all right."

My phone vibrated, and I tugged it from my pocket. I read the message on the screen and sent a quick text in reply.

"Who do you keep textin'?" Marx wondered. He lifted his chin to see my phone. In all fairness, anyone I might normally text was less than five feet away.

I angled my phone so he couldn't read it and squinted at him. "You're doing that nosy detective thing."

"I'm just askin' a question."

"To which the answer is none of your business," I replied with a smile. He frowned with suspicion, and I hopped off the table. "I'm gonna go find a different ball. This one's . . . um . . . finger holes are too big."

His lips curled up at the corners. "And it has nothin' to do with the fact that it's too heavy?"

It was definitely too heavy, and my arms were exhausted. "It . . . might be too heavy for some people."

He smiled at my deliberate refusal to admit that it was too heavy for me. "There's an eight-pound ball right there." I followed his pointing finger to a ghastly orange pumpkin ball.

"It's orange."

His brow furrowed in confusion. "Why does the color of the ball even matter?"

"Because it does." I walked away to scope out the options, hoping for something purple . . . or even pink.

"I do not understand women," Marx admitted beneath his breath.

Jordan laughed quietly as he sat down in the chair beside him. "Yeah, I don't either. But if I've learned anything about women over the years, it's that functionality isn't enough. It has to have character."

I agreed with that.

"It's an orange ball. It has plenty of character."

"It looks like a pumpkin."

Marx was quiet for a moment before saying, "Right. She doesn't like pumpkins."

I glanced at the message that came through on my phone and then looked at the front doors of the bowling alley. I spotted the woman in heels with her dark hair twisted into a bun on top of her head, dressed in a long black coat. The mere sight of her made me think "lawyer." It was definitely her.

I waved, and she notched her chin up before she started my way. I plucked a green ball off the shelf and walked back to stand beside Marx. When she approached, he blinked twice as if he thought he was seeing things, and then stood slowly.

"Shannon?"

Her red lips curved into a sad smile. "Hi, Rick. It's been a while." She stepped forward and embraced him in a familiar hug. Quietly, she said, "I'm sorry about Matt."

I saw the tears sweep across Marx's vision, and he tried to blink them away before she drew back. She turned her attention to me.

"Holly, it's nice to meet you. And thank you for the invitation. It's been ages since I've been here."

Marx gaped at me. "She's who you've been textin'? How did you even get her number?"

I hesitated before reminding him, "You called her on my phone at the precinct."

Shannon dipped her head apologetically. "I'm sorry about not answering your calls. I intended to call you back another time."

"Do you wanna join us for a game?" he asked.

She surveyed the group. "I would like that. Just let me grab some shoes, and then maybe we can do introductions." She draped her purse and coat over a chair and slipped away to retrieve her shoes.

Marx turned to me, and I shifted uncertainly at the unreadable expression on his face. I knew that it had been risky contacting Shannon, and I wasn't sure if he would be angry with me for invading his personal life or if he would just be happy to see her.

"Please don't be mad," I pleaded. "I just wanted—"

"Holly, I am . . . so very far from mad at you." He drew me into a gentle hug, and I stiffened in surprise, almost dropping the bowling ball on my toes. "Thank you," he whispered.

"Mmm . . . can you let go now?" I murmured uncomfortably.

I felt the quiet rumble of laughter in his chest before he released me, and I took a few steps back. "It's like huggin' a porcupine. The moment I wrap my arms around you I can feel all your needles stick up."

"I don't . . . hug. I'm not a hugger."

"Yet," he said with a small smile.

Shannon returned with her shoes and a bowling ball. I found a nice spot on a table by myself and took pictures between my turns.

My phone vibrated, and I pulled it from my pocket. I had a text message from an unknown number. Nerves fluttered in my stomach as I flipped the phone open to read it.

Do you smell smoke?

I frowned in confusion and then looked up when I heard Jordan say, "Yeah, this is Jordan." He pressed a finger into his left ear and walked away from the others toward me. "Hey, Beth Anne."

I hopped off the table and stepped closer to him, straining to catch her quiet words on the other end of the line.

He frowned and asked, "He's there now?" A pause. "Well, what did he want?" He listened for a beat, and then he covered the mouthpiece as he whispered to me, "Collin stopped by the shelter to pass along a message less than five minutes ago."

A chill slithered down my spine. "What message?"

Jordan's frown deepened, making him look older than his twenty-eight years. "He said 'one down, four to go.' Any idea what that means?"

I shook my head before remembering the anonymous text message that had more than likely come from Collin: "Do you smell smoke?"

"Something's wrong," I said slowly, the pieces coming together in my mind. "Tell her to leave. Tell her to get out. Tell her to get the women out." When he didn't speak immediately, I ripped the phone from his hands. "Beth Anne, you have to get everyone out of the building."

"Holly, he was . . ."

Something shattered in the background, and a shrill scream traveled down the line before it went dead.

The End

WHAT TO READ NEXT:

He'll get what he came for, no matter how many bodies he has to step over.

Collin Wells is relentless and ruthless, and he'll stop at nothing to get what he wants: his foster sister, the girl who always manages to slip through his fingers. Holly's foster brother has haunted her footsteps for years - taunting her, toying with her - and until recently, she never dared to stop running and build a life for herself. Now, everyone she loves is in danger. How can she protect the people she loves when her foster brother comes to collect?

About the Author

Jesus and laughter have brought C.C. Warrens through some very difficult times in life, and she weaves both into every story she writes, creating a world of breath-stealing intensity, laugh-out-loud humor, and a sparkle of hope. Writing has been a slowly blossoming dream inside her for most of her life until one day it spilled out onto the pages that would become her first published book.

If she's not writing, she's attempting to bake something—however catastrophic that might be—or she's enjoying the beauty of the outdoors with her husband.

How to Connect

Facebook.com/ccwarrens
instagram.com/c.c._warrens/
Website: ccwarrensbooks.com/
Email: cc@ccwarrensbooks.com

Note from the Author

Dear reader,

In the vast world of books to read, I'm honored that you chose to take this journey with my characters. I hope the trip was full of suspense, excitement, and laughter (especially laughter!)

If you're just jumping into this series, and you're curious how it all started, check out Criss Cross: A Holly Novel. Holly and Marx had an interesting beginning.

I love to hear from my readers, so please don't hesitate to get in touch with me through my Facebook author page or my Goodreads page.

If you enjoyed the book, reviews are helpful for authors and for potential readers. You can leave reviews in several places: Amazon, Goodreads, Bookbub, and Facebook.

Made in the USA
Coppell, TX
15 February 2024